Neither of them could resist this moment...

The night was soft, as gentle as the way Tom Sax kissed Juanita in the darkness. This was their second meeting. The first time they had sat together on a bench, talking, kissing, touching. This time he pulled her close, meeting her mouth eagerly, his kiss sweet and deep as he knelt to the ground with her, laying her back in the grass.

"You will think I am bad," she whispered.

"Never," he groaned. "Never, never. I love you, Juanita." He kissed at the silken skin of her shoulders and chest, his broad frame hovering over her. Carefully, he moved a hand to cup one of her full breasts through the flannel gown she wore. She gasped and whimpered at the touch, her whole body feeling like a fiery furnace.

"I want so much to please you, Tom," she cried. "I want to be a woman for you. But it would be wrong—"

"I would never ask you to do anything wrong. But I can't wait much longer, Juanita. I want you to be mine..."

☆

ALSO BY F. ROSANNE BITTNER

•

Savage Horizons
Frontier Fires
*Tennessee Bride**

Published by
POPULAR LIBRARY   **forthcoming*

F. Rosanne Bittner

DESTINY'S DAWN

POPULAR LIBRARY

An Imprint of Warner Books, Inc.

A Warner Communications Company

POPULAR LIBRARY EDITION

Popular Library® and the fanciful P design are registered
trademarks of Warner Books, Inc.

Cover illustration by Franco Accornero

Popular Library books are published by
Warner Books, Inc.
666 Fifth Avenue
New York, N.Y. 10103

 A Warner Communications Company

Printed in the United States of America

First Printing: October, 1987

10 9 8 7 6 5 4 3 2 1

If today I had a young mind to direct, to start on the journey of life, and I was faced with the duty of choosing between the natural way of my forefathers and that of the white man's present way of civilization, I would, for its welfare, unhesitatingly set that child's foot in the path of my forefathers. I would raise him to be an Indian!

—Chief Luther Standing Bear, Oglala Sioux, 1931,
  Land of the Spotted Eagle

This novel is the continuing story of Caleb and Sarah Sax and their children. It covers the years 1845 through 1865. Primary locations are: Bent's Fort, on the Arkansas River in present-day southeast Colorado; Sonoma, California, north of San Francisco; the central plains of Colorado and Nebraska; and old Fort Laramie in southeast Wyoming, which is where the famed meeting of thousands of Plains Indians took place for the signing of the Treaty of 1851.

This novel, as with all my stories, contains a considerable amount of historical detail. I do extensive research to ensure dates, locations, and major events in my stories are accurate. However, main characters and basic plots involving those characters are purely fictitious.

I loved you in spring, when you were young and budding,
  like the blossoms of the apple tree.

I loved you in summer, when you were full and ripe
  and beautiful,
    like a sweet, pink peach and the sensuous rose.

I loved you in autumn, when maturity brought a certain
  glow and warmth,
    like a golden leaf and warm cinnamon baking.

And I love you now, in the cold and barren winter,
  For when your eyes meet mine, I still see spring,
  And the budding blossom that drew me to taste
    its sweet nectar.

Yes, I love you still, in the winter of our lives.

—Author

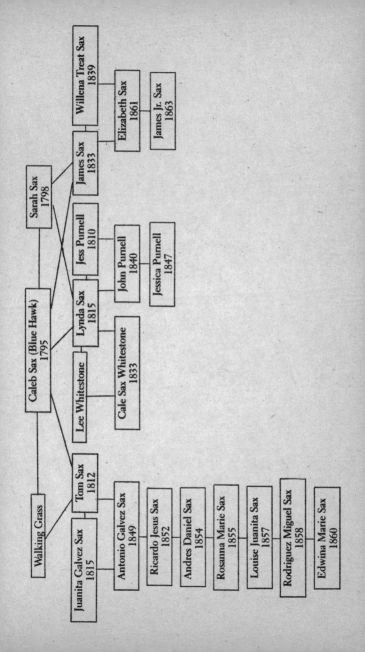

· Chapter One ·

Caleb Sax rose, blood dripping from his arms and hands. One of his best mares lay at his feet with her new foal beside her, both of them dead. In vain he had reached inside the mother to turn the foal; and he would never forget that feeling of warm life in his hands, followed by cold death.

As he looked away from the pitiful sight, Caleb saw them, four Cheyenne warriors looking down at him from a rise perhaps fifty yards away. They were mounted on grand, painted horses, watching him quietly. They wore nothing but loincloths and a little paint, two of them with feathers in their hair.

"You think they mean trouble, Caleb?" Jess Purnell asked the question. Jess was Caleb's son-in-law. He had come along with Caleb that morning to find the mare, because Caleb suspected there would be trouble with the birth.

"I don't know. I'm going to talk to them." Caleb looked down at the mare and foal again, feeling sick inside. Dancer was his best mare. Why did it seem the sight of the dead horses coupled with the almost ghostly appearance of the Indians on the rise were some kind of omen? He walked off toward the rise and the warriors without looking at Jess, his hands and arms still bloody.

Jess watched, saying nothing. He moved to his horse and rifle, pulling the weapon from its boot. But he knew he would not need it, as Caleb approached the Indians wearing no weapons. After all, they were his kind—Cheyenne. Caleb's own mother had been Cheyenne, and his Indian name was Blue Hawk—a name that carried respect and brought stories of the "old days" to the mouths of his tribe. There weren't many left anymore who remembered when Caleb used to live among them. After his young wife was killed by the Crow, Caleb had left his newborn son with the Cheyenne while he went on a mission of personal revenge, single-handedly attacking and killing over and over until his very name brought fear into the heart of the fiercest Crow warrior.

But that had been a long time ago, many years before Jess had ever met the man. He watched Caleb move up the hill toward the Indians. Jess could do nothing for now but stand and watch, ready for action if it was necessary.

As Caleb walked closer to the intruders, he thought how the steamy heat of the evening made them appear almost as a mirage, but they became more distinct as he came within a few feet of them. They looked down at him from horseback, but even though Caleb was on foot, they could see he was a tall and powerful man. He looked as Indian as they, dressed in buckskins, his long, black hair tied into a tail at the base of his neck, a thin white scar running down the left side of his face. That scar was put there by a white man when Caleb was sixteen—the first white man Caleb Sax had ever killed.

"What do you want?" Caleb asked the Indians in their own tongue.

"I am Gray Cloud," one of them, perhaps thirty, answered. He nodded to the two who sat on his left. "These are my friends, Bent Leg and Bear Man." He turned to an older man on his right. "This is my father, White Horse. We are from the Northern Cheyenne. You are Blue Hawk?"

Caleb nodded, looking at White Horse. "I remember the name White Horse. But it has been many years since I lived among the Cheyenne. Did I know you then?"

The older man nodded. "I was young like you. My own father, Sits Too Long, he remembers you best. He still tells stories about Blue Hawk."

Caleb felt the faint rush of desire to ride among them again but pushed it away. "I remember Sits Too Long. He must be very old now."

White Horse nodded. "Old and dying."

"I am sorry to hear that." Caleb detected a sadness that was more than just mourning the coming death of a loved one. "But surely you have not searched for me just to tell me about Sits Too Long." The conversation continued in a mixture of the Cheyenne tongue and sign language.

White Horse nodded. "Three moons ago we came here among our southern relatives. While we were here, we were told that the one called Blue Hawk was again living in Cheyenne country. We were going back north, for out in the villages there is much spotted fever and bad coughing. Many are dying. Most of our own relatives have been lost to death. But I have had a dream, and because of this dream I have come to see Blue Hawk before we go north."

Caleb sighed. Eighteen hundred forty-five had been a very bad year for the Cheyenne. Measles and whooping cough were ravaging the Indians, wiping out close to half the Cheyenne south of the Platte River. "I've heard about the sickness. It saddens my heart."

The Indian nodded. "White man brings it. I am afraid for my son."

Caleb nodded. "I understand that kind of fear. I have lost many loved ones, including two sons." Their eyes held, two men of kindred spirit. "You say you come because of a dream," Caleb spoke up.

There was great respect in White Horse's eyes. "*Ai*. But I also came just to look upon the one called Blue Hawk again, to help me remember the days when the Cheyenne were strong. Now, because white men come and kill the buffalo and divide up the land and bring disease, our strength is failing. It warms my heart to see the one called Blue Hawk still standing tall and strong in spite of his many years."

A faint smile moved over Caleb's lips. "I have been on this earth fifty winters—fifty hard winters."

White Horse nodded, his eyes moving to Caleb's bloody arms and hands. "The blood on your hands is from the birth of the foal?"

Caleb nodded. "The mother and foal both died."

White Horse met Caleb's blue eyes. He tried to decide if they were an ordinary blue made bluer by the dark skin and black lashes that surrounded them, or if they truly were a much deeper blue than he'd ever seen in any white man. How odd that this Indian of legend had such blue eyes—the eyes of his French trapper father.

"You live like a white man, Blue Hawk. But it will not always be so. The blood on your hands tells you this. Living against your spirit has been a struggle. I know this even though I do not know you well. It is in your eyes. You live like other white men, but that life has not been good to you. Your real desire is to live among us."

Caleb held his eyes. "I gave up Indian ways a long time ago—for a white woman."

A sudden gust of wind made some of White Horse's hair blow across his face. He shook it back. "I have heard. They say it is a great love you have for this woman. There are one or two who remember when you left the Cheyenne to go and find this woman you once knew as a child in the white man's world."

"I would die for her. And you are right. My heart lies with the Cheyenne. But as long as my woman breathes, I will live in the only way she can survive. But if I asked her, she would come and live with me among the Cheyenne. I won't ask it of her, because it would surely end her life much sooner. She is not well."

White Horse nodded. "I have come to tell you that in my dream you lived among us again. You rode against the white men with us. Your face was painted, and many spoke again with great honor about you as a warrior. You were alone. It is my duty to tell you of this dream, so that when the time for decision comes, you will know what to do, where you belong."

Caleb's chest tightened painfully. He had no doubts about the dreams of an old Indian warrior. He believed in dreams and visions as much as any full-blooded Indian. He knew what the dream meant, and the thought of being without his Sarah brought great pain to his heart.

"You will come back to us, Blue Hawk," White Horse continued. "You will die with the Indians among whom you were born. Your spirit will return to the earth. Your tears will mix with the rain; your blood will flow into the earth over which the Cheyenne have ridden since days we can no longer remember; your voice will cry out with the wind. You are still among us, Blue Hawk. You have always been among us. Our hearts are one."

The man touched his forehead as a sign of respect, as did Gray Cloud and the other two Indians.

Caleb stood almost transfixed. Surely the spirit of *Maheo* had given White Horse his dream and had sent the man to seek out Caleb before going back north. White Horse's understanding of his own spirit astounded Caleb. He vaguely remembered the man as a youth, but it had been over thirty years since he had lived among the Cheyenne. Surely it was a supernatural experience for the man to know so much about Caleb and his own inner struggles. That could only mean the spirits were calling Caleb—calling him back to where he really belonged. But he couldn't go. Not yet.

"Thank you for telling me of your dream. I will pray that the spirits will bless you and keep you and your son from the disease that has killed so many others. May the wind be at your back as you head north."

White Horse nodded. "I will see you again, Blue Hawk, when you are again Cheyenne."

The man turned his horse and rode off. The others followed, Gray Cloud giving Caleb a lingering look first, as though he looked upon some kind of sacred spirit. Caleb watched them until the horizon suddenly swallowed them and made it seem as though they had never been there at all. He looked down at the dried blood on his hands and arms, then turned around to see the mare and foal still lying dead on the ground, Jess still watching, standing near his horse.

For some reason Caleb had trouble making his legs move, but he finally managed to descend the small rise and walk back to Jess. His mind whirled with thoughts of Sarah. Was *Maheo* trying to tell him his days with the woman were numbered? No. Sarah was everything to him —everything.

"What the hell did they want, Caleb?" Jess asked when

he came closer. A chill swept through him when Caleb's blue eyes met his own. "Jesus, what's wrong?"

Caleb thought about explaining, but much as he loved Jess Purnell as a son-in-law, how could he truly explain to Jess what had just happened? This was something much deeper than anything the two had ever discussed. And perhaps there was no explaining it in words after all.

"It was just someone I used to know when I lived among the Cheyenne," he finally spoke up, his voice strained. "He's headed back north—heard I lived around here and wanted to see me again. Now let's get these horses buried."

"That's it?" Jess saw something more in Caleb's eyes. "If there's something wrong, Caleb, tell me."

Caleb managed a smile of appreciation for the man's concern. "That's all it was—really. I'm just upset to hear that a lot more Cheyenne are dying from measles than I thought."

Jess watched him go and get a shovel from the gear on Jess's horse. He sensed whatever had happened, it was better left alone unless Caleb chose to talk about it. Caleb returned and began digging. "This is a hell of a loss," he muttered, his eyes tearing. "I loved Dancer."

Sarah looked up from the basket into which she had been putting her clothes. The sun was setting fast now and a storm was coming, rolling in from the western mountains. She was glad her wash was dry, but she was worried about Caleb. He and Jess had been gone for hours.

Wind whipped about her skirt and face as she hurriedly took down the rest of the wash. Sarah never ceased to be amazed at how fast a storm could move in on these plains, or how quickly it would leave again, moving east to vent its fury on others in its path.

She stooped to pick up the basket and move it farther down the line. At forty-seven Sarah Sax had the appearance of a woman years younger, in spite of the hardships of having lived many years on the open plains of Texas and Colorado. Her reddish-gold hair was still thick but showed a hint of gray and had lost a little of its shine.

Her fair skin was no longer quite so fair. The prairie sun had seen to that. But it was still smooth, except for tiny age lines about her green eyes, eyes that still sparkled like a young girl's whenever she looked upon the man she had loved almost her entire life.

Surely it had started back at Fort Dearborn. Could it be true that place was a growing city called Chicago now? She and Caleb had been through so much since those childhood years when the uncle with whom she had been living brought home the nine-year-old half-breed Indian boy called Blue Hawk. Tom Sax had kept the wounded boy and named him Caleb; Sarah had helped teach him English and white man's ways. They had become like brother and sister, and then close, loving friends . . . and then lovers— lovers who had been cruelly separated for years until they found each other again later in life. That had been in 1832, thirteen years ago. Thirteen years was all they had really had together—thirteen years when it could have been thirty.

Now she was plagued more and more with spells of shaking and weakness, as well as bouts with pneumonia. Every time Caleb happened to come upon a doctor traveling through Bent's Fort, he corralled the physician and brought him to the small Sax ranch a half day's ride away to get another opinion of his wife's health. But no doctor could come to any particular conclusion, and all left tonics that were supposed to help a "woman's ailments" and give her more strength and energy.

None of them had worked, and from their smell and taste, Caleb guessed that most contained plain whiskey. Sarah was convinced the source of her problem was drugs forced into her years ago by her first husband, Byron Clawson, the man she was forced to marry after he had accomplished a plot to convince her Caleb Sax was dead. The baby she carried in her belly then, planted there by Caleb in a moment of tender, loving passion, had needed a father.

Would the horror of those years without Caleb ever leave her? She could only thank God that the son she and Caleb had after they were reunited did not seem affected by her ailments. James, twelve now, didn't have his father's Indian looks but his eyes were blue like Caleb's. The boy's skin was fair, browned only by the sun, not naturally; and his hair was a sandy color, with a reddish hint to it under the Colorado sun.

Sarah also had to thank God that she had found her daughter, the baby conceived in that passionate and youthful love affair with Caleb; the baby her husband had stolen away from her and put in an orphanage. Lynda was her name—the name given her by the orphanage. Several years later Lynda had found her mother in St. Louis where she was living, and together they had found Caleb in Texas with his Cheyenne son, Tom Sax.

Life in Texas had been good at first, until the war for Texas independence. Even though the men had fought in the war, the ensuing methodical extermination and exiling of Texas's Indians had left the Saxes nearly penniless and without a home, forcing them to flee that new republic and settle in Colorado.

Now there were just Caleb and Sarah, young James, and Lynda, who was married to Jess and had two sons of her own, and who remained near the parents she had never known until she was sixteen years old.

Tom, now thirty-three, had left for California, searching for the happiness he had been unable to find since losing his first wife, Bess, to cholera back in Texas.

Now Sarah could see Caleb and Jess finally returning. No other man sat a horse the way Caleb did. Sarah could see the fringes of his buckskin clothing dance with the rhythm of the horse's gait, could discern the ease with which he rode the animal. Most of the time he didn't even use a standard saddle, preferring the flat, stuffed buffalo-hide saddles Indians used, sometimes riding bareback.

Caleb was good with horses, the best, as far as Sarah was concerned. But starting up a new ranch and building a new herd at fifty years old was not easy, even for a man like Caleb. More and more settlement in the area had chased away the wild herds of horses from which Caleb had planned to rebuild his stock, breeding only the strongest and most beautiful horses from those he could round up on the free range.

Things had not gone as well as he had hoped, but to Sarah it didn't matter. All that mattered was that they had lived through the awful years of besiegement by those who threatened their very lives in Texas, and they were still alive and together. Except for Tom the whole family was still a unit. And even in his absence, Tom was still with them in spirit. He would always be with them. Few men were as close as Caleb and Tom Sax.

Sarah could see the weary, concerned look on her husband's face as he rode closer and dismounted from the big Appaloosa gelding.

"Take care of him for me, would you, Jess," he said then, handing the man his reins.

"Sure, Caleb. Sorry about the mare."

Caleb sighed deeply, removing a leather hat and wiping perspiration from his forehead. "So am I."

Jess rode off toward the cabin he shared with Lynda. Sarah could see her daughter hanging out some wash in the distance.

Sarah turned to Caleb. He towered over her, his huge frame silhouetted against a setting sun behind him. It was difficult to see his face and she shaded her eyes, noticing his own bloodshot eyes.

"You lost the foal?"

His jaw flexed. Handsome it was, square, strong, set under full lips that normally framed straight white teeth when moving into his usual warm, provocative smile. But he was not smiling today.

"We lost both of them."

"Oh, no! Dancer, too?"

Caleb just sighed again and walked past her to a pan of water that sat outside the cabin. He hung his hat on a hook and reached for a bar of lye soap, wetting his hands in the water and scrubbing them vigorously. He said nothing for several long seconds, working the soap up his arms to the rolled-up sleeves of his buckskin shirt, scrubbing some more.

Sarah watched, saying nothing. She knew he would tell

her more when he was ready. She noticed the dried blood on his arms and a little on his shirt. He rinsed off, then picked up a towel that sat beside the pan and walked to a watering trough nearby. He dipped his hands into the cleaner water and splashed some over his face, then picked up the towel and wiped off the water, running the damp cloth around the back of his neck.

"I don't know what happened," he finally spoke up, his voice troubled. "Who knows in these things? In all the years I've raised and bred horses, there are still things I can't explain. The foal was breech. I had to turn the damned thing myself. Hell, I've done it before." He threw down the towel. "And it always worked. But this time it didn't. I could tell when I turned it that it was already dead. I pulled on it and helped Mother Nature get the thing born. It was a nice-looking male, but it was dead. We tried to get the mother up then, but she just lay there and—" He shrugged and shook his head. "I felt so damned helpless. A man thinks he knows everything there is to know, and then he's confronted with something that makes him feel completely ignorant again."

Sarah moved closer, meeting the blue eyes she loved so much, feeling his pain. "I'm sorry. These things happen, Caleb. We know that. There will be other foals."

She saw the irritation in his eyes, the impatience. "That's what I told myself last year, and the year before that. But I can't find enough really healthy horses out there to begin with, and when I do, half of them don't breed well. It's like everything has been against us here."

"Caleb, you know what we agreed to about all of that. We agreed to be thankful we're all still together and no one was hurt. We'll be all right."

He turned away, staring out over the horizon. A small black, humpy line could be seen there, the distant ridge of the Rockies to the west.

"It's been three years, Sarah. We picked out this piece of land because it was close to Bent's Fort. We've all worked like slaves to get something going here. Tom even stayed on longer than he should have had to stay. But it seems as if I can't quite get back to where I was in Texas."

"No one expects you to build anything that big again, Caleb. We're surviving and our bellies are full. We're warm in winter and—"

He turned, his look of near anger cutting off her words. "That's not enough and you know it. You can't be working as hard as you do. I wanted more for you, Sarah. I had so much planned for you." He began unlacing his buckskin shirt, then reached down and grasped the bottom, pulling it up over his head, revealing a flat stomach and a muscular build that belied his fifty years. He was a tall, broad, strong man, who had lived hard and sometimes wild. He had not only fought in the infamous revenge against the Crow, but also the Comanche and the Mexicans in Texas. And his chest bore the scars of suffering the Sun Dance ritual in his teens while living with the Cheyenne. His handsome face was etched with the hard lines of living, and the thin white scar on his cheek seemed to get whiter as the rest of his skin got darker and more rugged with sun and age.

Sarah crossed her arms authoritatively. "There's no sense going over that again, Caleb. You know how I feel about it. Texas is behind us, and I've never asked for a grand life-style. Just finding you again and being with you is all that matters."

He tossed aside the shirt, putting his hands on his hips and looking down at her. To see them together—he so tall, dark, and broad and sometimes fierce looking; she such a small woman, soft and white—it was an almost humorous picture.

"I know how you feel," he answered. "And I love you for it. But even if you're satisfied, it still isn't enough for me. It's what *I* want for you. If they had let me alone in Texas, I could have given you the life you deserve. But when a man's life is more than half over, it's not easy to rebuild all over again."

She stepped closer, putting her hands to his waist. "You still have some fine horses to take to the fort next week, and Lynda made some beautiful quilts. I have two boxes of handmade clothes that will bring some good money in Santa Fe."

He put his hands on her shoulders. Sarah Sax was a talented seamstress, had even made a living at it in St. Louis during the years they were apart. The clothing she made was immaculately stitched, strong and lasting.

"You're busy enough with the general chores of a woman and making most of our own clothes. I don't like your putting in all those added hours just for extra money. You need your rest."

She reached up and grasped his wrists. "What's really wrong, Caleb? It's more than the dead mare and foal. Is it Tom?"

He studied her a long moment. She was still so beautiful to him. All he could ever see was the seventeen-year-old Sarah with whom he had fallen in love. She had always been so small, and now she seemed tinier than ever, losing weight as she aged rather than gaining, so that her waist was still slender and her skin still smooth, and her green eyes were still bright and provocative.

There had been times when she had cried over the fact she had never gotten pregnant again after having James. She had dearly wanted at least one more child. But whatever the physical reason for no more pregnancies, Caleb didn't care. He was glad their frequent lovemaking had not led to another conception.

"You're too perceptive, Sarah Sax. And you're right about Tom. I can't help but worry about him." He decided to let her think Tom was the problem. Why worry her with the story of White Horse's visit and the man's ominous predictions? If he told her about the dream, she would only suffer the guilt of thinking she was keeping him from the life he truly wanted to live—among the Cheyenne. That was how she would interpret it at least. It was true he missed that life, but to have Sarah was all that mattered.

"Tom Sax is a grown man who is more than capable of taking care of himself," Sarah was telling him reassuringly. "You'll be getting a letter from him soon telling you everything is just fine. And maybe he'll find himself a woman to love—someone who will make him as happy as Bess did. That's what we really want for him, isn't it?"

He leaned down and kissed her cheek. "Got any supper left?"

"You know I always keep something warmed. Maybe one of these evenings you can be here on time."

He grinned, sensing she needed the smile. They had drawn on each other's strength, as they always did. He would put White Horse's visit out of his mind. He could do no more than take a day at a time. But he would not give up his desire to make a better life for his Sarah. "Where's James?" he asked.

"He's out in the shed reading. You know James. He'd rather stick his nose in a book than go out on a roundup. He's got in the habit of going out there with a lamp and reading where he can be alone as often as he can. I swear if I didn't remind him of his chores, he'd let them go forever and even forget to eat. All he thinks about is those books. He surely has the equivalent of a good education by now, with all the reading he does."

Caleb said nothing. He and James were as different as night and day. He loved his youngest son dearly, but there was a growing barrier between them, and Caleb didn't have the slightest idea where it had all begun. Perhaps it was simply the fact that their spirits were not in tune. Caleb Sax was all Indian. James's looks and actions gave no hint that his father's Indian blood flowed in his own veins. Nor did he show the tiniest sign of Caleb's own Indian spirit.

"Cale around?"

"I think he's off with those Cheyenne boys again." Sarah shook her head as they headed toward the cabin. "That boy is going to break Lynda's heart, Caleb. He's so wild, and he's gone half the time."

Caleb only grinned. Now there was a spirit he understood all too well. His grandson Cale was all Indian, a son born to Lynda, and fathered by her first husband, a Cherokee man named Lee Whitestone. "There's no sense in trying to hold that one back, I can tell you," Caleb told Sarah as they went inside.

Caleb Lee Whitestone was named after his grandfather and father, and to save confusion, the family just called him Cale. Cale was just six months younger than his uncle, James. He would be twelve in December, and his looks and spirit showed no sign of the small strain of white blood that ran in his veins.

Cale's father was killed by Comanche Indians before Cale was even born, and several years later Lynda had married Jess Purnell. Since coming to Colorado, Cale seemed to be moving ever closer to his Indian blood and spirit. He had begun spending more and more time with Indian boys his age, mostly Cheyenne who camped around Bent's Fort and traded with the Santa Fe merchants.

Cale had a five-year-old half brother, John, born to his mother and Jess Purnell. John was a grand mixture of his Indian mother and white father, looking mostly white at first glance, but bearing the dark beauty of his mother. His skin was a soft brown, and his hair dark; but his eyes were a lighter blue, like his father's, and he carried Jess's broad, big-boned build.

"Well maybe when little John gets older he'll be more dependable than his half brother," Sarah was telling Caleb.

They went inside the small cabin, which consisted of one main room, a bedroom off that main room where Caleb and Sarah slept, and a loft above their bedroom, where James slept.

Sarah moved to the stove and Caleb came up behind, putting his arms around her.

"It's been a strange day, Sarah." He bent over, squeezing her close and kissing her neck. White Horse's words haunted him.

She smiled at his embrace, turning slightly and looking up at him. Caleb's mouth met hers in a kiss that told her her man needed her. She would never deny that need, not out of duty, but out of the sheer joy and pleasure she derived from his lovemaking.

His lips left hers and he smiled the smile that always melted her, but she saw a sadness behind it that she attributed to the lost mare and the fact that he missed Tom very much.

Caleb left her and walked into the bedroom to get a clean shirt. Far out on the plains wolves sniffed and scratched around freshly dug dirt where a mare and her foal lay buried. Even farther away more wild things moved—Indians—on their way north, constantly on the move now in a desperate struggle to preserve their way of life and what little freedom was left to them.

• Chapter Two •

A warm wind moved across the valley, carrying with it the scent of the Pacific as it gently moved over Tom Sax. The breeze and the sun felt good after his lonely and harrowing journey over the Sierras. No one would know up there it was supposed to be summer. Up there it was still very cold at night, and in the highest elevations pockets of snow dotted shadowed crevices, old, hard snow that never got the chance to fully melt before the next early mountain winter would just make it deeper again. The snows that did melt drained into the watersheds that fed the green valleys below, turning them into a farmer's or a rancher's paradise.

Tom gazed at one of those valleys now, a vast expanse of sun-warmed green that lay in quiet beauty. He breathed deeply of the sweet air. So, this was California. It was even more beautiful than others had described it.

Perhaps here he could start a new life. The stabbing pain of the memory of his sweet Bess was not so sharp now. Was it possible she had been dead ten years already? Texas, all his memories, everything had been left behind.

He adjusted his hat, studying the lovely scene below. Like his father, Tom looked all Indian, but he had never really lived like one. He carried Caleb's tall, broad build; and like his father he had a hard handsomeness to him that attracted women. He was dark, from his coffee-colored skin to his long, shining black hair to his wide-set eyes,

eyes that still showed the bitterness that lurked in his soul over what had happened to his family and their ranch in Texas.

But he could not live his whole life lamenting the past. He was thirty-three years old, and still, since Bess died, he had been unable to settle down again. The last few years his father had needed him to help get the family back on its feet after being forced out of Texas. Now it was time to be alone, to go on to something new. He knew horses and ranching, thanks to his father, and in the valley below he could see beautiful horses grazing on the rich green grass. They were golden like the California sun.

Palominos. He liked palominos. And already he liked California. A man could live a damned good life here, and right now it was mostly Spaniards and Mexicans who lived that good life. But it probably would not be long before Americans decided to get a taste of it. When Tom had left his family behind in Colorado, there had already been rumors that the war was not over between the United States and Mexico. Offers were being made by the United States to purchase vast new areas from Mexico, including most of California. But Tom knew Mexico would never sell. They still had not even acknowledged Texas's independence, let alone the fact that it was now a state. But now that it was, Tom Sax knew full well that if the U.S. could not buy more Mexican land legally, they would take it by force, just as they had taken his father's land in Texas by force.

He headed his Appaloosa gelding down the ridge toward the fields where the golden horses grazed. Perhaps there was work here for him. It looked like a huge ranch.

"Rancho muy grande," he muttered, studying the vast grazing land and several outbuildings in the distance. Even farther off he could see the main house, just a small dot far off in the valley. This was a big land, California. It reminded him of Texas in its vastness, but it was so much greener.

Tom stopped to dismount and remove his light buckskin jacket. He didn't need it now. He tied it to his gear and for a moment was tempted to strip down and ride through the valley half naked, feeling the sun on his skin. He supposed it was the Indian in him that gave him those temptations. But riding half naked into unknown territory run by strangers would not exactly be the best way to make friends and find a job.

He remounted, unbuttoning his blue calico shirt partway and adjusting his leather hat, then headed into the valley, his long black hair flying behind him as he urged the Appaloosa into a moderate run.

Caleb drove a last nail into the lid on the box of handsewn clothing. He had built the boxes himself, lining them with clean doeskin first and making sure the seams were good and tight so that the clothing inside wouldn't get wet in case of rain. Sarah had put too many hard hours into making those clothes to lose their value from careless packing.

It still irritated him that Sarah had to do seamstress work to help bring in more money. He worried about her. Her spells of weakness seemed to grow more frequent, and the visit from White Horse over two months ago still haunted him.

All his life it seemed people he loved were snatched away from him. And now he had to submit Sarah to the privations of life in an uncivilized land. It was true Texas had also been uncivilized when first she came to him there, but then he had land and power and many men to protect his own. There he had come so close to being able to give his Sarah the good life she deserved.

Now life was again a struggle. He didn't mind for himself, but it angered him that in these later years of life Sarah had to work so hard in their effort to start over. The frustration of it tortured his soul, and he cursed under his breath as he packed the clothing. Sarah had stayed up all hours of the night just to add to the supplies he would take to Bent's Fort and sell to traders going to Santa Fe. It was her contribution, something she insisted on doing to bring in more money.

He knew that if he were white, life would not be so hard for them. It was his Indian blood that got them chased out of Texas, his Indian blood Sarah's father had hated to the point of trying to have Caleb killed all those years ago, leading to their separation and her marriage to a cruel man. Still, he had never for a moment felt ashamed of being Indian. He was proud of that blood and made sure all his children felt the same pride. She would have it no other way. The Indian spirit in Caleb was part of what Sarah loved about him.

But there was one child who did not share that pride. James's memories of Texas and how they had been treated there had left scars. Caleb already sensed in James a denial of his Indian heritage. The boy did not look Indian. And for some reason Caleb had never been able to get close to his youngest son. James was not even as close to Cale as he had once been. When they were little, they were practically inseparable. But now Caleb could see the boys pulling in two different directions—James frustrated and angry over his Indian blood, and Cale proud of it. James refused to associate with the young Cheyenne boys who hung around Bent's Fort. Cale ran with them almost constantly now.

"Here are a few more things, Caleb," Sarah told him, coming out with a couple of small items on her arm.

He looked down at her. "You're looking prettier than ever today," he told her, keeping his voice cheerful. The remark was sincere. To him she still looked like the young girl he had run off with back in Missouri—a blossoming, ravishing young thing who had made his blood run hot. She still brought that warmth to his blood at night, when her full breasts were pressed against his naked chest and his fingers became entangled in her red-gold hair.

He put the clothes into the box, grinning over the way she blushed at his remark. "It's amazing to me that I still look pretty to you at all," she answered.

"Now that's ridiculous and you know it." He turned and pulled her into his arms. "We'll be back sometime tomorrow." He bent down and met her lips in a lingering kiss. Only hours before he had been inside her, enjoying the pleasures only she could give him. "And we'll continue what we were doing last night," he added, kissing her neck.

"Caleb!" she protested jocularly.

He squeezed her close, lifting her feet slightly off the ground, and Sarah laughed.

She looked into his handsome face, letting him hold her in his strong arms. "Don't be too upset with James for pouting over having to go to the fort with you," she asked him, instinctively wanting no problems between father and son.

Caleb sighed deeply and set her gently on her feet. "With Tom gone I have to leave a man here to watch over you and Lynda, which has to be Jess. Cale and James both know one or the other or both of them have to go with me to the fort." He put his arm around her waist and walked with her toward the cabin. "It used to be fun, Sarah. But now James says Cale always hangs around with the Indian boys, and he complains that there aren't any white boys his age to play with."

She put her own arm around his waist and squeezed, realizing how much it hurt him that James Sax made it very obvious he was ashamed of his Indian blood. "You can't force a person to feel the way you want him to feel, Caleb," she said carefully, hoping to soothe him. How she wished the two of them could be closer. She prayed for it every day. "He's just at the age where a young man starts wondering about a lot of things, doubting things, wanting to be his own man. You've got to let him get things straight in his own mind."

Caleb sighed and faced her again. "In the meantime I worry about you more than anything else." He glanced at the wagon and back at his wife. "I'm sorry, Sarah—about your having to make those clothes and all. They bring a damned good price. As soon as I get my herd built up again—"

"Caleb, we've been over this and over it. I don't mind."

She untied her apron as they neared the doorway. "Things will work out, Caleb. Now you take those clothes and the deer hides you cleaned and some of your best horses and get yourself to the fort before that supply train leaves for Santa Fe. And James will go whether he likes it or not. I've made up a list of things we need and so has Lynda. Come in and eat something now before you go."

She turned and marched into the cabin, adjusting and retying her apron. He gazed after her, realizing she had a way of leading him in spite of his strength and prowess. He had killed a lot of men, fought a lot of battles, but Sarah Sax had a way of making him follow. It made him remember when they were just children at Fort Dearborn and she had taken it upon herself to teach him English and the white man's ways. In times like this, when she lightly scolded him and marched away, she was like that little girl again, stubbornly taking command and not letting him falter or be afraid.

"Father, have you seen Cale?"

Caleb turned to see Lynda approaching.

"Isn't he cleaning out the stalls in the barn?" Caleb answered as the young woman came closer.

"No. Oh, Father, I think he's ridden off again ahead of you to the fort. Someday he'll just stay there with those Cheyenne boys and never come back. I just know it."

He grinned. "That's not so bad. He has to try things. He has to decide where he belongs."

Her blue eyes showed their concern. Lynda Sax Purnell was all of her father, with dark skin and a sultry, fiery beauty Jess Purnell had been unable to resist when he had met her in Texas. She was tall and slender with high cheekbones and her father's vivid blue eyes. It had taken many years for Jess, who had been a drifter, to break down Lynda's resistance and teach her to love again after losing Cale's father to death. But Jess's charm and rugged good looks, as well as his strength and goodness, won her over.

"Well, I'm afraid his decision will be to ride off someday with those Cheyenne boys and never return," she answered. "Every time he goes off like this I fear it's the last I'll see of him."

"Why don't you go help your mother with breakfast and stop worrying," Caleb assured her. "I've got to be getting to the fort soon. I'll look for Cale when I get there and give him a scolding for not telling someone before riding off like that. Are Jess and James in the barn?"

"Yes. And John is trying to help. It's so funny, his struggling with his little arms trying to rake out the stalls."

"He's a good boy, Lynda. I'm proud of both my grandsons. They'll both be fine men in their own right."

She met his eyes, her smile fading. "So will James, Father. But he's got to be the man of his choosing. I know his behavior has annoyed you lately, but be patient with him. He'll find his place one day. He loves you very much, you know. He almost worships you. But he thinks you don't approve of him because he's not all Indian like Cale."

Caleb studied her eyes. "He told you that?"

"Once. Not in those exact words, but I got the meaning."

"That's ridiculous. He's my son. He can be whatever he wants to be, as long as he doesn't hurt other people by doing it." He shook his head, looking toward the barn. "How is it you can love someone so much and yet have nothing in common with them, be so impatient with them?" He met her eyes again. "Has it been all that obvious, my impatience with him?"

"Only lately. I know you're upset over losing Dancer and the way other things have been going lately. Don't be too hard on James because of other problems, Father."

He smiled sadly. "The father is supposed to give the daughter advice, not the other way around."

She laughed lightly, but then her smile faded. "Father, can I ask you something personal?"

He frowned, folding his arms. "You can ask. It doesn't mean I'll answer."

She watched his eyes. "What did those Indians want— the day the mare and foal died? Jess told me some Indians came, and you talked to them, but you looked upset. He said you said it was just because of so many Cheyenne dying and that you knew one of them from when you were young." She tossed her head as though proud of the way she understood her father, sometimes better than even Sarah. "I say it was something more."

He sighed deeply, leaning against a hitching post. "That was over two months ago. Why are you asking now?"

She shrugged. "Because I knew you wouldn't tell me if I asked too soon."

"And I won't tell you now. It's too personal."

Her eyebrows arched. "That bad?"

He smiled sadly. "No. Not bad. Sad, maybe. But not bad. And don't ask me that in front of your mother. I never told her about that visit and I told Jess not to tell her."

"I know." She studied him lovingly. "You'll be with them again someday, won't you? You'll go back. You'll be Indian again before you die."

"I've always been Indian."

"You know what I mean."

His eyes showed slight irritation at the probing conversation. "I know exactly what you mean. And you're probably right."

"Not probably, I *am* right." Her eyes teared. "You and Cale. I can't blame my son for the way he is. He worships everything about his grandfather, you know. And he loves you so much."

"I know. And I love him, even when he runs off on me when I need him. I'll turn him upside down for that."

She laughed lightly. "I think he's getting too big for that. He's not even twelve yet, but he looks sixteen."

Caleb grinned. "I was the same way."

She smiled and shook her head. "I can just imagine." She moved toward the cabin then. "Go get those three troublemakers out in the barn and tell them to come and eat."

She went inside and Caleb looked toward the barn, where James and John jumped out of the loft into a stack of hay, laughing and tumbling. Maybe things weren't as serious with James as he was letting them be in his mind. Today the boy seemed perfectly happy, but then he would probably scowl when it came time to ride to the fort, whereas Cale was already undoubtedly playing Indian games with some of the Cheyenne boys.

The sprawling hacienda was even bigger than Tom had thought. He was quickly greeted by several Mexicans with guns, and he was wise enough not to draw his own pistol. Tom was familiar with the ways of men who owned such large ranches. Strangers were not to be trusted. No one was allowed to just ride to the owner's house without questioning. He would cooperate, and no one treated him rudely as he was escorted to the home of Antonio Galvez, who, he was told, owned the land on which he had intruded. His escort was courteous but watchful, and now one rode ahead of the rest to tell his *patrón* that a young stranger had come seeking work.

Tom's keen eyes absorbed the surroundings—a lot of land, horses, and men. This was no small enterprise. Whoever owned this spread was a rich man. Tom was glad he knew Spanish and was familiar with Mexicans and their ways. Years spent in a Mexican prison had taught him that.

A few young women, wives and daughters of the help, looked up as they rode through a spattering of small buildings that apparently were home for them. The little houses were well kept and solid. Some of the help looked more Indian than Mexican, and Tom forced himself not to look too long at any of the women, even those whose eyes told him they were quite pleased with the looks of the handsome young *forastero* who had come to the hacienda. Any one of them could be the wife or daughter of one of the men who were leading him to the owner. It would be unwise at this stage to get any of them riled up over a woman.

"El señor Galvez doesn't really need any more help," the apparent leader of the men told Tom. He was a cocky fellow that Tom already didn't like. Tom decided that if he didn't like the owner either, he would simply move on.

"Then why are you taking me to him?"

"Because it is your request. I am leader of these men here, but I am not the man who makes the final decisions on hiring or letting someone go. Those decisions are for the *patrón*. What is your name, señor?"

"I am called Tom Sax. What about you?"

The handsome young man looked over at Tom, a distinct coldness in his dark eyes. "I am called Emanuel Hidalgo." He looked Tom up and down. "You do not look like a true Mexican."

"I'm not. I'm three-quarters Indian. What's left is white.

My mother was full-blooded Cheyenne, and my father is half Cheyenne."

Hidalgo's eyebrows arched. "If you are looking to work for pay, señor, you have come to the wrong place. El señor Galvez uses Indians only as slaves. He treats them well. They have houses of their own and eat well. But they do not get pay, and they are the property of el señor Galvez."

Tom straightened proudly. "I've never been any man's property and I'm not about to start now."

Hidalgo grinned. "We will see."

Tom scowled at the statement and decided to change the subject. "Where in hell am I, anyway? I know I'm in California, but where in California?"

"You are in the Sacramento Valley, señor, not far from Sonoma. This is the northern part of California."

They were coming close to the main house, and then Tom saw her—a dark-eyed girl standing on the veranda watching. She was young, very young. But her rich beauty could not be denied, nor could the obvious fact that she was a ravishing woman in the making. This time it was difficult not to stare at the big, beautiful eyes that looked back at him curiously; impossible not to notice the velvety look of her young face, the glow of her dark hair that hung in waves to her waist, the blossoming bosom that nicely filled the bodice of her pretty yellow dress.

"Be careful with your eyes, señor, or the *patrón* will have you shot," Hidalgo told him then. "She is his daughter, and el señor Galvez watches her like a she-cat. Her mother is dead and she has no brothers or sisters. And she is not for the likes of an Indian."

Tom stiffened at the words. "I would say it is up to her father to decide who is worthy and who isn't," he answered, becoming more irritated at Hidalgo's impudence. "What's her name?"

Hidalgo flashed him a dark, warning look. "She is Doña Juanita Rosanna Galvez de Sonoma. She is fifteen and getting to the age where she can be married. When she does, she will marry me, Emanuel Hidalgo."

This time Tom's eyebrows arched. "You've already asked for her, and she has accepted?"

The man scowled. "I have not asked. I am simply telling you how it will be. And I am telling you not to look at her again."

Their eyes held challengingly, and Tom smiled then. "I thought the *patrón* made all the rules around here."

They halted their horses and Hidalgo moved smoldering eyes from Tom to the others. "You can all leave. I will stay until el señor Galvez decides what to do with this one. Get back to your chores, *pronto*."

The men left, a few of them stealing a glance at Juanita Galvez before leaving. Tom moved his own eyes in her direction again, not caring about Hidalgo's warning, which he was sure was meaningless. The man's statement that he would one day wed this girl was surely just his own personal dream and not a fact. And he did not strike Tom as being a gentle man. The beauty he beheld now should have a husband who knew how to handle such a sweet, untouched señorita.

He knew the ways of these people. This girl was innocent and would remain that way until married; and married only to a man of whom her father approved. He had no feelings for her himself, yet he suddenly did not like the thought of someone like Emanuel Hidalgo making a woman of the lovely child before him, and the little challenge Hidalgo had put before him only brought out the stubborn streak in Tom Sax. No matter what the odds, he would get a job at this place, and for pay, just to prove Hidalgo could be wrong about his beloved *patrón*.

A stocky, dark man came stomping out of the house, laying some sharp words on his daughter first for staring so blatantly at a stranger. He ordered her into the house. The girl smiled at Tom and whirled, running inside. He watched the movement of her firm, round hips beneath the yellow dress. It was a hot day, and she apparently wore no slips beneath it. He chastised himself for having manly urges for such a young thing, and he moved his eyes to her father.

"You are Antonio Galvez?" he asked.

"I am. What is it you want?"

"He has come seeking work on the ranch," Hidalgo answered before Tom could. "But he is Indian, *patrón*. I told him you do not hire Indians for pay."

Galvez cast the man a look of irritation. "I hire each man on his worth and skill, not whether he is Indian or Mexican or white," he snapped.

Hidalgo stiffened, and Tom kept a smile to himself, meeting Galvez's eyes squarely. "My name is Tom Sax, señor. And I am worth regular pay. I grew up on a ranch in Texas—my father's. We had thousands of acres, and my father raised some of the finest horses in the West. He still does, only now he is in Colorado. I know horses. I can ride down the wildest mustang and tame him. I know what to look for in a good steed. I could go to auctions and purchase only the finest mares and stallions for you. I can deliver a breech colt and I know how to treat sick and wounded horses."

Galvez nodded. "Texas? Did you fight against Santa Anna and help steal Texas from Mexico?"

"I never looked at it as stealing, señor. I was raised in Texas from a small child. I loved the land. We were good Mexicans, but Mexico would not help us against the Comanche and outlaws. They did not keep their promises and they threatened what was rightfully ours, our home and family. I did what I thought was right. I was at the Alamo, and my father fought at San Jacinto. I was captured before Santa Anna overcame the Alamo, and I spent several years in a Mexican prison. When I was released, a wealthy Mexican such as yourself gave me work and was kind to me. It was then I realized the war was not really between the two people, but a war of politics and power. Not long after, the Americans who had won Texas independence turned on my father because he was Indian, and we were forced to leave the Republic to save our lives. I had a wife in Texas, but she died. I am a man without a home now. I bear no bitterness toward the Mexicans any longer. In war a man seldom knows the real reason he is fighting."

Galvez nodded again. "You are a wise young man. I like the way you speak and the sureness of your words. You say the truth." He looked Tom over, admiring the young man's powerful-looking body and proud handsomeness. Antonio

Galvez was a man who knew how to judge other men, and this one was a good man.

"You claim to know horses well?"

"Working with horses is all I've ever done, señor. I've come to California to forget bitter memories in Texas and start a life of my own. I need work until I decide just what to do in this new land. I saw your hacienda and decided to see if you need any extra men."

Galvez pulled at a thick mustache. "Emanuel was right in telling you most of my Indian help are merely slaves. But they are not so independent as you seem to be. I like the way you talk. And I like the way you sit the horse you are riding. He is a fine-looking animal."

"He is one that my father raised from a colt. As I told you, my father raises only the best. And I only work for pay, like the next man. I will do my share. If I cannot work for pay, I will go someplace else."

"No." Galvez kept pulling at his mustache, leaving the veranda then and walking completely around Tom and his horse, closely studying both. Tom used the moment to glance at a window where a pretty young girl stood peering at him from between lacy curtains. She smiled and a wave of passion rippled through him that annoyed him considerably. What joy it would be teaching such a young thing about men, ever so gently partaking of her young, tender body and giving her pleasure in return. He quickly chastised himself for the thought.

"I will make you a deal, Señor Sax," Galvez told him then, coming around to face him. "The man who owns the ranch next to mine—Julio Baca—we have a friendly bet going. So far neither of us has won. If you help me win this bet, you have a job here at full pay."

Tom frowned. "How can I help you win?"

Galvez smiled. "I have a certain wild horse—a black stallion that has a mind of his own, if you know what I mean."

Tom nodded. "I have had experience with such animals."

Hidalgo shifted in his saddle, forced to hide his anger at the fact that Antonio Galvez seemed to like this new young stranger. He noticed Juanita watching from the window. If she were his wife, she would pay for looking at a man that way. How many nights had he dreamed about being the first one inside Juanita Galvez?

"My men caught the horse," Galvez was telling Tom. "But Julio claims it was caught on his property. We have agreed that whichever ranch employs the man who can train this horse will be able to keep the animal. So far none of my men have been able to train him, nor have any of Julio's men. If you can tame this animal, you have a job here."

Tom grinned almost boyishly. "I accept the challenge. I'll tame him."

Galvez laughed lightly. "Don't you want to see the animal first?"

"I don't need to. I'll accept your challenge without even a look. If I fail, I leave your land and do not get the job."

"This land, señor, is called Lecho de Rosas, 'Bed of Roses.' Wherever you ride on this land, you will find wild roses blooming. It is beautiful land, is it not?"

"It's the prettiest I've ever seen." Tom could not help glancing at Juanita again. She sensed his words were meant for her, and she dashed away from the window. "I would like to work at Lecho de Rosas," Tom added. "I'll tame the wild horse for you. Bring all your men to watch, if you want. And bring Julio. Is there a time limit?"

"Forty-eight hours. So far all the others have done is make the horse even wilder and angrier. He almost killed one of my men. He is a mean one, señor. Perhaps you will want to think about it first."

Tom shook his head. "I don't have to think about it. I'll do it. No one knows horses better than my father. I learned from the best. I'll tame your black stallion and he'll be your best stud. But if I do, I want the same pay as your more experienced men. I'm worth it."

Galvez's eyebrows arched. "You are not a man who wastes words or sells himself short. That is good, Tom Sax. I have many rules here and expect them to be obeyed, including staying away from my daughter, Juanita. She is very young. If you obey the rules, and do the job you say you can do, you will have the same pay as the others."

"But, Señor Galvez, he is Indian," Hidalgo exclaimed then, hardly able to control his jealous anger.

Galvez flashed him a warning look. "I make the decisions around here, Emanuel. You are always forgetting that, it seems." He put his hands on his hips. "Besides, if he does not tame the black one, he has no job at all. Considering the luck the others have had, I do not think we will be seeing any more of this one after he has tried his hand at that black devil." He smiled at Tom, then looked again at Hidalgo. "Give him a bunk and treat him well. I will make arrangements with Julio Baca."

Hidalgo turned his horse. "Follow me," he said to Tom, disgust in his voice.

"*Gracias,* Señor Galvez," Tom said to the man. "I will not let you down."

"We will see," the man answered with a grin. "We will see."

Tom turned and followed Emanuel Hidalgo, reminding himself it might be wise to never turn his back on Hidalgo. The man was definitely not someone who was going to help or befriend him. He was a man to be watched—not just for himself, but also around Juanita Galvez.

• Chapter Three •

James drove his father's wagon into Bent's Fort, Caleb driving a small herd of horses in its wake. Neither the wagon nor the horses brought much notice amid the grand mixture of traveling merchants and traders, trappers, and Indians who were milling about. James headed the wagon toward a caravan lined up outside the fort, prepared to leave for Santa Fe.

"Caleb! I was wonderin' whether you'd be comin' in," a whiskered man in buckskins called out.

"I'd have come a couple of days sooner, Willie, but the wife didn't feel well and she didn't get the clothes finished until just yesterday." Caleb pranced his Appaloosa closer and dismounted.

James watched with a mixture of admiration and resentment. His father was probably one of the strongest and most skilled men in these parts; but Caleb looked hardly any different from the Cheyenne men who hung around the fort. The men was so Indian; and James hated having Indian blood.

The boy stood up in the wagon to look across the wide, flat, grassy land that surrounded the fort, where tipis were scattered and smoke rose from campfires. He strained his eyes to try to find Cale. Indian women stood over the fires, while children and dogs ran about. James finally spotted Cale surrounded by young Cheyenne boys, all of them shooting arrows at a straw dummy. They seemed to be betting on whether or not they could hit their target.

James frowned at the way Cale got along with them so easily, laughing and shoving. James could see no future in hanging around with uneducated young Indian boys whose only goal was to run down a buffalo; who lived off the land and some of whom had probably taken part in attacks on whites, which seemed to be happening more and more lately. These Cheyenne even warred against other Indians, especially the Pawnee and the Crow. They didn't seem to care at all about settling down and realizing they must change their way of living. If only they would change, perhaps they would one day be better accepted by the white settlers who were fast filling this land.

But, James reasoned, maybe they would never be accepted. His own father had lived as well or better than most of the settlers in Texas, and what had it got him? They had still been forced to leave, just because they had Indian blood.

James scowled and sat back down. How could it be pos-

sible he was related to these wild people? He felt no fond-
ness for them nor any kind of attachment to them emotionally. He was white in every way; he had learned long ago
that to be recognized as having Indian blood meant disaster
and heartache.

"Them pretty dresses she makes sells like hot cakes
down to Santa Fe," the man called Willie was telling
Caleb. "Them Mexican women thinks our pretty American
women knows all about the latest fashions."

"Well, in my wife's case, they're right. Sarah hails from
St. Louis, you know, and for a lot of years she made her
living making clothes."

"Well, she's some fine seamstress. But a woman like
your Sarah don't need no pretty dresses to look good, that's
a fact, if you don't mind my sayin' so."

Caleb laughed lightly, walking back to the wagon to take
off the boxes of clothing. "James, why don't you go find
Cale? I'm sure he's around here somewhere."

The boy pushed on the wagon brake and jumped down.
"He's over there with those Cheyenne boys shooting
arrows," he grumbled. "They wouldn't want me around."

"Well, you won't know that unless you go over there and
see now, will you?"

"I'd rather stay here and help you, Pa."

Their eyes met. Caleb knew the reason but hid his disappointment. "If that's what you want. Take the boxes off
the wagon and carry them over to Willie Taylor's wagon.
I'll herd the horses into the corral and get a count and a
receipt from Willie." He turned away and walked back to
Willie, who was inspecting one of the mares as she grazed
peacefully.

"You sure got an eye for these beauties," he told Caleb.
"She'll bring a good price in pure silver, that she will."

"The more you can get, the better, as always. I've
brought some good deer skins, too. I'll be taking them and
a few buffalo hides into the fort to sell there. Some things
go to Santa Fe, but hides go east."

Willie nodded. "Hides is still wanted. But beaver
pelts—" He shook his head. "I'm afraid the old seasoned
trappers are gonna have to find themselves a new job. I

hear tell silk is takin' the place of beaver for hats. The demand has dropped real fast. It's affectin' a lot of people, includin' ones that run a place like this here fort."

Caleb looked around at all the activity. "I don't see any effects today."

"Well, you will, mark my words. And with more people comin' this way, the Indians is gettin' mighty restless. The day's comin' when we won't be able to be friendly with them no more, and all this tradin' will end. 'Course that won't make much difference to you, will it? To the Cheyenne you're pretty near a legend. I've seen how some of them look at you—the great Blue Hawk. 'Course most of them don't remember them days, do they?"

Caleb smiled sadly. "Quit reminding me of my age, Willie. I try not to think about the fact that most of the Cheyenne I knew then are gone. Fact is, I should have died myself more than once. I have no idea why I'm still walking this earth. I've got so many scars on this old body you can't find the good skin."

Willie laughed and slapped him on the shoulder. "Ain't a person here who'd guess your age. You're as strong as them young bucks out there who are full of fire and sass."

James looked up at his father at the remark. The older he got, the more incredible it seemed to have Caleb Sax as a father. "The boxes are loaded, Pa," he spoke up. "You want me to help you pick up the supplies for Mother?"

"No. I can do it. You can wander around and do whatever you want, Son. Make sure the team is tied and watered first."

"Yes, sir. Can I go help Mr. Benson at the supply store? Sometimes he pays me to help count pelts."

"Go ahead. Just be ready to leave in a couple of hours."

"Is Cale going back with us?"

"He certainly is. And he's going to get a good kick for riding off without telling any of us."

James ran off and Caleb gazed after him.

"Fine son you got, Caleb. And grandson. But they ain't much alike, are they?"

"No," Caleb answered rather absently. "They're nothing alike. Let's get a count on these horses, Willie."

They walked together toward Caleb's horse. "It's gettin' more and more dangerous to go to Santa Fe, you know," Willie said. "What with Mexico cuttin' off relations with the States and all. You know, I suppose, that we're claimin' the Rio Grande is the proper border between Texas and Mexico. It was Mexico's understandin' that the Nueces was the dividin' line. 'Course, Mexico never really has given up its claim on Texas anyway. The way I see it, another war is comin', and it won't be just over Texas. We'll get all of New Mexico and Arizona and maybe even California and most of this here Colorado Territory and maybe more. The States is tryin' to buy it all up, but Mexico won't sell."

"I've had my fill of wars, Willie. You can count me out of that one. Besides, it isn't right. The Americans got Texas. Now they want to grab up more." He grasped the reins of his horse and turned to face the man. "They've no right taking any of it by force if Mexico doesn't want to sell, Willie. I had to give up everything I loved and worked for down in Texas because of land-hungry Americans, and I even fought for Texas's independence. That's the thanks I got. The Americans will get no sympathy from me on this one." The two men walked together toward Caleb's other horses, which were scattered and grazing. "I have no doubt the Americans will move in on the big Mexican landholders, Willie, and take everything away from them. What is it about people with dark skin that makes most white men think it's all right to walk all over them and take what they want?"

"Danged if I know, Caleb. But you know I ain't that way. A man sets his own worth, and it ain't got nothin' to do with the color of his skin. You're as good as any man I know. It's too bad what happened in Texas, your oldest son spendin' all that time in prison down in Mexico and all. After what he done, it wasn't fair, all of you havin' to leave. By the way, you heard from him?"

Caleb eased up onto his horse. He used a small stuffed Indian-style saddle, covered with a blanket. "Not so far. He headed for California. That's all I know. He's surely there by now. I'll be worried about him if there is a war.

It's sure to involve California, too. I imagine he'll write soon and let us know where he's landed."

"He's a hell of a man, Caleb. He can take care of himself real good. He'll do all right."

Caleb nodded. "Tom has a special place in my heart, Willie."

"Well, I expect it was good he went off on his own for a while, Caleb. Mebbe he'll find himself a pretty little señorita to marry."

Caleb grinned. "Maybe. It would be good for him if he did." He rode around Willie to round up his horses and corral them. Willie would find a man to herd them south.

Willie Taylor was a good man, an experienced wagon master and trader. He didn't really own the items he carried on his excursions to Santa Fe, just a few of the wagons. He handled items that belonged to private enterprises like Caleb's as well as commercial merchants; Willie's suppliers depended on him to make good deals for them and get the best prices, and they trusted him implicitly to pay them all they had coming to them after he took a percentage for making the trip. Some of the wagons even belonged to the merchants themselves. All his suppliers realized Willie Taylor and his men risked their lives every time they journeyed south with valuables, and the return trip was just as dangerous, as they herded back horses and mules, and often carrying gold and silver along with colorful Mexican blankets, jewelry, and miscellaneous utensils that were in great demand in the States.

Caleb respected Willie and valued his friendship. Willie, once a trapper, had been one of the first to recognize that the business was fast fading. When the Santa Fe trade suddenly blossomed, he was there to take advantage of it. He had never told Caleb how old he was, but Caleb guessed him to be in his fifties. The man was hardy and humorous, but lonely inside. He had lost an Indian wife several years back, and had no interest in marrying again; but then Willie was not the marrying and settling type, at least not with a white woman. An Indian woman was probably the only kind who would understand and put up with the man.

Of course there were times when Caleb wondered how

Sarah put up with his own wild ways—the times when he would ride off alone to pray to *Maheo* and let his Indian spirit soar. Yes. It was just as White Horse had said. He belonged with the Indians. But as long as there was Sarah, nothing else mattered.

"How about a spot of whiskey," Willie yelled out to him then. "I ain't leavin' fer a bit yet."

Caleb rode out of the corral and dismounted, leaving his horse then and walking with the man. "Sounds good to me."

"I don't like what I'm seein' around these parts, Caleb. More and more of the Cheyenne and other Indians is gettin' hopped up on rotgut whiskey and it's just gettin' them in trouble. It's turnin' good men into useless beggars." He stopped and grabbed Caleb's arm. "There. Over there. You see?" He pointed to a buckskin-clad man who was holding out a bottle to several young Indian men inside the fort. "That's a new man been tradin' around here—sellin' sugared-down whiskey that's worth pennies in return for valuable buffalo robes. The damned Indians don't know the value of them skins to the white man, and that goddamn whiskey is bad enough to kill a man."

Caleb watched, his anger building. He had seen it happen before—white men buying off Indians with bad whiskey. And more and more the Indians were liking the white man's "firewater," for it helped ease the hopelessness some of them were beginning to feel. Many of them drank the whiskey because they thought it helped them contact the spirit world, made them feel stronger, until the next morning, when the rotten whiskey took its toll.

It was all going to get worse, Caleb was sure. As more white men came into Indian territory, bringing their diseases and whiskey and slovenly ways, the more the Indians were going to lose their sense of direction as well as their pride. And the white men damned well knew it.

"I'm a trader myself, Caleb, but I won't go gettin' rich off another man's ignorance. And I got too much respect for my red brothers to take advantage of them like that— make a fortune off them buffalo robes that I got for almost nothin'."

"What's that man's name?"

"Hank Tuttle. And they say he's ornery as a hungry bear. You didn't come here for no trouble, Caleb. Let it be. For every Hank Tuttle there's a hundred others, a thousand others. It's happenin' all over."

Caleb let go of his horse's bridle. "Well, it can't hurt to stop just one. Watch my horse."

"Damn it, Caleb, I didn't point him out for you to go over there. I was just makin' conversation, explainin' what's been happenin'—"

The words were wasted. Caleb was already walking toward the man. Willie sighed and followed, leading Caleb's horse. Caleb walked directly to the unsuspecting Hank Tuttle, who was himself a big, burly man, wearing a pistol and a big knife on his belt, and who looked several years younger than Caleb. The man laughed through yellowed teeth as he handed a bottle of whiskey to a young warrior and reached for the buffalo robe the young man held out to him.

Suddenly a strong hand was on Tuttle's wrist. "Pay this Indian the proper price for that robe," Caleb said firmly.

The man looked up at him, glowering. "Who the hell are you?" he growled.

"The name is Caleb Sax, and half my blood is Cheyenne. I don't like what you're doing, mister. These are young boys whose lives won't be worth a damn once they get started on that rotgut whiskey you're trying to sell them. Have you told them the kind of profit you'll make on those robes, or how that whiskey is watered down and full of sugar?"

Tuttle jerked his arm away. "I don't give a goddamn who you are or how much Indian blood you got, mister. Stay out of my business!"

"Well, I'm making it my business!" Caleb turned to the young Indian men, talking to them firmly in the Cheyenne tongue and grabbing the whiskey bottle from the man who held it. He raised it, saying something more, then smashed the bottle to the ground. Glass flew and whiskey splattered onto their feet.

The Indian men moved dark, untrusting eyes to Hank Tuttle. Tuttle grinned to himself. This Caleb Sax was much older than he, and if he could better the man in front of these young Indians, they wouldn't put much value into his words of advice anymore.

One of the Indian men spat at Tuttle, *"E-have-se-va. Ese-von na-ox-to-va! Maka-eta!"*

"Why, you little bastard! I ain't payin' you food nor money for them robes! You take the whiskey or nothin!"

The young man who was their apparent leader grabbed back the buffalo robe and waved the trader off. He stormed away, followed by the other Cheyenne men. One lingered, staring at the broken whiskey bottle, then looking up at Caleb with questioning eyes. Then he scowled at Tuttle and followed the others.

Tuttle turned angry eyes to Caleb. "You son of a bitch! Do you know how long it took me to gain their confidence? I can make a fortune off them robes! Who the hell do you think you are!"

"I'm one of them, that's who I am! And I don't like to see them getting cheated. Give them something of value for the robes—food, utensils, anything! They already go hungry in winter because game is getting more scarce. Whiskey isn't going to help them."

A few men had gathered around by then, mostly trappers and traders who were always game for a good fight.

"Tell *them* that," Tuttle argued. "If they're dumb enough to trade the robes for the whiskey, what do you care! Hell, they're a dyin' people anyway. And good riddance! I'm just helpin' them on their way."

A big fist landed on the man's jaw then. Tuttle flew backward, landing hard on his rump. He reached for his pistol, but couldn't get it loose before Caleb stood straddled over him, wielding a big knife.

"Go ahead, Tuttle! I'd just as soon slice through your throat as look at you!"

Tuttle hesitated. This man was older, but he packed a punch, and Tuttle had no doubt he could use the knife he was holding now. There would be a better time.

Caleb straightened. "Make up your mind, Tuttle. Go for

that gun and I'll slice you up before you can get it out of your holster! Or maybe you'd rather pull out that big knife you wear. Either one is fine with me."

"You'd better think twice, Tuttle," Willie spoke up, grinning. "That there is Blue Hawk, and he's killed his share of men. One more won't make much difference to him."

Men shouted, urging a fight. Such things were exciting entertainment after spending weeks and sometimes months out on hunting and trapping expeditions. Bent's Fort offered rooms, food, a chance to catch up on the latest news from Santa Fe all the way east. A good fight was simply additional entertainment, and men circled Caleb and Tuttle, holding up fists and whistling, some helping Tuttle to his feet.

Tuttle stumbled slightly when they let go of him, his mouth bleeding profusely. He was tempted to satisfy the crowd and land into Caleb Sax, but he knew the timing was bad.

"I ain't gonna fight you this time, mister," he grumbled. "But I ain't gonna forget this, either. You'd best watch the shadows."

"I've lived my whole life watching shadows." Caleb laid the flat of his knife against Tuttle's face. "Ride out of here, Tuttle. Bent doesn't like men selling whiskey to the Indians. And neither do I! And when Indians get drunk and attack innocent whites, it's men like you who should be hung for it, not the Indians!"

Tuttle turned his face away, spitting blood on the ground. To the disappointment of the crowd, he backed off. "We'll meet again. I guarantee it," he told Caleb.

Caleb shoved his knife into its sheath. "I look forward to it."

Tuttle shoved his way through the crowd and walked to a wagon nearby that was packed with crates of whiskey. The surrounding men mumbled about being cheated out of a good fight and dispersed, while Tuttle climbed up into his wagon and headed out of the fort.

A few Indians who had been among the crowd of onlookers laughed and waved Tuttle off, saying he was afraid of Blue Hawk; and white men heading back into the fort began arguing over whether or not it was right to sell whiskey to Indians. Willie just chuckled to himself, leading Caleb's horse back to him.

"Speakin' of whiskey and Indians, you still gonna have that drink with me?"

Caleb gazed after Hank Tuttle, trying to get rid of his anger. "Just one, Willie." He looked down at the man. "And the good stuff." He turned with the man to see James standing there, watching him with eyes that were too often unreadable.

"That was a good punch, Pa." James shoved his hands into the pockets of his pants.

"I thought you were helping Mr. Benson."

"He didn't have anything for me to do today. Can I go with you to the tavern?"

"I'd rather you went and found Cale first. Bring him back here. Tell him I want to talk to him."

James nodded reluctantly. He looked at Caleb as though he wanted to ask him something.

"What's wrong, James?"

The boy turned to watch the young Indian men standing off, trying to sell their robes. He was full of questions. Did he dare drink whiskey someday? Would it destroy him as it seemed to destroy Indian men? Was he expected to fight for them like his father had just done? And what about the trader his father had just run out of the fort? Would he come back and try to hurt them, as other men had done, just because they were Indian?

James had hoped they had left all that hatred and fear behind in Texas. James always wanted to ask Caleb questions like this, but he was always afraid to open up to this man who surely expected so much of him. He shrugged. "You okay, Pa? Did you hurt your hand?"

Caleb grinned, looking at his fist. A couple of knuckles were bloody and his hand ached. "I'm all right." He flexed his hand. "I'm just old enough to feel things a lot longer, that's all. I expect this hand will swell up and feel worse tomorrow."

James grinned a little. "I guess." The boy turned to walk

out of the fort to look for Cale, but Caleb called out to him. "James."

The boy turned.

"Is there something you want to talk about? I don't have to go with Willie."

The boy shook his head. "No, Pa. Go ahead. I'll go find Cale for you."

Cale, James thought. Always it seemed Cale somehow got in the way. And always it was because he was so Indian. It seemed strange to think of him as a nephew. They were only six months apart in age. They were more like brothers, and James was sure his father thought of Cale more like a son than a grandson. James's sibling jealousy made him equally convinced that Cale was favored over himself.

"He's gettin' mighty big," Willie spoke up. "I think he'll be big as you, Caleb. But he's sure got his ma's color with that red glow his hair takes in the sun. I swear, when I see you and James together, I can't hardly believe he's your boy."

An odd pain moved through Caleb's heart. "Sometimes I can't either." Caleb turned. "Come on. Let's go get that drink. I might be able to get back home tonight yet. We made good time this morning."

The men headed for the favorite drinking spot at the fort, while outside James walked toward a cluster of tipis to look for Cale. James was so full of questions about himself and his future, yet for some reason he could not bring himself to talk to anyone in his family about them. He felt more and more alien, and sometimes he was even angry with himself for some of the thoughts he harbored, especially the times when he felt ashamed to be Indian.

He walked among the tipis, scowling at women who looked up at him from cleaning hides and cooking over open fires. He couldn't understand why these people couldn't live like whites, and he was determined that as soon as he was old enough, he would leave all of this. He would be successful as a white man and would lead the good life that was always beyond their reach as Indians.

"James," someone spoke up.

He turned to see three Cheyenne boys grinning at him.

"I am looking for Cale."

"Cale." One of them nodded, then said something in Cheyenne. Most of these boys didn't even know English, only Cale and James's names. The one who had answered pointed to two boys wrestling in the dirt farther off. He grabbed James's wrist then, laughing and tugging James along toward the wrestling boys. They were all talking in Cheyenne then, and James fought the odd fear he had of these boys. They were so wild, and Cale was getting just like them. James wondered if he was expected to be like them, too.

Cale pinned the boy with whom he had been wrestling, holding him on his belly with his knee in the boy's back and one arm behind him. He laughed and jumped up, turning then to see James watching.

"James! When did you get here?"

"I came with Father. He had to drive the horses by himself because you weren't there to help. Father is angry with you and so is Lynda for going off this morning without telling anyone."

Cale shrugged. "Grandfather never stays angry long. Besides, he understands I like to be with these boys." He stood there dirty and sweaty, wearing only buckskin leggings and no shirt. Cale wore his hair long and tied into a tail at his back. He did not wear the blue quill necklace his grandfather had given him when he was born, a necklace Caleb considered sacred, passed down to Caleb by the Cheyenne mother who died at his birth. Cale apparently had taken it and his shirt off to wrestle.

To James, the necklace only proved Cale was favored. He understood none of the reasons why his father had given the necklace to Cale. There were many things about his father James didn't know and didn't bother to ask. At his young age he had only a selfish desire to be the favorite son, but it seemed his older brother Tom used to always come first. Since Tom had left, the attention seemed to turn to Cale.

"You should be with Pa. You knew he was going to

come to the fort today. Besides, what's the use hanging around with these stupid Indian boys?"

Cale frowned, looking sidelong at his friends for a moment. They were all smiling, unaware of the insult.

"They are not stupid. Why do you call them that?"

"Because they are. They don't go to school, and some of them just get drunk now. They don't even know the value of things. Pa got in a fight a few minutes ago with a whiskey trader. The stupid Indians were going to give him valuable buffalo robes for rotten whiskey. You shouldn't hang around with them, Cale."

Cale's face darkened. James and he had grown up like brothers. They had always been best friends. But it seemed ever since their family was harassed and forced to leave Texas, James had changed. Cale didn't much like him anymore.

"I'll hang around with anybody I want to," he answered, stepping closer. The boys were both big for their ages, and James met Cale's eyes squarely.

"What about me? I don't have anyone to play with anymore. You're always here with them," James pouted.

"You could be, too. Why don't you ever come with me anymore?"

"Because I don't like it here. I don't like being around them." James turned away. "Come on. Pa said I should come and get you."

Cale grasped his shoulder and forced him to turn back around. "You quit insulting my friends. They have been nice to you. You're part Indian yourself, or have you forgotten, my uncle?"

The words were sneered. James's eyes flashed with a pride of his own. "Well, I don't *look* like them, so I don't have to say I'm *one* of them!"

Cale shoved him. "I don't much like you anymore, *Uncle*. You act like you think you're better than the Indians. Well, you're *one* of them, and you'd better remember it!"

James shoved back. "I'll live my own way, and you can live yours! You just run with them because you think it makes Pa like you better!"

Cale dived into him then, and the two rolled on the ground. Indian boys began whooping and laughing, egging them both on as they circled the two boys, none of them quite sure what the fight was about. The boys were almost equally matched as they flailed away at each other, punching between wrestling holds. Neither seemed to be winning until Cale landed an especially hard blow to James's chest, knocking the air out of the boy.

James fell on his rear, holding his chest and rolling to his knees, gasping for air. Cale stood over him, waiting for him to rise and go at it again. His own feelings were mixed. He loved James like a brother, but the boy was so changed, and Cale's pride would not take insults from anyone, not even James.

James got to his feet then, shaking dirt from his hair and brushing more from his clothes. He looked at Cale, tears brimming in his eyes. "I'm going back," he choked. "You can come or not come! I don't give a damn!"

The boy stormed away, and Indian boys slapped Cale on the back and hailed his victory. But Cale gazed after James with an aching heart. He was losing his best friend, and he didn't know what he had done to cause it.

He said his good-byes, going to a stump and picking up his shirt and necklace, putting both on. He walked to his horse and leaped onto its back, then rode to catch up to James, stopping beside him.

"Get up behind me. I'll ride you in." He reached out his hand. "Come on, James. I'm sorry. But you shouldn't insult me and my friends."

James sniffed, quickly wiping at tears. "I don't have to hang around with them if I don't want to."

"That is right. But you don't have to insult them, either. They are my friends. And they are your friends, too. Their blood is in your veins. If you choose to pretend it is not, you will never be happy."

James stopped walking and looked up, meeting Cale's eyes boldly for several quiet seconds. He reached up, and Cale helped him mount up behind him. They rode into the fort to find Caleb on his own horse heading out to find them. Caleb noticed the boys and called to them, riding closer and frowning at their dusty, disheveled condition. He noticed James's red eyes.

"What's wrong?"

James looked down.

"We were wrestling with the Indian boys," Cale answered for him. "One of them knocked the air out of James, but James got him back good."

Caleb studied his grandson's eyes as he spoke. Cale was a poor liar. Caleb's heart ached at what he suspected was the real truth. "Everybody all right?"

"Sure," Cale answered with a smile. "James and I are the best, aren't we, James?" He turned to James.

"Yeah, sure," James mumbled.

"Well, you are in trouble with your mother," Caleb told Cale. "Take James to get the wagon. I'm not exactly pleased myself over your riding off this morning. From now on, come and tell us first. You'll have some extra chores to do for this one."

"Yes, sir," Cale answered dejectedly. He turned his horse to head out. James glanced at his father as they rode off. The man would be angry if he knew the real reason for the fight. But how could he explain it?

Caleb watched them both. Could he love anything more than he loved his sons and grandsons? How did a man explain there was really no such thing as a favorite? Some seemed more special than others, for certain reasons. But they were all loved the same and he'd die for any one of them.

He followed them out. From a distance Hank Tuttle watched, cursing under his breath at Caleb Sax. He decided he'd ask around inside and find out where the half-breed lived.

· Chapter Four ·

A host of Mexicans and a sprinkling of Indians and white Americans surrounded the corral, straining the wooden fence on which they were perched. Most were Galvez's men, though some had come from the ranch of Julio Baca. Tom waited impatiently, upset with the large number of men. He had not expected this many, nor so much commotion. How could he handle a wild horse with this much excitement going on around him?

He fidgeted with his leather hat in his hands. He wore a black shirt and black pants, with a red bandanna tied around his forehead. A turquoise stone necklace adorned the dark skin of his neck, and his rolled-up shirtsleeves revealed powerful forearms.

Juanita Galvez had been allowed to come, and now she studied every inch of Tom Sax while he was not looking, wondering why did this strange Indian man she had never met before tease her mind and dreams as he did? From the moment she had set eyes on him, she had sensed he was a man of honor and strength, and his handsome looks and build stirred new feelings in her, feelings her innocent body had never before experienced.

She glanced at Emanuel Hidalgo, secretly pleased at the jealous look on his face. She didn't like Emanuel. She didn't like how he looked at her and she didn't like his arrogance. He had wanted to be the one to tame the black stallion, but he had been unable to do so. Now she knew he was hoping this new man would also fail, which made Juanita pray all the more that Tom Sax would succeed.

Juanita sat next to her father in a wagon seat high enough for them to see over the fence and into the corral.

Her heart raced when the one called Tom Sax approached them. He met her eyes only for a moment as he approached. He nodded slightly, sensing the warmth his glance brought to her blood.

Tom forced himself next to focus his attention on Antonio Galvez, stepping closer. "I can't do it this way, sir. I didn't think there would be so many men." His words were shouted, even though he stood close, for the noise of the betting men surrounding them drowned out his voice.

"What do you mean?"

"There are too many men—too much noise. I'll never be able to work with the horse this way."

Galvez shrugged. "All you have to do is get on him and ride him."

Tom shook his head. "I don't do it that way."

"You are having second thoughts?" Emanuel Hidalgo asked. The man sat on the fence near to Galvez's wagon. "Perhaps the Indian is not so brave and good with horses after all. Already he thinks of excuses." He smiled down haughtily at Tom, who moved his dark eyes to Hidalgo.

"I haven't changed my mind about anything, Hidalgo. You have already proved you aren't man enough to master the stallion. So keep out of it."

Hidalgo stiffened with embarrassment and rage, and Juanita smiled. "You had better be careful how you talk to me, señor," Hidalgo warned. "If you stay, you will be working for me!"

"I will decide who works for whom," Galvez reminded Emanuel. He moved his eyes back to Tom, while Hidalgo fumed inwardly. "The horse is coming. You have not seen him before this moment, as we agreed. You have forty-eight hours. See what you can do, now that all the men are here. If you see it will not work, come back here and tell me what you wish to do."

Tom nodded. *"Sí, señor."*

He turned as two men on horses led the black stallion into the corral, each of them straining to hang on to a rope around the horse's neck. Men cheered and whistled, and some threw pebbles at the horse, which tossed its head wildly, tugging at the ropes. Someone closed the gate, and the two riders dropped their ropes and rode quickly through an opposite gate. The stallion snorted and whinnied, prancing about in the corral as the crowd of men egged it on with shouts and rocks. It charged a few of them, its eyes wide and wild, scaring the men off the fence, then turning to chase after some more. The men laughed and climbed back on, finding the entire moment a game.

Tom stepped away from the fence, eyeing the frightened horse as it skittered about. One man reached out and slapped the animal on its rump as though it were an act of bravery. The horse whinnied and bucked, and more men jumped away laughing.

It was then the horse spotted Tom. Juanita's heart raced, and the crowd quieted somewhat. Tom carefully bent down and picked up the trailing end of one of the ropes tied around the animal's neck. He twisted it around his hand, his eyes never leaving the animal.

"Get on him and ride him down," one of the men shouted in Spanish.

Tom seemed not to hear him. He slowly walked toward the horse, which stood its ground, watching him carefully as the crowd quieted somewhat.

"Caballo valiente," Tom said softly to him then.

"He's not brave, just mean," someone yelled, refuting Tom's words "brave horse."

A few more men laughed, but Tom only walked closer, speaking then in a language none of them understood. Juanita watched with her hands tight together, her whole body tingling, afraid she would see the handsome Tom Sax trampled to death. Emanuel's eyes moved from Tom to Juanita. There was no mistaking the look on her face, and he wanted nothing more than to see Tom Sax die beneath the animal's vicious hooves and teeth.

The horse snorted and whinnied, tossing its head as Tom came even closer, still speaking softly in Cheyenne. The crowd had quieted even more. Galvez smiled with satisfaction, and Julio Baca's eyebrows arched as Tom managed to get a position right in front of the horse without the animal's going after him. He slowly reached out and touched its nose, talking all the while.

No one could mistake the magic Tom Sax seemed to have with the horse. No one had gotten so close before. Galvez realized that there were certain men gifted in working with such animals, and they were few. This Tom Sax was apparently one of them. He had heard the Plains Indians were especially good with horses, and the surprising stories he had heard were that they tamed their horses by means of what this Tom Sax was doing now, rather than riding them down and whipping them into submission. Could it be true men like Sax shared a special spirit with the animals?

All was quiet for a moment while Tom petted the animal's nose. It was then Hidalgo looked across the corral at another man, nodding slightly. The other man slowly handed some firecrackers to a boy behind him who had been paid to set them off if Tom Sax got close to the black stallion.

A moment later there came the small explosions, startling the men as well as the horse. The black stallion whinnied in renewed fear, raising up on its hind legs. Men were shouting again, and Juanita screamed as Tom remained in front of the horse, backing away just slightly, still talking to it as it pawed at him.

Tom had to jump back then as the horse came down, but he stayed with the animal, still talking to it, ducking as it came at him with its teeth bared, then reared up again.

"Tell him to get out of there," Juanita said to her father.

Galvez looked at his daughter in surprise, seeing the frightened look on her face.

"He knows what he is doing," the man replied, looking back at Tom as he dodged and ran and ducked, still talking to the animal. The men were again shouting and whistling, and it became an impossible task to calm the animal. It reared again, one front hoof crashing down on Tom's shoulder. The blow threw Tom sideways to the ground, and Juanita screamed and stood up, shouting Tom's name. She thought the men cruel to just watch and laugh as the horse came down on Tom again. He rolled out of the way, then scrambled to his feet in obvious pain as men pointed and laughed and said he had failed, too.

Tom stumbled to a wooden inner fence that protected him from the animal and waited, holding his ribs. The men teased and goaded the horse enough to redirect its attention, and Tom walked briskly over to Galvez. Juanita's heart went out to him as he stood there dirty and panting.

"It cannot be done this way. I must concentrate. You gave me forty-eight hours, Señor Galvez. Let me take him into the hills, with only you and el señor Baca to watch from a distance so you can witness how I tame him. Within forty-eight hours I will ride him back to Lecho de Rosas myself. He is worth nothing to you the way he is. Tamed, he will be worth much." He wiped sweat from his brow, rubbing at his ribs.

"You are injured," Galvez answered.

"A bargain is a bargain. I can live with my injuries. Just have someone wrap my ribs."

Juanita blinked back tears and Hidalgo boiled with frustration. This was not going as he had planned. Galvez turned to another of his men and asked him to go and get Julio Baca. The horse continued racing around the corral, and Tom stayed close to the fence. Juanita wanted to speak to him, to tell him how brave he was and how sorry she was he had been hurt. She wanted to be the one to help him. But she didn't dare be so forward. She could do nothing but sit and ache for him as he bent over as though having trouble breathing.

Julio Baca returned with the messenger, and the men quieted again as the two *patróns* conversed quietly. Then Galvez rose.

"Señor Sax has asked that he be allowed to go into the hills with the horse, with only el señor Baca and myself as witnesses, while he trains the horse," he told the others.

There followed an outcry of protests. Everyone wanted to watch.

"The horse will get away and we will never get him back," Hidalgo fumed. "You cannot release him from the pens."

Galvez rose and looked down at the man. "This is the last time I am telling you not to argue my decisions, Emanuel. El señor Baca has agreed." He turned to another man. "Bring us three saddled horses and full gear for a night or two in the hills. And get someone to help el señor Sax into my house. Yolanda, my cook, can tend to him. We must leave soon."

"*Sí, señor.*" The man left, and Emanuel Hidalgo stormed away. Galvez turned to the crowd. "We will be leaving soon. El señor Baca and I will go with the Indian. We are men whose word can be trusted, but for those of you who have bet gold on el señor Sax's success or failure, you do not need just our word. Señor Sax has said he will return riding the black stallion himself."

Some of the men cheered and others laughed and said that would never happen in such a short time. A man came up to Tom, helping him through a gate, while some of the men called him names and said the stallion would finish him off before he ever tamed it. Others spit at the "Indian" for denying them the thrill of watching, while some wished him luck and called him a brave man.

Juanita was helped down from the wagon, and she hurried along with her father, begging him to let her go to the hills with him.

"It is no place for a young girl. You will know when we return who has won."

"You will not let the horse hurt him, will you?"

The man scowled at her. "I think perhaps you are too concerned about this Indian, Daughter. You do not even know him."

The girl reddened. "I only feel sorry for him. He loves horses, and he was doing well until those awful boys set off the firecrackers. It was unfair."

"With that I agree."

Tom walked behind the girl, not hearing the conversation but watching the gentle flow of her hips as she walked, enraptured with the lovely blue lace dress and the silken look of the skin of her arms. He had camped in the hills for two days while he waited for Galvez's messenger to come and tell him the men and horse were ready, so this was only the second time he had set eyes on Doña Juanita Rosanna Galvez de Sonoma.

He liked the long, melodic name. Everything Spanish

seemed beautiful and gentle and honorable. But perhaps in this case too honorable. Never would Antonio Galvez allow his daughter to be courted by an Indian, of that Tom was sure. He was foolish to even think of her in that way, yet perhaps if he could prove his worth as a man and make Galvez stop looking at him as an Indian, he could have a chance. But even then, he was twice Juanita's age. He had no right thinking of her sexually. She was still just a child. But he wouldn't mind waiting for her to mature. It would be worth the wait. And after all, it was very common for older, established Spanish men to marry very young girls. It was also a common practice among the Indians.

Minutes later he found himself standing in the kitchen, shirtless, a stout Mexican woman wrapping his ribs, which on the left side were already turning purple. "This is bad, señor. You should rest."

"I can't. I gave my word, and I'll not lose this for el señor Galvez."

"You are a foolish young man then. And look at your shoulder, all swollen and blue. Can you move your arm all right?"

Tom flexed it, grimacing in pain. "I can move it."

"*Sí*, with much effort. That horse will kill you, señor. You are too young and handsome for that."

Tom grinned, holding his arms up while the woman tied the gauze. "Thank you, señora, or is it señorita?"

The fat, aging woman laughed, her huge breasts shaking. "Señora for many years," she answered, blushing. "Sit and rest a moment. They are not yet ready to leave. I am going out to fetch a bucket of water."

The woman lumbered out the door and Tom looked around the huge, comfortable kitchen. A wood stove with several burners sat cooling at the moment, and shelves of home-canned foods lined one wall. There was fresh-baked bread on the table. Yes, this was a place of wealth, of fine clothes and full bellies and sweet sunshine. He liked it here more and more.

It was then his eyes caught sight of a blue lace dress at the doorway. He moved his gaze from the skirt upward, to see a pair of pretty dark eyes peeking around the doorway at him. "Are you all right, señor?" Juanita Galvez asked in her girlish voice.

Tom grinned. "I am fine, Señorita Galvez. Thank you for asking."

She moved farther around the doorway, blushing at the sight of his bare and muscular shoulders and chest. "I am not supposed to be here. But I wanted to tell you you are very brave, and I hope you come back riding the great stallion. I will pray for you."

Their eyes held a moment. "Then I'm sure I'll be successful," he told her.

She smiled, and his eyes moved over her in a way that made her tingle. "I . . . I hope you do not think me terribly bold to speak to you alone this way." She turned around. "I should not even be looking at you without your shirt."

Her innocence only made her more enticing. "I don't think you bold at all. I only think you're a very nice young lady with a soft heart. It was very gracious of you to come and wish me well."

She heard Yolanda returning then. "I must go!" She whirled, and her dress and petticoats made a swishing noise as she hurried out. Yolanda lumbered back inside with a bucket of water. "Do you wish a drink of water, señor?

"Sí. Gracias."

She plunked the bucket down and took a ladle from its hook, dipping it into the bucket and pouring the water into a glass, which she handed to him. "It is good, cold water from a natural spring."

Tom took the water. "Tell me something, Yolanda, and promise me you won't tell anyone I asked."

She grinned and giggled. "What is it, señor?"

"Señorita Galvez. Is she spoken for by that Emanual Hidalgo?"

The woman frowned. "She is a child. No one has spoken for her, but el señor Hidalgo would like to wed her. Everyone knows it. But she does not like him, and el señor Galvez would never force his daughter to marry a man she did not love."

Tom drank some of the water. "What if she loved someone her father would not approve of? Would he let her see the man? Would he put her happiness first?"

The woman studied him closely, then grinned broadly. "You are talking about yourself?"

Tom finished the water. "I never said that."

"You do not have to say it." The woman folded flabby arms over her breasts. "It is possible el señor Galvez would consider her happiness first. But he is a very strict man. He wants only the best for his daughter. If a man proved his worth in other ways, her father might approve of him." She gave him a wink. "I know I would approve if it were my daughter."

Tom grinned, trying to ignore the piercing pain in his side and hoping it wasn't anything dangerous.

"You be careful, señor. There are rules to follow with the daughters of wealthy Mexicans. You remember that. And you watch out for el señor Hidalgo. If he suspects you have eyes for that young girl, he will do something bad. Already he is jealous that you have been given permission to train the black one. I have been watching him these three days since you came here. He stomps around like a pouting child."

She set the bucket over on another counter. "Emanuel Hidalgo has a mean streak. He asked once to see my daughter, Marie. He took her riding, and then he tried to make her submit to him. He hit her and tried to force her. She scratched him and ran away. I think the only reason he did not come after her and force himself on her again was because he feared losing his job. I wanted to complain to el señor Galvez, but Marie begged me not to. She was afraid Emanuel would tell the *patrón* she is a bad girl. El señor Galvez gets angry with el señor Hidalgo sometimes, but he trusts Hidalgo's word and Hidalgo is a good foreman. He knows his job well."

Tom's eyes narrowed in anger. "Is your daughter all right?"

"*Sí*. She sees another young man now. It is kind of you to ask."

Tom looked toward the doorway through which Juanita had fled. "I'm glad Galvez doesn't allow Hidalgo to court

Juanita. If he touched her that way, I'd kill him," he said matter-of-factly.

Yolanda's eyebrows arched. "Such strong feelings for a man who hardly knows the girl."

"I know her well enough to know she's innocent and trusting—too trusting for a bastard like Hidalgo. The man she marries should be kind and patient."

The woman chuckled again. "I see what is running through your mind, señor." She sobered slightly then. "And why is it a handsome young man like yourself is not already married?"

Tom's thoughts turned to Bess. Such a long time ago it was. How could he still picture her so vividly? "I was— once. That was over ten years ago." He fingered the glass absently. "We were only married six months when she died of cholera. That was in Texas."

Yolanda's eyes actually teared. "I am so sorry, señor." She reached out and patted his shoulder. "Then you are a lonely man, who should marry again. A new woman and children would help you forget."

Tom smiled sadly and rose, putting his shirt back on. The fat Mexican woman made him feel comfortable. She was easy to talk to. "Right now I have a horse to break. I have learned to take life a day at a time, Yolanda. No one knows what tomorrow will bring." He buttoned his shirt. "But I will tell you one thing. In all these years, this is the first time a young woman has struck me in the way la señorita Galvez has done. I wish I could get to know her better, but that will probably be impossible." He winced as he tucked in his shirt. "Thank you for your quick doctoring."

"I am not so good at those things. You should see a real doctor, señor."

"I'll be all right."

Antonio Galvez came inside then to tell them everything was ready. Yolanda watched Tom walk out and returned to her work.

Outside the men mounted up. Two extra men would go along, one who worked for Galvez and one for Baca. Tied to their saddles were the two ropes that were looped around the neck of the black stallion. They got the stallion to follow along after much tugging and whistling, but their own horses balked and whinnied in return. Tom turned, removing a rope from his own horse and throwing it over the stallion's neck, pulling tight.

"You are too injured to help lead him," Galvez put in.

"I want to be sure he doesn't get away." Tom looped the rope around the horn of his own saddle.

Galvez studied him as they rode out, leading the whinnying, fighting stallion. This Tom Sax was a good and honorable man. It was too bad he was Indian. But that wouldn't stop him from putting the man in charge of training all mustangs if he was successful at taming the black one. Emanuel would be upset, but he had made the promise and he would keep it.

Juanita's heart swelled with pride and victory when Tom Sax returned two days later, riding the black stallion, just as he had predicted he would. Her father was beaming with excitement.

Galvez's men followed, more and more of them gathering as the men came closer. Those who had bet on Tom cheered for him and collected bets. Emanuel Hidalgo watched in dark fury, remaining at a distance, not about to congratulate anyone. Somehow, someday, he would show Tom Sax he was the better man, and he would have Juanita Galvez in his bed. His *patrón* had already obviously taken a preference to this Tom Sax.

Ever since Tom's arrival, it seemed to Emanuel that Galvez acted differently toward Emanual, and in Emanual's jealous mind, that meant he would slowly be replaced by the Indian. Emanuel liked being number one. He deserved to be number one. Tom Sax would not cheat him out of it. But for the time being, he could say or do nothing. He must cooperate with whatever Galvez chose to do. Tom Sax would have complete control over the horses and answer to no one but Antonio Galvez.

"By the time he got through talking to the horse and coaxing him, feeding him by hand—oh, you should have seen him," Galvez was telling one of his men. "When he got on that horse, it only bucked twice and then he rode off with the animal. It was a beautiful sight. Soon they came riding back, and for the rest of the morning el señor Sax rode the black beast until it obeyed his every command."

Hidalgo turned and walked away.

"Tonight you will sleep in the main house, Señor Sax," Galvez said. "You will dine with us and we will talk about horses. I will call in a doctor to examine you and be sure your injuries are not serious."

Tom dismounted in obvious pain. *"Gracias, señor.* But first I will bed down Valiente and make sure he is settled. I think I am the one who should do it for the next few days. I am still not certain he will not be mean to another man."

Galvez nodded. Juanita watched from a window. *Valiente.* So, Tom Sax had named the horse. Brave . . . valiant . . . just like Tom Sax.

It seemed hours to Juanita before they were all seated at the table. The doctor had pronounced Tom Sax to be healing, but he would require much rest and should not ride for several days. She was relieved. Tom sat there now in a clean yellow shirt and black pants. His belt was rich leather with turquoise stones set in it, and he wore the turquoise necklace at his throat again. His hair looked clean and soft, and it was pulled behind his neck.

Juanita stole glances at Tom as he ate, noting the fine lines of his handsome face, his firm jawline and lean, muscled neck. His eyes were dark brown and set deep and wide apart, framed with perfectly shaped eyebrows. His nose was straight and beautiful, and it was obvious he had once lived in relative wealth himself, for he seemed to know all the right manners. He was familiar with the Spanish, for he'd lived among them in Texas and in the prison in Mexico. She knew her father was testing him out with every statement and question, and Tom Sax answered everything in just the way he should. They learned more about the grand ranch his father had once owned in Texas, and he told Antonio and Juanita some of his past life, including the fact that he had once had a wife.

Juanita's soft heart went out to him, yet she was secretly

relieved that he was not serious about any one woman. She listened intently as he told about his family.

"So, I have a half-Cheyenne father and a white step-mother," he told them with a grin. "My family is very complicated. I am mostly Cheyenne. But my sister, Lynda, is mostly white, for Sarah is her mother. Sarah and my father had another child after they were reunited, a son called James. He's about twelve or thirteen now. And Lynda is married and has two sons—Cale and John. Cale is very Indian and very wild—almost the same age as James. John is more quiet and looks more like his white father. My half brother, James, doesn't look like he has any Indian blood at all. It gets a little complicated trying to explain my family."

Galvez laughed. "I can see that." Then he sobered. "There has been much tragedy in your life, Tom Sax, and in your father's. But tragedy is what makes a man stronger, if he is brave enough to bear the loss and keep going. I myself felt I had nothing to live for when Juanita's mother died. But I survived. I know how it feels to lose a wife."

Tom allowed himself to glance at Juanita for the first time. All evening she had been waiting for his eyes to meet hers, but she knew why he barely looked at her. "Yes," he answered, looking at Juanita. "It leaves a lasting pain."

It was as though he was trying to talk to her, to explain to her how he felt. How she wished they could talk alone. How she wished she could make him feel better and take away his loneliness.

Tom quickly looked away. "Speaking of my family reminds me I must write them. Is there someone to send a letter?"

"*Sí*," Galvez answered. "But this late in the year it might have to wait. Few men are willing to cross the Sierras now. From now until next spring a man could easily die up there."

Tom frowned. "I didn't think of that."

"We will see what we can do. Come. Let us go into the smoking room."

Tom finished his meal, then followed Galvez into another room for more talk about horses. It was late when he

finally retired. He walked wearily into his room and closed
the door softly, looking up in surprise to find Juanita standing in his room. A lamp was dimly lit, and she looked
startlingly beautiful in the soft light. She quickly put her
fingers to her lips to tell him to be quiet, then moved
closer, her bare feet making no noise.

All of Tom's sexual desires came alive, for her hair was
brushed out long and straight, hanging to her waist. She
wore a heavy robe, but he knew that beneath that was a
nightgown and beneath that . . .

Never had his desires been so disturbed—not since
being with Bess. There had been others, but not this wonderful, aching, heart-stopping feeling.

"I know I am bad for being here, but I know how hard it
will be to get to talk to you alone, señor Sax," she was
telling him in a near whisper. "I only wanted to say how
proud and happy I am for you—about the black stallion.
And I wanted to tell you how sorry I am about your wife,
and I hope one day you will be very happy again."

Their eyes held. He knew the real reason she had come
—hoping to hint to him that she liked him very much and
would gladly see more of him if her father would allow it.

"You shouldn't be here," he said softly. He reached out
and grasped her arms. "You're very sweet, but if you were
ever caught . . ."

She studied him with wide eyes, her lips trembling. "I
know. I just wanted—" Her eyes suddenly teared. "Oh, I
was very bad to come here," she began to whimper.

"No," he whispered. "It's all right." How he wanted to
carry her to his bed! "If I . . . if there is a way I can see
more of you, would you consent, Señorita Galvez?" He
strived to show her he had lost no respect for her, and he
knew she had no idea of the kind of thoughts that were
going through his mind.

She smiled then. "Sí," she answered quickly.

Tom grinned, bending down and kissing her forehead.
"Then you must give me time and not be impatient. Now
get out of here," he whispered, letting go of her.

He gave her a wink and she wiped at tears, wanting to
hug him and thank him. She hurried to the door then,

looking back at him once before carefully peeking out into the hall and looking up and down to be sure no one was there. She darted out, disappearing like a ghostly spirit. But she certainly had not been a spirit, and when Tom went to the door to close it, his body felt as though it were on fire. He would not sleep well this night. Of that he had no doubt.

• Chapter Five •

It was a hard winter on the Colorado plains. Just as temperatures sometimes climbed to sweltering numbers in the summer, so did they dip to a bitter, bitter cold in winter. June, 1846, brought a welcome warmth, a great relief to Caleb, who had helped nurse Sarah through a fight against pneumonia that had kept her in bed for weeks that spring and afterward had left her very weak.

The past winter had also brought a sad miscarriage for Lynda, who was trying hard to have another child for Jess. Carrying a baby had always been difficult for her, and the harsh winter on the open plains of Colorado had taken its toll, bringing Lynda's third miscarriage out of five pregnancies.

Now summer brought warm sunshine. Sarah was stronger, but Caleb was plagued with worry over when she might get sick again, and if and when he would ever be able to give her all the comforts she deserved. Lynda was recovered physically, but still suffered emotionally from the loss of another baby.

Caleb thought again about the letter from Tom, telling them what California was like. It had come just today and had arrived nearly a year after Tom's arrival in California. Winter snows had made the Sierras impassable. But the letter finally came, to Caleb's great relief. He wondered if California could really be as beautiful and warm and prosperous as Tom had made it sound. After the hard winter and nearly losing Sarah to death, California sounded inviting. It sounded even more inviting when Caleb realized how much he missed his eldest son.

Tom sounded very happy on the Lecho de Rosas, and from the way he had described Doña Juanita Rosanna Galvez de Sonoma, Caleb had no doubt his son had finally found someone in whom he had a strong love interest. But according to the letter the girl was very young and it was almost impossible to talk to her alone. If Tom cared for her, Caleb could only hope that somehow he could pursue that love. Tom Sax needed a woman—a wife, children.

An owl hooted somewhere in the distance. It was a warm night, and James had already fallen asleep reading in his bed in the loft. Sarah lay in bed reading over the letter that had come from Tom.

"Caleb, I think he's in love," she told him. "Isn't it wonderful? And it must have been so exciting taming that stallion. I wish we could have seen it! And doesn't California sound beautiful?"

"Yes, it does." Caleb undressed and crawled under the light blankets. He turned on his side, pulling the letter from her hands. "Beautiful enough that if things don't work out here in a couple more years, maybe we should think about going there, especially if Tom is still there."

Her eyes widened and she turned to face him. "Caleb! All the way to California?"

He reached out and stroked her red-gold hair. "Why not?" He leaned forward and kissed her forehead. "Don't worry. I'd take damned good care of you. I'd make the trip as easy as possible."

She frowned. "I'm not worried about me. It's just that you're just getting going right here. And this is the land you love. You don't belong in California."

He traced a thumb over her lips. "I belong wherever it's best for you."

She felt the warmth and love captured in his moving

blue eyes. "You're running away, Caleb; running away from what you really want."

"I'm only thinking about you: how hard it is here for you; the bitter winters; and never knowing from year to year how much money will be coming in. Tom's letter makes California sound like the best place in the world for raising horses. Mix that with the sunshine, which would be good for your health, and it gives a man something to think about."

"We have lots of sunshine here."

"But in winter the days are too çold, even with the sun. You need a place where it's warm all year round."

She ran a hand over his muscled arm and shoulder. "Caleb, give it some time. I'm all right, really."

"You weren't a few weeks ago. What about next winter, and the winter after that?" He kissed her fingers. Her knuckles were slightly swollen. "And I know you've had a lot of pain in your hands. I don't like your doing so much sewing."

She sighed, smiling softly. "Caleb, you're always searching. Sometimes I wonder if you even realize what you're searching for."

"I'm searching for a way to make a good life for you."

"No. It's more than that. You're searching for yourself —where you really belong. We both know where that is."

He put his fingers to her lips. "No more of that talk." He bent closer and kissed her eyes. "I've loved you since I was nine years old. You're my best friend, Sarah Sax, and I'm your own best friend. All that matters is that we're together—for just as long as we can keep it that way." He moved his hand behind her neck and kissed her cheeks. "I'm going to take the best care of you that I can."

"Caleb—"

He cut off her protest with a kiss, pressing gently, running his tongue over her mouth and moving on top of her. In all their years together he never ceased to work a certain magic on Sarah. Caleb took command, his very touch and movements making it impossible not to want him in return. They had not made love in weeks because she had been so weak. Now he would have her, and she wanted him just as much.

Their long abstinence made the fires burn hotter. He groaned with the want of her, and as his mouth continued to draw out her own desires, he handily removed his underwear and tossed it to the floor. His hand moved down to push up her gown, and he moved it over her bare hips and flat belly.

His lips moved to her neck and she whispered his name. His touch was always good, always beautiful. "I need you," he whispered.

Sarah stroked his long, black hair as he moved his face against her breasts. "I need you, too. I'm well enough now." She felt her cheeks getting hotter as he moved down, pushing her gown over her breasts and tasting the full nipples. He lingered there, as though he could take nourishment from the pink fruits; then he moved lazily over her belly, taking his time with her. After all, it had been a long time. He kissed at secret places, making her feel wanton. This man knew every inch of her, owned every inch, had explored every inch. He had been her first man, and in her mind her only man, for he was the only one she had ever loved.

She wanted to please him. She loved pleasing him, for she took her own great pleasure in return. Sarah was upset that she had been sick for so long this past spring. Would he find another woman if anything happened to her? No. There must never be another woman. The thought of it passed as a glorious explosion rippled through her loins, telling Caleb she was ready for him. He moved on top of her, pressing himself against her belly. He was a big man in every way, and sometimes she wondered how he fit inside her.

In the next moment he proved that he could, and again he worked his magic with her, filling her and moving rhythmically in that special way that took her to a world removed from reality. Whenever Caleb made love to her the room swirled with his dark beauty, and it seemed sometimes that she could almost hear drums beating, the shake of rattles. He whispered to her in the Cheyenne tongue, words she didn't even understand but were still beautiful to her. The words and his touch and the way he moved inside her made her gasp his name over and over, arching up to him in total abandon. He had such power, bringing out everything that was woman in her.

Sarah pulled herself up, kissing his chest, ignoring the scars there from the Sun Dance ritual and from various battles. He encircled her in strong arms, his skin looking so dark against her own. He pushed her back down, lying gently on top of her and pushing deep, his life spilling forth in great surges of love and need.

"Sarah, God, Sarah," he whispered, tangling his fingers in her hair. He kissed her over and over. "Don't leave me. Don't ever go away from me."

She knew he meant in death, and she prayed they would have many more years together. Such a strong man he was, yet so weak at the thought of being without her.

"I'll be here a long time yet, Caleb Sax," she answered softly. "And the way you live, I should be the one worried about losing you."

"I'm too damned mean to—" He did not finish. He rested on his elbows, hovered over her, kissing her hair. "Want to go to the fort with me tomorrow? If it's as nice as today was, it would be a good outing for you. You've been stuck in this cabin all winter and most of spring."

She smiled. "Oh, I'd love to go, Caleb. I need some material, and I haven't visited with anyone besides Lynda in so long."

"We'll all go then. Lynda already mentioned she'd like to go."

She pursed her lips. "And have you mentioned California to Lynda and Jess?"

"Just a hint. I think Jess has thought about it himself. It would be as good for Lynda as for you."

She sighed deeply. "Let's give it some time. Trading is good at the fort."

"It is now. But there is a lot of talk about another all-out war with Mexico, and you know what that could do to the Santa Fe trade. Either way, I'd give it another year. Part of the problem is Cale. He spends more and more time with the Cheyenne, and I have a feeling if we left here he'd want to stay behind. I'm not sure Lynda could bear that."

"I know. But he's with them so much now he's already gone from us most of the time anyway. That boy is so wild, Caleb."

"He's following his spirit."

Their eyes held. "And you?"

He brushed her cheek with the back of his hand. "I'm with the woman I love, and I have my family with me."

"Promise me something," she said softly.

"What's that?"

She traced a finger over his handsome lips. "Promise me you'll follow your own spirit, if anything ever happens to me."

"Sarah, don't—"

"Promise me. You know what I'm talking about, Caleb. Half of you belongs to the Cheyenne. When I'm gone, you must heed the call in your soul. Your life began with them. It should end with them. Promise me."

He sighed and smiled sadly. "I promise. But I refuse to think about it or talk about it."

He lay down beside her and she snuggled into his shoulder. "I love you, Caleb. I just want you to know I understand that side of you. As far as California, we'll do whatever you think is best. But right now I don't think I want to pull up roots again."

"Then we won't. It's just something to think about." He kissed her hair. "Tomorrow we'll go together to the fort. We'll celebrate your health and eat supper there. We'll have a good time."

She lightly stroked his bare chest with her fingers. "Caleb, if there is another war with Mexico, do you think Tom would be in any danger in California? It seems as if the American government is bent on grabbing up all the Mexican territory it can. Doesn't Mexico consider California theirs?"

He twisted her hair through his fingers, staring up at the log beams of the ceiling. "Yes, but they couldn't even control Texas, remember? They have even less control in California. It's too far away. I highly doubt there would be any real fighting there between Mexican soldiers and Americans. California is more on its own."

"But most of the people there are Spanish. Maybe they don't want American control. Maybe they want California to be their own country. Men such as the one Tom works for might fight an American invasion."

"That's possible. And considering the way Tom wrote about this daughter of his *patrón,* you can bet whose side he would be on."

Sarah laughed lightly. "Oh, Caleb, I'd love to know he was in love and married and settled again. He's been so restless and rebellious since Bess's death and those years he spent in prison. And your getting banished from Texas —that seemed to change him; it took away some of that good-natured, gentle spirit and made him harder. There's an angry spirit behind that handsome face that only the love of a good woman is going to calm down." She sighed and pulled away slightly. "And even without Tom's interest in that girl, I think he'd fight on the side of the Spanish anyway. He hates the Americans now for forcing you out of Texas and taking your land."

"I know." He closed his eyes. "God, I miss him, Sarah. I know he's a grown man, but to me he's just my Tom, my son."

She turned and hugged him around the middle. "Well, knowing you two, you'll end up together again. Tom will either come back home, or you'll go to California."

"Well, like I said, it's just a thought. I won't even consider it unless you've been good and well for several months. Besides, like I said, there's Cale to think about— and James. I'm not sure how he'd like moving again."

She closed her eyes. James. Her son had grown more quiet every year, and the barrier between him and his father worried her. She understood James's haunting memories of bad times in Texas and that he was confused about his Indian blood. And she also understood Caleb's love for his youngest son. They were so different. And what hurt most of all was that Cale and James hardly spoke anymore. That hurt Caleb more than anything. He had always been proud of his close, strong family.

"Maybe it would be good for James," she spoke up then. "The ordeal of a trip would keep him busy and maybe draw the two of you closer together. He doesn't seem to like it here much."

She felt him stiffen. "He doesn't like it here because he's around the Cheyenne and because Cale has taken up with them. He's jealous of them for taking away Cale's friendship, and he hates them because their own blood runs in his veins and he doesn't like to admit that."

"Oh, Caleb, I don't think—"

"It's true, Sarah, and you know it. He learned in Texas how most people feel about Indians. I'm not blaming him. He's my son and I love him. If he wants to go through life pretending he has no Indian blood, I'd never hold it against him. It's just that I want him to be proud. I don't want him to hate that side of himself, or hate Indians or—" He twisted her hair absently until it almost hurt. "Or hate me."

"Caleb, you're his father. He loves you dearly. That much I know for certain. He wants so much to please you. Remember when he was small and was so afraid of horses, but he rode one anyway because he wanted you to be proud of him?"

"I also remember screaming at him before that for being afraid in the first place. I don't think he ever forgot it—or forgot the day those squatters attacked you and Lynda and killed his dog."

"Those were bad times, for all of us. We all have scars from it. He's just got to live with the memories like the rest of us. God knows you and I have much worse memories. But love can overcome a lot of things, and no matter which way he goes, Caleb, the love of this family will bring him back and hold him to us." She rose up on one elbow and looked down at him, her long hair falling over soft shoulders and resting against his chest. "And no matter what happens—to any of us—it isn't your fault. You have spent half your life blaming yourself for what happens to those you love. It's the fault of society and prejudice, not you. You've loved us and provided for us the best you could."

Sarah bent down and kissed his chest. Her full breasts

brushed against his skin and she stretched out across his chest. He stroked her hair, studying its reddish glow.

He closed his eyes and pulled her tight against himself. "I love you, Sarah," he said in a near whisper.

Tom followed a maid down the long, cool hallway that led to Antonio Galvez's office. He was dressed in a neat black suit, his black boots polished, a little black string tie at the neck of his white, ruffled shirt, and a trim black hat in his hands. He was as handsome as the most striking Spanish gentleman, and his eyes snapped with respect when he was ushered into the room where his employer waited.

The Galvez home was sprawling and cool, made of stucco, many potted plants and beautiful vases placed perfectly in each room. Tom had not been back inside it since the four nights he had first spent there healing from the wounds the black stallion had given him.

The horse now made a fine stud breeder for Galvez, and Tom was allowed to ride the animal whenever he chose, a situation that angered Emanuel Hidalgo. Hidalgo rarely spoke to Tom, and whenever he got the chance, he would always mention to Galvez anything he thought Tom was doing wrong. But so far his points had been minor. Tom knew horses and was doing a fine job of breeding and buying for the ranch.

Tom nodded to Juanita's father as the maid closed the door behind him. "Thank you for seeing me, Señor Galvez."

Antonio turned from ther marble fireplace where he stood and stepped closer to Tom, his eyes taking inventory. The man suspected Tom's reason for being there. "You are looking very fine, Señor Sax. To what do I owe this formal visit?"

Tom swallowed, bowing slightly. "I would ask first if you are satisfied with my work."

Antonio smiled. "You know that I am. You are worth every piece of gold I am paying you." He reached down and took the lid from a silver cigar tray. "Would you like a smoke?"

"No, thank you, sir."

Antonio put the lid back and set his own cigar in an ashtray, clasping his hands behind his back then. "Well?"

Tom fingered his hat self-consciously. "I am wondering if . . . I mean . . . now that your daughter is sixteen, or so I am told, would it be possible to see her, visit with her, in the presence of others, of course."

Antonio eyed him warily. "Of course." He sighed deeply and walked back toward the fireplace, turning to look Tom over again. "I had a feeling that was why you had come. I am aware that you have respectfully kept your distance from Juanita, señor. I was also aware of the way you looked at her when you first came here; and ever since she asks about you all the time."

Tom had difficulty hiding his pleasure at the words. "And Juanita? Is she well? I seldom see her."

"She stays inside and studies, and I keep her away from the men. You can understand why."

Tom nodded, taking a deep breath for courage. "She is the most beautiful young lady I have ever set eyes upon."

Antonio rubbed his mustache. "I watch her carefully, Señor Sax. I love her, and I want nothing but her happiness. Some men of my station choose the man their daughter will marry, but that might mean Juanita would marry someone she does not love. I want her to be as happy as she can be—and I know that she would be very happy if I let you call on her." He paced for a moment, then stepped closer. "I have been waiting, wondering when you were gong to come with such a request. I have given much thought to the fact that you are Indian."

Tom stiffened. "I am proud to be Indian, just as you are proud to be Mexican. And just as I promised almost a year ago, I have proven my worth as a man. You told me yourself the day you hired me that you judge a man by his worth as a human being, not by whether he is Indian or Spanish or white."

Antonio nodded. "This is true. And that is why I give you permission to call upon my daughter. But you must do so only in the presence of me or one of Juanita's tutors or the woman who watches after her—Luisa. If I catch you alone with her, I will have you run off my ranch. Is this understood?"

Tom nodded, irritated at the order but grateful for that much. It was a start. "*Gracias.* I have nothing but the deepest respect and admiration for your daughter, *patrón.*"

Antonio grinned a little. "Of that I am sure. You are a good man, Tom Sax. I am glad I hired you." He frowned. "Tell me. What do you think of this thing of war with Mexico? They say Americans are already marching into Mexico, and that soon they will be here claiming California. We who own land here must decide whether to join with the United States willingly, or fight to keep to ourselves. We do not want to be part of Mexico any longer. Just as in Texas, they do us no good. They are too far away. But perhaps we can simply be our own country. We are not Mexicans or Americans. We are *californios.* At least that is what many of my friends choose to call themselves. Personally, I think it would be good to become part of the country called the United States. Otherwise they might try to take us by force as they did Texas and other lands around Mexico."

Tom nodded. "It's true they might. But you should set certain rules of land ownership and insist on them. To officially declare yourselves as wishing to be annexed by the United States is the same to the Americans as saying all of your land is now theirs for the taking. Believe me, I know what they will do. They will come here and try to take it all from you."

Antonio frowned. "But if we unite with them in a friendly manner, they would have no reason to try to force our lands from us. I am telling my friends it would be very profitable to become part of the American states. They are builders, and trade with them will be very profitable. We can give them much and get much in return. And peacefully bargaining with them will bring a quick solution and save bloodshed."

Tom's chest tightened. Something about the Americans coming to California made him uneasy. How well he knew how many of them felt about people with dark skin, and now that they had cruelly and systematically cast out the

Indians from the East and the South. They were doubtless determined to take even more land away from the Mexicans, for no good reason other than they wanted it and Mexico refused to sell.

"I am not so sure it would save bloodshed, señor. I hope you are right."

Antonio chuckled. "Of course I am. You will see. Soon there will be meetings among the *californios* to vote on these things."

"I hope it all turns out well, sir. I do worry about my own parents though. There are rumors that American soldiers will be moving through their area on their way to Mexico. I have seen enough of war. I hope we can keep it from coming here."

Antonio nodded. "*Sí.* I am hoping for the same." He broke into a grin and walked to a table on which several glasses and some brandy sat. "Now, let me pour you a drink. We will toast my daughter—and make a wish for a peaceful settlement with these Americans. We know that Mexican troops will do us no good here in California. So we will simply not have a war. It will be good." He poured some brandy into each of the glasses and turned with them, handing one to Tom. "To Doña Juanita Rosanna Galvez de Sonoma."

Tom smiled, his eyes shining. "I am very grateful, Señor Galvez. It will be a great honor for me to call upon her."

They touched glasses, and outside in the hall Juanita listened like an excited little girl. Her heart pounded wildly. Her father would actually allow Tom Sax to call on her! She ran off and up the stairs to try on dresses and decide which would be the best to receive him the first time he came to call. She hoped it would be very very soon. She had dreamed of nothing but Tom Sax for months.

How glad she was that it was not Emanuel Hidalgo who had been given permission to call. If only she could somehow find a way to be alone with Tom. Perhaps she could bribe Luisa into allowing them time alone without her father's knowledge. She was sure that if Tom Sax was alone with her, he would try to kiss her. Oh, what a wonderful thing that would be! The thought of it made her legs feel weak.

Several minutes later she heard footsteps in the hallway downstairs. She hurried out into the hall and leaned over the banister to see Tom walking toward the front door. She wanted to call out but knew it was not proper. He looked magnificent, and her eyes hung on him until he was gone.

Outside Tom walked toward the bunkhouse he shared with five other men. He had almost reached the doorway when Emanuel Hidalgo approached from another direction, calling out to him. Tom stopped and turned, reading the anger in Hidalgo's eyes as the man came closer.

"I saw you going to the *patrón*'s house," the man spat out, his eyes running over Tom's appearance. "And I saw how you were dressed. Since el señor Galvez is not holding a fiesta, perhaps you can explain the fancy clothes, Señor Sax."

Tom watched him warily. "I think you know why I'm dressed like this. I've asked to begin seeing Juanita. El señor Galvez has granted my request."

Hidalgo stiffened. "I don't believe you! You are Indian!"

"I am a man," Tom answered proudly. "A man el señor Galvez apparently thinks is worthy enough to see his daughter. You had your own chance to go and ask the same. Why didn't you?"

Hidalgo couldn't bring himself to tell Tom he had already done just that and had been turned down. Galvez had told him his daughter was still not old enough. Now the man had turned around and told this Indian that he could see Juanita!

Tom read the rage in Hidalgo's eyes. "I've never done anything against you, Emanuel. Why do you hate me so?"

The man's jaws flexed in heated anger. "La señorita Juanita Galvez is *mine*!"

Tom stiffened defensively. "You can't lay claim to her. No man can at this point. If you want to see her, then go ask. I can't stop you." He studied the man's eyes closely, seeing the hurt pride. "Unless you've already done so."

"You will go to hell someday, Tom Sax," Hidalgo sneered. "I will see to it!"

"I'm not at fault for decisions el señor Galvez makes, Emanuel."

"Until you came here, *I* was the favored one. Every night I dream about Juanita Galvez being my wife and you have ruined it."

"I didn't ruin anything. You had an equal chance. And I know what you did to Yolanda's daughter." He paused. "I'm glad Galvez had sense enough to turn you down. Juanita is too good for the likes of you."

"But not too good for an *Indian*?" Hidalgo lit into him then, shoving Tom back into some bushes. No one was inside the bunkhouse to see the two men roll over the bushes and land in sand just on the other side. Emanuel punched wildly at Tom, but Tom managed to get to his feet and jerk him up, landing a hard fist first into Emanuel's stomach, then his jaw, sending him flying backward. Emanuel sprawled into a bed of flowers. He rolled to his knees, then yanked a knife from his boot and jumped to his feet again, waving the knife at Tom, blood trickling from the corner of his mouth.

"Don't be stupid, Emanuel," Tom growled. "I've done nothing against you. All I've done is my job. You've still got your own position here, but if Galvez finds out about this, you could lose everything."

"It would be worth it!" The man jabbed the knife toward Tom, who darted back, then quickly kicked out, catching Emanuel's wrist and knocking the knife from his hand. Both men dived for it, but Tom came up with it and managed a quick slash before Emanuel could get away, cutting the man's shirt and leaving a thin, bloody line across his chest.

Emanuel's eyes widened and he stepped back. "You've heard about Indians and knives, haven't you," Tom sneered, his anger at full fury. "Well, it's true." He fingered the knife eagerly. "My father has killed men for less than what you just did to me. And I have also killed men! I'm tempted, by God, to kill again, but I might lose my chances with Juanita." He jabbed at Emanuel once more to frighten him, grinning when the man jumped back. "You get away from me, Hidalgo, and don't you ever pull a knife on me again. I'll not let you go next time."

He tossed the knife then, and it landed with a thud on the ground between Emanuel's boots. "Get the hell out of my sight!"

Emanuel ran a shaking hand over the cut on his chest, then bent down and pulled up the knife, giving Tom a dark look before turning and walking off.

•   Chapter Six   •

"Look there, Caleb. What's going on?" Jess spoke up. He and Caleb rode side by side as they approached the fort. James drove the wagon, with Lynda and Sarah on the seat beside him and young John happily taking in the bumpy ride in the back.

All of them noticed the large herd of cattle, foraging under soldiers' guard several yards from Bent's Fort, and a huge herd of horses beyond that. Just outside the adobe walls of the fort, squads of men, both on foot and on horseback, were drilling; and a literal village of Army tents was set up on the fields in the approach to the fort.

Caleb drew up his mount, and Jess halted beside him as James brought the wagon to a stop.

"Look at all the soldiers, Pa," James spoke up. "Why are they here?"

Caleb looked around. Tipis were clustered in circles in the distance, Indians come for summer trading. "Either there's a new campaign against the Cheyenne, or these men are on their way to Mexico," Caleb answered. "Let's ride in and see what's going on."

He moved his horse forward and the others followed. As they neared the huge, open wooden doors of the fort, Caleb spotted Hank Tuttle lingering at the gate, a bottle of whiskey in his hand. Tuttle eyed Caleb sullenly as the man rode through the gate with his family.

The Saxes moved through the entrance gate and inside the fort's thick adobe walls. The open courtyard bustled with activity—settlers, soldiers, traders, wagons, and horses. Chickens and dogs scampered about. Some Cheyenne stood aside, watching everything with a silent amazement, but also, Sarah guessed, with a good share of amusement.

For the most part Indians found the life-style of whites something of a curiosity, and she noticed one point to an employee of the fort who was frantically scurrying about, trying to clean up the horse dung that peppered the courtyard. It was an almost hopeless effort, and Sarah had to smile herself and share the amusement of the Cheyenne as they watched the man move from pile to pile. More men rode in, one of their mounts dropping a fresh sample of digested prairie grass. Sarah laughed aloud as the man with the shovel and wheelbarrow stared at the new "contribution" and finally threw down his shovel.

Outside the fort Hank Tuttle leaned to get a last look at Caleb Sax and his women. He had not forgotten the embarrassing confrontation with Caleb the year before. Men such as Sax could put him out of the whiskey trading business.

Tuttle hurriedly left then, his mind whirling with thoughts of revenge. His camp was farther off, and more men waited there for him, guarding the whiskey wagon. Because so many soldiers were around the fort now, Tuttle didn't dare ride in with a whole wagonload. His plan had been to sell a few bottles at a time.

The men with Tuttle were drifters mostly, ex-trappers with nothing better to do than freeload off Tuttle in return for guarding the wagon. Now, Tuttle surmised, they could become more useful. Perhaps they would be interested in something much more profitable than whiskey. The women with Caleb Sax were comely, and pretty women in these parts were rare. One looked very white. White women brought good money in Mexico. And if he had seen right, the other one was younger—a dark, provocative beauty from a distance. Maybe she was a daughter.

"I'll sell all the goddamned whiskey I want, and I'll sell the Sax women, too," Tuttle muttered. "And I'll kill that bastard."

Inside the fort Caleb studied the soldiers who milled about. The fort was teeming with them.

"Sergeant," he called out as a man with three inverted V-shaped stripes on the sleeve of his uniform walked past. "It is sergeant, isn't it?"

"That's right." The man glanced at Sarah, looking surprised that such a lovely white woman was with the tall Indian who had just called out to him. The soldier nodded to her, removing his hat. Sarah smiled and nodded in return. The man directed his gaze at Caleb again. "What is it you want?"

"My name is Caleb Sax. I trade here, live about a half day's ride from here. What's the reason for all the soldiers?"

The man straightened more. "We're on our way to take Santa Fe, mister. We're gonna claim her as American territory, then we'll move on to Mexico. Some of us might go to California."

Caleb looked down at Sarah and she read his alarm. "California? What is going on?"

"War, mister. We're here with Colonel Kearny. Some of our men are already on the trail to Santa Fe to stop any traders who have already left. They risk attack by Mexicans and by Indians being paid by the Mexicans. We're at war with Mexico, mister. President Polk himself sent Colonel Kearny to take Santa Fe. We're drilling now for the attack. Be leaving right soon."

"And trade with Santa Fe has stopped?"

"That's right."

Caleb looked around and sighed. "How about horses? Does this Colonel Kearny need any? I've got some to sell. I'll be bringing them in day after tomorrow."

"The army can always use horses, mister. The colonel is in his quarters. It's the biggest tent, the one with the flag on it."

Caleb nodded. "Thanks. I'll go talk to him."

The sergeant pushed back his hat. "We can always use scouts, too. You look like a man who knows this land."

Caleb shook his head. "No, thanks. I have a family. And I've had my fill of war. I did my share at San Jacinto. It's someone else's turn."

"San Jacinto! You were there? With Houston?"

Caleb nodded. "My reward was to get kicked out of Texas for being an Indian. You can understand why I'm not anxious to join another army."

The man glanced at Sarah again and he reddened at the remark. He met Caleb's eyes and swallowed nervously. "I'm sorry." He nodded a farewell. "Have a good day, sir." He turned and left, and James watched from the wagon seat, wondering where all the soldiers had come from. What was it like in the mysterious East where most such men originated? He had heard about cities and railroads, schools and even universities where a man could get even higher learning.

Cale rode in, two young Indian boys riding with him. He spotted his grandfather's wagon and headed in their direction, grabbing up his little half brother, John, out of the wagon and hoisting him up onto his horse. John laughed and grasped the animal's mane. Lynda watched from the wagon seat, as did James, who instantly turned away.

"Cale, you were supposed to be home two days ago," Jess told the boy, walking up closer.

Cale just laughed, handing John to Jess. "I was having fun," he told his stepfather. "I went on a hunt with Ten Stars and Buffalo Boy." He turned to the two young men with him and said something in their own tongue, nodding toward his family. They both touched their brow when he nodded toward Caleb. Lynda glanced at the painted, nearly naked young men.

"Cale, we need you at the ranch," Lynda told him, standing up in the wagon. "You must come home when we tell you to."

Cale looked at his grandfather. "I don't want to farm or ranch. I want to be with my friends. I want to ride farther north on the hunt."

Caleb walked closer. "It's getting dangerous out there for the Cheyenne, Cale," he told his grandson. "I know how you feel, but they can't keep living as they did before. You know there have been soldier patrols all over this area the last couple of years, and in the north too. The Cheyenne are getting blamed for a lot of raids and killing. Besides that, the Cheyenne are still at war with the Pawnee. You get too far north, and you're open to enemy Indians."

Cale just grinned. "I'm not afraid of any of those things. And there are plenty of places the Cheyenne can still ride free. Besides, Grandfather, if you could do it, you would be riding with us too. Tell me you would not."

Their eyes held, and Sarah watched from where she stood near the wagon, her heart going out to Caleb.

"The fact remains that we need you, Cale," Jess answered for Caleb. "Don't add to your mother's burdens by worrying her as you do. You're not even thirteen yet. Give her one more year before you go making decisions about what you're going to do with your life. She deserves that much."

Cale looked at his mother, reading her pleading eyes. "Just stay in this area at least until next year. There is fighting everywhere, Cale."

The young man sighed, turning to the Indian boys with him and speaking to them again in their own tongue. He turned to his mother. "I will come back in a while. Ten Stars and Buffalo Boy are leaving soon on a hunt. I have told them that out of respect for my mother I cannot go. But next year I wish to go on the summer hunt with them."

Lynda smiled through tears.

"You've made a wise decision, Cale," Caleb told his grandson.

"Your grandfather has to bring some horses in day after tomorrow," Jess told the boy. "You and James can help him. That will leave me free to stay with the women."

Cale nodded. "James and I have not worked together in a long time," he said, aiming his words at his young uncle.

James turned to face him. "That's because you're never home. Don't you care about your family, Cale?"

Cale's eyes flashed with anger. "I care—in ways you will *never* care," he sneered. He turned his horse, riding off with his friends.

Caleb turned to look at James, who met his father's eyes. "You let him do what he wants, Father, just because he's Indian like you."

Sarah turned in surprise at the remark, and Caleb just stared at his son in disbelief.

"And so are *you* Indian, James Sax," Sarah said sharply. "Don't you ever make such a remark to your father again."

James scowled and jumped down from the wagon. "I'm going to walk around and look at all the soldiers," he muttered, quickly walking off.

"James," Caleb called out, walking over to where the boy stood waiting. "I brought your mother here today to have a good day and celebrate her being well again," Caleb said firmly. "Don't spoil it for her."

The young man looked up at his father, his throat feeling suddenly thick, his cheeks hot. "I'm sorry, Pa. I didn't—" He looked down at his feet. "I didn't mean that the way it sounded. I only meant you understand the Indians better than I do."

"I know what you meant, James. But you've got to stop thinking of Cale as some kind of competition, James. You're my son and I love you, just the way you are. I've never asked you to be like Cale. You're a big help to me and you're a good son. I appreciate your always being around when I need you. Now come back and stay with us. We're going to have a big lunch—apple pie, the works."

The boy shoved his hands into his pockets and nodded. "Okay."

Sarah watched, her heart heavy.

Outside the walls of the fort Cale rode a hard race with Ten Stars and Buffalo Boy, dreaming of the day he could stay with the Cheyenne forever. They had plenty of freedom left. Surely this land would never become so settled that they could no longer roam the plains on the hunt and move north and south with the seasons. He loved this life. He wanted to live this way forever, to prove his manhood someday the way his grandfather had done by participating in the Sun Dance, to prove himself as a warrior. He loved his family, and James's remark had angered him. It was just that he didn't feel right living any life but among the Cheyenne. After all, his grandfather was half Indian, his own father had been a full-blooded Cherokee, and his mother was part Indian. There was nothing unusual about his spirit longing to ride free.

Lynda set down her brush and studied her long, straight hair in the small mirror of her dressing table. John lay sleeping peacefully in his bed in the second bedroom of their cabin. Cale, as usual, chose to sleep outside under the stars. She sighed deeply and looked over at Jess, who lay in bed on his back watching her, his arms crooked behind his head.

"What do you think, Jess, about Cale?"

He studied his wife's dark beauty. The Cheyenne part of her gave her such provocative looks—the lustrous dark hair, the high cheekbones; as well as the fiery temper and fierce pride that made living with her sometimes a challenge, and the wild passion that made every episode of making love something beyond ecstasy. He loved her more every day they were together. From Caleb she had inherited her astounding blue eyes and a greater height than the average woman's, which only made her build more willowy and desirable, her legs long and slender, her form nothing short of perfect.

"I think that by next year he's going to be beyond reach, Lynda. We should just be proud he knows what he is and knows what he wants to do with his life. That's more than we can say for James. He's one mixed-up young man. Cale knows exactly what he wants out of life, even if it might be dangerous for him."

She sighed deeply, rising and walking to the foot of the bed, removing her robe and draping it over the bed rail. "It isn't just the danger, Jess. It's the fact that there is no future with the Cheyenne. They don't understand that yet, but people such as us do understand it. Look what has happened to the eastern Indians. Some of the tribes don't even exist anymore." She moved around and sat on the edge of the bed. "I don't know. It seems so strange. All my life I wanted to find my mother and father. And now my own son wants to leave me."

"He's not leaving you. He's just being his own person. That's the way it is for most, especially a man. It's just hard for you to understand because you grew up in an orphanage."

She moved onto the bed and under the covers, stretching out beside him. "Are you sure you don't mind, Jess—always living near my parents? You talk about how Cale has to do what's best for him. What about you?"

He lay there silently for a moment. "I have you. That's all that matters." He wanted to say more, wanted to tell her how he longed to strike out on his own. But he never quite found the heart to do it. Being with her parents was the most important thing in the world to Lynda. She had lost so much in her lifetime.

He raised up on one elbow, looking down at her. "I love you, Lynda. And I understand how important it is to you to stay close to your mother and father. I'm doing what I would be doing if we lived a thousand miles away. Why not do it right here with them? It's all in the family, and what Caleb and I build together will be passed on to James and John, if they want it. I had no family at all until I met you."

"But what if Father decides to go to California as he mentioned?"

He lay back down. "Then I guess we go, too. The only thing wrong with that is leaving Cale behind. He'd never go, you know."

"I know. But even if we stay here, we would hardly ever see him. I guess I've already lost him, haven't I?"

"You'll never really lose him, honey," Jess told her, drawing her into his arms. "And we have John."

She kissed his muscled chest, lightly fingering the hairs on his chest as she spoke. "I know you want more children, Jess. I'm trying. I'm sorry about the miscarriage."

"Lynda, you can't blame yourself for a fact of nature that you can do nothing about. Maybe you'll have more, maybe you won't. We have John and we have each other.

And if having babies is going to harm you, then it doesn't matter to me if we never have another one. Your health is what's important."

She tilted her head and met his eyes. "You want to try again?"

He grinned, then laughed lightly. "Far be it from me to turn down a beautiful woman."

"Oh? How many have you had to turn down these last few years?"

"Dozens."

She smiled, moving her hand down over his chest to touch that part of him that brought out all her passions when they were one. "Then I had better keep you busy and make sure you're always satisfied, hadn't I?"

His blue eyes sparkled with love. At thirty-six, Jess was still a hard, handsome man. The lines about his eyes, put there by years of work under the open sky, only seemed to add to his rugged good looks. He made no verbal reply. He simply leaned down to meet her full, beautiful lips, groaning at the light movement of her fingers that brought out his manly desires. He pushed up her gown and moved on top of her, and her slender thighs parted, letting him inside.

It was all so easy and natural. They didn't always need to pet and fondle before doing this. After all, being one was the most wonderful part of their lovemaking. Sometimes, like tonight, it just happened, like breathing the air.

Their passion rose as Lynda arched up to Jess in rhythmic splendor. He raised to his knees, pushing her gown up over her breasts and moving his hands over them, down over her belly, then grasping her hips and supporting her as he pushed deeper, watching her voluptuous body shudder and sway beneath him. Her slender fingers grasped his forearms, and minutes later she groaned his name as the sweet climax of their lovemaking swept through her in warm pulsations that took her to a world removed from the realities of everyday life.

How she loved this man! He had been so good to her, so understanding, so supportive. How afraid she had been to love this way again, but they had been together ten years now, and she could not worry about things that might happen. That was what her mother and father had taught her. They had suffered so much more than anyone else in the family. Caleb and Sarah Sax understood the fact that life must go on and sorrow must not be allowed to consume a person's soul.

Jess bent closer, moving his arms under her back and kissing her neck.

"God, Lynda, it's always so good," he whispered, shoving hard and deep until she felt the gentle throbs of his own release. Again she found herself hoping that this time her body would accept his seed, that it would grow and blossom into another child.

He lay there quietly for a moment, then kissed her cheek. "I had no intentions of doing this, you know."

She laughed lightly, kissing his chest again. "You're just too easy, that's all. If other women do come around, I had better keep an eye on you."

He looked down at her, kissing her eyes. "Well, there aren't any as beautiful as you in this whole land, so it doesn't much matter."

She traced a finger over his lips. "Thank you, Jess, for letting me stay near my parents—for being so understanding all the time. I'll need your strength for the day Cale leaves and never comes back." Her eyes teared.

He brushed at one of her tears, just before they heard a gunshot. Jess straightened. Suddenly men were shouting and they could hear the thundering of running horses.

"Jess, what is it!"

"I don't know!" He jumped out of bed and pulled on his long underwear. "Get your robe on and go into John's room. Stay there until I come for you."

Outside in the darkness Hank Tuttle rode hard toward Caleb and Sarah's cabin, the men with him yipping and shooting, stirring up the herd of horses Caleb planned to take to the fort the next day.

"You're gonna pay now, you son of a bitch," Tuttle sneered, shooting at a window and shattering the glass.

· Chapter Seven ·

Caleb handed a rifle to James as the boy came scrambling down from the loft.

"What is it, Pa?"

"Somebody is stampeding the herd! Stay near the door and don't be afraid to use that rifle if somebody you don't know tries to get in here."

"Hey, Indian, come on out," Hank Tuttle shouted then, riding hard past Caleb's cabin and firing wildly through the windows.

"Stay against the wall, James," Caleb ordered, ducking down.

"Caleb! James!" Sarah shouted from the bedroom.

"Stay there, Sarah," Caleb shouted. "And stay down out of the way."

"What is it? What's happening?"

"Someone's trying to steal the herd. I've got to get outside."

"Pa, there's too many of them!"

"I got lots of whiskey, Indian," came the voice again from outside.

Caleb inched toward the window, peering out at a form in the darkness and wondering where Cale and Jess were.

"You'll want to get drunk like your relatives once all your horses are gone."

James listened with even more burning hatred and humiliation. It was happening again, someone giving them trouble because they were Indian.

"Sounds like Hank Tuttle."

"Who's that, Pa?"

"He's a whiskey trader I had a run-in with at the fort

once. The son of a bitch went and got himself some men to help him. Trouble is, I can't tell for sure how many. I've got to get outside. I'll go out a back window."

"Pa, what if they try to get in?"

"You just shoot at anything that moves. That thing will get off ten shots without reloading, and you know how to use it. Anyone gets in this house, they'll be close enough that you can't miss."

Caleb darted away then, moving through the bedroom. "Stay out of sight, Sarah," he said, heading for the window.

"Caleb, don't go out there!"

"I have to. James is in the other room with one of the repeaters. You'll be all right. Lock this window soon as I go out."

The window opened by hinges at the top. Caleb pushed it out and disappeared with all the stealth of the Indian he was. Sarah quickly closed and locked the window, then moved to the outer room to crouch down near James.

"Don't worry, Mother. Nobody will get inside."

"I'm not worried about myself. I'm worried about your father and what's happening over at Lynda's. And if your father loses those horses . . ." She closed her eyes, fighting tears.

"It's that whiskey trader Pa had words with last year," James mumbled, furious.

Two shots came through the window then and Sarah screamed and crouched lower. James shoved the barrel of his rifle through the window and fired twice.

Outside, Caleb darted to the corner of the cabin, seeing in the moonlight that men were breaking down the corral he had built for the horses he intended to sell to Colonel Kearny at Bent's Fort the next day. They were shooting and yipping, stampeding the horses out of the corral and toward the cabin. He had no time to wonder where Cale and Jess might be, sure only that they were somewhere close.

The horses thundered past the cabin and Caleb took aim, getting off three shots and felling a man with each one, glad for the moon's bright light. In the distance he heard more shots. That would be Jess. Remaining Tuttle men kept the herd running, and as they ran the horses off into the darkness, even more men suddenly rode out from behind outbuildings, heading for Caleb's cabin.

Caleb took aim just as someone rode past from the other direction, yipping in a familiar Cheyenne war cry. Caleb fired at the oncoming men, realizing the other rider had to be Cale.

"Cale, be careful," Caleb shouted to his grandson, who headed right for the intruders, fire spitting from the end of his own repeating rifle. With his and Caleb's own onslaught of bullets, more Tuttle men fell. Like a true warrior, Cale rode right into the midst of them and then suddenly fell to the side of his horse so that those who shot back at him only missed, wounding another of their own men.

Cale hung from the side of his horse until the animal thundered right through the middle of Tuttle men and beyond. By then the seven or eight men left were close to the cabin. Caleb raised his rifle but froze when he heard Sarah cry out his name in terror. Then he heard a gunshot from inside the cabin.

He inched around the corner toward the front of the cabin. "Sarah! James!" he called out.

"Give it up, Sax," came a voice from inside. "Give it up or they're both dead."

The rest of the men neared the cabin, and Caleb resisted an urge to fire at them. Somehow Tuttle had gotten into the cabin! Caleb couldn't take the risk that the man meant what he said about killing James and Sarah. What had happened? It should have been an easy shot for James.

He heard the door creak open. "Come around the front where we can get a look at you, Sax," came Tuttle's voice again. The man turned up the wick of an outdoor lantern that hung near the door, already lit. "Come around real easy and put down your weapon, else you'll be minus a wife and a son."

Caleb lowered his rifle, cautiously stepping around to the narrow wooden porch of the cabin. Tuttle stood there waiting, his own rifle pointed directly at Caleb while the rest of his men gathered close, remaining on their horses.

"Did Jim and the others get off all right with the horses, Joe?" Tuttle asked, keeping his rifle on Caleb.

"Sure did. They'll bring a pretty piece down in Mexico."

Tuttle nodded, grinning. "So will the women." He looked Caleb up and down. "I won't ask you again, Sax. Put down that rifle."

"Pa," James yelled from inside. "Pa, the gun jammed!" The boy sounded near tears. "The gun jammed, Pa. They hurt Mother."

"Shut your mouth, kid," someone growled.

Caleb's jaw flexed in unbearable anger. "What the hell do you want, Tuttle? You've got the horses, so why don't you just get the hell out of here?"

Tuttle laughed lightly. "You'd like me to leave it at that, wouldn't you, Sax?" The man glanced at one of his men. "Darryl, go on inside and get the woman. Be easy with her. And tell Billy to get the boy out here." His dark eyes flashed with victory as he held them on Caleb. "'Pears like your woman is some wounded. Had a little confusion inside when we went to get her. We'll have to fix her up before we sell her off to the Mexicans. I don't reckon my men will mind strippin' her down to take out the bullet first." He snickered again.

Caleb felt rage building inside him. The attack had been so quick, and there were so many of them. He couldn't afford to pay the extra men he needed to help watch his land and horses. Now this. Sarah! What had happened to Sarah!

His only hope was Jess and Cale. He prayed they would stay out of sight. The one called Darryl dismounted and went inside the cabin, while Caleb carefully laid down his rifle. From inside the cabin he could hear scuffling, James cursing someone to leave him and his mother alone.

"You'd better kill me now, Tuttle, if you've laid a hand on my wife and son," Caleb hissed. "Otherwise, no matter where you go, I'll find you, and by God you'll die slower than any man has ever died!"

Tuttle chuckled. "That boy of yours inside had a little trouble with his gun. He raised his rifle to shoot me, but low and behold, it didn't fire. Mine did—only your woman jumped up to protect her son and she took the bullet instead."

Caleb stiffened with rage and terror, and one of Tuttle's men dragged a screaming, kicking James out the door.

"Fights just like a wildcat." The man laughed. "Must be the Indian in him." The man gave James a solid punch to the face, knocking the boy backward down the steps. "Pour some whiskey on him, Joe." The man laughed again. "Long as he's got Indian blood, I reckon he likes the stuff. Might as well get him started on it. It'll help kill the pain he's gonna feel when he comes around."

The one called Joe took a bottle of whiskey from his gear and uncorked it, pouring it over James, who coughed and rolled over, putting his arms over his head. Caleb's mind swirled with indecision, unbridled fury welling in his soul at the sight of his abused son, a fury magnified when a second Tuttle man came from inside the cabin carrying Sarah. Caleb moved toward her, but Tuttle jammed his rifle barrel into Caleb's chest.

"Stay right there, Indian. She's goin' with us. She's worth a lot of money to us, if we can keep her alive."

Caleb watched in helpless fury as the man with Sarah handed her to the one called Joe, who set her in front of him, hanging on to her limp body to keep her from falling off the horse. There was blood on the front of her nightgown near her left shoulder.

"This will learn you not to mess with me and my whiskey business, Sax. Now you know I've got a long memory, and I'm gonna make you sorry you messed with me. I'm here to pay you back for stickin' your nose in where it don't belong. 'Course we'll have to mess you up some first—make sure you're in too bad a shape to follow us right away. While you're healin', you can think about your woman, lyin' naked while we take that bullet out of her— and the fine gold she'll bring us when we take her to Mexico, if she ain't too abused by us before we get her there. And that pretty daughter of yours will give my men much pleasure!"

They all snickered, as James groaned and got to his knees. In the distance Caleb could hear Lynda, fighting and screaming wildly, the men trying to bring her over cursing vehemently. Lynda Sax Purnell was not a woman who would go down easily, but with three men dragging her toward Caleb's cabin, the fight was in vain.

Caleb quickly counted as the men's attention was drawn to his beautiful half-breed daughter. Seven on horseback in front of the cabin, plus Hank Tuttle standing near the door. Apparently everyone had come out of the cabin, and the others had ridden off with the horses. He could find them and the horses later. All that mattered now was Sarah and Lynda and James. The three men who were dragging Lynda into the little group made a total of eleven.

"Here's the young one, Hank," one of the men shouted. "She's naked under this here gown. She's gonna bring us a fortune, if she don't kill us first."

They all laughed.

"Any others over there?" Tuttle yelled.

"Just a little boy. We tied him to his bed."

It had been a long time since Caleb Sax felt this much rage. Hank Tuttle would know the taste of revenge! Poor little John—only six—tied to a bed. The boy must be terrified!

Tuttle's gleaming dark eyes turned back to Caleb. "Where's your daughter's man, Sax?"

Sarah groaned Caleb's name and Joe gave her a jerk, telling her to shut up.

"Mother," James moaned, trying to get to his feet. One of Tuttle's men kicked and knocked him back down.

"My daughter's husband is out there somewhere, Tuttle," Caleb growled. "And so is my grandson Cale. Maybe you think you've won, but you aren't off my land yet, you bastard!"

"Well, with you walkin' in front of me and my rifle aimed right at the back of your head, I reckon they'll hold back till we're off your land. Besides, we've got both your women with us now."

One of Tuttle's men slapped Lynda hard, knocking her to the ground. He put a knee in her back and began tying her hands behind her back while another tied her ankles. They hoisted her up, throwing her belly-down over a horse. One of them mounted up with her, slapping her on the bottom. "This one is gonna be more fun than a house full of whores," he joked.

Caleb forced back black anger, struggling to think clearly. Apparently they had not got Jess or Cale. They were his only hope.

"Stu, Joe, Billy, you three stay close right here," Tuttle said, indicating the two who held the women and a third man. "The rest of you spread out. Find the young one's husband—and find the grandson."

"Somebody rode right through us, Hank—a full-blooded Indian if I ever saw one," one of them spoke up. "Got Ted and Trace, then dropped over the side of his horse like a shadow. He won't be easy to find."

"Find him, goddamn it," Hank barked. "He's the grandson. He's just a kid, you idiot!"

"Who are you calling a kid," came a voice near Tuttle.

From the corner of his eye Tuttle could see the barrel of a rifle protruding from the doorway of the cabin, pointed at his side. Black fear moved through him as though ice were moving through his veins. He heard the hammer of the rifle cock.

"Put the gun down, white eyes! It is you and your men who are the prisoners now, not us. And tell your man to put my mother and my grandmother down—gently."

There was a moment of intense indecision as all the Tuttle men still had their guns. James finally got to his feet, staring at the doorway.

"Cale," he murmured.

"You better do what the boy says," came another voice from behind Tuttle's men. "We might not be able to get all of you, but we can come damned close." It was Jess. "Any of you want to bet on which ones get it and which ones don't?"

Hank fingered his rifle restlessly. It was still aimed at Caleb Sax, whom he hated. "You two put down your guns," he warned. "Else Caleb Sax is dead. I'll blow his guts out right here!"

"Go ahead," Cale told the man. "He'd rather die than let

you ride off with my grandmother. Either way, you'll still be dead, Tuttle."

"Along with a few more of you," Jess added from the shadows.

Caleb grinned wickedly. "They're right, Tuttle. Go ahead and shoot. As long as I know you'll be killed, it doesn't matter much to me. All that matters is my wife and daughter. You'd better do what they say."

"The hell with this," one of Tuttle's men swore, giving his horse a kick and turning it. Jess fired and the man fell. The shot and the man's stumbling, screaming horse caused the other horses to rear and turn in circles.

Cale thrust his gun upward into Tuttle's to knock it away, afraid if he shot Tuttle point-blank the man's own gun would go off and hit his grandfather. Tuttle's gun fired into the air, and Caleb landed on the man at almost the same moment, knocking him down the steps.

More shots were fired, and James grabbed for his mother, hanging on to her while the man holding her kicked at him. The man finally let go of her, intent on just getting away. James hung on to her and lowered her gently to the ground.

"Mother," he wept, bending over her.

Jess had already fired several more shots, one of them downing the man who held Lynda, and now he was desperately grabbing at the startled, frightened horse that held her. Its rider had fallen off and the animal was turning in circles, whinnying and kicking. Jess managed to get hold of Lynda's shoulders as she screamed his name, terrified the animal would bolt her off and trample her. Jess grabbed her off in strong arms, falling to the ground and rolling away from the bucking horse, which finally ran off.

By then six more of Tuttle's men lay dead or wounded, some shot by Jess before he grabbed Lynda, and some shot by Cale. The rest rode off into the darkness. Jess quickly whisked out a pocketknife and cut the ties on Lynda's wrists and ankles.

Tuttle, although strong and vicious in his own right, had no chance against an enraged Caleb Sax. Over and over Caleb landed a foot or a fist into the man, grabbing him and hitting him again before Tuttle could get his breath to fight back. Blood poured down Caleb's face from the graze of a wild bullet, but he seemed unaware he had even been wounded in the melee. At the moment he was aware only of Hank Tuttle. He held the man's limp body by the hair of the head.

"Cale," he growled.

The boy ran up to his grandfather. "Grandfather, you're wounded! Did I do wrong?"

"No," Caleb panted. "You did just fine. Get your grandmother into the house and give me your hunting knife."

"Yes, sir." Cale whisked a knife from his belt and handed it to Caleb.

"Have Lynda help Sarah. I'll be right there." He dragged Tuttle's body off into the darkness.

Lynda stood torn, her mother lying on the ground, her little son still tied up over at their own cabin. She looked helplessly at Jess, who quickly embraced her. "Are you hurt?"

"I'm all right," she assured him. "Just—just so damned mad."

"What about John?"

"They didn't hurt him."

Jess closed his eyes, breathing a sigh of relief. "Everything will be all right," he told her. "I'll get your mother inside and you stay with her—get things ready." He looked over at James, who remained kneeling near Sarah. Cale was there, kneeling on the other side of her, holding Sarah's hand. "James, go to our cabin and get John. They've got the poor little guy tied up over there. Go get him and come back here with him."

James looked up at Jess, devastation on his face. "They shot her. They shot my mother, and it's my fault."

"It's nobody's fault, James. Go on now. Poor little John must be scared to death. I'll get your mother into the house. Get right back here with John. Your father will need some help. We're got to get that bullet out of your mother."

He gave Lynda one more reassuring hug, then walked with her over beside Sarah. He knelt down and took Sarah up in his arms, looking at a still-weeping James. "Go on, now. Go get John."

"How bad is my grandmother?" Cale asked.

Jess looked down at the growing bloodstain on Sarah's gown. "I don't know yet. Right now let's just get her inside." He walked past the two boys with Sarah, and Lynda hurried behind them. Cale and James faced each other. One side of James's face was already turning purple, and he reeked of whiskey, his long underwear covered with mud from the mixture of whiskey Tuttle's men had poured on him and the dust he had landed in.

"James, are you all right?" Cale asked in genuine concern.

James gave him a dark look, stiffening then when a man's screams came from somewhere in the darkness. Caleb Sax was getting his Indian revenge, making sure his enemy suffered mightily before he died.

"I'm all right," James answered, moving his eyes back to Cale's. "Thanks to you, apparently."

Cale scowled. "What do you mean? We all did what we could."

"We?" A tear slipped down James's cheek. "I failed him —father and mother both," the boy choked out.

Tuttle screamed again and a chill moved down James's spine. There was the Indian side of his father, and again his mother had suffered because Caleb Sax was Indian. It was bad enough that James was nothing like his Indian father and hated his Indian blood. But now he was disgraced. He had failed to protect his mother. And Cale, the Indian grandson of whom Caleb was already so proud, had been the one to save the day.

James stormed past Cale and headed for Lynda and Jess's cabin to get John.

Sweat beaded on Caleb's forehead, and Lynda reached over to press a cool cloth to his face.

"You should have let me tend to that wound, Father," she said, dabbing the dried blood on his face. He had come in, removed his bloody clothing, and washed thoroughly, but had refused to take the time to wash and bandage the deep flesh wound at the side of his forehead. In all the confusion he wasn't even sure how he had gotten the wound, but it appeared to be from a wild bullet.

He stood in clean pants but no shirt, bent over Sarah. Lynda had washed around her mother's wound, and Jess was in the room with them to help hold Sarah while Caleb cut into her. Cale, James, and John waited in the outer room while Caleb worked at removing the bullet buried in Sarah's shoulder.

"God, I don't want to do this again," Caleb said in a near whisper. He had dug for the bullet once, bringing heart-wrenching moans from Sarah's lips. He had been unable to find it. He had to search again. In these parts people had to tend to their own wounds, and it sickened him to have to put his Sarah through this pain. He was more sure now than ever that he had to find something better for her. The dangers of the elements, Indians, and outlaws in this land was too great. Now some of his horses had been stolen. If he couldn't get them back, it would be a hard year financially.

"It's . . . all right, Caleb," Sarah said weakly.

He swallowed. It was all he could do to keep from breaking into tears himself. He looked over at Lynda. "See if you can get a little more whiskey down her throat." He leaned closer to Sarah. "I'm sorry, Sarah. I'll try to get it for sure this time."

She managed a weak smile, meeting his eyes lovingly. "I know . . . you're doing your . . . best. At least it hit . . . nothing vital . . . and James didn't get hurt."

He leaned down and kissed her forehead. "You did a brave thing, Sarah Sax. You might have saved James's life. When I think of what could have happened—losing either one of you—"

"That won't happen," she whispered, her strength waning again. "You just . . . get this thing out of me and go . . . go after those horses. You can do it. You can find them."

Lynda raised her mother's head and helped her gulp down a couple more swallows of whiskey.

"Caleb, I think . . . your wife is . . . drunk," Sarah joked then. "I've never been . . . drunk before."

Caleb smiled sadly, then handed her the piece of rawhide to bite on. "Here we go." He looked at Jess, signaling him to again hang on to Sarah's ankles. Lynda put one knee on the bed and held her mother's wrists at each side of Sarah's body, keeping a firm hold as Caleb's knife again dug for the bullet.

In the outer room Sarah's shuddering groans pierced James's heart like a sword. He had said nothing, finally going to the loft and getting some clean clothes before he walked outside. Several minutes later Caleb came out of the bedroom, his face looking haggard, his eyes bloodshot.

"Are you all right, Grandfather?" Cale asked.

Caleb sighed and nodded. "I'll be better when I know for sure your grandmother will be all right. And when I get those horses back."

"I will help you. I can get some of my Cheyenne friends to help, too. That way Jess and James can stay here and watch things. How is Grandmother now?"

"She seems to be fine, as long as there is no infection. That's the biggest worry." He wiped at perspiration with a shaking hand. "That's the hardest thing I've ever done," he added, his voice choking. He breathed deeply, looking around the room. John lay sleeping in a big chair. "Where is James?"

"He got some clean clothes and went out. He was still pretty dirty. Those men poured whiskey all over him."

Pain moved through Caleb's eyes. "I know." He walked over to a hook on the wall and took down a buckskin shirt, pulling it on, sighing deeply. He moved his sad eyes back to Cale. "I don't know if we can stay here, Cale. For me it's fine. But I've got to find something better for Sarah. I know you like it here, but it's possible we'll have to move on. You'll have to decide whether to stay or go."

The boy nodded. "I know."

Caleb looked him over, realizing for the first time how big Cale was for his age. "You did a good job tonight, Cale."

The boy smiled proudly. "I snuck up on him good, didn't I?"

Caleb nodded. His eyes darkened with revenge then. "I

made a pretty bad mess of Hank Tuttle's body. Early in the morning I want you and Jess and James to dig some graves. None of them deserve burying, but we can't let them just lie around. Get whatever identification you can, and I'll report all this at Bent's Fort. Then we'll go after those horses."

Cale looked toward the door. "James feels pretty bad, Grandfather. He thinks it is all his fault."

Caleb rubbed wearily at his eyes. "What time is it?"

Cale looked at the mantel clock on the fireplace. "Three o'clock in the morning."

Caleb threw back his head and sighed deeply. "I'll go talk to James. Everybody had better get some sleep. We have a lot to do. Lynda and Jess are going to sleep here tonight in case I need them. They'll go up to James's bed and John can sleep between them. James can sleep down here in a bedroll. You go get your gear. You can sleep in here or outside, whichever you want."

He walked up and squeezed the boy's shoulder. "Thanks for your help, Cale." He walked outside with the boy and Cale headed for Lynda and Jess's cabin, where he had left his bedroll outside. Caleb could see James in the moonlight, standing near the well and splashing water on his face from a bucket. Caleb walked over to where he stood. As soon as James saw him coming he turned away, pulling on a clean shirt.

"You all right, James?"

"Yes, sir."

"I'm glad as hell nothing happened to you. I'm sorry about the gun. It's never jammed up like that before. It was just one of those things."

James shook his head. "No. It wouldn't have happened to you—or Cale or Jess."

"That isn't so. It could have happened to anyone. It's happened to me before. Not with that gun, but it has happened."

James turned, tears in his eyes. "Why don't you say it! Why don't you tell me I'm no use—that you hate me for what happened to Mother!"

Caleb shook his head. "I'm not saying it because it isn't true."

"Yes, it is!" The boy picked up the bucket of water and threw it across the well, banging it against the side of the stone wall. The water in it splashed out over several feet. He faced his father again. "Who really helped tonight? Cale! It's always Cale! I'm smart in the head, but Cale is smart in the ways you have to be smart to survive out here! I don't belong here, Pa. Sometimes it seems as if I don't even belong to this family! I was afraid of horses when I was little; I don't—I don't like being around the Indians; and when you and Mother need me most, I fail you! You say it's okay and that it wasn't my fault. But it was, Pa! It was! Besides that, these things are going to keep happening—because we're Indian. You heard what they said when they poured that . . . that damned whiskey on me." The boy sucked in his breath in a near sob. "Calling me names. I stunk like that goddamned . . . whiskey. . ."

"James, I'm sorry about that—"

"Don't be, Pa. Just don't be sorry. I'm the one who's sorry, because when I grow up I'm going someplace where there aren't any Indians and men who can break the law whenever they want—and someplace where nobody knows *I'm* part Indian! Maybe you can put up with these things happening to you all your life. You have to. Anyone who looks at you knows you're Indian, and Cale too! But not me, Pa! Not me. I can get away with it. I'm . . . I'm damned sorry I have to say it." His body jerked in another sob and he quickly wiped at his eyes. "I really am, Pa. But I'll never forget what happened in Texas: losing my home, losing my dog. And now—tonight. If I have a chance I'll never have to put up with that again."

The boy turned away, his shoulders shaking. His father just stared at him for several intense seconds before replying. "I told you back in Texas, James, that if you deny your Indian blood, you'll never be really happy. I still believe that. But you're approaching manhood now, and you'll have to make those decisions for yourself." He stepped closer, putting his hands on the boy's shoulders. "But I'll tell you here and now that whatever you decide to do, I'll always love you, and so will your mother. It won't change how we feel about you, not ever. You're free to do whatever you think you have to do whenever you're ready. But I know that if you go off pretending you've no Indian blood, you'll never be happy inside, and one day you're going to have to admit to what you are. Otherwise your spirit will never be free."

"I have no spirit," the boy mumbled. "I'm not like you and Cale and Tom."

"Yes, you are. You don't know it yet, but you are. Spirit is something deep in the soul. Every man has one, and there is no stronger spirit than the Indian spirit. It brings a man close to the elements, close to God, gives him strength in times when all true physical strength seems to be gone, brings out an ability to withstand pain and to face a truth that can sometimes be painful." He squeezed the boy's shoulders. "Right now, just believe me when I say you are not to blame for what happened to your mother tonight. Don't make her feel worse by telling her that. She would only worry about you more."

James sniffed and swallowed. "Will she be all right?"

"She will, as long as there's no infection. Tomorrow I want you to help bury all these bodies. Then I'm going to Bent's Fort to report all this, and Cale and some of his friends are going to help me find those stolen horses. I want you to stay here and help Jess guard the place."

"I might not be much good at that."

"You'll do just fine. It was the gun's fault, not yours. I'll give you that newer repeater I bought at the fort a few months ago."

James wiped at his eyes again. "Mother saved my life."

"She was doing what any mother would do—a natural reaction. It doesn't mean you did something wrong or that you owe her some kind of apology. We're family, James. Each one would lay down his life for the other. If the gun hadn't jammed, you would have shot those men who came inside and Sarah wouldn't have been hurt. Things just happen, James."

The boy shook his head. "Damned gun," he muttered.

"Come on." Caleb patted his shoulder. "Come inside

and get some sleep. You'll have to sleep on the floor in a bedroll. Lynda and Jess are going to use your bed so we'll all be together tonight." He started to turn.

"Pa?"

Caleb waited. James was still turned away. "What is it?"

"I'm sorry if I hurt you . . . about not wanting to be Indian. I . . ." He swallowed. "I love you, Pa. But I feel like . . . like that part of you isn't in me."

Caleb put a hand to his chest, feeling an odd pain. "Well, maybe someday in your search for the real James Sax, you'll find that part that's missing, James. I hope for your sake that you do."

Caleb turned and walked back to the house, feeling suddenly older and more tired. What else could he say to his son? He walked into the bedroom, where Sarah lay looking peaceful, breathing deeply in a heavy sleep. It hit him then full force what could have happened. A little lower, a little more to the left, and the bullet would have killed her. Or if she hadn't jumped in front of James in time, he would have lost yet another son. He had already buried two sons in Texas. He dreaded the thought of ever burying another.

He went to his knees beside the bed, putting his head down beside Sarah and holding her hand. He wept quietly.

• Chapter Eight •

In all of Tom's life he could not remember a more beautiful moment than this one—a soft summer dusk, sitting with Juanita in a gazebo that was enclosed with climbing roses. Their perfume filled the warm air, and in this place where not even mosquitoes bothered a man, he wondered if anything came closer to heaven than California. He had already learned to live with the only apparent danger in this land, earthquake. Still, it was not difficult to get accustomed to the occasional tremors that sometimes knocked dishes from the shelves but seldom did any worse damage.

Birds sang in nearby trees, preparing to nest for the night, and Juanita's ever present personal maid, Luisa, sat on a bench outside the gazebo. Tom rested an arm on the gazebo bench behind Juanita, facing her, smiling at the way she almost always kept her face turned away, as though if she faced him he might see the desire in her eyes.

"I wish there was a way we could meet alone," he told her, longing to touch her, hold her, meet her lips.

She twisted the lace of her dress nervously through her fingers, her hands resting in her lap. "So do I," she said shyly. "I . . . I have enjoyed seeing you, Señor Sax. All the things we have talked about . . . we know so much about each other's past and each other's dreams. We are like . . . good friends. But I have . . . I have also wished we could be alone."

He saw the flush of her cheeks. He grinned, moving his hand to lightly stroke her hair behind her head where Luisa could not see the movement.

"You're so damned beautiful, Juanita," he said softly. "I hope you'll keep seeing just me until you're old enough that I can . . ." He took a deep breath, hoping he would not frighten her away. "Old enough that I can marry you."

That remark made her look up at him, her dark eyes wide and dancing. "Señor Sax," she whispered in surprise.

He laughed lightly. "Will you quit calling me that? It's Tom."

Their eyes held. "Is it true? You wish to marry me?"

Tom glanced at Luisa, who sat reading a book. "It's true," he said in a near whisper. "But I don't think your father would want me asking so soon. It's just that—" His eyes moved over the pink, lacy dress, the way her full, firm bosom filled out the bodice. "It's just that the waiting will be very hard. Every night I think about making you my woman, Juanita—my wife. And I'm getting old enough that I must soon start having a family."

She blushed more and looked down. How she longed to know how it would feel to be kissed by him, held by him.

She had only a partial awareness of what it meant to be a wife, where babies came from. It was enough to make her both frightened and excited. The act was frightening, but the thought of Tom Sax being the one to make her a woman, the thought of giving him sons and daughters, filled her with a fiery desire she had never felt in her innocent young life.

"I would be honored to be your wife and to give you children," she said shyly, still looking at her lap. "When I think of how you lost your first wife I think how sad it all is—how long you have gone without a woman's love." She raised her eyes to meet his dark ones, feeling almost daring to actually look into his eyes and speak of love. "I weep for you sometimes. Now that I know you, Señor . . . I mean . . . Tom. Now that I know you so well, and we have talked about so many things, I feel older, wiser. And the thought of your suffering makes my heart sad. You are a good man. My father knows this. Perhaps he would consider—"

Their eyes held, and Tom felt ready to explode with desire. His whole body felt hot, and he trembled with the agony of not being able to take her into his arms and taste her mouth, feel her breasts against himself, and most of all to lay her down and teach her about making love.

"I will wait just a little longer," he told her. He took her hand, an allowable touch. It felt tiny and soft, and his felt strong and sure wrapped around her own. "I wanted you the first day I set eyes on you, Juanita." He kept his voice low so Luisa could not hear. "And now that I know you better, I know that I love you. I want you to be in my life forever, if you'll have me."

She felt spellbound by his dark eyes and handsome face. Suddenly it wasn't embarrassing to look straight into his true, loving eyes. "I want to be in your life forever, too."

"Your time is up, Juanita," Luisa called from the bench.

Juanita frowned, glancing in the woman's direction. "Yes, Luisa. Just a moment." She looked back at Tom.

"The time goes so fast," she whispered. "I hate it when I have to go."

Tom squeezed her hand reassuringly. "I am deeply honored, Juanita, that you want to be my wife. I must tell you that I have to go away for a while, but when I return, I intend to speak to your father about our feelings for each other."

"Go away? Where?"

"I am going to San Francisco. Your father says there is someone there who raises palominos—supposedly the finest a man could want. I am going to look them over for him and buy a good stud and mare for him."

She blushed slightly at the words. A stud and mare were for breeding. She had seen horses mate before. What was it like for humans? It seemed so appalling and frightening, yet sitting here with Tom's strong, warm hand wrapped around her own, she trusted Tom Sax would never let it be that way for her. She glanced over at Luisa, who had not yet moved to rise, then allowed her eyes to meet Tom's again.

"How long will you be gone?"

Tom sighed, rubbing the back of her hand with his thumb. "It's hard to say. A couple of weeks, I suppose, not much longer than that."

She daringly put her other hand over his. "I will miss you."

Tom glanced at Luisa, who was not looking, then leaned forward and gently kissed Juanita on the lips. He lingered there a moment, lightly moving his tongue over her mouth, wanting to remember the sweet taste of it, wishing he could part her lips and lay her back, kiss her until she was totally helpless beneath him.

It seemed to Juanita that a hot streak of fire moved through her insides in that very moment, and her eyes remained closed for a moment when he left her mouth.

"I love you, Juanita," Tom said in a near whisper.

She opened her eyes and smiled, but trembled with wonderful new desires, her eyes tearing from the joy in her soul. "I love you, too," she whispered. She blushed deeply then and looked at her lap. "I have wanted to say it for so long. I think I loved you the first time you rode onto my father's ranch looking for work. But I must seem such a child to you."

He reached out with his other hand and lightly touched her cheek with the back of his hand. "You are not a child, Juanita. You are a beautiful woman in the making. When I marry you, I will make you a full woman, and you will never have to be afraid of me, *mi querida*."

She clamped her hands tighter around his own, meeting his eyes again, smiling through tears. "I believe you."

He smiled back, the wonderful, handsome smile that made her legs feel like pudding. "We will be together, Juanita, and soon. I will do everything in my power to make it so."

She nodded.

"Juanita, we must leave now," Luisa repeated, finally rising.

Juanita continued to hold Tom's eyes. "Have a safe trip. I will pray for you."

He squeezed her hand. "You stay close to the house. Stay away from Emanuel Hidalgo. He has been giving me trouble and is very jealous. I don't trust that man, but there is nothing he can do as long as you stay close to your father. If I did not feel sure of your safety, I would not even go."

Her heart swelled with love. He would surely die for her if necessary. Of that she had no doubt.

"You know full well how Father watches me," she said then, laughing lightly.

Tom rolled his eyes. "I most certainly do."

They rose, and Tom squeezed her hand once more, wanting to hold her. But Luisa was watching. "I leave early in the morning," he told her. "I probably won't see you before I leave, so I will just have to dream about you until I return. When I come back, I will make those dreams come true, Juanita. I promise you that."

"Come, Juanita." Luisa gently took hold of her arm. Luisa liked Tom, but she also liked her job. She was well aware of the love Juanita felt for the man and would have liked nothing better than to let them be together for as long as they wished. But she had her orders.

"*Adiós,* Tom," Juanita told him, reluctantly letting go of his hand.

Tom nodded, feeling an odd apprehension as she left him, a sixth sense that something was amiss. He glanced around at the shadows, always feeling that Emanuel Hidalgo was watching. But Emanuel had been gone a couple of days, and Tom wondered where he was and what he was up to. No one seemed to know.

He watched Juanita, studying the tiny waist and the way her dress swayed as she walked, envisioning how she must look naked . . . like a goddess, he was sure. At least he knew he could go away and not have to worry about her safety. This was a big ranch with a lot of men. Hidalgo could not get near her. And maybe the man wasn't even coming back. Maybe he had decided that if he couldn't have her, he would rather not be around her at all. It was a nice thought, but something about Hidalgo's pride told Tom the man would not give up that easily. As far as Tom was concerned, he could not marry Juanita soon enough, not just because he wanted and loved her, but because Emanuel Hidalgo would realize once and for all that his dreams of having Juanita for himself were hopeless.

Caleb drew his Appaloosa to a halt, ten Cheyenne warriors with him. They were all young and eager, angry that the soldiers had all but put a stop to their normal summer migration because of the Mexican war and Indian attacks along the Santa Fe Trail. The Southern Cheyenne insisted they were being blamed for atrocities committed by other Indians, but their complaints were for the most part ignored. The younger men camped around Bent's Fort were restless, happy to help the elder warrior Blue Hawk find and bring back his stolen horses.

Caleb sensed the wild anger these young men felt over recent soldier campaigns against the Cheyenne. They would not stay put long, of that he was sure. They felt this land belonged to them, and they would continue to use it and to raid settlers who intruded upon it. But when they broke loose again, Cale would most likely be among them. His grandson would ride off someday for good, never to return. And a part of Caleb Sax would go with him.

One of the young men pointed. "Scout," he said in his own tongue, then signed the word.

Caleb nodded, waiting as two riders approached. Cale and another had left the day after the raid on Caleb's ranch, immediately setting out to track down the culprits who had stolen Caleb's horses. Much as he hated to leave Sarah, Caleb waited only two more days. Time was essential if he was to get the horses to Colonel Kearny before the soldiers left for Santa Fe. Sarah understood and was doing much better than he had expected. So far there was no infection, but Caleb was still worried and anxious to get back. He had been gone three days, and they had ridden nearly fifty miles north, following an easy-to-read trail left by Cale and his friend, who from a distant rise had spotted Caleb and the others finally coming. Now they rode close, looking excited.

"We have found them, Grandfather," he said victoriously. He signed to the others present, showing *many horses, many men.* They all nodded.

"Hopo! Hopo!" one of them said excitedly.

"Wait," Caleb told him, making the sign for *halt.* "We have to be careful," he said in the Cheyenne tongue. "We will hide and wait until dark. They don't expect Indians to come at dark." He turned to Cale. "How many men are there?"

"Maybe six. I heard them arguing what to do with the horses. They have been waiting for the one called Hank Tuttle to show up. Now they know he is not coming." He grinned. "If they knew what you did to him, they would be running fast right now with their tails between their legs." He repeated the statement to the others in their own tongue, and the young men snickered, feeling great respect for Cale's grandfather.

"Do you think they'll wait for one more day?" Caleb asked him.

Cale nodded. "I was close enough to hear them talk. They are so stupid! They did not even know I was there. I could have taken two or three of them right then and there."

The boy sat proud and straight. Ever since the night of

the raid, when he rode right into the outlaws like a true warrior, he felt more manly. His story had drawn approval from his peers, and more than ever he wished to stay with them and become one of them.

Caleb motioned for them to follow him a few yards back down into a narrow ravine where they could not be spotted. "We will camp here until the sun is down," he told them, dismounting and offering all of them some tobacco. "I am grateful for your help."

They tethered their horses and then took the tobacco eagerly, some chewing on it, others packing some into long pipes they drew from their parfleches, intending to smoke it. Cale's friend Ten Stars asked for some whiskey.

"No," Caleb told him. "I didn't bring any with me. The firewater is bad, Ten Stars. It makes a man weak and do stupid things."

Ten Stars shook his head. "It gives him power." He held out a fist. "Makes him strong and brave."

"It only seems that way. Why do you think so many white men try to sell it to you? It's because it makes you weak and easier to defeat in battle. It turns warriors into women. I got into all this trouble because I stopped a white man from selling whiskey at the fort. Why would I put myself and my family in danger doing that if I didn't truly believe the whiskey was bad for you?"

Ten Stars looked over at Cale. "He tells you true," Cale told him. "My grandfather cares about the Cheyenne."

Ten Stars shrugged and threw up his hands. "What is left for us? They do not let us ride and hunt as we used to do. The whiskey makes us feel good, takes away the sadness in our hearts and makes us happy."

"It's a false happiness, Ten Stars," Caleb told him. "Don't let the whiskey traders fool you. They are your enemy. Remember that."

Ten Stars plopped down and pulled two leather pouches from his own parfleche, dipping a finger into one of them. He smeared red marks across his cheeks. "Tonight we will be warriors," he muttered.

"Kill only if you have to. The soldiers know you're all with me to help me get back my horses. That's all. If you kill these men deliberately, take any scalps, you'll all be in trouble and so will I. Kearny couldn't spare any men to help me, so I brought all of you. Don't deceive me. Don't make the Cheyenne look bad. Your chiefs are struggling to make the soldiers and the government believe it's not the Cheyenne who are making so much trouble lately. I think our numbers are enough to scare them off, especially now that they're restless over Tuttle's not showing up. We'll watch the white men run away and we'll take my horses home. There will be a reward of food and tobacco for you. I can't afford to give you much more."

"We are glad to have something to do," Buffalo Boy spoke up. "It is better than sitting around that fort."

Caleb stuffed and lit a pipe of his own. "If my woman were not hurt, I would keep going—do a little hunting with you. But I have to get back to her."

One of them grinned, a twinkle in his eye. "How is it the warrior Blue Hawk is married to a white woman?"

Caleb puffed on the pipe for a quiet moment. "It is a long story. But her heart is as good and true as any Indian woman's. Someday all of you will have a good woman at your side, and you will understand how I feel."

"Is it true you once had a Cheyenne wife?" one of them asked.

Caleb felt the old pain. How many years ago had he loved and married Walking Grass? Well over thirty winters. He nodded, staring at a colorful stone that lay nearby. "She was my first wife. I was very young, hardly any older than most of you. She was the mother of my oldest son, Tom." He eyed all of them, grinning inwardly at the way they all stared at him. Indians loved to tell and to listen to stories. Many stories had been told about the warrior Blue Hawk, and he didn't doubt that by now they had been exaggerated to the point of making him sound superhuman. "You would all like Tom. He is very Indian, like Cale. And he is handsome because his mother was so beautiful."

There was a moment of silence.

"It is because of her that you rode against the Crow,"

another spoke up then, "is it not? The Crow killed your Cheyenne wife?"

Caleb nodded, amazed at how the pain of that day could still stab at him as though it had happened only yesterday. His blue eyes glazed colder with remembered hatred. "Hatred and vengeance were great in my heart, so great that I hardly knew what I was doing. I was one man against a nation of Crows, riding out alone. But I made the mistake of hating so much that I began attacking them without first praying to the spirits for guidance. I was acting on my own and not following the signs, not listening to the spirits who guide a warrior in battle. For this I finally suffered a terrible wound that almost killed me." He studied them individually. "Remember that. Never ride into battle without prayer and sacrifice, without your own spirit being right with *Maheo*, or when the signs tell you it is not the right time."

Cale held out the blue quill necklace he wore around his neck. "Grandfather gave this to me when I was born. His own Cheyenne mother gave it to him at birth. She died, and he never knew her. It is over fifty winters old. This necklace has magic. It helped my mother find my grandmother and grandfather. It brought my family together and now it is mine. It is a special gift that will always bring me health, a gift I will one day pass on to my own son."

Ten Stars finished painting his face for the "battle" to come. "Have you celebrated the Sun Dance," he asked Caleb, eyeing him daringly, still a little miffed about not getting any whiskey.

Caleb met his eyes. "I have. I was about your age."

Ten Stars slowly nodded. "One more summer. I am going to suffer the Sun Dance and so is Cale. We will be accepted then as true men, true warriors."

Caleb glanced at Cale. This was not the time to discuss participating in the Sun Dance. He did not want to voice any protest in front of Cale's friends. But he knew Lynda would fly into a motherly rage at the suggestion her son go through such torture.

"It is good," he spoke up, relieving Cale with his approval. "I will be proud when Cale participates, even though I know the pain and suffering it will bring. The Sun Dance is something you will never forget. It will bring you a power and spirit that the firewater can never bring you. Through the Sun Dance you will be stronger. Your strength comes from inside, Ten Stars—from a strong spirit, a strong heart—from touching the spirits through sacrifice and pain. You will have a vision, and you will know what to do with your life."

Caleb leaned back against a rock and closed his eyes. "Rest now—all of you. Tonight we must be quiet like the gentle winds, invisible, quick. Tonight we get back the horses."

They all listened and obeyed. Among the Cheyenne the elders were always respected, especially when they had the reputation of Blue Hawk. It was true he lived among white men, but his heart rode with the Cheyenne, and all the old chiefs predicted that one day this Blue Hawk would return to the Cheyenne.

Sarah awoke to the touch of Caleb's hand against her cheek. He was leaning over her, his long black hair tied to one side of his head with a blue-beaded strip of leather. She could smell the dust in his buckskin clothing and saw by more dust on his face that he had not stopped to wash or do anything else when he had gotten back. He had come straight to her.

"Caleb! Are you all right?"

He smiled softly, leaning closer. "That's supposed to be my question. Lynda said you had a fever last night."

"It's gone now. I even sat up and ate a big breakfast this morning."

He leaned down and kissed her forehead. "Good."

"Did you get the horses back? Did anyone get hurt?"

His blue eyes danced with an almost boyish excitement. "I got them. Cale and his friends had a grand time scaring off Tuttle's men. They ran like rabbits when they heard all that war whooping and shooting. Nobody got hurt. I'm afraid I have to leave you again, but I'll be back tonight yet. I'm going to ride on in and see if Kearny is still at the fort. It's possible I can still sell the horses."

She reached up to touch the creases of dust in his handsome face. "Oh, Caleb, you must be so tired. You should stay at the fort once you get there and wait till morning to come back."

He stroked her hair gently. "No. I've been away long enough. I was worried sick about you. I'm just sorry you ever got hurt in the first place. You gave me a hell of a scare, Sarah Sax."

She smiled reassuringly. "You're the one who's always telling me I'm stronger than I think."

He closed his eyes and sighed, pulling back the covers and unbuttoning her gown to pull it away from her shoulder, relieved there was only a light bloodstain on the gauze. "I'll take a better look when I get back. We've got to start exercising that arm right away." He leaned down and kissed her shoulder.

"Will I have a bad scar, Caleb?"

He struggled to hold back the renewed anger he felt at the thought of Tuttle's shooting her. "Not too bad," he assured her. "Besides, woman, Lord knows you have to look at enough scars on me. One little one on you isn't going to matter much."

"But I'm losing my youth. I hate to have a scar—"

He touched her lips. "Sarah, do you really think any of that matters to me? They could have cut your nose off and it wouldn't change how I feel about my woman. Now get some rest. No more talk about scars or anything else. You know how beautiful you are to me." He kissed her softly then. "I'll be back later tonight. If you're already asleep I'll try not to disturb you. I'll just crawl into bed and wrap my arms around you and go to sleep. Every time I'm away from you that's all I can think about."

He kissed her once more, a more possessive kiss. "Hurry back," she whispered. He kissed her eyes, thanking the spirits that she was better.

Their eyes held for a moment. "I'm getting you out of here, Sarah. If you have a good winter, we're going to

California. I've thought about it more and more, and I can't help thinking it would be good for you there."

"Don't get all upset over it, Caleb. I'm fine. And if we stay right here in Colorado, we'll do just fine."

"I don't think so. Trade with Santa Fe is practically at a halt, and who knows when it will pick up again? And all this trouble with the Cheyenne. I don't like any of it. Life is going to get harder here for a while, not easier, and I hate what it's doing to you."

She smiled lovingly, her eyes teared. "Caleb, please stop worrying so. Take those horses to the fort and get your money. We'll talk about it when you come back."

He kissed her once more. "How is James?"

Her eyes teared more. "I'm more worried about him than about myself. He feels so bad, Caleb. And now he's more withdrawn and moody than ever. I feel as if it's partly my fault."

"No, honey, it has nothing to do with you. It's much more than that. I talked to him the night it happened, but then I was so wrapped up in your injury and had to head out." He sighed. "I'll talk to him some more when I get back. You rest."

"Is Cale all right?"

He straightened, grinning. "No sense worrying about that one. He's just fine and full of the devil. I'm afraid we might as well not plan on seeing much of him anymore. It's hard to let go, but I can't help smiling when I watch him. There's no holding that one down, Sarah."

"I know."

Their eyes held, both realizing that already another young one was preparing to leave the nest.

"They'll grow up and leave us, Caleb—and then it will be just you and me, the way it started," she said softly.

She saw the pain in his eyes. Their younger years were not at all what they should have been. They had lost their best years. Now they were just doing their best to make the most of what was left to them.

His eyes seemed to tear, and he looked as if he wanted to say more, but he just turned and left.

· Chapter Nine ·

Caleb removed his clothes, glad he had already taken the time to pay for a bath at the fort. He knew he would be late getting home and he didn't want to disturb anyone, least of all Sarah. Before leaving Bent's Fort he had washed his hair and worked the grime out of his pores, then put on new bleached buckskins for which he had just done some hard bartering with an Indian woman. Now he tossed the new clothing onto a chair, removing even his underwear. It was a hot night.

Lynda had let them in, and now everything was quiet. James, who along with Cale had helped take in the horses, had bedded down in the outer room. Lynda and Jess were sleeping in the loft, which they always did whenever Caleb had to be away. They couldn't be sure he would get back that night, and Lynda would not think of leaving her mother alone. James was recruited to the floor, but he didn't seem to mind. Cale, much to Lynda's disappointment, had stayed behind at the fort with Ten Stars and Buffalo Boy.

Caleb looked through the curtained doorway again to be sure James was asleep. There had been little conversation between James and Cale on their trip to the fort with the horses. Caleb knew James still felt responsible for what had happened to his mother and felt less capable than Cale. Caleb had tried to talk to the boy all the way home, but there seemed to be no getting through to him. It was becoming impossible to share the warm closeness he had always had with Tom.

He turned away, wondering what more he could do. Perhaps nothing. Perhaps it was only a matter of time and healing, a matter of James's deciding for himself the kind of man he would be. Few understood better than Caleb Sax what it was like to be a man of two worlds. But maybe it was harder for James because he looked all white.

He moved to the foot of the bed, studying a sleeping Sarah. How beautiful she looked. For the life of him he couldn't see that she looked much different from when he had first fallen in love with her over thirty years ago. Did James blame his father for his mother's hard life and past suffering? He didn't need James's accusations for that. He was having a hard enough time living with his own guilt for the same feelings. He would never choose for anything bad to happen to his Sarah. He had only loved her. But the rest of the world had declared it was wrong for an Indian to love a white woman, and they would not change their minds, not in his lifetime, probably not in anyone's lifetime.

He tried to concentrate on happier thoughts. At least Sarah was getting better, and he had sold the horses to Colonel Kearny. He had brought home some supplies, and a gift for Sarah—a lovely gold and ivory brooch, which had cost him plenty. But it was worth it. It wasn't often that he splurged on something that wasn't really necessary, but he wanted to do something to make up for Sarah's suffering. His heart ached at the memory of having to dig out the bullet from her shoulder and bring her the hideous pain.

He walked around and blew out the lantern Sarah had kept turned up for him, then crawled under the light blanket that covered her, trying not to disturb her. But she gave out a sleepy little moan and spontaneously snuggled closer, her back to him. He turned and reached around her, kissing her hair and running a big hand gently over her belly and breasts through the soft, flannel gown. She came more fully awake and turned.

"Caleb. What time is it?"

He kissed her cheek. "Very very late. I didn't mean to wake you," he answered in a near whisper.

"It's all right. At least it's all over and you're home to stay."

He nuzzled her neck, moving his hand up to grasp some of her thick hair in his fingers. "That's one thing for certain. Now get some sleep. We'll talk in the morning." He kissed her lips lightly, then stretched out on his back, sighing deeply. "I can't believe how well you're healing, Sarah. It's only been nine days. Thank God nothing vital was hit."

She reached over and touched his chest. "Caleb, I—" She suddenly started crying and he rose up on one elbow, leaning over her.

"What's wrong, Sarah?"

She couldn't reply right away. He pulled her close, being careful of the bandaged shoulder. He kissed her hair, waiting for her to speak.

"Just . . . a late reaction, I guess," she finally whispered, sniffing and wiping at her eyes. "It could have been you or James. Thank God no one in the family was badly hurt."

He kissed her gently. "Don't cry, Sarah. I've always hated it when you cry." He kissed her eyes. "The worst part is that most of the time I'm the cause of it."

"No, Caleb. That isn't true. You're the only real happiness I've known." She reached up and touched his face in the darkness. "Make love to me, Caleb," she whispered.

He took her hand and kissed the palm. "You aren't strong enough."

"You can be careful. I have hardly any pain, Caleb, unless you actually touch my shoulder." She sniffed again. "I want to know you're really here—that everything is all right."

He grinned and gently stroked the hair back from her face. "Well, I am really here, and everything really is all right. You need your rest, Sarah."

"Please," she whispered. "I need you to make love to me."

He knew her well enough to know that if he could see her face in full light it would be crimson. It was not like her to be so bold, in spite of all their years together. He held back an urge to laugh and tease her, sensing a certain need in her that went beyond sexual desire.

He moved his hand along her leg, pushing up her gown and gently stroking secret places. "Are you sure?"

"Yes." She breathed deeply to relax, relishing his touch.

His fingers probed gently and she leaned up to kiss his chest. "I want you inside of me, Caleb." She knew the words sounded brazen, but she also knew he would understand. He moved carefully on top of her, finding it easy to be ready for her. He guided himself inside of her slowly, worried that his movements would bring her pain, but she was breathing deeply and rhythmically with every thrust.

He raised up on his knees so as not to put any weight on her, grasping her under the hips, doing all the moving for her so that all she had to do was lie there and enjoy. Her smooth moistness told him he was bringing her pleasure and not pain, and moments later he felt the warm, grasping pulsation of her climax, so sweet that it brought a groan to his own lips.

He was tired from the long night's ride. Every bone ached from the ordeal of the last several days. But right now none of it mattered.

He leaned closer, resting on his elbows and leaning down to meet Sarah's mouth, searching its depths with his tongue while his life spilled into her in great surges of his own emotional relief.

"I love you, Sarah," he whispered, leaving her mouth but letting his lips linger on her cheeks and eyes, then nuzzling her throat before he moved off her. He pulled down her gown and held her close. "Are you all right?"

She was suddenly very tired. "I'm all right," she said sleepily. "I should get up and wash."

"Just stay right where you are. I'll help you wash in the morning." He pulled the blankets up around her neck. The early morning hours had taken on a chill.

"I love you," she whispered.

He stroked her hair, realizing only minutes later that she was asleep again. She was like a little girl sometimes, cuddling up to him as though the only safe place to be was in

Caleb Sax's arms. He thought about the gold and ivory brooch, but she was already asleep. He would give it to her in the morning.

Juanita held her rosary close to her breast, praying again for a safe journey for Tom. He had only been gone five days, but it seemed like forever. She felt his presence as though he were in her room, and she wished so much that he were. Things had suddenly changed on the ranch; the lovely peace she had always known there seemed somehow gone. She wondered if something bad had actually happened in only the last few days, or if it was just Tom's absence that made her feel so anxious.

Luisa had been fussing for the past four or five days about the *americanos* who were getting very demanding, saying there had been fighting somewhere between Americans and *californios* and clucking that the world was coming to an end. Juanita's father felt it was nothing for his young daughter to be worried about, so it was impossible to get a straight story out of the man; but Juanita sensed her father's deep concern. There had been meetings in his study with other Spanish landowners, meetings held late at night and in secret. Juanita felt an odd fear of the unknown, and more than ever she wished Tom were with her to hold her. She would gladly run away with him if he came for her, but she knew that in his good heart he still wanted to do the right thing. He would try to talk to her father when he returned and convince the man to let them be married.

She went to the mirror and brushed out her hair, smoothing her green cotton dress and going out into the hall. Perhaps if she spoke to her father first, told him how she felt about Tom, she could pave the way for when he would return and ask for her hand.

The house was quiet. She walked through the sprawling bedroom wing of the graceful stucco mansion and through a cool hallway to her father's study. She had heard him come in minutes ago. Through open windows and doorways she could hear birds singing peacefully and could see roses blooming outside. An odd chill moved through her, because for an unexplainable reason she sensed something terribly wrong in spite of the beautiful morning.

She breathed deeply and knocked on the door to her father's study. She heard his voice. *"Entra."*

She slowly opened the door and peeked inside, meeting her father's dark eyes. "What is it, Juanita? I am busy."

"Father, I . . . I wish to talk to you . . . about Tom."

His eyebrows shot up and he put down his pen, leaning back in his chair, his dark eyes studying her closely. "You have come to tell me that you love him and that he loves you."

She looked at him in surprise, stepping farther inside, her cheeks looking crimson in spite of her dark skin. "How did you know!"

The man smiled rather sadly. "I was in love once myself, you know—with your mother. Besides, I have been asking Luisa what your visits are like."

Juanita swallowed, looking at the floor. "I think when Tom returns . . . he will ask you for permission to marry me, Father."

Galvez sighed deeply. "And I am afraid I would have to say no, Juanita. You are still too young, and I have perhaps made a mistake letting Tom Sax see you. He is at an age where he will be very anxious to start a family."

She raised her eyes to meet her father's. "But I love him, Father! Some women marry even younger than me! Please give us permission."

Her eyes teared in desperation, and Galvez rose from his chair. "You should not be discussing these things with me, Juanita. It is something between Tom and myself. I will consider your feelings, but you have not been seeing Tom long enough to be so certain of your feelings. In another year—"

His words were interrupted by shooting in the distance. He frowned and hurried to a window, calling out to one of his men. "Ramone! What is it?"

It seemed to him that the man took his time answering. Ramone showed little concern as he looked up from the hitching post where he was tying his horse. "I am not sure, *patrón*, I will go and see."

"Well, get going then—*pronto!*" Galvez turned away from the window, failing to see Ramone pull a rifle from his gear and head into the house. "Get to your room, Juanita! There is some kind of trouble."

The girl had barely any time to turn before the door burst open and Emanuel Hidalgo stood there, rifle in hand. Juanita gasped and stepped back.

"Emanuel!" Galvez frowned, stepping closer. "What is this!"

The man smiled, an evil glitter to his dark eyes that made Juanita shiver.

"I decided, *patrón,* that I did not like the thought of waiting another year, perhaps longer, to enjoy the favors of your daughter and to have the joy of owning land!" He stepped inside the room, waving the gun at Galvez, two men behind him.

Juanita felt her chest tighten almost painfully, her muscles trembling and her ears beginning to ring when Emanuel turned his gaze to her for a moment, looking her up and down hungrily.

"I am confused, Emanuel," Galvez spoke up. "Put that gun away!"

Emanuel looked back at the man with great contempt. "You have ordered me around long enough, Señor Galvez," he sneered. "Lately I have come to realize that my *patrón* would never consider Emanuel Hidalgo worthy of being part of his family. So I said to myself, perhaps with this new trouble with the *americanos* there is a way I can have what I want much sooner, if I cooperate with them. So I tell them, if Emanuel tells you the easiest way to take over the estate of Don Antonio Galvez with little or no bloodshed, will you award Emanuel a piece of Galvez land and his daughter?" He grinned more when he heard an odd choking sound from Juanita's throat. "And they said, yes, we will let you have that much. Antonio Galvez has much land, much cattle and horses. We would like very much to break his power. It will help us in our cause, for we must crush the wealthy *californios.*"

He just stood there a moment, letting it all sink in as more gunshots came from the surrounding hills and outbuildings. Then they heard Luisa scream from somewhere in the house, followed by shouting. The heavyset woman was running through the house calling for Juanita.

"Shut up, you fat mama," they heard someone yell. There was the sound of a blow, and there were no more screams from Luisa. Juanita broke into a cold sweat, looking around desperately for a place to run. Her father moved his hand toward an open drawer, and Emanuel's gun fired. Galvez flew backward against the wall.

"Father!" Juanita stared in disbelief as the man's body slid down the wall. She ran to him, leaning over his bleeding body. "Father! Father!"

Galvez looked at her with wide, teared eyes. "You . . . you were right . . . my daughter," he choked out. "Tom. He will . . . come. Go with him."

His body shuddered and Juanita leaned over him to hold him, but someone grabbed her arm painfully and jerked her up. Emanuel shoved the barrel of his rifle against her throat. His eyes were wild and victorious, his grin hungry. His handsomeness was totally erased by the sneer of his lips and the coldness of his heart. "Now you will finally be mine, Doña Juanita Rosanna Galvez de Sonoma."

She struggled to get away, but he jammed the rifle hard, half choking her and burning her neck, the gun barrel still hot from just being fired.

"I have a few things to do first, my sweet Juanita. My men will take you up to your room to wait for me." He took the rifle away, handing it to one of Galvez's own men, who was in on the plot and who now stepped closer, grinning as Emanuel forced Juanita's arms behind her back and kissed her savagely. She twisted wildly, but he only kissed her harder, hurting her lips and making her teeth cut into them until they bled. He finally released her, throwing her on the floor.

"Take her upstairs," he told the other two men. "Strip her and tie her to her bed." He gave them a black, warning look. "Do not touch her! I will be the first. If either of you touch her I will kill you!"

Juanita struggled to her feet. "Tom Sax . . . will come," she wept. "He will kill you for this!"

"Your beloved Tom will never get back in time, bitch," Emanuel sneered. "Besides, he does not care about you. He only wanted to get under your skirts. Only *I* will be first at that! When he learns this, he will no longer want you."

Juanita stared at him a moment, trying to understand it all. Tom! How could he save her now? Was it true he would not come to help her, would not want her? She would not believe it. Surely he would come any moment. He would never let these men touch her! The thought of it brought vomit to her throat and terror to every nerve, bone, and muscle in her body. It was supposed to be beautiful. It was supposed to be with Tom. Not this way—

She started to run, but she was dazed and frantic and no match for the two men who helped Emanuel, both of them men her father had trusted. Each man grabbed an arm and dragged Juanita, kicking and screaming, out of the room. Emanuel watched coldly, feeling an almost painful passion at the thought of finally possessing her. He would show the haughty bitch! Now it was Emanuel Hidalgo who had the power!

He picked up his rifle and hurried through the beautiful, cool hallway, grinning at the sound of the still screaming and crying Juanita. He hurried outside. Lecho de Rosas was crushed. Part of it would belong to him now, and so would its young heiress! It had all been so easy. He was glad for the Mexican war and the Bear Flag revolution. Now he was free—his own man. And soon Juanita Galvez would find out just how much of a man he was! She would submit eventually. He would make her feel so good she would wonder why she always ignored him before. She would pay now—pay for turning him away—pay for wanting an Indian!

He hurried outside, where already several of the attacking Americans were herding Galvez men into a circle. They would be arrested and held until it was certain there would be no Spanish uprising against the American settlers.

Emanuel walked up to the big man the Americans considered the leader of this raid. His name was John Hughes, and to Emanuel's delight the man had no scruples. He had been easy to deal with. Hughes and his men had destroyed Lecho de Rosas, with Emanuel's help from the inside and the promise that Emanuel could have Juanita. Emanuel did not fear Tom Sax now. If Tom was after the ranch and the money, there would be none of those things left after today, nor would his precious Juanita be a virgin any longer!

Hughes gave out a rebel yell of victory, riding up to Emanuel. The attack on the Galvez estate had not been sanctioned by anyone truly in charge. It had been planned by Hughes and his ruffians, who were simply volunteers out to gather the spoils that could be realized from the wealthier Spaniards. This would not be the only *ranchero* that would go down under Hughes and his men. And with the current, though minor, revolution going on, it gave men who were no better than outlaws a chance to reap some of the benefits.

Emanuel's hunger for power had taken him to Sonoma seeking Americans who would be willing to overrun the Galvez estate. Emanuel's information on just where guards were posted, how the *ranchero* was laid out, and the best time of day to attack, had helped Hughes and his men move in in a matter of minutes with no losses on their side. Emanuel knew the best time to attack was while Tom Sax was gone.

"Señor Galvez is inside," Emanuel told Hughes. "He is dead."

"You find the daughter?"

Emanuel nodded. "You can take what you want from the house, and you can have any of the horses and the cattle that you wish, even claim some of the land. Just leave me the house—and the girl."

Hughes nodded. "You were right. They didn't hardly put up a fight."

"That is because they are so ignorant as to think you *americanos* will be friendly to them and treat them kindly if they give no resistance and cooperate. Señor Galvez did not think there would be any real fighting. He was a fool!"

Hughes laughed. "We'll herd these men up and walk them to Sutter's Fort. Frémont can decide what he wants to do with them. We'll be rounding up some cattle and horses."

Emanuel grinned, raising his rifle victoriously. "Take what you wish, señor. I already have all that I want." He turned and hurried back toward the house. Hughes looked toward an upstairs window from which he thought he had heard a woman's screams.

"Hidalgo," Hughes shouted.

Emanuel turned.

"That little filly you wanted—any chance of sharing her once you've had your fill?"

Emanuel grinned. "Bring back some good whiskey, señor, and we will talk about it."

Hughes laughed and looked at the upstairs window again. The screaming had stopped.

· Chapter Ten ·

Tom rode into Sonoma, proudly leading the two palominos he had purchased for Galvez. He was tired and thirsty and decided to stop in Sonoma for a couple of drinks and a visit to the bathhouse behind the barbershop before returning to the ranch. He wanted to look his best in case Juanita was watching and waiting when he returned.

He had not ridden far down the dusty main street before he noticed a flag perched atop one of the buildings, a flag bearing a star and something that looked like a bear. He frowned, realizing something was amiss. The sleepy little town was teeming with horses and wagons, and a few cannon sat at the end of the street. Those who were Spanish walked around quietly, dipping their heads, women hiding under shawls and scampering about as though afraid.

Tom took inventory, noticing a lot of rough-looking men

standing about. They were not Spanish. They were white
—Americans—the rugged, buckskin-clad type very much
like the ruffians who had come to Texas to help that republic gain its independence. What were so many of them
doing in Sonoma? Were the rumors he had heard in San
Francisco about Americans taking over California true?
People even said an American fleet would soon land on the
coast.

He dismounted in front of a tavern, tying his Appaloosa
and the two palominos. He walked inside the tavern, where
several white men sat around a table eating peaches from a
basket and laughing about the "greasy Mexican" from
whom they had stolen the fruit. The peaches gave off a
sweet scent, but the smell did not erase another odor—the
scent of danger. The men all looked warily at Tom, and a
couple more who had spotted him outside walked through
the doorway as Tom approached the bar.

A short, nervous-looking Mexican stood behind the bar
wiping his hands on a towel. "Can I help you, señor?"

"Give me a whiskey."

"Sí, señor," the little man answered.

"What's your name, mister?" one of the Americans
asked.

Tom turned, watching the man carefully. "Maybe that is
my business."

The man rose from his chair. He was huge, tall and
heavyset, and he sported a thick beard. He seemed all hair,
hair that surrounded cold gray eyes and wide lips.

"I'm John Hughes, and everything that happens here is
my business now, mister. We've come here to protect the
American settlers."

Tom frowned. "American settlers? Protect them from
what?"

Hughes's eyes moved over Tom. "Protect them from
being overrun by the fancy rich Spaniards around here.
Seems some have been talking about taking over American
claims and making the Americans leave. You the kind that
would do that?"

Tom kept a defensive pose. "I have no interest either
way. I am from Colorado. I just bought a couple of horses

in San Francisco—intend to start my own ranch." Tom decided not to mention Galvez and his ranch. These men were looking for trouble. He would not draw their attention to the Galvez estate.

Hughes's eyes moved over Tom as though to sum him up. "You see that flag outside?"

Tom nodded. "I saw it."

"Well, that's the flag of the new Bear Flag Republic. That's what us Americans are calling California now. Just a precaution."

Tom frowned. "A precaution?"

"Against the Spaniards. Word is the United States will soon be at war with Mexico—maybe already is. Now that means the Spaniards here might turn against us. Not that they care about Mexico that much anymore. What they think is that Mexico will probably lose, and they'll lose their own protection as a result. So they figure they'll get together and protect themselves against the Americans who might come here after they defeat Mexico and try to claim California. These Spaniards here call themselves *californios*. Now you wouldn't by any chance be one of these *californios,* would you?"

Some of the others snickered.

Tom watched them, trying to think. Something had happened here he didn't know anything about. Were the Spaniards contemplating war against the Americans, or was it the other way around? He knew there had been conflict, but most *californios* were all for simply peacefully joining with the United States if it came to that kind of choice. Even Antonio Galvez intended to handle the whole thing peacefully.

Tom's anger began to build at the realization that the Americans had probably decided that was not good enough. They were going to push this—use it as an excuse to take over valuable Spanish land for themselves. Immediately he was alert, and his first thought was for Juanita and the Galvez estate.

"I told you I have no interest either way," he said carefully.

"You got to be one or the other, mister. You're either

American or you're a *californio*," Hughes told him, deliberately trying to egg Tom on. "Now judging from your appearance, it ain't likely you're American now, is it?"

They all laughed then, and the little Mexican behind the counter set a glass of whiskey on the counter, then moved back, sure there would be trouble.

"I am American," Tom answered calmly. "But not your kind of American. I am a true American," he said proudly. He didn't care what these men did or thought. They were the kind who had forced his father out of Texas, and he hated them!

"Now what is that supposed to mean?" Hughes asked with a grin.

"It means I am Indian," Tom replied.

The men sobered, and Hughes's eyebrows shot up in surprise. He stepped back a little more. "Well, well. Now the way I look at it, an Indian is even lower than a *californio*, wouldn't you say, boys?"

The others nodded, some snickering again.

"Please. Let the man drink his whiskey and go," the Mexican behind the bar told Hughes.

"You shut up, you greasy little tit," Hughes growled at him. "You want to be arrested like the others?"

The little man turned away.

"What others?" Tom asked warily.

Hughes rubbed at his beard. "All the traitorous *californios* we can round up, that's what others, especially the rich ones. They're the ones with enough power to chase out the Americans. California is going to be part of the United States once this thing is over. Until then us Americans are getting together to protect ourselves. We've got the help of one of our own kind—a John Frémont. He's at Sutter's Fort right now—a government man sent here by President Polk himself. He's set himself up as our leader."

"I heard of this Frémont when he first came. He was supposed to be on a peaceful mission for the U.S. government, making maps or something."

"Well, once we all knew there might be war with Mexico, he agreed to help us stay a step ahead and start right now to secure California."

"And what have you done to secure it? Have you attacked the Spanish landowners?"

Hughes scowled. "We haven't attacked anybody but them who are a real threat. We're here to keep the peace, not start a war. We're holding Sonoma and we're here to protect any Americans that need protecting."

Tom felt an urgent need to get to Juanita. Had the Galvez estate been targeted? This was the very thing he had once warned Galvez about. Now he was frightened for Juanita. This would be just like Texas. Once the Americans took over, many of the original Spanish citizens would be destroyed or cast out. If that happened to Galvez, what would happen to Juanita?

Apparently the Americans had the help now of John Frémont, whose own men were brash, hard frontiersmen who knew how to fight and how to use knives and guns. The *californios* didn't want Mexican control any more than the Americans did. They wanted to rule California themselves. But now so did the Americans, and Tom well knew that what the Americans wanted, they almost always got in the end. He picked up his whiskey and quickly drank it down, keeping his eyes on the one called Hughes.

"It seems to me I heard this Frémont came here as a mere surveyor for the army," he told Hughes. "How is it he has become the leader of the Americans in California? We do not even know if war has been declared against Mexico."

Hughes scowled. "You talk mighty pretty for just a dumb Indian who's not concerned."

"I fought against the Mexicans in Texas. I was at the Alamo, but I was captured before the mission was taken. My father fought at San Jacinto." He relaxed a little more when he noticed a hint of respect come into the eyes of a couple of the men, but Hughes still scowled.

"So what?" Hughes spoke up. "You're in California now, not Texas. You saying you're ready to join us against the Mexicans in these parts?"

Tom set his glass aside. "I am saying I have had my fill of war, mister." He wiped his lips with his shirtsleeve and headed for the door.

"Fine looking pair of palominos you got out there, mister," one of the other men spoke up. "We'll be addin' them to our collection."

Tom stopped and turned, fire in his eyes. "What did you say?" It was then he realized that while he had headed for the door several guns were pulled on him.

"I said them two horses will make a nice addition to some of the rewards we've been gettin' for helpin' out the Americans."

It was all Tom could do to control an impulse to pull his own pistol and start shooting. But he forced himself to remain clearheaded. He must keep Galvez out of this! He must stay alive and get to Juanita. Drastic measures were apparently being taken by these American invaders.

"Those horses are worth a lot of money," he hissed at the man who had spoken to him. "And they are *mine!*"

The man just grinned, and the rest of them chuckled. "Not no more," another told him. "We seen when we come in that they didn't have no brand on them. We'll sell them to the highest American bidder and split up the reward. We can't let nobody with dark skin have such a fine pair of horses. He might start himself a ranch and end up a rich man. We got to nip all this in the bud, don't you see?"

They all laughed harder, and Tom secretly swore a mighty vengeance.

"You have no right to take those horses," he snarled.

Hughes walked closer. "Right now we can do anything we want, mister. I've got me a whole army of men, all volunteers willing to come here and help hold California for the Americans. These men aren't getting paid. If they want those horses, they can have them—and anything else we choose to take from anybody who wants to give us trouble."

Tom felt on fire with rage. Juanita! If not for Juanita he would risk shooting them all down! But he must not do anything foolish. All that mattered now was to get to Juanita and get out of this area completely. He would leave it up to Galvez what to do about the horses. The man had plenty of men. He could take care of it however he chose.

"You are all nothing but a bunch of thieves," he sneered.

He turned and barged through the doors to see two men in buckskins blatantly leading away the palominos. How he longed to draw his gun and shoot them both in the back! He never should have stopped first in Sonoma.

He went to his own horse and mounted up, and the men in the tavern came outside, still laughing. "Get your ass out of town, Indian," the one called Hughes shouted.

Tom backed his horse, glaring at Hughes with eyes that gave the man the chills and wiped the smile off his face. Tom decided to check the urge to take his case further. He could do nothing until he knew if Juanita was all right. He jerked the reins and turned his horse to ride out of town.

"Go on back to Colorado," one of the men behind him yelled. "They've got plenty of Indians there!"

He heard more laughter, and his fury knew no bounds. In only a moment they had stolen away the beautiful palominos for which Galvez had paid so much money. They had apparently taken over the whole town and the outlying area, which might include the Galvez estate.

How he hated men like Hughes and those with him. He would get Juanita to safety, and then if Galvez wanted to try to get his horses back, he would help the man. Perhaps if they talked to the one called John Frémont, they could get some help. Surely this Frémont had no idea some of the Americans were taking such drastic and unfair measures.

Hughes watched Tom disappear, then turned to one of the men. "Saddle my horse, will you? I'm heading back to the Galvez place. I'm getting an itch to have another turn at that pretty little gal Hidalgo's keeping there."

The other man shook his head. "Hidalgo charges too much in whiskey and cash for that one."

"She's worth it." Hughed rubbed his hand across his chest. "I haven't seen anything that pretty in my whole life. If I leave now I can get there by night."

"You think that Indian will be any trouble to us?"

"Hell, no. He's just a damned worthless drifter and only one man. I expect he'll head on back to where he came from. We've pretty much got this whole territory under control, Bailey—and that Frémont says help is coming by way of the coast. California belongs to us now. Men like

Galvez and that Indian and the others learned that the hard way. The days of the wealthy Spanish landowners are over."

They both laughed and went inside.

Tom headed toward the Galvez ranch, debating whether to go there first or to Sutter's Fort to talk to John Frémont. Did Frémont know what the men in Sonoma were up to? Surely he would not condone horse stealing and whatever other theft must be taking place. Maybe Frémont and his men would protect the innocent people who were suffering from this American takeover. And if he talked to Frémont first, he would know better what to tell Antonio Galvez. Perhaps Frémont would help get back the palominos. The last thing Tom wanted was to go back to Galvez without the horses. Maybe Galvez would be so angry he would not consider talking about marriage to Juanita.

Tom headed for the fort. He was sure he could reach it by nightfall, and it was not that far from the Galvez estate. He could be back at the ranch by the next day, perhaps with some help from Frémont. His mind fought his heart, which told him to go directly to Juanita. He struggled to decide what was the most logical thing to do—what would be most helpful to Antonio Galvez—and that was to go to Sutter's Fort first. He wanted to be sure Galvez acted rationally and did not go riding into Sonoma after his horses, risking an all-out battle with Hughes and his men.

He rode steadily, hoping his already weary horse could make the last few miles before dark. After several hours he spotted smoke from a campfire not far ahead. The presence of ruffians looking for trouble in the area made him wary, and he slowed his horse. He veered into some brush, heading along the foot of a high bank that would keep him hidden from whoever was camped up ahead. He rode for close to a half mile, then dismounted, deciding it wouldn't hurt to check on who was camped on the other side of the ridge. A man had to know his odds now. Whoever was camped there could be part of more American volunteers, and they were no more than a day's ride from the Galvez estate.

He dismounted and tied his horse, ducking through the underbrush and making his way up the barren ridge dotted with scrub grass and wildflowers. He reached the top, carefully peering over and spotting the campfire again at the foot of the ridge. There were three men sitting around it, talking loudly to each other.

Tom moved back down out of sight and walked closer, then moved back to the top, removing his hat and lying on his belly to watch and listen.

"I say we just go in there and clean them out!" one shouted in Spanish.

"There are too many of them!"

"Not anymore. Many of them left when they herded us to the fort. They took what they wanted and left! My wife and children are still there and I am going back! And what about that poor Galvez girl? God only knows what has happened to her!"

The entire conversation was in Spanish, and the voices sounded familiar to Tom. He scooted closer, moving down behind a huge boulder above the men. He daringly peered around the boulder, recognizing Andres Terres, a Galvez ranch hand who lived in a small house on Galvez land with a wife and small son. Tom's heart pounded harder. He recognized the other two men also—Jesus Vasquez and a man called Rico. Tom knew Jesus the best, had worked closely with the man, who helped Tom with the injured and ailing horses and helped in breaking in new horses.

What were these men doing here, arguing about Andres's wife—and "that poor Galvez girl." Did they mean Juanita? His desperate fear and curiosity left no more room for caution. He stood up, putting his hat back on. "Jesus!" he called out.

The three men looked up, backing away slightly. Tom hurried down the hill, and Jesus called out his name. "Tom! It is Tom Sax!" Jesus smiled and reached out a hand as Tom stepped up closer to the fire.

Tom grasped the man's hand and shook it fiercely.

"What the hell are you men doing here, Jesus? What has happened!"

A terrible sadness came into Jesus's eyes as he withdrew his hand and turned to look at the other two men. He looked back at Tom, then glanced at the hill behind him, as though wondering if he was alone. "How did you find us, Tom?"

"I just came from Sonoma, where a bunch of American volunteers have taken over the town. They're flying some flag with a bear on it and saying the town belongs to the Americans. They took the palominos I bought for el señor Galvez and told me to leave town. What is going on?"

Jesus sighed deeply and Rico turned away. "Those men have already been to the ranch," Andres spoke up, putting up a fist. "There were many of them, Tom, and they attacked suddenly, shooting down men, burning buildings, running off stock. They killed el señor Galvez and herded the rest of the men together, including us, and walked us to Sutter's Fort as prisoners! Only two days ago we were released," the man sneered. "They said we were no longer a threat! They left us with no horses or guns! We have walked this far. My wife and children are still back at that ranch. I am going to get them, and I don't care how many of the Americans are left there!"

Tom just stared at the man in near shock. Americans on the Galvez ranch! Galvez himself killed! It was all so difficult to comprehend! He began to tremble with a mixture of rage and desolation. He turned angry eyes to Jesus. "Juanita!" he said in a desperate whisper. "What happened to Juanita!"

Jesus rubbed at his eyes and turned away. "God only knows by now, Tom. The reason they were so successful was they knew all about the place—knew the buildings, how many men there were and where they were. They had . . . inside help."

Tom felt a black fury enveloping him. "Hidalgo!" he hissed.

Jesus nodded, looking back at him. "*Sí.* He helped the Americans. Once we were taken to the fort, we realized the one truly in charge—some man called Frémont—he does not understand what some of the American volunteers are doing. It is true he has declared California for America, but I do not think he is part of what these other men are doing. He—"

Tom grasped his shirt front. "When. When did it happen? Where is Juanita?"

Andres grasped one of Tom's arms. "Take it easy, Tom. My wife is there, too. I am just as concerned. We must think clearly so we can help them."

Tom's eyes filled with tears as they drilled into Jesus. He let go of the man, turning away and hunching over, making an odd groaning sound. "I am sorry, Jesus." Tom threw back his head and breathed deeply. "Tell me—all of it."

Jesus ran a hand through his hair. "They came a few days after you left. As I said, it was a complete surprise. Men were shot down in cold blood. Some big heavyset man seemed to be in charge. I think his last name was Hughes."

"Hughes." Tom turned. "I met a man in Sonoma called Hughes. He's the one who let his men take the palominos."

"It could be the same man. We think by now most of them are gone. They took what they wanted. Many rode off with much loot that same day. Others herded the rest of us together and made us walk to Sutter's Fort. We were held prisoner there until just two days ago when they finally let us go. We walked all the way here. We have been trying to decide what to do—how to go and get Andres's wife."

"And what about Juanita!" Tom hissed. "Did you see her?" He moved his eyes to Rico and Andres. "Any of you?"

Rico sighed, shoving his hands into his pockets. "She never came out of the house, Señor Sax," he said quietly. "I . . . I heard some screams from somewhere in the house. And I . . . I heard Hidalgo talking to that man Hughes about her . . . about . . . about letting Hughes and his men have . . . turns with her when he was done with her himself . . . for money and whiskey."

"My God!" Tom groaned, turning away again. "I knew

it! Somehow I knew it deep inside." He hung his head. "My God, I failed her."

Jesus frowned with concern. "It would have happened no matter if you were there or not, Tom," he told the man. "There were so many of them. It was well planned. You should not blame yourself."

Tom shook his head, clenching his fists. "I had such a strange feeling when I left . . . like something terrible was going to happen. But I ignored it," he groaned. "I thought she would be so safe there. Even when I heard talk in San Francisco about Americans taking over California . . . I did not worry so much about it." He breathed deeply. "I was going to ask her father for her hand in marriage . . . now . . . my poor Juanita! My God, what have they done to her?"

Jesus felt like crying. He looked at Rico and Andres, who both felt the same fury.

Andres stepped closer to Tom. "If you want to go and get her, señor, I will help you. My wife is there, too. I want to go and get my family. I think by now there will not be many men left there. They will move on to other places. It might be possible to take them. Perhaps if we can make it to my house, my wife will be there and she can tell us how many men are left."

Tom's breathing deepened as he fought to stay in control. "This is war," he said quietly. "War. If Juanita has been abused; if she is badly hurt or dead; I am going to war against these Americans!"

He turned and looked at the three men, a wild, almost demonic fire in his dark eyes that made them all step back slightly. "My father once made war against the Crow—one man against all of them," he growled. "He struck terror in their hearts! I will do the same to these Americans who have come here to rob and kill and rape. I was on my way to Sutter's Fort to talk to this Frémont. But I will talk to *no* American now, for I no longer *wish* for peace! Everyone at that ranch will die, and *I* will do the killing!"

Rico swallowed. "I bet on you when you broke the black

stallion, señor. I think you are a man who does what he sets out to do. I wish to help you, señor."

Tom's jaw flexed in repressed emotions. He slowly nodded, turning his eyes to Andres.

"I also want to help, Señor Sax."

"And so do I," Jesus spoke up. "But we have no horses —no guns."

"There is a ranch not far from here—run by American settlers." Tom sneered the words. "I will go there tonight and steal three horses. When we get to Galvez's land, we will go in at night." He pulled out a huge hunting knife from where it hung at his belt. "This will silence whatever guards they have posted, and their guns will become your guns. Then we will move in on the rest of them—take them by surprise." He gripped the knife tightly. "And Hidalgo is mine—all mine!"

Jesus nodded. *"Sí,* Tom. We understand."

Tom shoved the knife back into its sheath. "Soon it will be dark and I will get the horses. In the morning we ride until we are close to Galvez's land, then move in after dark." He looked from one to another. "You are all sure you want to do this? You do not have to."

"I do," Andres answered. "My wife and sons are there."

Tom nodded. "A man protecting his woman is a man who can be trusted." He looked at Rico.

"I will go," Rico assured him again. "It is wrong what they have done, especially to the innocent young girl. They stole my horse and weapons and walked me to that fort, calling me names all the way. I will go."

Tom looked at Jesus. "You know I will help you, Tom. You are my friend."

Tom could not stop the tears from welling in his eyes. He reached out and Jesus took his hand again. *"Gracias, amigo,"* Tom told him. He turned to Rico and Andres, telling them the same. "I truly believe God sent me this way first so that I would be warned about what had happened and would find help. We will succeed, my friends, because God is with us." Tom held up his fist. "Of this I have no doubts. We have His power behind us."

Tom slowly lowered his fist, fighting an urge to break down. He could not do that now. He had to stay strong. He couldn't let this get the better of him—not yet. There was no time for tears now. That would have to come later, after Emanuel Hidalgo was dead. And his death would be a slow one indeed.

• Chapter Eleven •

The night was still as Tom and the three men who had agreed to help him moved toward the cabin of Andres Terres under cover of darkness. Earlier in the day they had scouted the estate from the surrounding hills. There was little activity. The vast outlying grazing lands had been vacated.

They carefully moved through the empty pastures toward the house.

As the four of them moved even closer to the main house, they could see that several outbuildings had been destroyed by fire, perhaps to further discourage other Mexicans from trying to move in on the ready-made ranch and make a home there. The bunkhouses were gone, but a few cabins remained. Andres was relieved to see that one of them was his own.

They made their way closer, quietly walking the horses they had stolen the night before. The Americans who had stayed behind, and, Tom hoped, Emanuel Hidalgo himself, all seemed to be congregated in the main house. Apparently they expected no trouble. That was fine with Tom. Surprise would be their best aid.

Andres left his horse with the others and darted to his cabin door, tapping on it lightly, while the rest of them waited in the bushes. It opened slowly, and one of his young sons peeked out. Behind the boy stood Andres's wife, holding a butcher knife defensively. Her eyes widened when she saw her husband, and she whimpered his name. The man ducked inside, and Tom and the others could hear almost hysterical weeping, combined with a torrent of sobbed Spanish words.

"She says the bastards raped her," Jesus spoke up, the woman's words coming to them clearly as they waited outside the cabin.

"I am glad I came along," Rico hissed through gritted teeth. "Andres's wife is a good woman. They had no right!"

Tom remained silent, his own rage and torment almost unbearable. If they had raped Andres's Mexican wife, they had most certainly done the same to Juanita; and for Juanita it would be so much worse, never having known a man. He closed his eyes and hung his head at the thought of the pain and horror she must have suffered.

They waited several minutes until Andres finally opened the door and signaled for them to come inside. They tied the horses and hurried in. Andres's wife was closing the curtains. Tom met Andres's tear-filled eyes.

"They raped my wife," he groaned. "I will kill every one of them!"

Tom glanced at the young woman, who remained turned away from them, busying herself with preparing some food. He could feel her unnecessary shame. He moved his dark eyes back to Andres. "Hidalgo is mine. Remember that."

"That is fine with me," the man growled. "It was the American men who abused her. You can have Hidalgo. I want Hughes—their big fat leader! She says he returned last night from Sonoma."

Tom put a hand on his shoulder. "Keep a clear head, Andres. If you don't, we might fail."

The man breathed deeply, wiping at his eyes. "My wife is fixing us something to eat. We are all weak from so much hard riding and little food or rest. I think we should eat just a little. Come. Sit down."

They all moved to sit around the table, removing their hats. Andres's little boy came to sit on his father's lap, and a baby slept in the corner of the room in a cradle. The little boy clung to his father as though terrified he would go away again.

"My little boy saw it all," Andres said in a broken voice. "My Rosa says he has not spoken since."

Tom rubbed at his eyes. "Does your wife know how many there are?"

Andres turned to her, rattling off questions in Spanish. She finally turned, and faint bruises were still evident on her face and arms. She hung her head as she spoke.

"They are careless now," she told them in Spanish. "When I go out to hang wash or work in my garden, I see no one around. They have not come around me since those first two days." She rubbed her hands against her dress nervously. "I wanted to run away... but I did not know where to run. I have no money. And I knew that if they let my Andres go, he would come here looking for me. So I waited." She finally raised her eyes and looked at Tom. "Since those first two days they have all been at the big house. They drink. They laugh. They play cards. And they..." She looked away again. "At first I could hear her crying, screaming... begging. Even this far away I could hear her. Then all of it stopped. She makes no sounds anymore. Sometimes I wonder if she is dead." She looked at Tom again, seeing the horror and devastation in his eyes. "I am sorry. I feel so sorry for la señorita Juanita. I pray for her every day. I hope she is alive and that you can help her. There are eight or ten of them over there, including Emanuel and two of Señor Galvez's own men who helped—Ramone and Chico. Usually someone sits outside the front door to keep watch. But since the American soldiers came by ship and raised the American flag, they think everything is over, so they are not alert."

The room seemed filled with Tom Sax's rage. "Well, everything *isn't* over, is it," he choked out. He looked at Andres. "What are the chances of your wife's helping us?"

The man frowned. "What do you mean?"

"It's a big house. We dive into one room, some in other rooms will get away. In order for our identity to never be known, they *all* must *die*! That means we have to be sure we've got them all in one place. I know it's a lot to ask, but if your wife could ... could go over there, make them think she's going to give them a good show. They would call the others in, all gather around to watch."

Andres shook his head. "It is too dangerous. She could get killed when the shooting starts. Besides, she has been through enough. I could not ask her to do that."

"We just want to get the men in one room. We could give her some kind of signal before the shooting starts so she could maybe saunter to one side of the room, then duck down or run out."

Andres kept shaking his head, and his wife, who spoke no English, asked him what Tom was saying. Andres reluctantly told her and she put a hand to her throat and turned away. The room fell silent while she stirred a pot of reheated chili. Then she turned and faced Tom.

"I will do it."

"Rosa!" Andres looked at her in surprise, and she looked back at him sternly.

"I will not forget what they did, Andres," she told him. "And what happened to me was even worse for la señorita Juanita because she is so young and innocent; and because they do not stop with her. For all these days she has been living in hell in that house. We must help her, and these men must die. And if you are going to go over there and help el señor Sax kill them, I want to be sure it is done in a way that is safe for my husband. And el señor Sax is right. They *all* must die!"

The man sighed, rubbing at the back of his neck. "What about the boy?"

"I will explain to him. I will tell him it is very important that he stay here and be very quiet and watch the baby. I will make him understand it is important, because we are going to get rid of those bad men."

Andres looked at Tom. "You have the final say, Andres,"

Tom told him. "She's your wife. I won't hold it against you if you say no. I'll just have to think of some other way."

The man thought for several long, quiet seconds while Jesus and Rico said nothing. "All right," Andres finally spoke up. "I think it can work. But all of you must promise you do not fire one shot until my Rosa is out of the room. She could get caught in the cross fire."

Tom nodded. "Agreed." He looked up at Rosa and spoke in Spanish. "You are a very brave and honorable woman. I will not forget this night. If this works out, you and Andres take whatever you need from the house—money, if there is any left—food—whatever. You take it and go far from here. You should find enough money and goods to start over someplace else and make a good life for yourselves."

A tear slipped down Rosa's cheek. "I don't really care about that," she answered. "I just want those men dead. It is a terrible thing they have done—to me and my frightened son—and to the little girl in that house. I want to help however I can."

"I am grateful, Rosa. I know God will be with you."

She wiped at the tear. "I think tonight He will be with all of us, señor." She sniffed and turned back to the pan of chili. "Now, all of you, take a moment to think and plan. I will give you something to eat. The night is still young. It will be easier to take those men if you give them more time to drink first. In an hour or two they will be mostly drunk, and a drunk man does not aim his gun well."

Tom had to grin at the very wise statement, and he admired her courage. "A good point." Tom looked at Andres and the others. "Check your guns, my friends. You have stolen them from the guards and they are not familiar to you. I want every shot to count. And remember, when we move in and start shooting, no one hesitates for one moment. None of them must be allowed to get away. And do not kill Hidalgo or Hughes. It is important they are just wounded—for the time being. It is only fitting that they both die slowly."

His dark eyes glittered with near joy at the thought of

vengeance, and they could almost see the war paint on his face, even though there was none there.

Tom waited outside the window with a pounding heart. Inside the sprawling main room of the Galvez mansion ten men had gathered, laughing and clapping, Emanuel himself strumming a guitar while Rosa whirled around the room, swaying her hips seductively, holding a bottle of whiskey in one hand.

"My husband has not come back," she had told them earlier, feigning tears, weeping against the chest of John Hughes himself. "I cannot forget what you did to me," she told him in a sultry voice. "I pretended to fight you, but all the while I was on fire for you."

Emanuel interpreted her words for Hughes, and the man threw up a cheer and dragged her into the room. "I thought I'd had my fill of this one," he told the others. "But now I'm not so sure."

"Ah, that one is loose. She has had two babies. The one upstairs, she is better."

Rosa had begun turning about the room, moving her hips seductively in front of each man.

"Well, I'm tired of that lifeless thing upstairs," Hughes had answered. "I'm ready for a real woman—one who's grateful and does some of the moving herself. And no woman moves like a hot Mexican señora."

They all began laughing and joking about it, some of them who had been playing cards dropping the game when Rosa stepped right upon their table and danced over the money and cards.

"Hey, this could be good," one of them spoke up.

There were six of them in the room at the time. One of them went out and yelled upstairs. "Get down here, men. No sense guarding that little filly up there. She ain't goin' nowhere. Come see what we've got down here."

The one man who had been sitting outside the entrance to the house looked around a moment, then went inside, deciding there was nothing to guard and curious about the drunk Mexican woman who had come to their door.

Tom watched the men fill the room. He waited, letting

them become engrossed in Rosa's dance, his heart aching for Andres, who also had to watch and relive the horror of what these men had already done to his wife.

Rosa swirled and gyrated, lifting her skirts seductively, drinking a little whiskey. She looked down at Hughes then. "I will let you make bets," she told him, letting Emanuel interpret again. "All of you can bet on whom I will choose tonight. Whomever I pick, he gets all the money, and the rest of you can watch us." She rubbed a hand over her abdomen, breathing deeply. "Whomever I choose, I will wear him out."

There was more cheering, and the betting began. Rosa held John Hughes's eyes, making him believe he would be the one she picked. Those who had not been a part of raping her the first time pulled out her skirt as she danced around the table, peeking under it and making howling noises. She had deliberately worn nothing under the skirt. Her ruffled top was cut low, revealing full cleavage. She looked toward one of the windows as they all put out their money, and she made a circular sign with her hands and arms, indicating to her husband and the others outside that all the men were in the room now.

Tom crouched under the window and carefully laid a rose on the sill. Rosa saw the signal, and she moved from the table to the floor and swayed across it toward the doorway. "All of you line up for me," she teased. "I want to look you over."

Emanuel told the Americans what she had said, and they all eagerly gathered in a half circle around the table. Rosa sauntered to the doorway, looking them over carefully, pulling the ruffled top down over her breasts to her waist. They all stared, grinning and waiting. Suddenly she ducked out of the door.

All the men stood gaping at the doorway, momentarily confused. A fraction of a second later fire spit from rifle and pistol barrels and men screamed, bloody holes exploding in backs and chests and heads. The main room could be closed off by two polished oak doors, which Rosa quickly shut.

Most of the men inside were not even wearing their

guns, and those who had not been hit scrambled for holsters that hung over the backs of chairs, or rifles that stood against the walls. But good aim at close range and the element of surprise were all that Tom and the others needed. Bodies reeled about the room, none of them even making it to the doorway. Blood seemed instantly splattered everywhere. Wine and whiskey bottles shattered and furniture tumbled as men fell.

In a matter of seconds the room was silent. Andres burst through the front door, and Tom could hear him say, "Rosa, thank God you are not hurt."

Tom climbed through the window, studying the bloody sight without an ounce of regret or revulsion. To him it was a beautiful sight. Someone in the corner moaned and started to rise, grasping for a rifle. It was Emanuel. Tom hurried over to where he lay and kicked him over onto his back. The man stared up at him in total shock. "Sax!"

Blood poured from Emanuel's legs and left arm.

Tom grinned. "Nice to see you again, Emanuel."

The man's eyes instantly teared and he began to tremble. "You . . . you have hurt me enough, Tom Sax," he almost wept. "I did not kill her. She is all right. Please. You can just take her and go. Look . . . look what you have done to me. I will probably bleed to death. You do not need to shoot me again," he begged.

Tom lowered the rifle barrel, pressing it against the man's privates. Hidalgo whimpered. "Don't worry, Emanuel. I'm not going to shoot you again. And you're probably right about bleeding to death." The man looked somewhat relieved, watching Tom pleadingly. "You *will* bleed to death. But not from these wounds, and not from my gun. I will finish the job with my knife. And I will give you three guesses what gets cut off first."

The man's eyes widened and he cringed backward, whimpering with pain. Tom turned to Jesus, who stood beside him. "We messed up, señor. Hughes is dead. We were supposed to save him for Andres."

"Are the rest of them dead?"

"*Sí, señor.*"

Tom looked over at Andres, who came in then with his

arm around his wife. She cringed at all the bodies. "Watch him," Tom told Jesus, indicating Emanuel. "I have to go see about Juanita. I will be back for this one. He's mine. Remember that." Emanuel sobbed as Tom walked up to Andres and Rosa. "I'm sorry about Hughes, Andres."

The man shrugged. "It was probably my own bullet that killed him. I tried to hold back, but when I leveled my rifle on him, I could not stop shooting."

Tom turned to Rosa. *"Gracias.* It is a good thing you did tonight. Go on back to your children." Tom looked at her husband again. "Take what you need and go, Andres. Never mention my name, and I will never mention yours."

The man nodded, putting a hand on Tom's arm. "We will not see you again after tonight, señor. God be with you. I will pray that one day you and la señorita Juanita can be happy and together."

Tom looked toward the stairway where all remained silent. The thought of what he would find upstairs filled him with absolute terror. She must still be alive. The men had talked about being tired of her just lying there and not responding. They apparently had continued to use the girl however they chose.

"Perhaps that can never be," he said sadly, his voice choking.

Rico came out of the kitchen down the hall. "There is no one else around, Señor Sax. I think we got them all."

Tom looked back at Jesus. "Strip him down," Tom told Jesus, regarding Emanuel. "I want him to lie there and think about what I'm going to do to him. I'll be back in a few minutes." He turned and headed past Andres and Rosa, wondering how he got his legs to work at all as he climbed the winding staircase toward Juanita's room.

The door to her room was open a crack, and a lamp was lit inside. Tom pulled out his revolver, just in case of trouble.

"Juanita?"

He heard a woman whimper.

"It's me, Juanita, Tom."

"Please . . . do not hurt her," came a woman's voice from inside. Tom recognized it as Luisa's. He pushed open the door to find the old woman sitting on the edge of the bed, bent over a young girl, cradling her in her arms.

The woman looked at him in wide-eyed terror, then blinked in slow recognition. "Tom!" Her voice almost moaned with weary sorrow. "Tom Sax!" She let go of the young girl and slowly rose, looking past him out into the hallway. "All the shooting . . . I did not know what to do. I thought you were someone come to kill us. But praise be to God, it is Tom Sax, come to save my Juanita."

He slowly holstered his pistol, looking at the pitifully tiny figure in the bed. Her bare arms were stretched over her head and tied to bedposts. The wrists were bloody from the rough hemp rope that held her. She was clumsily covered with a quilt, and she lay staring at the ceiling.

"My God!" His words came out in a pitiful groan. He walked closer, moving to the bedside and bending over her. "Juanita," he whispered.

"She cannot hear you." Luisa sniffled. "She has been like this for many days. They come . . . and use her. And she just lies there. They made me stay with her . . . made me wash her for them. They kept a man here all the time to watch over us. Many times they hit me, telling me if I tried to help her get away, they would do terrible things to me. Every day I thought they would stop coming. But every day they came again—first one, then another. Emanuel Hidalgo, he was the most cruel. He did such very bad things to her. He broke her spirit, Señor Sax."

"Juanita," Tom whispered. He quickly pulled out a knife and cut the ropes that bound her, then was overwhelmed by her pitiful state. He collapsed over her body, enveloping her in his arms and weeping openly. He rocked her, repeating her name over and over. This was even worse than he had imagined. Luisa wept behind him, realizing the nightmare was finally over.

Tom had no idea how long he lay there. Finally Luisa was touching his shoulder. "You must take her away from here, Señor Sax. You must take her out of this house and never bring her back."

Tom reluctantly let go of her, his whole body trembling.

He threw back his head and breathed deeply for control. "She doesn't . . . speak? Doesn't know you?"

"I am not sure whom she knows, señor, or what she hears. She only stares. She makes no sound, not even to cry. I cannot even begin to tell you how terrible it was . . . especially those first days when she was awake. I think it is God's blessing she is this way . . . that her mind has slipped to another world."

Tom's chest heaved in one great sob and he wiped at his eyes, leaning over the girl and gently stroking the hair back from her face. "Juanita? It's me, Juanita. It's Tom." He leaned down and kissed her forehead. "Nobody will ever hurt you again, Juanita."

There was no response. He moved slightly away, hunching over and feeling sick to his stomach.

"You . . . you will help her, señor?"

He rose from the bed, walking to a dressing table and in one swoop of an arm slamming everything off it. "Damn," he growled. "Damn! Damn!" He picked up a vase and threw it at a huge mirror that hung on the wall, smashing it. Juanita made no move, no sign of being aware of the noise.

"Tom! You all right up there?" Rico called up.

He stared at the doorway, his chest heaving in great gasps of unbridled rage. He walked to the door, looking back at Luisa. "Clean her up and dress her. I'll be back in a while." He turned and went out.

For the next forty-five minutes Luisa gently washed and dressed Juanita, while somewhere outside a man screamed in ways she had never heard—screams of horror that sent chills down her spine. Sometimes she could hear crying and begging. Once she moved to the doorway and looked over the banister downstairs, where two men stood. She recognized them as Galvez's men—Rico and Jesus. "What is happening?" she asked.

Jesus looked up at her. "Luisa. How is the girl?"

"She is very bad, señor. Her mind—" She shook her head. There came another scream from outside. Jesus looked from Luisa to Rico and back to Luisa. "It is el señor

Hidalgo. El señor Sax is repaying him for what he did to Juanita."

Luisa put a hand to her chest and nodded. She went back into the room, and several minutes later Tom returned. Luisa noticed he had changed clothes, from black shirt and pants to a blue calico shirt and brown pants. He had apparently washed for his hair was still wet, tied into a tail at his neck. The wild look still in his eyes was almost frightening, but the woman knew he meant it for Emanuel Hidalgo, not for herself.

"Emanuel Hidalgo is dead," he told her flatly. "He will never touch her again, nor will the others. They are all dead."

She nodded. "The screams of Señor Hidalgo were music to my ears."

Tom's eyes moved to Juanita. "And to mine." He walked to the foot of the bed. Juanita lay there dressed in a pretty yellow dress that buttoned to her neck. Her long hair was brushed out behind her over the pillows. "It is all my fault," he said, great sorrow in his voice. "I should not have gone off and left her behind. But I wanted to do everything the proper way, for her sake. I wanted it all to be nice for her. I was going to give el señor Galvez some time to think about it, marry her the right way. If I had . . . only known—"

"But you didn't know, señor," Luisa told him. "You had no way of knowing this would happen. You must not blame yourself."

"There is no one else to blame."

The woman stepped closer. "You loved her, señor. That love will help her heal. One day she will be well, and you can be together."

His jaw flexed as he tried to stay in control, and a tear slipped down his cheek. "What do I do now, Luisa? How can I help her?"

The woman put a hand on his arm. "There was once an old priest in Sonoma that she liked very much. She has known him since she was a very little girl. Now he is at the Saint Christopher Mission in San Francisco. Perhaps you should take her there. Perhaps the old priest and the nuns there can help her get well. God's love, and your love, will heal her, señor. You will see."

He blinked and swallowed. "Saint Christopher's? What is the priest's name?"

"Father Thomas Juarez."

Tom looked away. "What about the cook—Yolanda? She was a nice lady."

Luisa looked down. "She ran outside when they first came. She was killed by a stray bullet."

Tom nodded, looking about to collapse. "She had a daughter."

"*Sí, señor*. Emanuel and his men—they . . . they raped her, too. She killed herself and they buried her."

The room hung in bitter silence.

"Señor, they killed the *patrón*. Juanita has no one but you to help her."

Tom turned to face her, his dark eyes hollow-looking and circled.

"I will take her to the mission in San Francisco. Will you go with her?"

The woman nodded. "*Sí, señor*, of course. I will not leave my Juanita. But she will be a long time getting well, I am afraid. What will you do, señor?"

He thought about the riffraff that would surge into California now that it had been declared a part of the United States. "I will continue to get my revenge," he said in a near growl.

"But you have done that, señor. You have killed el señor Hidalgo."

He looked at her, his dark eyes wild again. "That isn't enough! It is more than what has happened to Juanita. My first wife suffered because of war and hatred. My whole family suffered. The whites just take and take and take, Luisa. I have lost all I can because of them. My life is destroyed, and people are going to suffer!"

Her eyes teared, and she touched his arm. "Juanita needs you, señor. When she is well, you must be there."

"Until then I will be making up for what happened to her."

"I do not like what you are saying, senor. Your heart is bitter now. Someday it will heal. Do not do something foolish that will get you killed. What would Juanita do then?"

He shook his head. "I have already failed her."

"No, señor. This is not your doing. It is the way life is. Nothing you do will change what a man feels in his heart."

"Perhaps not. But it will help heal my own heart! Once my own father rode a path of vengeance against the Crow Indians! Now I will do the same—only it will not be against Indians! It will be against *white* men!"

He turned and went to the bed, gently wrapping Juanita in a quilt and lifting her. Luisa saw that there was no arguing with him at the moment.

"Did you pack some of her things?"

"*Sí, señor.* I have two bags." The woman hurriedly threw on a shawl and picked up two carpetbags.

"Do you know how to ride a horse, Luisa?"

"*Sí,* I can ride."

"We can't waste any time. I will carry Juanita with me. We have to get into the hills tonight yet. We will stay away from the main roads until we get to San Francisco." He turned, Juanita in his arms, his heart aching at how light she felt. She was skin and bones. "You must never mention my name in any of this—nor Rico's or Jesus's or Andres's."

"You know I would not, señor."

"They will know Mexicans did this, but they will never be sure who. The rest of Galvez's men have scattered, and Andres and Rosa will also leave tonight." He carried Juanita out into the hall and down the stairway. Rico and Jesus waited in the hall.

"How is she, señor?" Jesus asked.

"I'm not even sure. I'm taking her to a mission in San Francisco, Jesus. Then I will be back. Wait for me at the cave I told you about."

The man nodded. "We will wait."

"Did you find any money?"

"There was much in those men's pockets. We gave much of it to Andres. We found a safe but it was empty. We saved some of the money on the men, and we found more in their saddlebags. We put it all together. It is for Juanita. She will need it. It belongs to her. Most of it must have been her father's money."

"You are kind and generous," Tom told them. *"Gracias.* Take a little for yourselves. When you go, leave all the horses. You don't want to be seen riding stolen horses."

"Sí."

"As soon as I get Juanita to the mission, I will let Luisa's horse go. I am riding my own Appaloosa with my father's brand, so my horse cannot be traced to Galvez. When I get back we will have to find some mustangs for the two of you and break them so you can have your own horses without someone else's brand on them."

Jesus nodded. "The black one—he jumped a fence and ran off when they first attacked. Valiente is gone, señor."

Tom thought about the beautiful black stallion he had worked so hard to tame. He had done it mostly to impress Juanita. He no longer felt like that victorious man.

"It is best," he told them. "He should be free. I wouldn't want anyone else to get their hands on him."

"They couldn't if they wanted to, señor. He remained as wild as ever, except for you. Maybe someday you will find him again."

"It doesn't matter anymore. Nothing matters but revenge. You two think about what I told you while I'm gone. You can always change your minds."

"No, señor. We will ride with you. And I bet we can find others who will want to do the same. Maybe these Americans have won California, but we will not let them forget who this land really belongs to. It will be a long time before they can settle happily here."

Luisa frowned. What were they planning, to wage their own personal war? There was too much hatred in the air this night for her to speak up against such a plan. Perhaps on the way to San Francisco she could talk some sense into Tom Sax.

"Thanks for your help," Tom told both men. "Get the hell out of here now and keep to the hills."

Jesus nodded. "We will pray for the girl, señor."

Tom's dark eyes were bloodshot and filled with great sorrow. "She will need your prayers. I fear she will never get well." His voice broke and he walked out. Luisa followed. Jesus and Rico followed them out, and Rico hurriedly gathered up the money for Juanita, stuffing it into the carpetbags Luisa had packed and tying the carpetbags onto the horses. They helped Luisa mount up. The woman was weary and half sick herself, but she forced herself to keep going for Juanita's sake. She understood how important it was to get away tonight.

Tom handed Juanita to Jesus, then mounted up. Jesus handed the girl up to him, and Tom was overwhelmed by how small and young she seemed. He perched her sideways, holding her in one arm, then reached up to gently close her eyelids. To his relief they stayed closed. Her staring eyes filled him with sickening rage and guilt. At least with her eyes closed she looked more at peace.

He picked up the reins of his horse and turned to Luisa. "Are you ready?"

"*Sí, señor.*"

"I'll go as easy as I can. It's dark and dangerous. I know a place where we can rest safely before going on tomorrow."

"I will be all right, señor. It is only Juanita that I care about. Do not worry about me."

"You are a good woman, Luisa—as good as her own mother would have been."

"I am glad her mother is not here to see this. It is a blessing she is gone."

Tom gently kissed Juanita's cheek. "Yes. It is a blessing." He rode off into the darkness and Luisa followed.

The Stars and Stripes hung over the town of Sonoma, replacing the Bear flag. The Americans had claimed California. There would be more fighting, but Tom didn't care about that now, nor did he ever care in the first place who claimed California. All he cared about was right there in his arms, and he had lost her to a world he could not reach.

· Chapter Twelve ·

"She looks so pretty and innocent lying there," Tom said brokenly.

He stood in a small room in a wing of the mission where the nuns resided. Juanita had been bathed and she lay in a small bed now, wearing a clean white robe, her hair shiny and clean. It graced her shoulders and the pillow. To Tom she looked like an angel, and he was glad that at least now she was at peace.

Father Juarez studied the agony on the face of Tom Sax and had already read in the man's dark eyes a hungry vengeance.

"Now you think that killing the men who harmed her is not enough," he spoke up quietly. "You are thinking you must go on killing."

Tom tore his eyes from Juanita and faced the man. "How else am I to live with my own guilt?"

The priest frowned. "Guilt?"

"All of this could have been avoided. I failed her, Father Juarez! I should have taken her away with me. I should not have left her! Something deep inside me told me not to go, but I left anyway."

"You didn't know this would happen, my son. These things are the tragedy of war. No one man is expected to predict the future—that is God's knowledge alone. No one else knows what will happen from one day to the next. This is not your fault. You love her. And in spite of what happened to her, you still love her. You are a good man, and still a young man. She will need you when she is well again. Do not go out and do something that will bring your death. That would be harder for her to bear than what has already happened."

Tom fingered his hat in an outward reaction to the horrible guilt and thirst for vengeance that boiled inside. His breathing quickened and his eyes were red and tired.

"For one thing it is possible she might never get better," he answered, his voice low but burning with sorrow. "She might even die, Father Juarez. And if and when she does get better, she will never want me. I failed her. But I will not fail in avenging what has happened to her. I can do that much at least."

"And how would you do that? Wage your own war against the Americans?"

Tom towered over the short, stocky priest. "Why not? I am Indian, Father Juarez. My father is part Cheyenne, and my mother was a full blood. Warring in the name of vengeance is in my blood. My father did it many years ago— against the Crow who killed my mother. Now I will do the same!"

He turned away and walked to the side of the bed. A nun moved back to allow him room, and he bent over Juanita, touching her cheek gently. "I will be back, Juanita," he said gently. "I will keep coming back until you are awake and know me—and then you can decide how you feel about me, if we can share the love we once had." He leaned closer and kissed her forehead. "I love you, Juanita," he whispered, the tears coming again. One fell unwantedly and dripped onto her cheek. "I will always love you. That is a promise. Even if you wake up one day and hate me, I will still love you." He touched her hair gently.

He straightened, quickly wiping at his eyes with his shirtsleeve. He turned and faced the priest, breathing deeply to keep from breaking down in front of the man. "Promise me you will pray for her—several times a day."

"You do not need to ask me to do that. I have known Juanita since she was born. I baptized her. She is like a daughter to me. My heart is heavy for el señor Galvez and what has happened to his men and his land—but most of all his daughter. He would want many prayers for her. Of course I will pray." The man stepped closer. "And I will also pray for you, my son. I see hatred and revenge in your eyes. Such things come to no good end. You must free your heart and soul of this hatred."

Tom put on his hat and walked to the door, then hesitated, turning back around. "Guard that money well. Use whatever you need to take good care of her. The rest belongs to her." He glanced at Juanita once more, then back at the priest. "If she does come around, tell her I . . . tell her I love her and will be back. Tell her I will not blame her if she chooses not to see me."

He walked out and closed the door softly. He had already said his farewells to Luisa. It was done. He could not change what had happened to Juanita. He could only make amends by riding a path of revenge in her name. She was in God's hands now, but what Tom Sax had in mind had nothing to do with God. And if he burned in hell forever for it, so be it.

Cale sat alone, leaning against a cottonwood and listening to the flow of the creek nearby. It was March, 1847, and there was still fighting deep in Mexico as American troops marched ever closer to Mexico City. Kearny had easily taken Santa Fe and had marched on to California. Now the family waited anxiously for word of what was happening there, since Tom was there and they had not heard from him in many months.

Trade had improved again with Santa Fe, but now that it was American territory, the high prices Mexicans once paid for American goods there had dropped, making things more difficult for his grandfather financially. His grandfather's continued threat to leave Colorado and go to California weighed heavily on Cale, who had made many good friends among the Cheyenne. He wanted to stay in Colorado. If his grandfather moved, his mother and Jess would go with him, and Cale would be left with the very difficult choice of staying with the Cheyenne or going to California. Either way he would lose something very precious to him.

He had come to this place to think about that decision. He had walked here from the Cheyenne village where he had spent a good share of the winter, sharing Buffalo Boy's tipi with the young man's mother and father and young sister, Séhe.

This had brought still another problem to the growing and changing young man that he was. Although Séhe, whose name meant Snowbird, was only eleven, she had lately and very subtly taken on a beauty that disturbed him strangely. She was just a little girl, wasn't she? Yet only a few nights ago she had changed her tunic in front of him, thinking he was asleep, and he had noticed with surprise that her chest was no longer totally flat. There were soft little bumps there, surely the beginnings of breasts.

Never before had he been so acutely aware of women and how they were shaped. He had suddenly realized how beautiful his own mother was, and some of the young Cheyenne wives. Girls his own age were difficult to look at, as it was forbidden to look straight at a young maiden once her "flowing time" had begun and she was eligible for marriage.

To his own shame and chagrin, he didn't even totally understand what "flowing time" meant, and he wondered when it would come to Snowbird. He did not look forward to that time. They were good friends, and although he teased her incessantly about how men were far superior to women, deep in his heart he admired the strength and pride he saw in Snowbird, in spite of her age. When her own flowing time came, he would no longer be able to look at her or speak to her, and he would miss her very much. But what bothered him most, and also surprised him, was that he did not like very much the idea of some older warrior taking her for his wife. Somehow it seemed she belonged to him, yet both were far too young for any kind of commitment. Besides, since Cale was not a full-blooded Indian, he realized it was possible Snowbird's mother and father would never approve of him as a mate for their daughter.

He angrily broke a twig. "I will show them," he muttered. "I will be a great warrior someday. Already I am a good hunter." He sighed deeply, picking up another twig. As was the custom, Buffalo Boy's uncle, Spotted Horse, had taken on the task of teaching the boy Indian customs, and how to hunt and make war. The man had kindly included Cale in much of his instructing because Cale was the grandson of the respected warrior Blue Hawk. Cale had already proven himself capable and learned just as fast if not faster than Buffalo Boy himself. Buffalo Boy tended to be overweight and a little lazy, whereas Cale was energetic and eager.

He twirled the twig between his fingers, wondering if he should tell Caleb about Snowbird. Would his grandfather laugh at him? No. Not Blue Hawk. He would understand. And the more Cale thought about it, the more he realized that if his family moved on, he would stay behind with Buffalo Boy and the Cheyenne. After all, leaving would mean leaving Snowbird, and somehow he couldn't do that. Nor could he consider living totally in the white man's world now. His heart was leading him elsewhere, his spirit telling him where he really belonged, even to his belief that he must participate in the Sun Dance ritual. He wanted to be Cheyenne—all Cheyenne. He did not want anything less.

How many times had his grandfather told him he must follow his heart? Cale was perfectly aware of what the future held for the Cheyenne, but surely the real problems were many, many years in the future. Surely they would live as free as they did now for most of his own life. There had been a lot of trouble from the soldiers, but that was because of the Mexican war. That would all change once the war was finished—most of the soldiers in the area would leave, and the Cheyenne would have all their old freedom back. They rode the land from Colorado into the Dakotas; and together with their friends the Sioux and Arapaho, they were very strong.

He loved his life, loved his Cheyenne friends—and in some ways he was beginning to realize he loved Snowbird. Not as a man loves a woman. They were too young for that. Now he loved her the way a boy might love a sister. And he realized that there had been a time when his own grandfather had loved Sarah the same way. Could this strange feeling he had for Snowbird be the beginning of something much deeper?

Girlish laughter interrupted his thoughts. There was a rustling and much chatter not far away, and he realized it was the time of day when the women came to the stream to bathe. He knew he should leave, but also realized they could not see him from where he sat. The new curiosity that had been aroused in his deeper thoughts in the night about women held him in place, even though better sense told him to leave. These were full-grown women, as well as a few of the young maidens not yet taken. If ever he wanted a good idea of what it was like to look upon a naked woman, this was his chance. Perhaps there was something secret about them he didn't know.

Why did it arouse all his senses lately when he thought of young women? He was only thirteen. But then again he was also almost a man in the eyes of the Indian. Once he killed his first buffalo and suffered the Sun Dance, he would have proven himself well.

But for the moment he did not have the manly wisdom or strength to resist his racing curiosity. He realized no one knew he was here, and against all better sense and even his own deep respect for these women, he found himself crawling among underbrush and darting from tree to tree to get closer to the creek.

This was the place of the "big timbers"—*Hinta-Nagi* to the Cheyenne. Here was where many of them camped in winter, where trees sheltered them from cold winds and provided plenty of wood for fires. Spring had come early this year, and it was already warm. Some of the women had apparently decided to brave the creek and go all the way into the water this time.

Cale lay on his belly, watching through the bushes, his eyes widening as several of them stripped off their tunics. They wore nothing under them. They chatted and laughed, some going into the water and screaming as they splashed each other. Cale stared in awe at round, bare bottoms and full breasts, and he wondered at the V-shaped dark patch of hair nestled deep between their thighs. Somewhere in that place lay the most secret part of woman, the place where a man connected with her in the way he had seen animals connect.

What a magical thing woman was! A man planted himself inside of her and released the odd substance he had released more than once, quite by accident deep in the night. Surely that was what carried man's seed. And somehow that substance found its way deep into a woman's belly and mated with her egg, growing into a baby that made her belly fat. He remembered his own mother being fat with young John, his half brother. And then somehow the baby got born. Did it come out between her legs, the way man went in to make it in the first place? He had seen calves born, horses, puppies. It couldn't be much different for human babies.

He had a tremendous curiosity now as to how it might feel to mate with a woman. The Cheyenne were quite open about such things. Buffalo Boy's mother and father had mated several times deep in the night while Cale and Buffalo Boy and Snowbird slept nearby. They thought of it as simply a part of ongoing love, a fulfillment of their love for each other, a natural instinct. Cale thought about the sounds they had made, as though the act was a mixture of pain and ecstasy.

He spotted Snowbird. Love and respect made him quickly close his eyes, but a power stronger than his own will made him open them again. She was beautiful, though such a child yet. Her skin looked so smooth, and she didn't have any hair where the older women had hair. Her breasts were just tiny buds, but her thighs and bottom were shaped perfectly, firm and beautiful. Surely she would one day make a very lovely young woman. Somehow he had to prove his own worthiness soon, for when Snowbird came of age, he must make sure some older man did not claim her for himself.

His mind was made up now. If his family went to California, he would not go with them. He was almost a man now. He didn't really need his mother anymore, and he must learn to get along on his own. After all, that was what he had already been doing for a long time now.

His whole body felt warm and almost painfully alive as he watched the women, and he decided he must have a good talk with his grandfather about women. He loved and respected his stepfather Jess very much. But it always seemed so much easier to talk to Caleb. Caleb was Indian like himself. His grandfather understood him better than anyone else in the family.

Suddenly Cale cried out when someone very strong pulled him to his feet by the hair of the head. Cale's head and scalp screamed with pain as he was jerked around, and he stared straight into the wrinkled face of old Yellow Neck, one of the ornerier and older warriors, who was a respected dog soldier.

"You have done a bad thing this day," the old man snarled through yellow teeth. "You must be brought before the elders!"

Cale was speechless and devastated. Old Yellow Neck began walking back to the village, still grasping Cale by the hair of the head and yanking him along, half dragging him part of the way as Cale grasped at the man's hand and stumbled along backward with him. There was no releasing the firm hold Yellow Neck had of his long mane, and he didn't dare hit the man or put up too much of a struggle.

Cale knew that what he had been caught doing could bring him great punishment, possibly even death, and Yellow Neck just might decide to make that decision himself here and now. He was a very strong man. Cale did not want to offend the Cheyenne any worse than he already had by fighting against a respected warrior for something he was guilty of doing—sneaking a look at their women while they were naked—worst of all, setting his eyes upon the young maidens not yet taken.

"I am sorry, Yellow Neck," he panted, squinting against the pain. "I was just sitting there. I did not follow them deliberately. I was already there when they came."

"Then you should have left! You have brought yourself much shame, grandson of Blue Hawk. Your grandfather would be very angry with you! The men of the council will be very angry! You have lost much honor this day!"

Cale wanted very much to cry, but he didn't dare. Nothing would bring him more shame than to go whimpering to the council and begging their pardon. Admitting to what he had done and asking for the proper punishment would be much more honorable. He would take what he had coming to him and hope that somehow he could still be accepted in the village.

Why had he not listened to the wise voices in his heart that told him to leave? What was the strange power that had made him do something so blatantly against the rules of the Cheyenne? How could he have been so stupid? He was surely more angry with himself at this moment than the Cheyenne would be. Somehow he had to make up for this, unless they killed him. His only saving grace might be that he was Blue Hawk's grandson. And at the moment his first concern was that Yellow Neck would not pull every hair from his head before they reached the village. Standing bald before the council would be even more disgraceful. The only thing to be glad about at the moment was that his grandfather would not be there to witness his shame and disgrace.

The drums beat and Cale waited in the center of the circle of women. The decision had been made. The women would mete out Cale's punishment, for it was the women who had been offended. Cale knew how vengeful Cheyenne women could be. The loose women of their own tribe were usually badly beaten and banished from the village. And he had seen an Arapaho man, who had forced himself upon a Cheyenne woman, beaten nearly to death by the rest of the women of the tribe.

He could not help wondering where Snowbird might be as the older women circled closer to him, waving their sticks and stones. His loyal friend and Snowbird's brother, Buffalo Boy, had deliberately stayed away, realizing Cale's shame would be great enough without his best friend watching the beating. But was Snowbird watching this belittling punishment? He didn't dare look, for to scan the whole circle of women would make him appear cowardly, as though he might try to run away from what was coming.

Snowbird did watch, but from the shadows where Cale could not see her. Her lips puckered and tears came to her eyes as the women's sticks came down on Cale. He put his arms around his head to ward off the stones the women threw at him, and Snowbird's heart hurt for him. She didn't care that Cale had looked at the women. Buffalo Boy had told her two other boys he knew had done the same thing, but they had not been caught. Surely it was just a part of boys becoming men, and somehow deep inside her innocent body there stirred pleasant flutters at the thought that Cale might even have seen her.

The thought made her face red, for surely she looked puny and childish next to the grown women. She couldn't quite understand why she even cared what Cale would think. He was just a good friend. But lately her own mother had scowled on Snowbird's speaking to the boy, and both Cale and Buffalo Boy were gone more than they were around, learning warrior ways, hunting, becoming men much faster than Snowbird was becoming a woman.

She watched Cale bravely take the blows from the women without running or crying out. She was proud of that, proud that before the council he had bravely admitted his guilt and had sworn that after taking his punishment he would prove he was brave and honorable by participating in the Sun Dance. The elders had told him he was too young, but Cale told them he was the grandson of Blue Hawk and eager to prove he carried the same courage and spiritual strength as his grandfather. After all, he wore the blue quill necklace given him by Blue Hawk. He wore it even now as the women, from the very young to the very old, vented their wrath on the young boy.

Snowbird sniffed and rubbed her eyes as the women descended on Cale until she couldn't see him at all. Finally they walked away from him. He was crouched on his knees, struggling to get up and obviously in a lot of pain. Even by the light of the fire Snowbird could see bruises already appearing. She wanted to run to him but knew she dared not. She watched him finally get to his feet and stumble out of the light of the fire to his horse. As she ran around two tipis to keep him in sight, he rode off into the darkness toward his home in the white world. She wondered if he would keep his promise and come back.

· Chapter Thirteen ·

Caleb led the roan mare into the narrow holding pen, and Jess closed the wooden gate behind them. Jess pulled the hot iron shaped in an *S* from the coals, perched himself on the top of the wall of the pen at the horse's left side, and quickly shoved the hot iron hard against the horse's left rump. The animal whinnied and reared, kicking to get away but having no place to go. Jess kept firmly shoving the brand for another few brief seconds, then released it and jumped down, shoving the brand back into the coals.

Caleb opened the front gate and pulled the rope from the animal, whistling and urging it out of the pen and into the corral with other freshly branded horses. Its flesh still smoked, but its pain would soon be forgotten.

"That's the last one, Caleb."

Caleb opened another gate and walked out of the corral, turning and looking over the horses. "They look good, but it's still a small herd, Jess. Then again if we head for California, it's small enough that we could take most of them along and maybe sell them at one of the forts along the way."

Jess leaned against the fence and took a pipe and a pouch of tobacco from his pocket.

"Caleb, I'm afraid this isn't the year to think about California, unless you want to go on ahead and leave me and Lynda behind."

Caleb turned in surprise to face the man who had been more than a son-in-law. Jess Purnell was also a friend, and without his help survival would have been a lot harder.

"What's wrong, Jess?"

Jess lit the pipe and puffed it a moment. "Nothing is

really wrong. Actually, it's good news. Lynda is pretty sure she's pregnant again."

Caleb's eyebrows arched and he smiled, leaning against the fence himself and folding his arms. It was a warm day, and he wore no shirt. Jess never failed to be struck by the man's firm, powerful physique, in spite of his age and the hardships he had suffered.

"Well, congratulations, Jess. This is kind of a mixture of good and bad news. I'm happy as hell for Lynda. I know she's been wanting another child. But that sure puts an end to plans to head west."

Jess nodded, puffing the pipe again before speaking. "I'm afraid it does. You know how delicate her pregnancies are—three miscarriages and two difficult births. She wants this baby, and with Cale gone so much, I think it would be good for her. She knows she's losing Cale, and she knows that if we do leave Colorado she'll likely be leaving her oldest son behind."

Caleb sighed, tossing his long hair behind his back when the wind started to blow some into his face. He looked out over the vast plains to the east, and Jess could easily picture the man with his face painted, riding a big horse across those plains.

"Life sure gets complicated when a man has a family," Caleb commented. He turned back around to face Jess, a sad smile on his face. "Constant decisions. Circumstances keep me here, yet I can't help worrying about Tom out there in California. All I ever got was that one letter. He sounded so happy. I guess if I hadn't had that damned dream, that sure feeling that he needed me—"

"I know. It's always been that way between you two. But you sent that reply months ago. Your messenger should be coming back sometime this summer with word on Tom."

Caleb leaned against the fence again, looking at the horses. "I just wish I knew what was going on in Sonoma with the war and all. Tom has a knack for getting involved in messes like that."

"Like his father?"

Caleb grinned and shook his head. "Yes, like his father."

He looked at Jess again. "You've been a good husband and father yourself, Jess. I know this baby means a lot to you, even more to Lynda. And when it's born it will be important to her to have Sarah with her. I wouldn't think of leaving without my daughter and her family. We all go together or we don't go at all. Tom's a grown man, something that has always been hard for me to get through my thick head. He'll just have to manage on his own. I just hope he isn't in some kind of really bad trouble, or wounded."

"Well, maybe you'll hear from him yet this summer. And if the birth goes well, next spring we could think about heading west."

"That all depends on how the winter goes for Sarah, and how the new baby is doing. I won't jeopardize any member of this family."

Caleb deliberately checked his disappointment. He wanted to get Sarah to California, sure her health would improve there. But he would not spoil the joy of Lynda's pregnancy, nor do anything to risk another miscarriage.

"Rider coming," Jess said.

Caleb looked out across the north ridge to watch a lone rider approach. "It's Cale. That should make Lynda happy." Caleb looked at Jess. "Don't worry about California. Lynda is going to have a baby, and that's something to celebrate. I'll try to get Cale to stay here tonight, and we'll have a big feast." He reached out and squeezed Jess's shoulder. "I'm glad for you, Jess. You've been loyal to the family, a good husband to Lynda. I know what a stubborn thing she can be sometimes."

Jess grinned. "No one can say Lynda doesn't speak her mind."

Caleb smiled, stepping away to greet Cale as he came closer, but his smile quickly faded when he realized the boy was dirty and badly bruised over his entire body. He slowed when he saw his grandfather, but he did not stop completely. His dark eyes showed shame and turned away as though he couldn't face Caleb.

"Cale," Jess spoke up anxiously. "What has happened to you!" The boy rode past them. "Cale! Come back here."

The boy finally halted his mount, reluctantly turning the animal and trotting it back to the two men. Jess reached up and grasped the bridle. "What the hell happened? Did white men do this?"

Cale's eyes moved to Caleb's. "No," he half mumbled. "It was not white men." He swallowed, then straightened, obviously struggling not to cry. "I will show them! I will show them I am a man, as good a warrior as any of them!" He turned his horse and rode toward the barn.

"What do you think happened, Caleb?"

"Apparently the Cheyenne did this," Caleb answered, gazing after his grandson. "You had better go tell Lynda he's back." He looked at Jess. "I have a good idea what happened. It's something to do with Indian custom. Maybe I'm the one who should talk to him."

Jess nodded. "I'll go inside and talk to Lynda."

The two men parted, Jess heading for his own cabin, Caleb heading for the barn.

Cale was angrily removing the bridle, blanket, and gear from his horse. As he slammed the bridle over a hook, he noticed his grandfather approaching. He picked up a currying brush and began brushing down his horse in vigorous strokes.

"You keep brushing him that hard and you'll brush the hair right off his hide," Caleb told the boy.

Cale hesitated, then continued with lighter strokes. Caleb stepped closer, leaning against the wall of the stall. "Want to tell me what happened?"

Cale swallowed and blinked. "I might as well. You will just find out some other way that your grandson has disgraced you."

Caleb subdued a grin, waiting for the boy to go on.

"Women did this," the boy grumbled. He stopped and threw the brush into a corner. "Women!" He turned and leaned into a corner, looking away from his grandfather.

"Well, the only thing I can think of that they would turn the women loose on you for would be if you offended some young maiden. Who was she?"

The boy didn't answer right away, and Caleb waited patiently.

"It wasn't just one. I was sitting alone by the creek when many of them came there to bathe. I knew it was wrong to look, but I couldn't help it." He punched at the wall and never did Caleb Sax have to struggle so hard not to laugh out loud. He knew it would be the worst thing he could do to his already greatly disgraced grandson. "That stupid old Yellow Neck caught me and dragged me before the council. They voted to let the women punish me."

Caleb reached over the wall of the stall and stroked the nose of Cale's horse. "Cheyenne women can be pretty damned mean when they want to be. I take it they used some nice big sticks on you."

Cale began toying with a piece of splintered wood, pulling it away from the main board. "Sticks and rocks," he mumbled.

Caleb moved around to the outside of the corner where the boy stood. "You all right? Nothing is broken, is it?"

The boy continued to hang his head. "I am all right. It is my pride that hurts the most."

Caleb reached out and touched his shoulder. "I know exactly how you're feeling, Cale."

"No, you don't." The boy pulled away.

Caleb sighed and moved inside the stall. "Yes, I do, Cale. I wasn't much older than you when I had to run away from Fort Dearborn where my adoptive white father had been raising me. I was caught in a very embarrassing situation with a white girl. Her father walked in on us, and as soon as he did she started yelling rape. Being Indian, everyone believed it easily enough, but it wasn't true. At any rate it was either run or get hung."

The boy turned to face him. "Really?"

Caleb grinned a little. "It was my first experience with a woman. I was too stupid to see through her and realize she would get me in trouble. She wasn't exactly the innocent type, but I was so struck by how wonderful it was to be with her at all that I didn't stop to think about her behavior." He leaned against the wall of the stall. "At any rate, my shame was very great. I felt like the fool of the year."

Cale sighed, turning away again. "It has only been lately I've thought about . . . women. There is one special one—she is only eleven summers now, but she is very beautiful. I didn't think about her any other way until one night I saw her take off her tunic." His voice dwindled and he shrugged. "Is it bad to want to look at a woman with nothing on, Grandfather?"

Caleb's heart ached for his badly bruised grandson. "Of course it isn't bad, Cale. It just means you're beginning to experience the emotions of a man instead of a boy. You want to know things—to learn. Who is the little girl?"

Cale leaned against the wall, his back still to Caleb. "Her name is Snowbird. She is Buffalo Boy's sister. We are good friends, or at least we were until now."

"If you were good friends before and she is good and true, that won't change. Your grandmother and I started out the same way, you know. We were childhood friends, like brother and sister. And then the day she was forced to leave Fort Dearborn and go to St. Louis, she cried because she didn't want to go, and she hugged me. I'll never forget that moment, Cale. I held her close and smelled her hair, and I felt something I'd never felt before. It made me feel guilty, just like you're feeling guilty. Now I know it wasn't a bad feeling— nothing to be ashamed of. And neither should you be ashamed. Do you think you're the only young Cheyenne man who has been caught taking a peek at the women?"

The boy sighed deeply, turning around but looking at the ground. "It is worse for me because I am not a full blood —and more disgraceful because I am the grandson of Blue Hawk and should be stronger."

Caleb folded his arms. "Did you own up to what you did and ask for the proper punishment?"

"Yes, sir," the boy mumbled.

"And did you stand still and take the blows without try-ing to run?"

The boy raised his eyes finally to meet his grandfather's. "Yes."

Caleb nodded. "Then you have made your atonement. For their part it's forgotten, and you faced it like a man."

The boy's eyes teared. "That is not enough."

Caleb frowned. "What do you mean?"

"I mean—" He searched his grandfather's eyes. "Are you going to go to California, Grandfather?"

Caleb unfolded his arms, trying to determine what the boy had in mind. "No. You probably don't know it yet because you're gone most of the time. But your mother is going to have a baby, Cale. We can't go this year."

His eyebrows arched in surprise and the boy grinned. "A baby? That is good. She wants another baby." He stepped closer. "It is even better than that, because it means you will be home this summer."

Caleb frowned. "What do you have in mind, Cale?"

The boy straightened proudly. "I want to show them I am a man, not a sneaking coward. I want to take part in the Sun Dance celebration this summer. Can I do it, Grandfather? Will you come and help me? Watch me?"

Caleb sobered completely, stepping closer. "Cale, you're awfully young for that. Do you understand what will happen to you?"

The boy held his chin proudly. "I understand. I will fast for many days, and then I will be taken to the Sun Dance lodge, where they will put sticks through my flesh with rawhide tied to them. They will pull me up by the skin then, and I will hang there until the sticks tear away from my flesh, and through all the pain and hunger I will grow very weak and have a vision, and I will know what I am to be and know for certain where I belong."

Caleb felt a stabbing pain at the thought of his grandson suffering. "You know I don't like leaving your grandmother, Cale."

The boy's eyes remained pleading, and Caleb could not help being proud that he wanted to participate in the most trying ritual of the Cheyenne. "You could come right back as soon as it is over. They are going to have the celebration at the South Platte this year instead of going farther north. That is not so far from here, Grandfather. Please say you will let me and that you will come."

"Only if your mother approves. It makes her very sad to know she will lose you completely to the Cheyenne, Cale."

"You can talk to her. She listens to you, Grandfather. Please talk to her. Make her understand I love her very much. I love all of you. But it is something very deep in my heart, this feeling I have to be Indian. You must make her understand that. You can do it because you know how I am feeling. And now that I have been disgraced, it is even more important that I do this, to win back my honor and respect, and to be a man in front of Snowbird."

Caleb put an arm around him and led him out of the stall. "I'll talk to her."

"Thank you, Grandfather!" The boy hugged him around the middle. James came into the barn just as they were embracing, and he stopped for a moment, watching them and scowling, feeling the old jealousy he always felt over how his father felt about Cale. Caleb noticed his son, saw the look on his face, and read it with an aching heart.

"James. Did you bring in that old red stud that's been giving us so much trouble?"

The boy walked closer almost reluctantly. "I found him," he mumbled. When he got closer, his eyes widened at the sight of Cale's bruised body. "What happened to you?"

Cale stepped back, looking helplessly at his grandfather. Caleb knew the boy didn't want his family to know what had happened.

"Cale had a little run-in with a couple of Indian boys. It's all straight now. Just a little betting on a shooting contest that got out of hand," Caleb answered for his grandson.

James smiled in a near sneer. "Were they drunk?" he snipped.

Cale frowned. "No. They were not drunk."

James turned away, taking down a bridle. "Well, it serves you right. I could have told you that if you hang around with that kind long enough you'll get into a lot of trouble." He walked to a stall and began fitting the bridle onto a black mare.

"What do you mean by 'that kind'?" Caleb asked his son.

James glanced at him, then looked back at the horse, always angry with himself for feeling somewhat awestruck and almost afraid of his father. "I just mean those ruffians who know nothing but fighting and gambling and drinking and making war."

"You don't know anything about them." Cale spoke up before Caleb could answer. "They have a way of life that is beautiful and would even be peaceful if the white man would let them alone. They know a freedom no white man knows —

a peace that comes from the inside, a closeness to the spirits. They need none of the things the white man needs to survive. *Maheo* provides all that they need in the land and the animals."

James scowled at him. He didn't want to hear any of it, for he was sure his grandfather favored Cale over his own son. "Don't talk to me about *Maheo* and the strong and brave Cheyenne." James wondered himself why he was speaking the way he was in front of his father. "I don't look Indian and I don't intend to *be* Indian or let any strangers know I have Indian blood!"

Cale stepped closer, fists clenched, while Caleb just stared at his son. "You will never be at peace as long as you feel that way. I wish you would come with me and Grandfather— come to the Sun Dance. I am going to make the sacrifice, James. I am proud to be Indian, and so should you be. Come with us! Let us ride together as when we were younger and good friends. You were always my best friend, James."

James leaned against a post, looking from Cale to his father. "It's true? He's going to make the Sun Dance sacrifice?"

Caleb nodded. "It's true. Come with us, James."

The boy's face grew darker. "You don't want me with you. It's a special time for you and Cale. You've always liked him better. Now he will truly be your favorite, because he is making the sacrifice."

"Don't talk stupid, James," Caleb told him angrily.

"It isn't stupid. I am not Indian, Father, and I have no desire to go live with a bunch of them and watch that barbaric ritual of manhood." The words poured out unwanted, out of bitter jealousy. He didn't want them to come, yet he could not stop himself. " You think Cale is wonderful now because he will make the sacrifice. And you think I am weak and worthless. Well, I'm not! Someday I will be very successful all on my own, and while Cale is riding with the Cheyenne and all of them are dying, I will be a successful man enjoying the luxuries only a man with no Indian blood can enjoy—luxuries my own mother can never have because of you!"

Caleb flinched almost as though someone had hit him. His fists clenched. Never before had he been tempted to hit one of his own children, but now he held himself in check. It was Cale that could not. The boy hauled off and punched his uncle James roundly in the chest, knocking him against the horse he had been getting ready to ride. James slid down the side of the animal and fell hard on his rump, but was immediately up again, glaring at Cale.

"Go ahead to your stupid Sun Dance," he hissed, tears coming to his eyes. "Take my father with you and make him proud! He has never been proud of me! Go and live with the Cheyenne so that I don't always have to be compared to you! Go away, Cale, and stay away!"

Caleb stepped closer, reaching around Cale and grasping James's arm. "How in God's name can you say I've never been proud of you?" he asked angrily, his eyes wide and hurt. "I've always been proud—of all my children and grandchildren, each one for what he or she is as a human being! But right now I *am* ashamed of you—for your cruel words and selfish attitude!"

The boy jerked away. "I saw you hugging him. And you have just said you will go to the Sun Dance ritual with him. You have always thought Cale was better than me."

"That isn't true, James."

"Yes; it is! Why did you have to be my father! Why did an Indian have to be my father!"

Their eyes held challengingly. Caleb struggled to keep from hitting his son, and he could see by the boy's eyes he regretted what he had said, but James said nothing in the way of an apology. He whirled and jumped up onto the back of the horse he had bridled.

"See?" he sneered. "I can ride, too. I can do a *lot* of things, Father."

The hurt in Caleb's eyes pulled at James's heart, but for some reason he wanted it to be there, wanted his father to suffer. It was only right, for he himself would suffer the rest of his life just because he had Indian blood.

"I am through with my chores for the day." James turned his horse and rode past them out of the barn.

Cale turned and looked up at his grandfather, his heart aching at the hurt and sorrow in the man's eyes. He touched Caleb's arm. "I am sorry, Grandfather. It is my fault."

Caleb looked down at him, touching his shoulder. "Don't ever say that, Cale. You are what you are, and you have never done one thing to cause this. There is a terrible restlessness in James's heart that nothing can help—not even my love. He has never forgotten the hurt in Texas, and for a while I wasn't much of a father then."

"He should understand how hard it was for you, too. He is selfish." Cale looked down at his fist. "I should not have hit him. It is not the first time we have fought." He met his grandfather's eyes again. "Maybe you should not go to the Sun Dance with me."

Caleb put an arm around him. "I will go. I do my best for each member of this family, Cale. Apparently that isn't enough for James. I'm through trying to cleanse the bitterness from his heart. That's something he has to do himself. My heart aches for the suffering he's going to experience by denying his own blood. I don't know anymore how to help him."

"Then we must pray for him. At the Sun Dance we can pray for him. There is powerful medicine there. The spirits listen well."

Caleb took hope in the words, proud of how understanding Cale could be, proud of the man he was becoming. He couldn't bring himself to spoil this major decision Cale had made with troubles over James. He could do nothing but love his son, but apparently that was not enough.

He wondered if he should just pick the boy up, sling him over his lap, and spank him like a child. But he had never hit any of his children, and he could not get over the regret that maybe some of it was his fault after all. Somehow, somewhere, he had failed James. And like other bewildered parents who suffered similar problems with their children, he couldn't quite place when and where it had happened.

They walked outside and a bird cried out overhead. Caleb looked up to see a hawk, his sign. A chill moved through him, for he realized he was himself being untrue to his real calling. Only Cale was doing that. He remembered his own vision of a hawk, changing from blue to red and white, a voice telling him he would forever be tortured by being a part of two worlds—that one day the two must come together into one man.

"Grandfather! A hawk," Cale said almost worshipfully. "It is a good sign. Maybe it means it is right that I go to the Sun Dance."

"It means more than that, Cale."

The hawk disappeared into the sun, and Sarah called from the house. He looked at her across the distance. Sarah. His beautiful Sarah.

"Let's go talk to your mother and grandmother and Jess about what you want to do."

"You won't tell them what really happened to me?"

Caleb grinned. "I won't tell them."

"What about James?"

"James has made his own decisions, just like you're doing. Every man has to live with those decisions, Cale. There is nothing more I can do about it. I just hope whatever he does he doesn't hurt his mother. I don't mind his hurting me."

They walked toward the cabin. Caleb looked back to see the hawk flying off in the distance toward James, disappearing over the rise.

• Chapter Fourteen •

Everyone sat around the supper table in strained silence. James had not returned, and Cale ate as though his entire body was in pain. Lynda kept looking at him with teary eyes, finally setting aside her fork.

"Cale, I can't keep going through this. Now, I can only guess what happened to you at that village, since neither you nor grandfather will tell me." Her chiding blue eyes moved to her father, whom she loved to the point of worship, but with whom she was also very angry at the moment. "All I know is this is the end of it. You will not go back to that village!"

The boy set down his own fork, while Jess and Caleb and Sarah all exchanged looks. When Lynda set her mind to something it was difficult to change it, as Jess well knew from when he had first tried to court her and she had thought he was an enemy of her father's. But Cale was just like his mother when it came to stubbornness. Now his dark eyes held her blue ones daringly.

"Yes, I *will* go back, Mother," he answered firmly, watching her eyes widen with indignation. "I respect your wishes, but Cheyenne mothers of men my age don't try to tell them what to do. It's disgraceful."

"Disgraceful! Men! You're only thirteen years old! I'll grant you seem much older and your build defies your age. But you're still thirteen. And as far as disgraceful, look at you! Look at what they've done to you! How can you think of going back?"

"It was just punishment for something I did wrong," he answered, raising his voice sightly. "It won't happen again. They are a people with rules and I was treated fairly. Besides, I will be fourteen this year. And I intend to show them the kind of man I am, so that this will never happen again. I am going to participate in the Sun Dance ritual this summer. Grandfather is going with me."

"Caleb!" Sarah blurted out his name in surprise at the news none of them knew anything about.

Caleb quickly swallowed a piece of meat, feeling his daughter's wrath as her eyes, as blue and sometimes as icy as her father's, turned to him in surprise and desperation. "What is my son talking about?"

Caleb frowned at Cale, who pouted and hung his head; then Caleb looked at Lynda. In all his years of fighting and killing, he wondered if he had ever faced a challenge quite like this. He sighed deeply and leaned back in his chair. "Cale wants to take part in the Sun Dance this summer, and he has asked me to be there."

Lynda just stared at him a moment, breathing heavily.

Caleb glanced at Jess, whose eyes said "good luck with this one," and Caleb suppressed an urge to grin.

"And you both decided all of this without asking me, his own mother?" Lynda voice was high and strained with an effort to keep from screaming the words.

Caleb leaned forward, resting an elbow on the table and leaning closer to his daughter, who sat just around the corner from him on his left. "Lynda, I was going to talk to you alone. I didn't mean for it to come out this way."

She just blinked and stared at him.

"Lynda, the boy wants very much to do this. There is nothing you could do to show your love in any more powerful way than to let him—to be proud of him in the way a Cheyenne woman would be proud of her own son's decision to do such a thing."

"Does he realize what they will do to him?" she asked, her voice shaking.

Caleb reached out to grasp one of her hands. She did not pull away. "Of course he does. And I've been through it myself, Lynda. With me there, I know he can get through it. For a Cheyenne boy it's the most important event in his entire life. And if it's in his heart to do it, you have to let him."

Jess reached over and put an arm around her shoulders, while young John watched his mother in confusion, shoving half a biscuit into his mouth so that his cheeks bulged while he chewed and listened.

"I'll lose him forever then," Lynda protested.

"Lynda, if you refuse to let him do this, you'll lose him in the worst way," Jess told her gently. "I don't understand all this Indian stuff, but Caleb does, and he understands how Cale is feeling. If you keep trying to hang on to him and keep him in our world, he'll be resentful and unhappy. He's three-quarters Indian, Lynda. He *wants* to be Indian. Caleb understands better than any of us the tortures of living in two worlds." Sarah felt an odd pain in her chest at the words.

"Cale knows exactly what he wants to be, Lynda. Even if you're apart physically, the love and honor between the two of you will be so much greater," Jess told her.

Caleb squeezed her hand. "Jess took the words right out of my mouth."

"But . . . he's a part of Lee." She quickly wiped at more tears, sniffing and meeting her father's eyes again. "You'd be with him?"

"Every minute."

"You'll teach him—about ways not to feel the pain?"

"He's my grandson, Lynda. You know how much I love him. Do you think I would let him suffer any more than is necessary?"

"And you'll make him come home after—just for a little while, so I can see for myself he's all right?"

"Whatever you want."

Their eyes held, and she realized this was as important to her father as it was to her son. She could not help sensing the secret pride that went with the Sun Dance, and her own Indian blood made her feel some of it herself, in spite of her love and protectiveness making her want to tell her son no. She had to ask herself now what an Indian mother would do, but she already knew without asking. Caleb squeezed her hand reassuringly, and she knew by his eyes what would make her son love her more than he had ever loved her. She sighed deeply, looking at Cale.

"If it is so important to you, and if your grandfather is going to be there, then I suppose you must do it."

Cale grinned. "Thank you, Mother. I have told all my friends about my mother, that she is more beautiful than any of the women in their villages, and just as strong and wise. Buffalo Boy said you were too white—that you would never let me do this." He tossed his long hair behind his shoulders. "Now they will see! They will see how brave and honorable I am, and I will be the most important one at the Sun Dance, because my sponsor will be my own grandfather—Blue Hawk! They will all envy me."

Caleb looked over at Sarah, seeing the hint of fear that she always showed when he had reason to get mixed up with his Cheyenne relatives—the fear that he would ride off with them and never come back. She knew better, yet could never quite get the thought out of her mind.

"I didn't mean for it all to come out this way," Caleb

told her quietly. "Cale spit it all out before I had a chance to talk to anyone."

She forced a gentle smile. "No matter which way it came out, you would have done it anyway."

"I don't like going away, Sarah. But this is important to Cale, and I don't want him to go there alone."

The pain moved through her chest again. Cale—their first grandson—so proud and handsome and free-spirited, just like his grandfather.

"This supper I made was supposed to be to celebrate the fact that I'm going to have another baby," Lynda said quietly. "Things didn't turn out exactly as I had planned." She looked at her father. "And I'm sorry I spoiled your plans for California."

Caleb gave her a smile. "Knowing you're having another baby means a lot more—to me and Sarah both. And I know what it means to Jess. Besides, with Cale wanting to participate in the Sun Dance, I couldn't have left anyway. You may be losing your oldest son to the Cheyenne, but I have a feeling that deep inside you'll be happier knowing Cale is living the life he truly wants to live."

Just then James came riding up. Sarah caught the mixture of anger and hurt in Caleb's eyes as he glanced toward the door, then resumed eating as James came inside. The boy hesitated at the door and Sarah looked up at him. "James Sax, where have you been? We're nearly finished with supper."

The boy reddened slightly, glancing at his father as though wondering if someone had told on him about something. His eyes moved to Cale, who scowled at him and returned to his food.

"I felt like riding, that's all," the boy told Sarah. "May I still eat?"

Sarah looked from her son to Caleb and Cale, feeling the certain tension. She was sure angry words had again been exchanged between James and his father. Sarah knew James's shame over his Indian blood hurt Caleb deeply, but the man in turn felt somewhat guilty that James had such problems about his own identity, as though it was his fault and so he had no right chastising the boy for his disrespectful behavior.

"Sit down, James," Sarah said calmly. "I'll get you a plate. Lynda, you sit still and finish your food. I can fix James's for him."

James hung his hat on a hook. "I went to our cabin first—figured you were all over there," he said, trying to make pleasant conversation. "How come you're making supper tonight, Lynda?"

Lynda met her young brother's eyes, also sensing the tension between Caleb and the boy. "It's a celebration. I am going to have another child."

James grinned at first. "Hey, that's great." Then he sobered. "But . . . we won't be able to go to California, will we?"

Caleb met his eyes. "You *want* to go?"

Sarah set a plate in front of James and he stared at the food. "I just want to get out of here—away from . . . things."

Caleb frowned at him. "Yes, I suppose you do. I don't need to guess what the 'things' are you'd like to get away from. I think they're called Cheyenne." He set aside his fork and rose while everyone looked at him in surprise and James reddened. "I'm going out for a smoke. You care to join me, Jess?"

Jess sensed the man's need to get out of the room. "Sure, Caleb." He patted Lynda on the shoulder and rose, getting his hat. Caleb moved to the door, turning and looking at his family.

"Several things have happened lately that seem to be designed to try to tear this family apart, but it's not going to happen. Cale may leave us, but we won't ever really be apart, because he is a fine, proud young man who is following his heart and who loves his mother dearly for understanding. We can only be proud of him. Lynda is going to have another baby. We're gaining a new member in the family, and that is always something to celebrate. As far as California, it apparently will just have to wait. We'll just have to trust Tom to our prayers. And no matter what James decides to do with his life, it will be his decision, just as Cale has made his own choice. I will not let whatever any of you do interfere with the fact that we all are Saxes and we are family, and wherever any of us goes in life, the love we share will give each of us the strength he or she needs to survive, and we can all be together—in spirit."

He turned and left, and Sarah gazed after him, realizing something very moving had prompted the speech he had just given. She glanced again at James, who sat staring at his plate, and it pained her heart to realize the rift was deepening between her son and his father. Young John climbed down from his chair and ran around the table to climb onto the lap of his bigger Indian half brother. James watched Cale as he picked the boy up.

"What *really* happened to you, Cale?" he asked sarcastically.

Cale met his eyes challengingly. "That's my business."

"And my father's? Everybody knows how close you are," James quipped.

"James, that will be enough," Sarah spoke up, a quiet anger evident. "You and your father could be even closer, if you would let it happen. That is no one's fault but your own."

James said nothing. He picked quietly at his food for a few minutes, wondering what his father meant by "losing Cale." Life might be a lot better for him if Cale would stay out of the picture. "You going away, Cale?" he finally asked after swallowing a piece of chicken. "For good, I mean?"

Cale handed his little brother a piece of meat. "You don't have to try to act like you care. You know I am going to take part in the Sun Dance. You heard—out by the barn." He accented the words as though to remind James of something more, and James glanced at his mother's discerning eyes. He looked back at Cale.

"So? What about it?"

"So I will probably stay with the Cheyenne after that."

James took a bite of biscuit and swallowed. "We all knew you would. You think you're all Indian. You might as well live with them."

"And what are you, James?" Cale asked in a near sneer.

James scooted back his chair and rose. "I am James Sax." He leaned closer. "See this face? You see any Indian in it?"

Cale held his eyes steadily. "No. But there is Indian in your heart, and in your blood! One day you will realize that and you will be very sad that you pretended it was not so."

James snickered. "I highly doubt that. And the fact that you see no Indian in me answers your question. You asked what I am. I am white. You made your choice, and I made mine."

Cale nodded. "Yes. Why does that mean we can no longer be the good friends we once were, James? I miss the fun we used to have."

Some of the arrogance left James's eyes and he looked somehow deflated. He turned around. "I miss it, too. But things were different then. We were in Texas and we had a good life there. It's all different now." He looked at Lynda. "I'm glad about your baby. And I'm sorry I spoiled supper. It seems as if I'm always spoiling things." He turned back to Cale. "Is Pa still going with you?"

Cale nodded. "Yes. You could go, too. Grandfather would like that."

"I doubt it. He'll be with the Indians. I don't know him when he's like that. Besides, he likes being alone with you. He and I don't have much in common anymore."

"James, that's enough," Sarah said sharply. "You go back to our own cabin and wait for me there, do you understand?"

The boy glanced darkly at her, then looked down at the table. "Yes, ma'am." He hurried out, slamming the door.

In the distance Caleb and Jess stood against a fence, smoking pipes. They watched James storm toward Sarah and Caleb's cabin.

"You had words again?" Jess said quietly to Caleb.

Caleb nodded, puffing his pipe a moment. "I can't talk to him at all anymore, Jess. I swear I'd rather have the kind of problems you and Lynda have with Cale than the kind I have with that boy. At least Cale loves and respects you both. I have no doubt how much James loves his mother.

But he doesn't seem to hold much for me anymore. I was very tempted earlier today to hit him for something he said. I don't like feeling that way about one of my own children. I guess that's the Indian in me. They never hit their children. Pure shame over doing something wrong seems to be enough punishment. But I went wrong somewhere with James. And he doesn't seem to feel any shame at all when he insults his own father and his own blood."

"You're wrong there, Caleb. That boy all but worships you and he doesn't even know it. He keeps his true feelings buried way, way down deep. You can't do a damned thing about it, and you shouldn't feel guilty or wrong for that. You've done nothing but love him. He's just got a lot of learning to do before he begins to understand what's really important in life. We're losing Cale to the Indian world. And I think you'll lose James to something else—a search, perhaps. But he'll come around." He sighed deeply and turned to rest a foot on a fence rail. "Thanks for what you're doing for Cale. I'll watch the women. James can help me there. Maybe I can bring in one or two men from the fort. There are always men around who'll work for a meal."

Caleb nodded. "I'll try to get back as fast as I can. Depends on how Cale is."

Jess frowned. "How bad is it, Caleb? He'll be all right, won't he?"

Caleb kept watching the house, where James had gone inside. "I'll make sure he's all right. But it's a very difficult ordeal. Most grown men wouldn't think of going through it. Personally I'd rather he waited. But he's been shamed and he's anxious to make up for it."

"What really happened to him?"

A faint grin passed over Caleb's lips. "You've got to promise not to tell Lynda. The boy would be devastated."

"I wouldn't think of telling her."

Caleb sighed deeply. "It would be humorous if it wasn't so serious to Cale. I'm afraid he got caught doing a little peeking at some young maidens who went to the creek to bathe. He was taken before the council, and it was decided the women themselves should do the punishing. And believe me, Indian women can be real vicious when they choose to be."

Jess contemplated the story for a moment, then began to grin. "Cale was peeking at naked women?"

Caleb grinned more. "I'm afraid so. Sounds like a pretty normal, red-blooded boy to me, wouldn't you say?"

Jess began to snicker. "I'd say so." He laughed more then. "Women did that to him?" His laughter became more uncontrolled. "Jesus Christ, now I know where Lynda gets that temper," he said between laughs. "I sure hope I don't ever make her that mad! I'd hate to say I was beat on by a woman!"

The picture it brought to mind made Caleb laugh even harder himself. It felt good to laugh, for deep inside he wanted to cry. He watched his own cabin as the refreshing laughter moved through him, wondering when the last time was James had laughed. The more he thought about it, the more he realized he could not remember the boy laughing, even in the good years. He had always been so serious, even as a child. Jess's laughter helped him push away the agony he felt over James. Jess was laughing so hard by then he could hardly get his breath.

"Hell, if I had the opportunity, I'd peek, too," he told Caleb, wiping at tears of laughter.

"And I'd be right beside you."

He continued to laugh along with his son-in-law, but he was watching Sarah walk briskly toward their own cabin.

Sarah walked into the cabin with a determined sureness, turning and closing the door behind her. She held James's eyes as the boy stood at the table facing her.

"Don't you love me, James?"

The boy frowned. "You know I love you, Mother."

"I find that hard to believe. Don't you realize that every time you hurt your father, you also hurt me?"

James sighed deeply, fingering the back of a chair.

"You had words with him again, didn't you? What kind of disrespectful things did you say to him this time?"

James looked at her with tear-filled eyes. "He loves Cale more than me. He always has!"

"That is nonsense! My God, James, after all this family has been through, how can you not see how much Caleb Sax loves every member of his family, *especially* his son. He has lost so much. So much! And I will not stand for your hurting him any more than you already have!"

"But *he's* the one who has hurt *us*—especially you. It's all his fault."

She stepped closer, never more tempted to hit her son. "How dare you suggest your father would ever deliberately hurt anyone he loved! None of the things that have happened are his fault. It's the fault of society—of prejudice and hatred and war! Your father has no control over those things. The only thing a man can control is his own choice in life, and that is what you must also do, James. If you don't want to admit to being part Indian, that is just fine. Your father has told you to do what is in your heart to do. We have always given you that freedom. But I will not stand for your insulting or hurting your father again—not in any way, word, or deed!"

James stared at her, frowning at the firm, determined look in her eyes. She was different this time, angrier, stronger. "I'm sorry," he mumbled.

"Sorry is not enough. If you want to continue living in this house with your mother and your family, you will apologize to Caleb, and you won't tell him I know or said anything to you. And you will promise me never to hurt him again with your selfish, spiteful words!"

"What do you mean, if I want to continue living here?"

"I mean exactly what it sounds as if I mean! You are my beloved son. I would die for you, and so would your father, I might add. But that doesn't mean I have to allow you to keep disrupting this family and hurting your father. Your father works hard for you and has even denied himself things that he needs in order to put money aside so that you can further your schooling, something we both know you want very much to do. You will repay that with respect for your father, or you will leave this house and this family and make your way alone, *without* the money we have set aside for you!"

The boy watched her green eyes and saw firm determination there. He swallowed, realizing she meant every word. "Father . . . set aside money for school?"

"Are you going to do what I have told you?"

He sighed deeply. "Yes, ma'am."

"And you will also apologize to Cale. You had no reason to speak to him the way you did tonight. You will wish him luck at the Sun Dance, much as you might detest what he is doing. It is his choice and in his mind an honorable thing to do. It's important to him, just as your schooling is important to you. And you will stop this ridiculous jealousy you feel for him. I am ashamed of the selfish and childish way you have acted."

James blinked, his eyes tearing slightly. "I don't always mean . . . sometimes things just come out wrong, Mother."

She wanted to soften, as she usually always did. She wanted to embrace him. But at the moment being firm seemed the only solution. He had to believe she meant it when she said he would not be allowed to live with them if he hurt his father again.

"That happens to all of us at one time or another, James. But we don't repeat such things over and over as you have. I will remind you that you are still riding a beautiful Appaloosa—the horse your father brought to you when we had to flee Texas. He bought that horse from Mr. Handel with money we needed very badly, just because it was a pet and you missed that animal dearly. I will never forget how happy you were when you saw that horse, or the way you looked at your father. What happened, James? What put all this bitterness in your heart?"

The boy shrugged and swallowed. "I don't know. I guess it just didn't change the fact that we had to leave in the first place—because of our Indian blood. All those bad things that happened—those men who hurt you and my sister and killed my dog." The boy blinked and swallowed again. "And then those men who stole our horses and shot you. It's always because we're Indian. I just don't understand how Pa can keep being proud to be Indian and be so excited that Cale wants to live with the Cheyenne and take part in that pagan ritual."

"Then I suggest you start at least trying to understand,

James Sax. And even if you can't, you will show some respect for others' feelings and the way they choose to live. Your father would much rather be with the Cheyenne himself, but he gave up that life for me. I won't have you making it all more difficult for him by adding to his problems with your inconsiderate ways. Do we understand each other?"

The boy sniffed. "Yes, ma'am."

"Good. Now you can go outside and bring in some wood. I'm almost out."

The boy turned and went out, and Sarah gasped with repressed sorrow, breathing deeply to keep from breaking down. She didn't want James to see her being weak, not at this crucial moment. Moments later he came back inside with the wood and she ordered him to get more, going outside herself and calling out to Caleb as he approached the house. She put on a smile for him.

"I made a cake for Lynda. Let's take it back over," she told him. "There have been enough words between us this evening. Lynda wanted this to be a celebration, and we will make it one." She hugged him around the middle and Caleb glanced at the doorway, from which James had emerged. The boy hesitated before speaking.

"You got any chores for me tonight, Pa?"

Their eyes held, Caleb wondering at the changed attitude in his son. He looked down at Sarah, who was smiling but also pleading with her eyes to leave well enough alone. He leaned down and kissed her cheek, then looked back at his son. "No. Just get that cake your mother baked and carry it back over to Lynda's. We aren't through celebrating."

James managed a smile and went inside. Caleb looked down at Sarah. "You all right?"

"I'm fine," she answered with sureness. "Just promise me you'll come back after you go with Cale to the Sun Dance. Don't set your eyes on some pretty little Indian maiden. I know all about how older warriors often marry the young girls."

He grinned, bending down and kissing her lightly. "I've got my own young girl right here. And how could I not come back? I'm only happy when we're together." He embraced her tightly. "I'm sorry I didn't get a chance to talk to you first."

"Just be careful out there, Caleb. It's so dangerous for the Cheyenne now. That's my biggest worry with Cale. Life just isn't the same for them anymore. They're a hunted people and things are only getting worse."

"I know. But don't worry about old Blue Hawk here." He looked up to see James coming toward them with the cake. The boy came closer, looking up at his father.

"Let's go surprise Lynda," he told his parents.

Caleb kept an arm around Sarah and put a hand on James's shoulder. "Don't you dare drop that thing."

James managed to grin as they walked back toward Jess and Lynda's cabin. Caleb looked down at Sarah, his mind full of questions. But he sensed those questions were better left unasked.

• Chapter Fifteen •

Crickets screeched into the night air as Caleb sat near Cale, watching Buffalo Boy's mother carefully paint his grandson's entire body with colorful flowers. Both Cale and Caleb wore only loincloths in the hot night, and Caleb had painted his face with stripes in his prayer color, white. Buffalo Boy's family had agreed to help Cale prepare for the ceremony, and Snowbird watched quietly and proudly from the shadows beyond the light of the tipi fire as her mother painted nearly every exposed area of Cale's body, using clays and flower pollens for color.

In spite of several days of fasting and a loss of weight, Cale's body still had a hard, strong look to it. He was taller and broader than most boys his age. Snowbird could see he got that build from his grandfather, whose white father's blood had given him his height. Her family had been glad to aid Cale, for he had become like another son to them, and since his grandfather was the legendary Blue Hawk, they felt even more honored to sponsor the boy. They were anxious to see Cale make up for the disgrace he had suffered at the hands of the Cheyenne women and to have him fully accepted into the tribe, for Cale and Buffalo Boy were very close.

Snowbird secretly dreamed of one day marrying the tall and strong grandson of Blue Hawk, but she dared not be so bold as to mention such a thing, for she was much too young to be thinking of marriage. Perhaps one day, when she became a woman, Cale would come and ask permission to court her. He would bring her father buffalo meat, robes, and horses. Cale was good at catching wild horses, something his own grandfather did for a living. Horses were the greatest gift of all, and she dreamed of Cale's bringing many to her father's tipi one day.

"Grandfather," Cale spoke up, his voice sounding weak and his eyes closed. Buffalo Boy supported one arm that Cale held out to be painted.

Caleb sat cross-legged, watching the ritual painting, keeping a good eye on his grandson and realizing the suffering he had already experienced in going several days without food and the last two days without water. "I'm right here, Cale."

"Do you think I will have a vision that will give me a new name—an Indian name? I would like an Indian name."

"It often happens. Just remember you can't really tell anyone your vision, not even me. But if you feel it is a vision that calls for changing your name, you can tell me that much."

Cale took a deep breath against the mixture of dread and excitement he felt every time he thought about what he would be doing the next day. "Pray hard for me, Grandfather. I don't want to cry out. I would be disgraced."

"You won't cry out. Every time you feel a need to cry out, you will blow hard on your whistle."

"I don't have a whistle."

Caleb untied a small leather pouch from his waist, opening it and reaching inside. He reached out and took Cale's free hand, placing a carved bone whistle in it. "You have one now."

Cale opened his eyes, looking down at the whistle, then glancing at the leather bag and meeting his grandfather's eyes. "That is your own medicine bag!"

Caleb smiled and nodded. "It is. That whistle was given to me when I participated in the Sun Dance. I have carried it around with me for over thirty-five years. Every warrior needs his own medicine bag, Cale, filled with things that give him power and strength. My medicine bag has kept me alive, and its power helped me find Sarah again, brought me a daughter I never knew I had—your own mother. Now I am getting older, and it will be many years yet before I live truly as an Indian. If and when I do, it will mean your grandmother has left me in death, in which case I will have no need for the luck of the medicine bag, because life will mean nothing to me without Sarah. It is time to give my power to others, and I can think of no one more worthy than my grandson, who has chosen to be Cheyenne."

In his weakened condition Cale's eyes teared. Caleb squeezed the whistle into his hand and held his hand tightly. "No tears. You will mess up White Bird Woman's beautiful painting."

Cale managed a smile. "Thank you, Grandfather," he said in a broken voice. "You should not do this. I already have the quill necklace."

"These are things that should go to someone who loves the People, believes in them; someone who will help carry on the Cheyenne customs. I know your father was Cherokee, but to be Cheyenne is to be Indian, the same as Cherokee. And that is the most important thing to remember—the race. Don't let it die, Cale. I see a future where the white man will do all he can to wipe out all Indians and their culture along with them. Don't let it happen. Teach your children not to let it happen. The white man can take away the land, but he can't take away what is inside, Cale—the spirit, the blood. Make it live on."

The boy sniffed and nodded. "I will do all that I can, Grandfather. The things you have given me are such great gifts—a necklace given you by your own Cheyenne mother, the bone whistle you used at your own sacrifice. Yet you have given me a much greater gift. You have given me your love and guidance and some of your power. Please, make my mother understand why I am doing this. And . . . and tell James that no matter how he feels, he will always be my honored uncle and my friend. My feelings for him will never change, and I will pray that whatever he does with his life, he will be happy."

Caleb felt the old ache of loving a son whom he knew he was losing in the worst way. "I will tell him."

Buffalo Boy lowered Cale's arm. The painting was finished.

"Now we can only wait and pray," White Bird Woman said.

Cale held up the whistle, showing it to Buffalo Boy. "A gift from my grandfather. He used it when he also took part in the Sun Dance, many years ago when he was not much older than me."

Buffalo Boy's eyes widened, and he made a little hissing sound of awe as he touched and studied the whistle. "You must have a medicine bag, Cale, in which you will collect things that are good luck charms and will give you power," Buffalo Boy told him in the Cheyenne tongue. "I will make one for you."

Cale looked at him in surprise. "You would do that?"

"You are my good friend. We are like brothers. And I envy you, having the courage to do what you are doing. I will someday, too. But I do not feel ready yet. Not many do this at your age."

Cale straightened, puffing out his chest. "Then it will be even more proof of my bravery—and it will more than make up for my disgrace."

"Your disgrace will be forgotten after tomorrow, Cale."

Cale met his grandfather's eyes and smiled. "*Ai*. After tomorrow I will be an honored warrior, part owner of the sacred Sun Dance Medicine Bundle. After this I can help the priests conduct future ceremonies. And I will bear my scars proudly." His eyes dropped to the scars over his grandfather's breasts, the scars on his upper arms. He met the man's eyes again, realizing how painful his ordeal would be. But Blue Hawk would be watching, as well as Buffalo Boy, and Snowbird. He had not looked at her, but he knew she was watching. He must be a man. "After tomorrow there will be no more doubts about whether I am worthy to be a Cheyenne. After tomorrow I will feel no white blood."

Caleb nodded. "In the morning the dancing begins."

Their eyes held. "You feel good being here, don't you, Grandfather?"

Caleb smiled. "Yes. It is good to be here, Cale." He thought lovingly of Sarah, patiently waiting for him to return. How familiar all of this felt: the tipi, the painting, the medicine bag, the wonderful summer ceremony of the Sun Dance. It had been so many years, and when he had done this, he had been showing off for his beautiful Walking Grass, Tom's mother.

That made him think of Tom. Tom. What had happened to his precious first son? Other responsibilities kept Caleb from going to California to find the man. He could only pray for him, as he must pray now for Cale. If only he could know what was happening in California. But for now Cale needed him here.

James looked up from the fence he was mending to watch his father and Cale approaching. "Jess! They're coming."

Jess looked out over the northern plains to see the two riders. He knew Caleb's outline well enough by now to know who it was. "I'll go get Lynda. You go get your mother."

Both men dropped their tools and mounted their horses, riding toward the cabins, which were a half mile to the south. A man Jess had hired to stay near the cabins when he had to be in the fields stood up from his chair on Sarah's porch, cradling his rifle warily until he realized it was Jess and James coming. Jess headed for his own cabin, and

James rode up to his mother's, dismounting and tying his horse.

"They're back, Carl," James told the man before going inside. "Mother," he called out, barging through the door. "Father is coming with Cale!"

Sarah's eyes widened with joy. She hurriedly untied her apron, walking into the bedroom to get a look at herself in a mirror. She pinched her cheeks and patted the sides of her hair, which was pulled up into a heavy bun. She felt like a young girl, getting so excited at seeing Caleb. It was always this way. But this was especially exciting. He had been with the Cheyenne, and she always worried about losing him to that world, even though she knew better than to think he would ever not return to her. But he had been among Indian women, with their brown skin and long, dark hair and quiet strength. Did he ever wish he had married that kind of woman or wonder what his life would have been like if Walking Grass had lived?

She heard the door slam as James ran back outside, and she hurried out herself to see Lynda walking from her own cabin, leading John by the hand. Jess walked beside them. Lynda was already seven months pregnant, and so far she had carried the baby well. Sarah gave James a warning look not to spoil this moment, but James's own curiosity overwhelmed his feelings of jealousy over Cale.

Grandfather and grandson came closer, and if they did not already know who they were, all of the Saxes would have thought the two men approaching were wild Cheyenne come to do them harm. Cale had chosen to be as Indian as he could be, striping his face in blue, his chosen prayer color because his grandfather was Blue Hawk. Both were dressed in buckskins, and Cale wore the blue quill necklace, as well as the bone whistle, which was tied on a piece of rawhide string around his neck. He wore a red headband, and his spotted horse was painted with signs of the summer celebration—a sun, tipis, arrows, a buffalo, and a blue hawk. Sarah noticed something was different about the blue quill necklace. There was a new stone hanging on it, a lovely, round, reddish stone with something carved on it.

Caleb's horse was also painted. His hair hung long and straight, with a red headband tied around his forehead and white stripes painted horizontally on his cheeks. He was as Indian as any true Cheyenne, and Sarah's heart swelled with pride, as well as ached with the old guilt of where this man truly belonged. He had been with them for several weeks, but he had returned. His moving blue eyes met hers as he rode up to her, sitting tall and beautiful on his mount, like a warrior come to steal her away. But then he had done that, many years ago. He smiled and dismounted, immediately embracing her.

"You are all right?" he asked.

"I'm fine. I've been fine. And so is Lynda."

He kissed her hair and turned to look up at Cale, all of them staring at him proudly. "This is Heammanahku. In our tongue that means Bear Above." Caleb looked at Lynda. "From now on that is what you must call your son. He is no longer Caleb Lee Whitestone. I don't think Lee would mind, and Bear Above hopes that you don't mind. He has survived the Sun Dance with great honor, and he has had a vision, from which he took his name."

Lynda stared at her oldest son, her eyes tearing. He looked much thinner, but well. He wore his hair long, but one side was braided behind his ear with beads wound into it. "Are you all right?"

Cale grinned. "I am fine, Mother. It has been four weeks since the celebration. One of my wounds was infected and it took me longer to heal than I had thought it would. Grandfather helped me get well. He helped me through everything." He looked at Caleb lovingly before looking back at his mother again. "I will stay two days—no more. Then I go back. I have much to learn." His eyes moved to James, and he tossed his head. "How do I look?"

"Like an Indian," James answered. "Kind of scary."

They all laughed lightly.

"Then maybe if the day comes that I have to fight white men," Cale answered, dismounting, "I can just scare them away with my looks."

No one knew what to say, for none of them wanted to

imagine young Cale fighting white soldiers. Yet surely that day was coming.

"Warriors do not openly show their affection," he told his mother. "But since I am not among Cheyenne, I guess I can hug you."

Lynda smiled through tears, embracing her son, the young man who was all she had left of her first husband. "Your father would be very proud of you, Cale—I mean, Bear Above. You will have to let me get used to your name."

"I understand." He let go of her, looking down at her swollen belly. "You are all right, too?"

She reddened a little, putting a hand to her stomach. "Yes. I think this is going to be a good one."

Cale grinned, picking up a wide-eyed John and swinging his brother around, holding him in one arm as he shook hands with Jess.

"I'm glad that everything went all right for you, Bear Above," Jess told him. It seemed strange that he had already lost fatherly control over this young man. But then it seemed Indians did everything sooner than white men. What was it about the Indian spirit that could never quite be captured or controlled?

Cale turned to James, putting out his hand. Their eyes held, and James finally reached out. Cale grasped his wrist and James grasped Cale's firmly. They held for a moment.

"So. We go our separate ways, James. I wonder sometimes—if Grandfather and all of you move away from here, will I ever see my childhood friend again? Will we ever be as close as when we were boys in Texas?"

James swallowed back his emotions. "Probably not. You've chosen a dangerous life, Cale." He rolled his eyes. "Bear Above."

Cale kept hold of James's wrist. "Look at me. Could I have chosen any other and be happy?"

James smiled a little. "No. I guess not."

"For me, living among the Cheyenne will not be as dangerous as trying to live among white men. You can live among white men safely. Just don't forget who your relatives are."

There was a tense moment of silence. James did not answer the statement, and Cale put a wiggling John down and turned to his grandmother, embracing her.

"You remind me of a young Caleb," she told him. "We all love you, Bear Above. You can come to us anytime. Always remember that."

"I will remember. And you will see me often as long as you are here. I will often be around the fort with Buffalo Boy and his family." He held out the new stone on his necklace. "See what Grandfather made for me? He calls it a sun stone. It is round, representing the endless circle of life. And into it he carved a bear, representing my vision."

Sarah studied the stone, touching the quill necklace lovingly. The necklace meant so much—a sort of powerful link for all of them. It was so old, and so much a representation of the heritage of Caleb Sax. "It's beautiful," she said softly. She patted Cale's shoulder. "You are much too thin, Bear Above. Lynda and I will prepare a supper that will fatten you up by tomorrow morning."

They all laughed, but Caleb caught the torment in Lynda's eyes. Jess embraced her reassuringly, and Caleb was relieved at how understanding the man could be. As long as she had Jess, and if the baby was born healthy, his daughter would survive the trauma of losing her precious eldest son to another world. Lynda was a strong young woman, a survivor—a Sax.

"We will eat at our cabin," Sarah told them. "I don't want Lynda doing too much work."

Young John took the horses, proudly showing that he was getting big enough to help with some of the chores. Caleb turned to Sarah, seeing in her green eyes a sudden new concern. She reached out and took his hand, leading him away from the others. His heart tightened. Had she been sick again or was something wrong with Lynda? She turned and looked up at him.

"I'm glad it all went well, Caleb, and I'm relieved to see you back in one piece. And the stone—such a lovely gift. I know it came from the heart." She sighed deeply. "There are more soldiers in the area. Some even came here, asking if we had had any trouble with renegade Cheyenne. If it wasn't so serious, I would have laughed." She tried to smile, but her eyes teared and she looked down.

"What is it, Sarah?"

She swallowed, looking back at him and watching his eyes. How she hated giving him bad news. "Our letter to Tom—it came back."

He frowned. "Came back!"

"Yes. The messenger found Lecho de Rosas, but the land had been broken up and taken over by Americans. He said—" She swallowed before continuing. "He said they told him there had been some fighting there—that the owner, Antonio Galvez, had been killed. Those who live there now don't even know exactly what happened after that. They only know that later several American volunteers and two or three Mexicans who had apparently settled into the Galvez mansion were found murdered there—almost execution-style. Everyone who had anything to do with the ranch was gone, including Juanita Galvez. No one seems to know what happened to her, where she went, or who could have killed all those men."

Their eyes held, and she saw the terror in his own, mixed with the fire of his own remembered vengeance. "If something happened to that girl, I have a damned good idea who could have been involved in those murders— someone who would most certainly seek revenge, just as his father once did!" He turned away, clenching his fists. "Damn! Something terrible has happened, Sarah. Maybe he was hurt in all that fighting. Maybe that's why he hasn't written."

"But the girl is gone. Who else could have taken her but Tom? And if he did, that would mean he's all right, Caleb. We have to believe that."

Caleb stared out at the purple mountains in the western horizon. "Did the man say how things were in California in general?"

"Fairly peaceful now. The Americans have claimed it. Most of the trouble was in the Los Angeles area. A Commodore Stockton is apparently in control there, after some kind of dispute between him and Colonel Kearny. Kearny is on his way back east now with someone by the name of Frémont. There is very little fighting left, other than some raids by guerrilla *californios* against American settlements."

"*Californios?*"

"That's what the Spanish faction who don't want American rule call themselves. There have been some vicious raids, and they say only a handful of *californios* seem to be responsible. They have begun calling them Los Malos, The Bad Ones."

He turned to meet her eyes, and she saw his lonely sorrow. "He's all right, Caleb, I just know it," she assured him. "It's just as before—when we thought he had been killed at the Alamo. You refused to believe the worst then, and you were right. And just as then, I'm sure there is some good reason you haven't heard from him. I'm sure he'll get a message to you soon."

He looked past her, absently watching Jess and Cale talking. "I don't like this, Sarah. A bunch of American volunteers attacking that ranch and killing Señor Galvez, and now the girl is missing. Something terrible happened to her. I feel it. Tom must be suffering some terrible anguish. That would explain my dream a few months ago, when I thought he cried out to me."

She sighed deeply, wishing she could somehow relieve his worry. "I have to make supper, Caleb." She touched his arm. "All we can do is keep the faith and wait to hear from him. We will. I know we will. Poor Lynda felt terrible when the letter came back. She feels as if it's her fault we can't go to California. We can't let her feel too badly about it. Tom means very much to her. They were close. That's why I didn't want to bring this up in front of her. I wanted you to get your emotions under control before we go have supper."

Caleb grasped her arms, leaning down and kissing her hair. "We can only wait—and pray," he told her, "and be glad that at least Cale is all right and all of us are well." He embraced her. "I missed you, Sarah. I hate being away from you."

"And I hate it when you go away."

He pressed her close, and she felt his power, his need. Caleb would want her tonight. And she, him.

"Go ahead with supper. I'll be there in a while."

She managed a reassuring smile. "I wish I hadn't had to tell you about the letter. I thought it best to get it over with."

"It's all right."

She turned and left reluctantly.

"Los Malos," he muttered. "The Bad Ones." Surely these "bad ones" were *californios* bent on revenge for some great wrong. It reminded him of his own days of warring against the Crow, and his anxious heart and discerning mind could not help linking Tom to the guerrilla raiders. It could explain why they had not heard from him. A man bent on revenge thinks only of that and nothing more, not even his loved ones. He could only pray his suspicions were only that—suspicions. Raiding against the Americans could be very dangerous business, and Tom surely had more sense than to get mixed up in such a venture.

• Chapter Sixteen •

The wagon train of supplies moved slowly through the valley, just as the sun nestled behind the next mountain. The men driving the wagons intended to make camp soon. Tomorrow they would be in Sonoma, bringing the latest in clothing and machinery from the East for the Americans in California. There were twelve huge, lumbering wagons, each pulled by several pairs of mules and loaded down with all they could possibly carry. Two men rode in each wagon seat, one driving, the other riding shotgun against Indians and possible outlaws. They had heard of Los Malos, but there had been little raiding lately, according to a scout, and most of that had been farther south. They slowed and began circling to make camp.

That was when the shooting began. The outlaws appeared seemingly out of nowhere, emerging from the surrounding hills like ghosts and descending upon the party of traders so quickly that they had no time to get organized.

Seven drivers went down immediately. Their attackers wore black hoods so that none of them could be recognized. There were eight outlaws all together, and only one was bareheaded. His face was painted, every inch of it, half black and half white, with yellow stripes across each cheek. It was as good or better a disguise than a hood, and to his victims he was every bit the wildest of Indians. His hair was long and black, and his shirtless chest was also heavily painted. His white, even teeth showed a grin nothing less than evil as he aimed his repeating rifle or revolver with sure accuracy and let out a war whoop every time his weapons met their mark.

Three more drivers went down, and the elusive attackers suddenly retreated into the hills, leaving the remaining fourteen teamsters frightened and bewildered. They waited through the night, keeping watch, sure there would be another attack. They pulled in their dead and buried them by lantern light, all of them nervous and shaken. But everything remained quiet.

"What do you think, Lenny?" one of them spoke up after shoveling in more dirt over his dead friends. "They're as cunning as damned Indians, but most of them were dressed like Mexican bandits."

Lenny lit up a thin cigar. "Mexicans—*californios*—no doubt about it. But their leader, the Indian, that part I don't understand."

"How do you know he was the leader?"

"Pretty damned obvious, the way he was painted. Besides, he had a certain arrogance the others didn't have— more daring. You see how close he got? And yet none of us could hit him."

"Maybe he's just a Mexican painted up like an Indian for the hell of it."

"Could be. But he has that air about him and that wild look that smells of true Indian, the way he was painted up—shirtless and all. And the way he rode."

"You think it's that bunch they call Los Malos?"

"They fit the description. But the last we heard, they were farther south."

"Apparently they get around."

"What I don't understand is why they keep it up. It won't change anything. California belongs to the Americans, and that's that. What's the sense in all this damned killing?"

They both stared at the fresh mound of dirt that covered the common grave they had dug for their friends. "Things like this—it smells of plain old revenge, Lenny. Plain old revenge. I mean, it makes sense, you know? The scout said the only ones who get attacked are Americans."

Lenny shivered. "Gives me the chills." He looked around into the darkness beyond the lantern light. "Come to think of it, we haven't seen our scout all day or tonight. Why didn't he warn us of this?"

They looked at each other. Neither had to ponder the answer.

"I'll be glad as hell to reach Sonoma tomorrow," Lenny said.

Lenny's "tomorrow" brought an early-morning attack that caught several of them sleeping. Five more teamsters went down, and the other nine who slept scrambled for their rifles, finding it difficult to believe that twenty-four men had been overwhelmed by only eight of the enemy.

Those eight rode in closer now. Lenny took careful aim at the painted Indian, but just as he was about to fire the man fell to the side of his horse, and Lenny's bullet whizzed through thin air. He cocked and aimed again, but the Indian was also aiming, his pistol in one hand while with the other he held on to his horse's bridle, perched precariously on the side of the mount. The pistol fired, and

Lenny went down, staying alive long enough to see the Indian ride up even closer, now fully mounted again. He looked down at Lenny.

"American swine," he sneered, his white teeth gleaming through the hideously painted face. "You took my woman from me, and you will suffer for it!" He rode his horse over Lenny, pulling a torch from where it was tied to the side of his mount and lighting it. He threw the torch on the top of the wagon beside which Lenny had been shooting. He rode his horse past the man, then quickly jumped the animal over the tongue of the wagon to chase down one driver who was running away. He aimed his revolver, taking an easy bead on the man's back. "Hey, *Vehoe*," he shouted, using the Cheyenne name for "white man."

The man turned, his eyes wide with terror. He raised his pistol, but the Indian's fired first, opening a hole in the man's forehead.

The Indian whirled his horse then, pulling another torch from his gear and setting a second wagon on fire, then reaching down and unhitching the team of mules. He didn't mind killing Americans, but he couldn't bring himself to let the animals die from the heat of the fire.

His friends were doing a good job of finishing off the rest of the Americans, and four more wagons were already burning, their teams also unhitched.

Minutes later, all twelve wagons were in flames, and some mule teams were running off, still attached by harnesses. Only one driver was left alive. He crawled in panicky circles as the outlaws surrounded him, calling him names in Spanish, laughing at his fear. The man finally got to his feet, breathing deeply for courage, waiting for his fate. He stared at the Indian, who approached, looking down at him arrogantly. The Indian aimed his pistol close to the man's face, and the man stood shaking and looking ready to cry.

"Please . . . let me go," he squeaked.

The Indian grinned, suddenly gently releasing the cocked hammer and holstering the gun. "I will let you go. You are perhaps a day or two's walk from Sonoma." The wagons raged in flames by then, billowy, black smoke rising high into the sky, the flames eating up thousands of dollars of valuable supplies. "You go there," the Indian continued. "You tell them what happened here. Tell them it will happen again and again, until the Americans have paid for what they did to the *californios*. You tell them it might be better if they left California."

The man stared at the Indian, amazed at his good English. His accent was slightly Spanish, but everything about his looks was Indian.

"Who the hell are you?" he choked out.

"That is for the Americans to wonder about."

The man's shirt was soaked with sweat as he backed away slightly. "The Bad Ones. You're The Bad Ones—Los Malos—aren't you?"

The Indian grinned more. "Los Malos! Is that what they call us?"

The American nodded.

The Indian began laughing, saying something in Spanish to his hooded men. They all began laughing, exchanging the phrase between them. The American started to grin himself, until the Indian suddenly sobered, riding closer to him, his eyes looking wild. He reached down and grasped the American by the front of the shirt, yanking him close against the side of his horse and bending close to him.

"I will tell you who the bad ones are," he sneered. "You Americans! You came here and murdered at will, raped our women and stole our land! Do not call *us* the bad ones, *señor!* You stole Indian land back east, and you stole Texas, and now you want more! You will not stop until you have it all!" He shoved the man so hard that he landed on his rear. The Indian backed away then, signaling his men and riding off.

The American watched until they disappeared as quickly as they had appeared. He breathed a deep sigh of relief, overjoyed that he was still alive. He turned to see the wagons burning so hard that they roared, and he shook his head at the considerable loss. He got up then, hurriedly removing a mule from its harness and scrambling to find a

canteen. He saw one hanging from the side of a burning
wagon. He ducked toward it and grabbed it off, the heat of
the fire singeing his hat. He grabbed the mule by the harness and pulled.

"Come on, you jackass, let's go. You're coming along in
case my feet give out."

He headed for Sonoma.

Several hours later, deep in the foothills of the Sierras,
seven men removed their hoods, and the eighth washed the
paint from his face.

"Did you see how that man was shaking, Tom?" one of
the others asked the Indian.

Tom Sax grinned, wiping his face with a towel. "I saw,
Jesus." He put down the towel. "We hurt them bad today.
That was a big shipment."

The others, including Rico, agreed. Tom, Rico, and
Jesus had added men gradually over their several months of
retaliatory raids, men as bitter and angry as them; men who
had lost wives and sons, daughters and land; men wiped
out and ruined by American occupation of California. They
were all loyal *californios*, some actually believing they
could eventually make the Americans leave. Tom knew
better, but he would not take away their hopes. His own
goal was simple revenge for Juanita.

"How was la señorita Galvez the last time you visited,
Tom?" one of them asked.

Tom sobered. "A little better. She moves around and
takes care of herself now—feeds and dresses herself, all
that. But she still won't talk, and when she looks at me—"
He turned around, pulling on a shirt. "She always starts
crying." He stared at the Sierras rising, only three or four
miles away. He slowly buttoned his shirt. "She looks at me
with such love sometimes, but when I try to touch her she
screams and runs away. I can't tell for sure if she even
recognizes me."

"She will, Tom," Rico spoke up. "You will see. Someday she will be the Juanita you once knew."

Tom shook his head. "I don't know if that can ever happen." He walked to his gear. Seventeen. Juanita was only seventeen. Would she be like this for all the years she had left to live? Would he ever hold her again or even have the glorious privilege of making love to her, as he so ached to do? He took some paper from his supplies, as well as a quill pen and a bottle of ink. He had to finish his letter to his father and find someone to carry it to Colorado. He knew full well how worried Caleb Sax would be by now, for he hadn't written in a long time, and if Caleb had sent a letter to Lecho de Rosas, its carrier would have found the disaster there and relayed it back to him.

The last thing Tom wanted was for his father to come looking for him. For one thing, Caleb belonged with the rest of the family in Colorado. They needed him. And for another, he didn't want his father to know what he was doing here in California. Caleb would worry even more, and he would most certainly try to discourage him.

Tom Sax didn't want or need any advice or discouragement. He was determined to taste the sweet honey of revenge over and over. He would not stop until Juanita was well. That was his vow to himself, and he would keep it. Los Malos would raid and burn and kill until Juanita Galvez was a whole woman again, or until Tom Sax himself met his death during one of his own raids. With Juanita the way she was, it mattered little to him now if he lived or died.

Sarah ignored the pain that had returned to her joints. The baby was coming and her daughter needed her. Jess and Caleb paced outside Jess and Lynda's cabin, feeling the helplessness all men feel when a woman is having a baby. It was October, 1847. Cale had been gone over two months. He had returned to the Cheyenne he now called family, and Caleb guessed they had gone even farther north, following the buffalo, which were already becoming more scarce.

Seven-year-old John helped James turn a herd of mares from a corral out to pasture. John was strong for his age and had learned early to ride. Jess was proud of his son, who had his father's stocky build, and blue eyes. Jess had himself been orphaned at a young age, and for years he had drifted, never dreaming he would someday have a wife and a son. Now a second child was being born. Lynda had been in labor for twenty-four hours now, struggling to give birth to the child she had prayed for months would go full term and be born healthy.

"Why do we do these things?" Jess asked Caleb, nervously lighting a pipe.

"What things?"

"Get married, have babies. Jesus, a man has a choice to be free as a bird and move from woman to woman, and what does he do? He marries one particular woman and gets himself all tied down, then goes through the hell of listening to his woman lying there screaming with pain—and why? Because he made love to her and got her pregnant. If she survives that, you've got sons and daughters and all that new responsibility, and the thing just keeps going and going."

Caleb only smiled, sitting down on a hitching post and taking a thin cigar from the pocket of his buckskin shirt. "You know damned well why we do it," he told Jess, lighting the cigar. He puffed on it quietly for a moment. "You go along with no one to think about but yourself, and then all of a sudden one woman comes along who strikes you in a certain way—and she can't be had easy like the others. There's only one way to have her and that's to marry her."

For several minutes both men sat thinking their own thoughts, until Sarah finally came to the door. She noticed a look of near worship in Caleb's eyes when he turned to look at her, and their eyes held for a moment. A lovely warmth moved through her at his discerning gaze, and she wondered what the two of them had been talking about. But there was no time for questions. Jess was looking at her anxiously. He stood up. "What's wrong?"

Sarah smiled. "Nothing. You and Lynda have a daughter. Lynda and the baby are both fine."

Jess's eyes teared. "There's no heavy bleeding this time?"

"Nothing unusual that I can tell. I still have to clean them both up. I just thought I'd let you know right away. I'll let you know when you can come and see them."

Jess turned and looked at Caleb, letting out a war whoop and running off the porch to go and tell John. Sarah met Caleb's blue eyes and he walked up the steps, putting a hand to her waist. "You all right?"

Her eyes teared. "Oh, Caleb, we have another grandchild! Isn't it a miracle? I just wish—" She hugged him around the middle. "I wish Tom could be here, or that we would hear from him. Everything would be so perfect then."

He ran his hands over her back, kissing her hair. He knew she was in pain and not telling him. And Tom. Where in God's name was Tom?

"A granddaughter. Our first granddaughter. I'll be damned," he muttered.

Sarah looked up at him and he met her lips, suddenly hungry for this woman who had come into his life and brought so much happiness in his later years. He kissed her hand, then moved his lips to her cheek, her neck.

"Caleb! What has got into you—that look on your face when I came to the door—"

He laughed lightly, kissing her cheek again. "I just love you, that's all." The baby started crying and Caleb grinned. "That's a nice sound." He kissed her once more lightly. "Go clean them up. I want to see my new grandchild."

He let go of her and she hurried inside, and Caleb looked out over the plains again, wondering suddenly if he would ever hear from Tom or see his eldest son again.

"Caleb, where are we going?" Sarah rode in front of him on his horse. "What if Lynda needs me?"

"We won't be far, and Jess knows where we are. They're having a good time enjoying that new baby girl, and James can fend for himself."

It was dark outside, but Caleb knew his land well as he headed to a grassy ravine nestled among cottonwood trees near the river about a mile from the house.

"You mean you told Jess you were riding off with me?"

"Sure. He's an understanding man."

"Caleb!"

He knew her face was reddening and he laughed lightly. "Sarah, for the last two weeks you've been under a strain, waiting for that baby to come. And the delivery wasn't easy for you. Lately I feel like we haven't really been together, there have been so many other things to think about. Tonight we put aside Lynda and Tom and James and all the rest. Tonight it's just you and me. And it just seems easier to forget about problems if you can leave the house and get off alone."

She leaned against his chest, smiling lovingly. "What a nice thought for you to have. Thank you, Caleb."

They rode on quietly as he headed into the trees. It was dark, and this could be a dangerous land, but she was never afraid when she was with Caleb Sax, never doubting his ability to handle himself and protect her if the need arose. She felt suddenly excited as a young girl. They were alone, and she was with her man, the man she loved with the same passion as the young, handsome half-breed who had swept her away so many years ago.

He reached the place he wanted and halted his horse, dismounting and lifting her down. But he didn't put her on her feet. He brought her close, meeting her lips in a searching kiss. She knew Caleb was deeply worried about Tom. It seemed that when he was worried more than usual about someone he loved his passion increased. But she would not mention Tom. She would simply enjoy the moment.

He slowly lowered her, and she met his eyes in the moonlight that filtered through the trees. It was early autumn and the mosquitoes had nearly vanished because of an early frost they had had the week before. But now it was warm again, the night perfect and romantic, with a full, luminous moon.

"It never really changes, does it, Caleb? We've been through so much—so much pain and loss. And yet here we are. The love has never changed. It's just as wonderful and sweet as when we first realized it was there." She ran a hand over his strong arms, breathing deeply, feeling exhilaration at the realization that he could so easily hurt her but knowing he never would. He could be as wild and vicious as the most uncivilized warrior, yet here she was in his arms. "In my whole life I'll never forget how you looked that day you came to see me in St. Louis. You look hardly any different, Caleb."

"And neither do you." He kissed her forehead.

"Oh, Caleb, sometimes I'm half crippled like an old lady. You must tire of it."

"I wouldn't tire of you if you couldn't even get up out of bed. But you're better now and tonight we will celebrate."

He let go of her and took a blanket down from his horse, spreading it out on the grass. Then he took a bottle of wine and two glasses from his parfleche. "I bought this at the fort the other day." He held out the bottle.

"Caleb Sax. You know I don't drink."

"Oh, you've taken a nip or two for pain. What's wrong with some for simple pleasure?"

They sat down on the blanket and he uncorked the bottle, pouring some into each glass, handing one to her. "The man at the fort assured me this is good stuff—imported from France and shipped here from St. Louis. I paid a pretty penny for this stuff, so drink up, woman."

She laughed lightly and took a sip. "Do you think we'll go to California next spring, Caleb?"

"Who can tell? It's hard to plan anything anymore. We'll see how you and that new baby do over the winter."

She breathed deeply, drinking more wine. "This is good wine."

Caleb grinned to himself, pouring her a little more. He knew she still had the pain in her joints, and he wanted her to feel no pain tonight—only pleasure. He kept her talking, never mentioning the past—only the future. He drank a little more himself, but filled her glass faster than he filled his own, until finally she was giggling.

"Caleb, this is so crazy, coming out here in the middle of the night." She laughed. "What if someone comes along?"

"Out here? What's going to come along? A deer, maybe?"

She laughed again. It was not like her to laugh so readily, and he knew the wine was having its effects. He leaned forward and kissed her in the middle of a sentence, and she returned the kiss with great passion, laughing while her lips were still on his and pushing, making him fall backward. She lay on top of him, still balancing her glass, then quickly gulped down the rest of the wine.

"Caleb, do you know what I want to do?"

"What," he answered with a grin.

She sat up, pulling her dress from under her, sitting on top of him as he lay there on his back. "Something I've always been too bashful to do."

He just stared at her lovingly. He could see her well now in the moonlight, which made her even more beautiful. She took the pins from her hair and let it fall over her shoulders, then unbuttoned her dress. Neither talked anymore. She opened the dress and pulled it to her waist, then stood up on unsure feet, removing it the rest of the way. He sat up and took off his shirt, then eased out of his buckskin pants and his loincloth. He lay on his back again, watching her take off her underclothes and toss them aside, the wine she had drunk taking its effect.

"Am I terrible?" she asked.

"No," he answered, his voice husky with desire. "You're beautiful—and wonderful."

"You've done this to me." She smiled and sat down across his legs. "You purposely got me drunk, Caleb Sax."

He ran his hands over her slender thighs. "You're exactly right."

She tossed her head. "Well, I don't care. It feels good." She leaned forward, kissing him like a wanton woman. He returned the kisses gladly, moving his hands over her bottom and massaging her in places that brought out all her passion and removed all inhibition. It was always hard for her to do something daring and different. She was too much of a lady.

"Caleb," she whispered, leaning farther forward and offering her breasts. He cupped one in his hands, leaning up and gently sucking on the full nipple, making her gasp with the pleasure of the lovely sensation that brought to her whole being. He moved to the other breast, gently taking emotional nourishment from it.

A sigh of passion exited Sarah's lips as she moved her mouth back to meet his. She felt his hands searching, exploring, then guiding himself into her. She groaned with the pleasure of it, sitting up and moving with him rhythmically. In her light-headed, ecstatic state she thought to herself that she was riding her grand stallion, galloping across the plains on the most beautiful horse that ever existed. Her mind reeled with a mixture of Caleb and the horse—both wild and beautiful. She rocked in ecstasy as his hands moved over her thighs, massaged her belly. In minutes she felt the splendid pulsations of her climax that pulled at him in gentle desire. She lay over him.

"I want you on top," she whispered.

Caleb grinned, rolling her over. He moved with hard thrusts, and she panted with the same rhythm, groaning his name over and over until he could no longer hold back the glorious release, pouring his life into the woman he loved beyond his own life.

The rest of the night was a wave of sleeping and making love. Morning came all too soon, and Sarah fussed at the fact that she had drunk too much wine. Caleb teased her about her headache and told her she had better "sleep it off." She quickly dressed, embarrassed to be outdoors and naked, and the whole time Caleb continued to tease her.

"Personally, it was one of the most enjoyable nights I've ever had."

"Caleb, stop it," she said almost bashfully, buttoning her dress.

He loaded their things and helped her walk on unsteady feet to their horse.

"Caleb."

"Hmmm?"

She faced him but hung her head. "I remember . . . doing something very brazen. Did I really, or do I just think I did it?"

He chuckled, lifting her and plopping her on the horse. "You did it," he said matter-of-factly. "And I wouldn't mind doing it again. Moments like that don't happen often. You were wonderful, wild as the most wanton woman could be." He mounted up behind her, putting an arm around her and noticing she wasn't smiling. "Hey." He peeked around to see her face red and her eyes teared. He kissed her cheek.

"Sarah, don't make such a thing of it." He sobered. "I love you. You're my wife and my life. It was beautiful. I couldn't help teasing you. I'm sorry." He gave her a squeeze. "What's wrong with giving your man pleasure, and taking your own, when we love each other as much as we do?"

She managed a smile, putting her face against his chest. He kissed her hair. "I love you, Sarah. Thank you for a wonderful night."

"I love you, too," she whispered.

He rode forward, noticing James riding out to meet them before they even reached the cabin.

"Oh, my God, Caleb, our own son! He'll know what we've been up to. I'm a mess!"

"Jesus, Sarah, he sleeps right above us at home. Do you think he doesn't know we still make love?"

"Pa! Pa, a man brought a letter! It's from Tom!"

Caleb's heart pounded and he kicked his horse into a harder run to catch James quicker. James handed him the letter. "We didn't open it yet. Hurry up, Pa!"

Caleb stared at it a moment, seeing his son's name in one corner, his eyes tearing.

"Oh, Caleb, he's alive! He's finally sent a letter!"

James studied his mother's disheveled look and red eyes. Never would he understand why his beautiful mother put up with the hardships loving a man like Caleb Sax had brought her. But he respected the love they shared and felt a little embarrassed at the obvious reason they had been at the river all night.

Caleb dismounted, lifting Sarah down and quickly opening the letter.

· **Chapter Seventeen** ·

Caleb read Tom's letter silently at first, then looked at Sarah. "Something isn't right." He looked at the letter again.

"Read it to me, Caleb, before I die of curiosity," Sarah told him.

"Yeah, Pa, hurry up and read it."

Caleb frowned. "The news isn't very good," he told them both before he began reading.

"Dear Father, I am sorry I took so long to write. There has been a lot of trouble in California. The Galvez ranch where I was working has been taken over and divided up by the Americans. El señor Galvez was killed and my Juanita was abused in the worst way men can abuse a woman. She is recovering at a mission in San Francisco, and I go there often to see her. She is slowly getting better."

"Oh, dear God," Sarah groaned.

"I am working here and there, trying to stay close to her," Caleb continued. *"I pray for the day Juanita and I can marry and that somehow you and Sarah can meet her.*

"I hope this letter finds all of you well. If it were not for Juanita, I would come home to see you. But I am sure you understand why I cannot come. My grief for Juanita is great, but please do not worry about me. I am fine physically.

"I am sorry, but I cannot tell you where to write me. If I give you the name of the mission where Juanita stays, I am afraid you will come looking for me, and that is not necessary. I myself wander from job to job, so have no address.

Please believe me when I tell you not to worry. When all is well again and Juanita and I are settled, I will write and tell you where I am. I ask only for your prayers now, not your presence. Pray not for me but for Juanita. I fear she may never get completely well. It was a terrible thing for her. She was so young, just a child really. I am sorry to bring you such sad news, but I hope to write you with better news soon.

"I do not think I could have gotten through this terrible thing without the knowledge of what you yourself have been through, Father, and how you survived; nor without the strength your love gives me. I thank you for the things you have taught me about strength and survival.

"Please give my love to everyone. My thoughts are with you always. I will write again. Love, Tom."

Caleb lowered the letter, meeting Sarah's concerned eyes.

"My God! Poor Juanita," she said in a near whipser. "The poor child!"

Their eyes held a moment, and she saw the anger in Caleb's. "Bastards," he muttered, turning away. "He's lying, Sarah. He's not working and just sitting around waiting for her to get better." He faced her again, his eyes ablaze with a wild vengeance. "He's his father's son. He was angry before he even left! He's making sure people pay for what happened to Juanita. Tom is not the kind of man to let something like this go so easily. He's part of those outlaws who have been attacking Americans in California. I know it! I just know it. It all makes too much sense!"

She put a hand on his arm. "Caleb. At least you've heard from him and you know he's alive and you know what is going on. He has asked you not to worry and not to go there. Whatever he's doing, it has to be his own decision. He has to find his own way."

His eyes suddenly teared and he turned away. "He has to be going through hell, Sarah. If something like that happened to you or to Lynda, I'd be crazy with vengeance! And if he is part of those outlaws—"

"Caleb, you spent more than half your life protecting

Tom, clinging to him because he was all you had, worried you'd lose the last bit of life and love you had left to you. But he's thirty-five years old, Caleb! You can't go out there and protect him again. Whatever is going on, he has decided what to do, and in so many words he has even asked you not to interfere. Stay out of it, Caleb. Stay out of it and wait until you hear from him again. For God's sake don't ... don't go there and leave me here to worry if you're alive or dead!"

Her voice broke and she turned away. Caleb frowned, turning around and putting his hands on her shoulders, the letter still in one hand.

"I'll leave, Pa. I'll go tell Jess and Lynda what was in the letter."

James rode off and Sarah broke into tears. "I'm sorry, Caleb. It sounds so selfish. But for so many years I've worried about losing you again. I'm terrified of your going off for a long time. Maybe it would be ... like the last time. Maybe you'd never come back. I know it's terrible of me to come between you and Tom."

He sighed, reaching around and crossing his arms over her breasts, hugging her from behind. "You aren't coming between us. And you're right to tell me not to go out there. He doesn't want me there."

"All we can do ... is pray he'll be all right," she sobbed. "And that poor girl."

He sighed and kissed her hair. "Maybe next spring we'll be able to go there—all of us. It would be good for him to have all of us there. Maybe by then Juanita will be all right."

She turned and hugged him. "Oh, Caleb, I'm just tired, from Lynda and last night and all. I didn't mean it. If you think you need to go—"

"No. You're right. And I'm needed here too much. Besides, we made a promise never to be apart again for a long time." He lifted her chin and kissed her lips. "Everything will be all right." He put a hand to the side of her face. "I'm not going anywhere."

Their eyes held and she reached up and touched his

handsome face. "Poor Tom. He finally found someone to love, and now this."

Caleb pulled her close, his heart heavy for his son. But Sarah was right, and that was the hell of it. He could only wait and pray that somehow Tom Sax would find peace and happiness and rise above the hell he had to be going through now.

The raiding continued through the winter of 1847–48. Ranches, supply trains, everything that aided in American settlement became a victim. Crops and barns were burned, and there were even bank holdups. The name Los Malos began to strike fear in the hearts of American settlers, especially those in the more remote areas. Their only comfort was that women and children were always spared; although, as happens in any panic situation, untrue rumors of atrocities against women began to circulate, putting an even uglier brand on the renegade *californios*. The rumors were started from crimes committed by outlaws with no particular mission other than to rob, rape, and murder, allowing The Bad Ones to be blamed. And so, although the vengeful men led by the painted Indian were responsible for great destruction to the Americans, more hideous crimes were blamed on the renegades.

No one doubted that Los Malos were the culprits behind every crime against the Americans. Settlers began to unite. Law and order came to several communities. And meetings were held, where plans were made to try to capture Los Malos and end the murder and destruction for which they were responsible.

All the while, a well-groomed and handsome Tom Sax made regular visits to the St. Christopher Mission to see Juanita, who was slowly recovering. No one recognized the handsomely attired young man as the wild, painted Indian who led the dreaded Bad Ones. The contrast was amazing, but Father Juarez was highly suspicious, although he would never reveal those suspicions to another human being. His heart went out to Tom, who had suffered so greatly, and who now suffered from bitter hatred and the useless determination to find his revenge.

It was January, 1848, when Tom visited again after a two-month absence, during which the raiding had been more heated than ever, reaching as far south as Los Angeles. Father Juarez greeted him in the sanctuary of the mission, where Tom sat alone in a pew, looking lost and lonely in the great room with its statues of the Mother Mary and Christ and its domed ceilings, painted with biblical scenes. The graying and rotund priest quietly approached him.

"Hello, Tom. It is good to see you, my son."

Tom looked up at him with red, watery eyes. He immediately rose. "Hello, Father. I am sorry I was gone so long this time. How is she?"

Though they kept their voices low, their words still echoed in the huge sanctuary.

The priest smiled, motioned for Tom to sit back down. He moved into the pew to sit beside him. "You will be surprised. She is almost normal. She is speaking, and she remembers it all now." He sobered. "It was a terrible few days for her when it all first came back to her. But the sisters have stayed with her faithfully, praying with her, loving her, helping her see that none of it was her fault and making her realize God still loves her and she has nothing to be ashamed of or for which she needs to be forgiven. She is much stronger now, and she has gained a little weight."

Tom brightened, turning and quickly wiping at his eyes, breathing deeply so as not to break down in front of the priest. "What about me? Did she remember me? Ask about me?"

"Oh, yes. We talk about you often."

Tom met his eyes. "Does she . . . still love me? Or does she hate me for not being there when she needed me?"

The father smiled sadly. "She could never, never hate you, my son. She holds no one to blame. She is just . . . more peaceful now, but I am not sure she can ever get over the memories, the nightmares. She still loves you, Tom, but do not expect the kind of love you are talking about. When you talk to her, you will understand what I am telling you. She is changed, and you must love her from a distance, at least for now."

Tom frowned. "What do you mean?"

The priest put a hand on his arm. "You talk to her. It is something you must talk about alone. And be patient with her, Tom. I am sure you will be. You are such a good and strong young man. The sisters are with her now, helping her get ready to see you. While we wait, I wish to talk to you about something else."

"What is that, Father?"

"You, Tom. I want to talk about you."

The young man looked away. "What about me?"

The priest sighed deeply. "Tell me truly, Tom. Are you a part of this gang of renegades called Los Malos?"

Tom looked at him in surprise, and their eyes held for a moment before he answered. Tom turned away again. "I cannot lie to a priest." He looked back at him defiantly. "Yes. I am a part of it—*more* than a part of it. I am the leader." He looked around warily, his dark eyes suddenly defensive and cautious.

The priest put a hand on his shoulder. "Do not worry. No one would suspect, and I care too much for you to ever say a word to anyone. The only reason I suspected is because I remembered how you were when you first brought Juanita here—so full of hatred. And not long after that, the raiding began." He squeezed Tom's shoulder. "It is wrong, Tom. You know how wrong it is."

Tom swallowed, leaning forward with his elbows on his knees. "I know. I try to stop, but I can't, Father. I keep... remembering her... the way I found her... what they did to her. And it isn't just Juanita. It was Americans who destroyed my father's ranch and wealth in Texas and turned him and the family into wandering nomads. My father has never been able to quite get back on his feet since then. The Americans seem to think they are superior to anyone with dark skin." He shook his head. "My father was one of the first settlers in Texas. He lost a wife and two sons and a son-in-law there. He struggled against Comanche raids, drought, disease... and I lost my first wife there, to cholera. We fought so hard to make it work, and then they just came along one day and said we had to leave." He sighed deeply. "I am sorry, Father, but I cannot forget those things or forgive them. Perhaps someday I will be able to, but not yet. If I go to hell for it, then so be it."

"I do not believe God would send you to hell, my son. If I, mortal soul that I am, can see the goodness in your heart, the gentleness in your countenance, the integrity and honesty in Tom Sax, the man, then surely God can see it much more. But what you are doing will not change anything, Tom, and it is wrong to take the lives of people who are perfectly innocent of the atrocities a few others of their kind have committed. Surely you know that. And more than that, the things you are doing will one day lead to your getting yourself badly hurt, perhaps killed . . . or hung. You must stop, Tom. The settlers are gathering their forces, setting traps. They are determined to capture Los Malos. Stop now, before it is too late."

Tom shook his head. "No. I made a vow that I would never stop until Juanita is completely well and is my wife. She might be better, as you say, but until we can find the love we shared before this happened, I cannot stop."

A nun came into the sanctuary then, announcing that Juanita was ready to see Tom. Both men rose, and the priest took Tom's hands. "Think about what I have told you, Tom. My prayers will be with you. Give it up, Tom."

"I appreciate your concern, Father. But I can't stop. Not yet."

Father Juarez frowned. "They are accusing you now of raping and murdering women and shooting down little children."

Tom's eyes widened, and his jaw flexed in anger. "We have not done those things." He drew his hands away. "Father, I swear to you, we have not done those things. It is someone else!"

The father reached out and touched his arm. "I did not say I believed it, Tom. I am telling you how dangerous it is getting. You are hunted men now. It is only a matter of time before you are caught."

Tom's breathing quickened with the desperate anger of being accused of things he had not done. He held the priest's eyes. "It does not matter. If I cannot have Juanita, nothing matters."

The priest sighed sadly and turned. "Come. I will take you to her." He motioned for Tom to follow, leading him through the sanctuary to the several rooms adjoining it where the nuns resided. He led Tom to one of the wooden doors and stopped in front of it. "Remember," he said quietly, "be very patient. Remain calm. It has not been long that she has been so much better. Do not touch her unless she wishes to be touched."

Tom nodded, his heart pounding with anticipation. Juanita! She was better. She would know him. Surely she would get well now and they could be together in the way he had always dreamed of being with her. The priest left, and Tom lightly tapped on the door.

A small voice told Tom to come in, and he suddenly felt weak and sweaty. He slowly opened the door, overwhelmed with love and desire at the sight of Juanita sitting near a window, wearing a cream-colored lace dress and looking to Tom like nothing short of an angel. Her dark hair was brushed out long and shining, and her milky dark skin looked creamy, her complexion more perfect than he realized. With the little weight she had gained she was the comely young woman with whom he had fallen in love. The terrible gaunt look was gone, as were the circles under her beautiful brown eyes.

At first they just stared at each other, but then she looked down at her lap. Tom quietly closed the door, then stepped closer.

"Don't come too close," she said quietly.

He frowned, feeling suddenly awkward and almost afraid. She seemed so delicate. He wasn't sure what to say, how she might react to him. "You . . . you look so beautiful, Juanita. It's true then? You . . . know me now?"

She kept her head down. "It is true. I . . . remember things. The only thing I do not remember is the many days . . . after they . . . first came. And I do not remember your coming for me . . . or my first weeks here." She twisted her hands. "I am just sorry about the way you must have found me—"

Her voice broke and his heart went out to her. He wanted so much to move closer, to hold her. But she looked as if she might run away at any moment.

"It's all right, Juanita. None of it matters. Surely you know that. If anything bad comes from this, it is that you should hate me for not coming sooner. Every time I think of it . . . that I could have saved you from all of it . . ." His voice began to choke. "It eats at me inside," he almost hissed, "until sometimes I think I will be sick to my stomach. I will never forgive myself. Never! And no man could be more sorry."

She shook her head, wiping at a sudden tear. "You have nothing to be sorry for. You could not have known. I have never blamed you, Tom."

He stepped just a little closer, kneeling down. "Look at me, Juanita. Please look at me and tell me you forgive me."

She swallowed, sniffing and meeting his tear-filled eyes with her own. "There is nothing to forgive," she said sadly, wiping at still another tear.

Their eyes held, and she felt flushed with embarrassment at the realization of how he must have found her, what he knew had happened to her. But he looked so forlorn himself that she could not help obeying his request that she look at him.

"Tell me you still love me, Juanita," he said in a near whisper. The statement was almost begging.

Her small body jerked in a sob and she looked at her lap again. "I will always . . . love you. As the most wonderful man I have ever known; as a good friend and as someone with whom I once could have been happy. I love you more dearly than anyone I will ever know again. But I cannot love you in the way you mean. That . . . that is all over, Tom."

His heart beat so hard he could feel it. He wanted to grab her, shake her, squeeze her close to himself and order her not to say such things. He felt a rush of fear and desperation at the words.

"Don't say that, Juanita. You're only saying it because

the bad memories are still so fresh in your mind. In time—"

"No. Time will make no difference. I am stained. The only way I can make up for it is to live a life of purity from now on. Perhaps Father Juarez did not tell you. I . . ." She continued to twist her fingers, staring at her lap again. "I have decided to stay right here at the mission . . . to be a nun. There is peace here. I can be purified. God will remove my stains—"

"No!" He stood up then. "Don't talk that way! I need you, Juanita."

She shook her head, more tears coming. "You are a good man . . . a strong man. You will love again, and—"

"I will *not* love again! Don't do this to me, Juanita, please. All these months I've waited for you to get better, visited you faithfully. Just give it time, Juanita." He reached out and touched her shoulder and she jerked away, jumping up from her chair and moving away from him.

"Please don't . . . touch me," she whimpered, backing up and looking at the floor.

He breathed deeply for control, clenching his fists in despair and helplessness. "Juanita, I love you. I love you just the same as I loved you before any of this happened. To me nothing is different."

"But it is," she whimpered. "It is all different and it cannot be changed." She crossed her arms in front of her, beginning to breathe in rapid, frantic gasps. "It cannot be changed! I am staying here, and I will never . . . never marry. I am so sorry. I love you. I truly do. But I love you only as a good man who helped me."

He just stared at her, sensing that if he touched her again she might become overly upset.

"Juanita, please don't send me away with no hope for the future."

She sniffed, wiping at her tears with shaking hands. "I cannot . . . give you that kind of hope," she squeaked. "I am so sorry. Go back to Colorado . . . to your father. Someday you will find another—"

"No," he said firmly but calmly. "There will not be another. Unless I can have you, I will not have any woman at all."

She felt her cheeks flush again, feeling sad that Tom was so beautiful standing there, looking so lonely and vulnerable. No woman could ask for a better or more handsome man. But she could not bear the thought of even this gentle man doing to her what the horrible men had done to her. Her own shame was so great she could think of nothing more than atoning for what had been done, sure that giving her whole life to God would help erase the ugliness, the horror of it all.

"Then I . . . must pray for you," she said in a shaking voice. "It is . . . all I can do." Her dark eyes turned pleading. "The war is over, Tom. I am trying to also end the war in my soul. If you truly love me, you will understand. You will go on with your life."

A tear slipped down his cheek. "I have no life without you. But I will honor your wishes," he said, straightening and speaking in a voice full of resignation. "You are right. I do love you enough to respect your wishes in giving yourself to the mission and to God. But it leaves me with nothing; nothing but emptiness and hatred. Death means nothing now." He fought another urge to go to her and hold her, turning instead and walking slowly to the door, staring at it as he spoke. "I am glad you are better, Juanita. I have that much to be glad about. I suppose what you have decided is just another punishment for me, a proper one. I don't deserve to have you now. I failed you."

"Don't say that," she whimpered. "It has nothing to do with you, Tom. You must believe me. It is just . . . how I am . . . what I feel. I would not be a good wife for you now. What I am doing—it is best for both of us."

He sighed deeply, shaking his head. He opened the door.

"Tom!"

He turned to take a last look at her, so beautiful, so precious. How he loved her. How he wanted her.

"Will you . . . come back?"

His dark eyes moved over her and he swallowed against a great, aching lump in his throat. "There is no reason to come back," he said quietly. "You have made your decision. It would only make it all harder if I came back."

"But ... how will I know if you are all right?"

He struggled against more tears. "It won't matter, will it?"

Her chest jerked in a sob. "It will always matter," she whimpered.

"But not for the right reasons. Good-bye, Juanita. I love you. I will always love you."

"Good-bye," she whispered. "Thank you ... for what we had ... for helping me ... bringing me here. You are a good man, Tom Sax. I will pray for you. One day you will also be healed. You will love again. I know it in my heart."

He just shook his head, turning and going out. He felt as though a stone was tied to his heart. Nothing had turned out as he had hoped. He told himself that perhaps in time it would all change. He could come back in a month or two, and she would think differently. Yet after what she had been through, perhaps he had no right coming back again and trying to change her mind. If staying at the mission and becoming a nun would help her and make her happy, who was he to ruin it for her? But without her, there could be no joy in life for him. The only relief he could get now would be death. He would go and find it, meet it gladly just as his own father would do if he lost Sarah.

Tom walked out, saying nothing to Father Juarez. He mounted his horse to ride back to the mountains and rejoin his outlaw friends. There would be more hell to pay.

Juanita watched from a window, sinking to her knees and weeping bitterly, grasping her rosary and praying in great earnestness for Tom Sax.

· Chapter Eighteen ·

"Oh, Caleb, I've ruined it all. I've ruined it!"

Sarah lay in bed, perspiring heavily and putting a hand to her chest as though the gesture would somehow help her breathe better. The spring of 1848 was not really a spring at all, but rather a miserable continuation of winter, which had refused to leave and had brought a late, wet storm, as well as another bout with pneumonia for Sarah Sax. This occurred when Caleb was preparing to sell whatever excess items and horses he could and pack what was left into a wagon and head north to Fort Laramie. There they had planned to join one of the several wagon trains that headed for California and Oregon every year.

Caleb had heard plenty of stories about more and more people heading farther west every year, and spring was the time to leave if one wanted to get over the Sierras before early snows hit those ominous mountains. But Sarah had taken ill, and Caleb knew that even if she again survived the pneumonia, she would be left weak for several weeks, too weak to make a trip west and suffer all the hardships that would involve. She simply would not be strong enough in time for the journey.

"You haven't ruined anything," he assured her. "Besides, little Jessica is probably too young. It might be dangerous for her, too. Maybe this is God's way of telling us this just isn't the year to go." He leaned close over her bed, kissing her cheek.

Tears ran out of her eyes and down the sides of her face into her hair. "But it's always . . . next year. And you want so much to find out about Tom. I don't know why you put up with me."

221

"Sarah, stop it." He grasped the sides of her face. "You're worn out and sick, and you're making too much of it. All that matters is your health." He felt the unwanted lump in his throat, the desperation that always engulfed him when he feared for her life. All winter she had suffered more than usual from the unrelenting pain in her joints that made it difficult sometimes for her to even get out of a chair. Now the pneumonia. "Just get well, Sarah," he told her, his voice full of emotion. "You get well, and next winter we'll pamper you like a woman of royalty. We'll get you through the winter and then get you to California." He sat down carefully on the edge of the bed. "From all the things I hear about California, it's the best place in the world for you, if I can just get you there. I can't think of anything better than a place where there is always sunshine and warm weather. They say sometimes you can smell the air off the ocean." He swallowed back the lump. "Remember how we used to love Lake Michigan when we were little, how we could smell the water and the fish sometimes?"

She managed a dim smile. "That was . . . such a long time ago," she whimpered. She began coughing, the deep, choking cough that made her have to sit up and bend over. Caleb held her, smoothing the long hair back from her face. There was a hint of gray in her tumbling red-gold tresses. He held her close, cradling her head against his chest until the awful coughing subsided. It left her even more weary, and he helped her lie back against the pillow, fluffing it for her with one hand while he supported her with the other. She settled back and Caleb picked up a jar of ointment a traveling doctor had left with them.

"Oh, Caleb, that stuff smells so awful."

He unbuttoned her gown. "Soon as this fever goes down I'll bathe you and wash your hair." He dipped his fingers into the greasy salve and began gently rubbing it onto her chest, his dark skin a stark contrast to the soft, lily-white skin of her breasts.

He leaned close again. It was the middle of the night, and he wore only the bottoms of long underwear, his broad, muscled chest bare. The sight of Caleb's handsome face, his perfect build and still solid body, all brought a pain to her heart, the pain of not being a woman who could match him physically.

He gently stroked her cheek with the back of his hand. "You're my best friend, Sarah Sax. You have been that since I was nine years old. I need you in so many ways." His eyes teared. "Get well, Sarah. That's all that matters. I'll be right here for whatever you need."

"But . . . the ranch . . . the horses and chores—"

"Jess and James are handling things just fine. And John rode a full-grown horse earlier today. I would have told you when it first happened, but you were sleeping and I didn't want to disturb you."

The tears came again and she closed her eyes. "Oh, Caleb, the trip and all our plans—"

He leaned down and kissed her tears. "That's not as important as your being well. That's what the trip is for in the first place, you know—to get you to a better climate."

"But Tom—"

"The war with Mexico is over. It's been several months since we got his letter. Maybe things have calmed down now." He had to think positive thoughts. He couldn't bear to think of the possibility that his son had been a part of The Bad Ones, that he might have even been caught and hung by now. And what had happened to the poor young girl called Juanita? The answers would have to wait. His Sarah was sick. She needed him close by, needed the strength only Caleb could give her.

"I'm going outside for a smoke." He tucked the blankets around her neck. "You rest. And you get well, or I'll be very angry with you."

She met his beautiful blue eyes with her green ones, the whites of her eyes red from fever. "I love you . . . so much, Caleb," she whispered. "We'll go next year, I promise."

He leaned close and kissed her eyes. "I love you, too."

She took a deep breath, her chest rattling with phlegm. "You should be sleeping. Now I've made you lose your rest."

"Stop worrying about me. You know how I am. I have sleepless nights whether you're sick or not. And Lord knows I can manage without a full night's sleep. I've done it many times."

He got up and turned the lamp dimmer, then picked up his pants from the foot of the bed and walked as quietly as possible across the wide planks of the cabin floor. He pulled on the pants and took a buckskin shirt from a hook on the wall and put it on, then pulled on his wolfskin jacket. He checked the pocket to be sure his pipe and tobacco were in it, then walked outside.

The night was cold but clear. The late snow lay in a hard crust now, and Caleb guessed that in Colorado's dry climate the snow would be gone by the end of the next day. He stuffed and lit his pipe, then stepped down off the porch, looking up at the wide heavens and at what seemed billions of stars. He thought how as a youth, while living with the Cheyenne, his Indian relatives read those stars, saw signs in them, and used them to determine what to do.

He drew on the pipe and sat down on the steps of the porch.

"Pa?"

Caleb turned with a start. "James! What are you doing up?"

"I heard Mother coughing."

Again Caleb could see the accusations in the boy's eyes. Everything that happened to his white mother he blamed on his Indian father.

"She's got a fever." Caleb turned back. "I intend to stay awake until the fever breaks."

James wrapped his jacket closer around himself and stepped closer. "We won't be going to California then, will we? Mother will never be better in time."

Caleb took the pipe from his mouth, resting his elbows on his knees. "No, I don't expect we'll go. Maybe next year."

James swallowed. "Pa, I . . . I don't want to go there. I want to go east, maybe go to a higher school, learn city ways and all, get a good education and a job someplace different."

The boy waited, his heart pounding with dread that his

father would insist he go to California. Several long, silent seconds passed.

"Have you told your mother?" Caleb finally asked.

"No."

"Well, wait until she's well. It won't set easy with her. It will be hard enough leaving Cale behind."

"You'll have Lynda and Jess with you, and John and Jessica. And once you get out there you'll probably find Tom. You're always happier when you're with Tom."

Caleb frowned, turning to look at the boy, sitting sideways to get a better look at him. "You've always thought I favored Tom and Cale over you, haven't you?"

James swallowed again. He wanted so much to please this man, and at the same time he hated him for being Indian. Why did his love for his father come out all wrong? What made him hold it back? "It's all right. Everybody probably has somebody that's special, even though they love everybody in the family."

Caleb held his eyes. "It isn't that way, James. You've convinced yourself of that, and I stopped trying a long time ago to make you understand that it isn't that way at all." He studied his son, who had shot up in height the past summer and winter and was close to fifteen now but looked much older. "Maybe it's best that you do go east. As much as I love you, James, there is something invisible between us—something that maybe only being apart can heal. If it's something I've done, I'm damn sorry."

The boy shook his head, swallowing back tears. "No, Pa. You didn't really do anything."

Caleb rose, looking down at his son. "Except be Indian. Right?"

James turned away. "Maybe," he said quietly. "I'm sorry, too, Pa."

Caleb put a hand on James's shoulder. "You go east, James, if that's what you want. I have some money saved to help you get started, but you'll have to find work to keep going on your own. I hear there are all kinds of jobs there for a young man who wants to work. And that's something you've never shunned. You've helped me, and God knows you suffered things in Texas that maybe you'll never get over. Maybe getting away from it all will help. I'll always love you just the same."

The boy only sniffed and quickly wiped at this eyes. "I have to go, Pa. It's just something I feel as if I have to do."

"I know. Just give your mother more time. Wait until next spring."

"I thought . . . maybe later this summer I'd leave. If I wait till next spring, it would be too many good-byes for Mother."

"You'll be only fifteen, James."

The boy shrugged. "Lots of boys my age strike out on their own. Jess was alone at thirteen. And you went west at sixteen and joined up with the Cheyenne. Cale's already with the Indians where he wants to be. Why can't I go east?" He turned and faced the man. "I can read and spell and do figures real good. I bet I could get a good job easy back there, and I could go to school on the side."

His eyes lit up with excitement. Caleb could tell even in the dim moonlight. James had not been happy ever since leaving Texas. It tore at his heart to think of the boy's leaving, but to try to keep him would make him just as unhappy as it would have made Cale if he had been forced to stay. They were young men biting at the bit to strike out on their own—find their own way. In this land children grew up very fast.

Caleb sighed. "All right. But you had better let me break your mother in on this one first. And wait until she's completely well. And you write us as soon as you can so we will know where to write and let you know when we get to California and we can keep in touch."

James smiled sadly. "Thanks, Pa."

Caleb studied him intently. "Your mother came to me in Texas by choice, James. She gave up a lot because she loved me. And the love we found together again produced you. That makes you very speical to us. No matter what you think of your Indian blood, you remember that your own mother, who has no Indian blood at all, is proud that blood runs in her son's and daughter's veins. But it has always bothered you. I hope to God you find out what you want out of life. Whatever it is, it isn't here. But then someday maybe you'll find out it *is* here after all. Sooner or later a man goes back to his roots, James. You think about that."

The boy looked away from him. "I . . . I will, Pa." He turned to go inside.

"James."

The boy turned.

"You're a Sax. But that's the name my adoptive white father gave me. Before that my name was Blue Hawk— still is. And you are the son of Blue Hawk. Remember it. Don't dishonor it."

Their eyes held a moment before the boy turned and went back inside.

Caleb stared at the door, tears welling in his eyes.

"Something does not smell right about this one," Tom said quietly. He crouched in the rocks above the camped circle of wagons, another supply train from the East. Tom turned to Rico. "They have not even posted any guards. it is as if they want to be attacked."

Rico shook his head. "We have not been raiding in this area for a long time. They just think no one will come, that is all."

Tom looked back down at the wagons, his dark, fiery eyes looking almost evil staring out from the heavily painted face. This time even his chest and arms were painted. He wore no shirt, just buckskin pants and moccasins, and a heavy belt of ammunition for his repeating rifle and pistol.

"It's a trick, I tell you. Father Juarez told me the Americans have come together and held meetings, trying to figure out how to catch us."

Jesus Vasquez crouched on the other side of Tom and waved him off. "You are letting the father get to you, my friend. I agree with Rico. I say we attack, burn those supplies after we kill the drivers, and take what we need.

They moved stealthily back to their own circle of men, and Tom looked at each one of them as he spoke.

"I think the wagons below are a trap. Rico and Jesus disagree. It is up to all of you whether we go in. We will take a vote. If we are going in, it must be soon, before it is too dark to see all of them. My vote is no."

They all looked at each other, then gave their votes, beginning with Rico. "I say yes."

"Yes for me," Jesus put in.

"Yes," said the next man.

Four more yes's outvoted Tom. He raised his rifle. "We go then," he said quietly. "Get mounted. Hit hard and fast, as we always do. There are only six wagons and only ten men. Jesus, Rico, and I will wait on this side. You others use the rocks for shelter and move around the other side. Give the call when you are ready and we will go in."

The others nodded, moving off at a quiet walk and leading their horses by the reins, careful to avoid the sound of thundering hooves and not to stir a lot of dust. Tom crouched with his friends and waited.

"I think she will change her mind," Jesus said in a near whisper as they crouched beside their mounts.

Tom looked at him. "Who?"

"Juanita Galvez. You go back, Tom. Give her a little time and go back."

Tom turned his eyes back to the edge of the rise over which they would ride any moment and attack the supply train. "I do not think so. They destroyed her, and I shall destroy them."

Jesus sighed. "We must stop, Tom. We cannot go on this way forever. We have seen much revenge. I am tired. I want to find a woman, settle down."

Tom looked at him in surprise. They were good friends now, all of them, especially Tom, Rico, and Jesus. Tom felt the pain of losing even his friends, yet he could not blame them. None of them had the intense need for vengeance that ate at his own heart.

"I cannot truly blame you." Tom sighed deeply, looking at Rico. "And what do you wish to do?"

Rico shrugged. "I am homeless. But I, too, am tired of the fighting. It gets us nowhere as far as getting rid of the Americans. More and more of them come. It cannot be stopped, Tom. It is done."

Tom's eyes teared and he faced forward again, finding it

difficult to look either one of them straight in the eye. He loved them like brothers. "That much is true. Both of you should do what is in your heart to do. For myself, I must continue, even if I continue alone. My father did the same thing once—made war against the Crow all alone. I will do the same, and now that I cannot have Juanita, I pray that someday I will die fighting for her honor." He swallowed. "After today both of you are free to do what you wish, as are the others. Take what you need from this wagon train—money, supplies, whatever. Use it to get yourselves settled again."

The whistle came, sounding only like a bird to the men below. Tom whistled back. "Let's go!"

They quickly mounted up and kicked their horses into a full gallop, as did the rest of the men from the other side. The men sitting around the campfire in the circle of wagons looked up in surprise and scrambled for their guns, but already three of them were down. It seemed to Tom this would be as easy as other attacks had been, but suddenly the canvas over three of the wagons was flung back, and several men with rifles raised up and began firing from each wagon, aiming in both directions.

Tom's eyes widened in horror as Rico and Jesus both screamed and went down, Rico flying from his mount, Jesus and his horse both going down in a tumbling, dusty heap, the horse whinnying and screaming, its nostrils flaring and its eyes wide with pain.

"A trap! It's a trap," Tom yelled to those on the other side. But two of them had already fallen. There was no time to guess how many men there were in the wagons, perhaps five or six in each, and they knew how to shoot. These were not mere settlers and wagon drivers. They were trained men.

So many shots were being fired, the sound was like a constant roar. Horses reared and dust rolled. Pain suddenly ripped through Tom's left thigh, and his horse reared and stumbled sideways.

"It's him! It's their leader," someone shouted.

"Get the bastard! We'll hang him!"

Tom took a quick look at Rico and Jesus, who both

looked dead. Bullets whizzed by him as his horse circled frantically. He thought about riding straight in, letting them fill him with their bullets, but suddenly Juanita's face was as clear to him as if she were standing before him. It was all he could see amid the volley of shots and shouting.

From then on everything happened as though he were dreaming all of it. He turned his mount, unsure if the animal was also wounded. He ducked to the side, amazed that at the moment he actually felt no pain in his leg after the initial hit. He headed his horse up the rise and over it. Whether by luck or a miracle of God, he felt no bullets in his back, and his horse was still on all fours.

Juanita! He only knew he had to get to Juanita and the safety of the mission. He wanted to die, and yet something would not let him deliberately end it all right then and there. It would have been so easy. He remembered men shouting to saddle horses, cursing that they were not prepared to give chase. That was good. That gave him a little time. He rode hard, oblivious to the gaping wound in his left thigh, or the fact that the bone was shattered and he was bleeding dangerously. In his dazed state he still somehow thought clearly enough to realize he would have to find shelter quickly and tie off the wound before riding to the mission. Otherwise he would leave a trail of blood.

He headed for a nearby river. He would ride through it for a ways so that he left no tracks or blood. His horse splashed into it, and the cool water felt good against his wound. He reached down and splashed water onto his face. Somehow later he must find a way to wash off the paint.

Behind him men were ready to go after him, and his friends lay dead, all but Rico, who still had some life in him.

Juanita lit another candle. Every day she had lit a new one for him, praying for his safety. After Father Juarez had told her the shocking news of Tom's activities, she also prayed he would stop before it was too late. The nuns sang their nightly prayers. How she wished Tom could find this kind of peace. And how she regretted having to turn him away. But that could not change.

She knelt and prayed, running through her rosary beads faithfully. Everything was gone—done. This was all she had now. She would not see Tom Sax again, never be the woman she once dreamed of being. All that she owned was gone, except for the money Tom had salvaged for her after attacking the men at her father's home. She prayed again for her father, prayed that God would welcome him into heaven, and she lit yet another candle for him.

She prayed for an hour, as she did every evening before going to bed.

"Juanita!"

The voice of Father Juarez interrupted her prayers, and she turned in surprise at the plump man as he hurried down the aisle of the sanctuary, looking alarmed. He came close, trying to keep his voice down.

"Come quickly! Tom is here, and he is badly wounded."

Her eyes widened and she quickly rose. "How badly is he hurt?"

The man shook his head. "He has lost much blood. It is his leg. I do not know how long it has been since he was wounded, but the wound is already badly infected. He is asking for you. Some of the sisters and I managed to get him to a bed." He put a hand to her waist and led her down the aisle. "Hurry!"

She walked with him, her heart racing with fear. Tom! The worst had happened, but at least he had come to the mission for help. What if he died? Or what if he lost his leg? How could she forgive herself?

"Father, what if men come after him?"

"He arrived alone. I saw no one chasing behind. The sisters have removed everything from the horse and taken it far away and set it loose. No one outside this mission will even know he is here. We will have to treat him ourselves. We cannot even take the risk of getting a doctor. Some of us have treated wounds before. We will do our best. It will help for you to be with him."

He hurried her into a room at the back of the church. Before they even entered it she could hear Tom crying out her name, groaning with pain. She hurried inside with Father Juarez, then gasped at the sight of him. He was already stripped naked, his face, chest, and arms smeared with paint and dirt, as though he had clumsily tried to wash it off but did not succeed. He was so dirty and bloody that she was hardly aware of his nakedness. His chest heaved in great gasps of pain and desperation as the sisters worked quickly to wash him and prepare to treat the hideous wound.

At first Juanita stood frozen. Toms' left thigh was grotesquely swollen, dried blood mixed with a yellow-green discharge around a gaping wound making her feel ill.

"We might have to remove the leg, Father," one of the sisters spoke up.

"No! No! No!" Tom screamed the words. "Juanita! Where is . . . Juanita!"

The girl hurried to his side. He had done so much for her. She must be strong now. He needed her. She could not be his wife, but she could be his friend now, his strength.

"Tom. I am here." She leaned close.

He reached up and grasped her arm, opening frightened bloodshot eyes. "Don't let them do it," he begged, his eyes tearing. "Don't let them take my leg."

He squeezed her arm so tightly that it hurt, but she said nothing. She touched his dark hair, smoothing it back from his forehead. "I won't let them," she said softly.

"Stay with me," he pleaded. He shuddered then with pain as one of the sisters began washing the wound. He sucked in his breath in gulping sounds. "Stay . . . with me."

She had no idea why, but she bent closer, kissing his cheek. "I will stay with you," she told him calmly. "I will not leave you."

His breathing calmed a little. "I don't care if I die," he groaned, a tear slipping down the side of his face. "I just . . . wanted to see you once more . . . be . . . close to you, Juanita."

His eyes closed and he continued to grip her arm with surprising strength. "Don't let go of me," he muttered.

She knelt beside the bed, putting her head down and managing finally to make him let go of her arm. She took his hand and held it tightly between both her hands. "I won't let go," she promised. She began praying while the sisters frantically washed him. There was a general discussion of what should be done, and Juanita looked up at Father Juarez.

"I promised him they would not take his leg. You must do whatever you can to save it, or let him die. He is not the kind of man who would want to live with only one leg."

The old man nodded.

The infection had to be cauterized if there was to be any hope of saving the leg. Even then there was no guarantee. The room was filled with Tom's screams and the smell of burning flesh. Through it all Tom clung to Juanita's hand, until finally he passed out.

Suddenly the room was quiet. Everything that could be done was done, and Tom lay unconscious in the bed, washed and covered. Juanita was alone with him, and never had she prayed so hard as she prayed now for Tom Sax to live.

• Chapter Nineteen •

Juanita never left Tom's side through the night. She fell asleep with her head on the edge of the bed and her hand still holding his. In the wee hours of the morning she awoke to the soft chanting of Father Juarez, who was administering the last rites. Her heart quickened at the deep circles under Tom's eyes, the yellowish look to his normally healthy dark color.

"Father," she whispered, raising her eyes to meet the priest's. Her own immediately teared.

"It does not look good, child. We cannot tell whether he will live. It is important to save his soul. Although he thought his cause was good, he has taken many lives. But I am sure that God will see into his good heart and will welcome him with open arms."

Juanita stood up. "He can't die! He can't," she said through tears, keeping her voice to an urgent whisper. "What will I do? It would all be my fault."

The priest shook his head. "Not your fault, child. What he did was his choice. I warned him where his hatred and bitterness would lead. He has brought it upon himself." His heart went out to her at the desperate look on her face. She had suffered so much. "Pray with me, Juanita."

She shook with the effort of holding back a torrent of tears, kneeling beside the bed again and taking Tom's hand. The priest continued his ritual. When he finished he came around to Juanita's side of the bed, touching her shoulder.

"I sense in him a wish to die, Juanita."

The girl looked up at him with tear-filled eyes. "But why, Father? Why would he *want* to die?"

He watched her sadly. "You do not know?"

She hung her head, breaking into tears, and the priest bent down and grasped her arms, making her rise. "Do not blame yourself, Juanita. But think about what is in his own heart. He loves you very much, and sometimes when a man is so badly wounded, it is only the desire to live that determines whether or not he *will* live. Think about how you truly feel about this man, your true reasons for turning to the church. It is possible God has brought him here this way for a reason. And you, Juanita, could be what decides whether or not he lives. You could give him reason to live, child; or reason to die."

His words rang in her ears as he left her alone with Tom. She checked her tears, trying to think as she stared at the man she once loved, once desired in ways she was sure she could never desire a man again. She realized more fully than ever how much he had also suffered, only in different ways than she had suffered. She daringly allowed herself to remember what it had been like to let him kiss her. It had been so sweet, seemed so right. But that was a different Juanita, one who had never known man. Now she had known the male species in all the intimate ways a woman could know man, only it had all been ugly and vicious. Surely not even Tom Sax could make such things beautiful and sweet for her again, nor could she even contemplate lying that way with him and letting him try.

And yet she loved him so. That had not changed. The priest had said she could help Tom live, and she knew that it was probably true. Was that why God had sent him here? Was she to reconsider some of her decisions? It was all confusing and frightening. His screams of pain still echoed in her ears, as her hand still ached from his tight grip.

"Stay with me, Juanita," he had said over and over. He was so lonely, in some ways just as lost and broken as she.

He stirred then, groaning with pain. It was the first time he had moved or uttered a sound in hours. His face broke out in perspiration and she quickly wet a cloth and gently patted his face. His movement gave her a tiny bit of hope.

"Juanita," he whispered.

"I am here," she said softly.

His breathing was light, and his whole body shuddered. "My . . . leg."

"They did not take your leg, Tom. I promised you they wouldn't."

"Can't feel . . . move it . . ."

"The wound is still very bad, Tom. You must give it time."

His eyes slowly opened. She wondered if she should get Father Juarez, but she also did not want to leave him. His eyes were red with fever. "Promise me . . . you will visit my grave," he whispered.

She swallowed back a lump in her throat. "There will be no grave to visit. You are not going to die, Tom."

"It would be . . . best . . . lose my leg . . . lose you . . ." His eyes closed again.

"I told you you will not lose your leg." She set the cloth aside, summoning all her courage. He looked so pitiful, and she didn't care about anything other than that he must live. She had to do something to make him try harder. She leaned closer, wondering where she found the words. "Tom, look at me."

He opened his eyes again. In his pain and confusion he

wondered if she was just Juanita in angel form. Perhaps he had already died. "Please live, Tom," he heard her saying. "If you live, I promise I will marry you."

He studied her, struggling to determine if this was real or a dream or the path to heaven.

"Do you hear me, Tom? I do not want you to die. If you still want to marry me, I will be your wife, if only you will get better and live. Please, Tom. Please, don't die." He saw the tears in her eyes, felt her soft, tiny hand touch his face. It all seemed so real.

Juanita watched the love growing in his eyes, could almost feel a new surge of energy moving through him. It was done. She had made the promise and could not take it back. Was it what God wanted? If it was, then surely he would give her the strength to keep the promise and to be a woman for this man. At the moment she could not imagine how she was going to manage, but she knew that if any man would understand and be patient with her, it would be Tom. But then maybe he wouldn't even remember the promise. He was so deep in pain that this moment might be forgotten when he was better.

"Tell me . . . again," he muttered.

She took his hand. "I will marry you, Tom, if you live. Please do not die. I could not bear it."

His eyes slowly closed. "My Juanita," he whispered, slipping again into blessed unconsciousness.

Jess moved a hand under Lynda's gown and over firm hips and the smooth skin of her flat stomach. She was warm and relaxed as she slowly moved out of the deep sleep of early morning and turned toward him, curling up against him.

"What do you think you're doing, Jess Purnell?"

He nuzzled her neck. "I just had this urge to make love," he said softly. "I like this time of day—everything quiet and sleepy." He moved on top of her, and she realized he was naked.

"Jess, I'm not even awake," she weakly objected as he pushed up her gown.

"Go back to sleep if you want," he teased, moving between her legs.

She laughed lightly. "Shall I pretend this is all just a nice dream?"

"Well, I should hope a dream and not a nightmare."

She started to laugh more, but his lips met her mouth, and in a moment he was inside her, both of them quickly on fire and moving in rhythmic desire beneath a heap of warm quilts.

Jess loved his tall, beautiful, dark wife in every way a man could love a woman. He felt her pulsating climax, and much as he tried to prolong her pleasure, his was so great in this weak, sweet moment of the morning that his life soon poured into her in his own ecstatic climax. He groaned with the almost painful throbbing, grasping her hips and kissing her hair. Then he relaxed, nuzzling Lynda's neck and remaining inside her for several seconds.

"I love you, Lynda," he told her softly, pulling away from her but remaining close beside her to envelop her in his arms.

She ran her fingers over his muscled forearm. "I love you, too." She rubbed at her eyes and turned to face him, thinking how handsome he was with his thick, sandy hair all tossled and his whole countenance relaxed and sleepy. She kissed the thick hairs of his brawny chest. "What got into you, Jess Purnell?"

He grinned and gently massaged a hand over her breasts. "I don't know. The thought of what it would be like if I didn't have you, I guess."

She settled against him, lying on her back and staring up at the ceiling, pulling the covers close around her neck. "Well, you do have me."

He sighed deeply, lying on his side with his arm over her chest. "Yeah, but you can be pretty stubborn, Lynda Sax Purnell."

She frowned. "What is that supposed to mean?"

He swallowed as though suddenly nervous. "It's just . . . I've been thinking, Lynda . . . about California and all. If things go right over the winter, we'll be going come spring."

"And?"

He kissed her hair again. "And ever since I've known you—been married to you—we've stayed near Caleb and Sarah for your sake. I know how you feel. You grew up wondering who and where your parents were, dreaming of what they would be like. When you found them, it was the first security and love you had ever known. But you have me now and your own family—John, little Jessica. And you're a grown woman."

Her heart tightened, and she told herself to wait, think, remember how much she loved this man. "You don't want to go to California?"

He rubbed her arm. "I'd never do that to you, Lynda—make you be that far away from them. After all, you've already had to give up Cale. But when we go, maybe . . . maybe you and I could settle in some town a little bit away from wherever your folks end up . . . close enough to visit but far enough to have something of our own."

Her eyes teared, and she felt like a foolish little girl. How long had Jess thought such thoughts? How long had he stayed close to her parents simply for her sake, because he knew how much she loved and needed them?

"It's really up to you, Lynda. It's just that I'm almost thirty-eight years old, and I've never had something of my very own. I could have. But I knew you wanted to be near Caleb and Sarah, so I settled for working with Caleb and sharing the load. I've never minded all that much. I love the man. I'd die for him, and I think he'd die for me. But I'm a man, Lynda, and I have a need to know I can manage on my own. I want to own something that's just mine, something I can hand down to John and Jessica. If we go to California, Caleb will end up being near Tom if he can find him, and I can understand that. But I want to do something of my own, Lynda. It's like . . . like I've always been a Sax instead of Jess Purnell. It's like I should have taken your name instead of you taking mine."

He waited, ready for an explosion. Being close to her long lost parents meant a great deal to her and no one understood that better than Jess. Could she understand how he was feeling?

He sighed deeply and lay back against the pillow. "Lynda, this has just been building up inside me. I love your folks like they were my own, and I'm willing to go to California if for no other reason than to help them get there safely. But I've got to have a place of my own once we get there."

A tear slipped down the side of her face. "Tell me the truth." She swallowed to keep from crying harder. "If I insisted we stay on with them, would you leave me to find whatever it is you're looking for? Is it just . . . the drifter in you talking?"

He reached over and put a hand to the side of her face. "No, it's not the drifter. It's just Jess Purnell, the man. And if I left, it would be to find that man, not because of a need to wander, and certainly nothing to do with you. I love you and I need you, Lynda. I don't want to be apart from you —ever, if I can help it. I don't doubt I would probably bury all these feelings and stay on with Caleb, if that's what you insisted on doing."

She breathed deeply. "Jess, I've never thought of you as a Sax. And if I've made you feel like one, I'm sorry. I guess I just took it for granted you were happy with things the way they were. You never let on—"

"I didn't let on because just winning your love was challenge enough. I wasn't about to try to take you away from your folks at that time. Then we had all that trouble in Texas—and more problems when we came here. Then Cale ran off." He sighed, toying with her hair. "It's just been one thing after another. There was never a right time to bring it up. But if I don't do something about it when we go to California, and while I'm still young enough to work my own place, I'll never do it."

She closed her eyes against more tears. "I never realized . . ." She turned to face him and he turned also, drawing her into his arms and letting her cry against his chest. "I'm sorry, Jess. All those years in that orphanage when I had that blue quill necklace, I used to make up dreams about what they were like. I never let myself believe they didn't love me. When I found them and found the hell they had gone through, I learned how much they would have loved me if we could only have been together..."

"I know. But honey, those are lost years now. You're a grown woman with a husband and children of your own. You can't go back and be the little girl your mother never got to hold and raise. And from now on I'd like us to be Purnells, not Saxes. That doesn't mean we can't always remind our children that they also have Sax blood in them. There's certainly plenty in that to be proud of. But I also want them to be proud to be Purnells."

"Of course you do," she whispered. She sniffed, using a quilt to wipe her tears that fell on his bare chest. "Jess, you should have said something a long time ago. I've been awfully selfish, haven't I? When I insisted on helping with the ranch back in Texas, when everything was folding under and then I lost that baby because of it—you should have said something right then. I lost it because I was so devoted to Father, when I should have been thinking more about you and your needs."

He stroked her hair, overjoyed inside that she was more understanding than he had expected. But he knew it was only her love for him that was speaking; that she would always rather be near her parents. He had given something up for her for years. Now she was willing to do the same.

"Those were bad times, Lynda. We were all under a strain. But it's all behind us."

She kissed his chest again. "You do what you need to do, Jess. I'll go along with whatever you decide."

He moved back a little, meeting her moving blue eyes, Caleb Sax's eyes. "You sure?"

She smiled through tears. "I'm sure. I've not been a very good wife, have I?"

"You've been everything I wanted and more." He kissed her forehead. "And if we get out there and find out some bad news about Tom, we don't have to leave out on our own right away. I realize what we find out there will make a big difference in whether or not it's right to leave Caleb."

She snuggled against him. "Tom means so much to him. It worries me that father has had another dream about Tom's being in trouble. Mother said he woke up sweating the other night, sure Tom had called out to him again. Father is usually right when he has those feelings. He's so strong spiritually."

"Well, maybe we'll get another letter before winter sets in."

"I hope so, for Father's sake. Mother says he's so restless, and James's wanting to go east isn't helping anything. That will be hard on both of them."

"I think the boy should go. Maybe once he's away from familiar things, he'll be able to think more clearly about his life."

She looked up at him again. "Is that how you feel?"

He traced a finger around her lips. "Sometimes."

She leaned forward and kissed his cheek. "I love you, Jess. Don't keep things from me. Nothing is more important than being with you and knowing you're happy. But maybe it's best we don't say anything until we get there and find out about Tom. It means waiting over a year yet, Jess. We can't leave until the spring, and it will be late summer by the time we get there."

"It doesn't matter. Just knowing you understand makes me feel better about everything. I can wait a little longer."

He kissed her lightly, then found himself kissing her harder, loving her more for accepting his feelings so readily. She returned the kiss with fervor, wanting to show him how much she loved him, thinking how terrible it would be to live her life now without Jess. He was so much man, and she wanted him to know she thought of him as the separate, wonderful human being that he was. It seemed right to seal their new agreement, and her own new awakening to the man who was her husband, by making love once again.

It was late summer of 1848. The past three months had been agony for Tom Sax, who had had no feeling in his injured leg those first few weeks. Gradually the feeling returned, and it became evident he would not lose his leg. But the wound would leave an ugly scar on his left thigh, as well as leaving his leg stiff and slightly shorter than his right.

Through all the pain and rehabilitation, Juanita was with Tom almost constantly. Watching his suffering and being forced to be near him all helped in her own healing. Gradually she remembered the kind of man Tom really was and saw all the things she loved about him, as well as loving and admiring his strength and determination to be a whole man again.

But old fears still made her hope at times that he would not remember her promise. He had never mentioned it, and in fact behaved more like a close and sincere friend than a man who loved her. She wondered if perhaps he was only afraid to say or do anything more. In spite of his injury and the long, slow struggle to walk again, it was a time of sweet friendship, and a time for a cleansing of the souls. They prayed together often, each asking for help in forgetting the ugly past.

To their relief no one came searching for Tom. Juanita convinced him to cut his hair to a neat, shoulder-length cut, worried that keeping it at its near waist length would draw attention to him as an Indian. With his hair shorter he looked more like a Mexican. It was important that people forget about the painted Indian who had led The Bad Ones. The rumor had spread that the Indian must have crawled away somewhere and died from the wound his attackers were sure he had suffered. Father Juarez, Juanita, and the sisters could only hope everyone would believe that to be the truth and would put the missing "Bad One" out of their minds and stop searching for him.

Tom finally reached the point where he could walk with the help of the sisters and Father Juarez, and he insisted that someone make a cane for him so that he could try walking with no one's help. Juanita found just the right tree branch for a sturdy cane, sawing it off herself with a small hand saw, then cutting off the tiny stems that grew from it and cutting it to a height she hoped would be right. She brought it to Tom, where he sat in an open court at the center of the mission. It was a beautiful, sunny day, and roses bloomed everywhere.

The sisters had helped Tom walk to the inner gardens, where he eased into a heavy wicker chair. They left him there, and he put his head back to feel the sun on his face. He thought about his father, feeling guilty for not having written the man. It had been months. But he was determined not to write Caleb until he was well and walking on his own. Now it was getting almost too late. Winter would soon set in in the Sierras, and he would be hard-pressed to find someone willing to carry a letter over those menacing peaks before spring.

Father Juarez approached him, interrupting his thoughts with his footsteps. Tom smiled. "Hello, Father. Where is Juanita?"

"She will be along soon." The priest frowned, sitting down on a stone bench nearby. "I have some news, Tom, that might concern you."

Tom leaned forward, resting his elbows on the arms of the chair. "Is something wrong? Are they looking for me again?"

The priest shook his head. "It is hard to say. We have a newspaper here in San Francisco, you know. Today I saw in it an article that one of The Bad Ones survived the ambush—a man named Rico."

"Rico! He lived?"

The priest nodded. "Apparently the only reason his wounds were treated was to save him for a show before the public. They wanted a sacrifice, Tom, someone they could jeer at, watch hang."

Their eyes held, and Tom realized what the man was telling him. He thought of what a good friend Rico had been. They all had died—all his friends—all because of Tom's own need for vengeance. The last raid. If only they had not gone on that last raid. His eyes teared and he looked at his lap.

"They saved him—and then they hung him," Tom said, more a statement than a question.

"I am sorry, Tom. Yes. He was hung at Sonoma. They say he went to his death refusing to tell the name of the man who was his leader."

Tom looked at the man again, a tear slipping down his cheek. "Do you think it's true, or perhaps a trick?"

The priest shook his head. "I don't know. I can only pray it is true. Either way, I thought you should know."

Tom nodded, and Father Juarez rose, touching his shoulder for a moment. "It is done now, Tom. God understands."

"I can only hope He does," he answered quietly.

Father Juarez saw Juanita coming. He hurried to intercept her, quietly telling her the news. Her eager smile faded, and she walked past the priest, approaching Tom hesitantly. Father Juarez left them alone, glad that at least Tom's coming to the mission had given Juanita a purpose in life and seemed to have had a healing effect on her.

Juanita moved closer to Tom, holding the handmade cane awkwardly, feeling his pain. "Father Juarez told me," she said softly. "I'm sorry about your friend."

Tom quickly wiped his eyes and breathed deeply before meeting her eyes. "It was cruel—saving him like that just so they could hang him." She saw some of the old hatred returning to his dark eyes. "Bastards," he hissed, looking away again.

She knelt in front of him. "Let it go, Tom. It is done." She pushed the cane into his arms. "Look. I made you a cane."

He studied the sturdy branch, placing his hand on it.

"See how it's curved on the end? It was as if God led me right to this branch. It's perfect."

He took another deep breath, putting on a smile for her. "Should I try it?"

"Yes." She smiled. "But be very careful."

Their eyes held. "You always make me feel better. You cut and trimmed this yourself?"

She nodded her head, her eyes beginning to sparkle. "Come on. I will help you stand up."

She took his arm, and between her and the cane he used his good leg to get to his feet. Then she carefully let go of him, and he stepped out on his own with slow, halting steps. Perspiration broke out on his forehead, and it was obvious he was in pain.

"Not too much," she warned.

"You, uh, you better help me get back to the chair."

She hurried to his side and he put an arm around her small shoulders, leaning on her as she helped him back to the chair. Before he sat down his arm moved down to her waist, surprising her when he suddenly drew her close.

Her face flushed and her heart pounded. It was the first time he had done anything to hint at old, manly feelings.

"Don't be afraid, Juanita. Look at me. Please look at me."

Her breathing was quick, and her arms hung stiff at her side. Her full breasts were pressed close against his chest. "I . . . can't—"

"Look up at me, Juanita."

She swallowed, slowly raising her eyes to meet his.

"I have said nothing before now. But you are stronger, and I cannot take this loneliness any longer. Hearing about Rico—it only makes me know how much I need you." She was so close. Now that he felt better, he had thought more about her as the woman he wanted for his own. "You made me a promise when I lay near death. Tell me it is true— that I didn't just dream it."

She swallowed, unable to take her eyes from his hypnotic hold. "It . . . it is true."

A faint smile passed over his lips, even though there were tears in his eyes. *"Mi vida,"* he said softly. "Tell me you will not break that promise."

Her own eyes teared. "I will not break it. But . . . I am afraid," her voice squeaked.

He only held her tighter, and she was surprised that his strength was more comforting than frightening. Their eyes held, and she realized he was bending closer. She should turn away, she thought, and yet she could not. In the next moment his lips were gently meeting her own in a kiss as light and tender as ever a man kissed a woman. This was nothing like the cruel, vicious acts of Emanuel Hidalgo and the others. Most of them had not even bothered with kisses. A kiss was a tender introduction, an act of love and devotion. The kiss lingered, and she did not turn away.

He left her mouth, kissing her cheek, her eyes. "You tell me, Juanita. You are too delicate for me to decide. You tell me when you are ready to be my wife, and we will have the father marry us. We have time yet. I have more healing to do. I am not in any shape to be a husband in every way, so I guess we're kind of even for now, aren't we?"

She felt herself blushing and she dropped her eyes, suddenly hugging him around the middle. "Help me, Tom," she whispered. "I do love you so, but I am so afraid."

He encircled her in his arms, resting his cheek against the top of her head and breathing in the scent of her hair. "Trust me, Juanita. Trust me, and know that I love you beyond my own life. There is nothing wrong in loving a man with your body and letting him love you back. It is never wrong when it is for love, a way of giving pleasure to the one with whom you wish to share your life, taking his seed and letting it blossom into a child both can love. We both need that, Juanita—each other, a family. Soon I will write my father and tell him we are together and happy. Maybe he will even come to California. I tried to talk him into it once."

He felt her tremble. "It's all right, Juanita. It's all going to be all right. I love you too much to rush you. I am a patient man. I just want to know you're mine. I want you forever at my side. I will never leave you again or let you out of my sight."

From a shadowed alcove Father Juarez watched, his eyes tearing. It was good to see them in an embrace. They would be all right now, as long as Tom was never singled out as the leader of Los Malos.

· Chapter Twenty ·

"Are you sure you have everything you need?" Sarah fussed, walking over and straightening the collar of James's shirt.

"Mother, you checked a million times."

She met his eyes, her own tearing; then she suddenly embraced him. "Oh, James, are you sure you want to do this? To me you're still just a boy."

He sighed, hugging her back and patting her shoulder. "I have to do it, Mother. We already talked about all that. And I grew up a long time ago, back in Texas. I really want to do this, Mother." He pulled away. "I'll be all right. It's a really big supply train I'll be with, all the way from Bent's Fort to St. Louis. I won't be in any danger, and besides that, I'll actually be working for them and making money on the way. Ole Willie Taylor himself is the train master. You know how much Pa trusts him. Willie will watch out for me."

She squeezed his arms, breathing deeply to keep from breaking down. "It could be months before I see you again —maybe even years. You write to us right away, while we're still on this side of the mountains so your letter will reach us quickly, before we leave for California. We'll have to know where to write and let you know how to find us." She swallowed back an urge to scream. What good would it do to tie him down and force him to stay? It would only fill him with resentment, especially toward his father. He was young and reckless and excited, and she had to admit he was intelligent and capable. It was only her own motherly instincts that made her want to grab him and never let go.

"I promised I would write," James told her, sounding impatient.

"And you have the money your father gave you?"

"Yes, ma'am."

She swallowed again, blinking back tears. "It's so strange —all those years I never had my Lynda to raise, hold, love. I didn't get to have her for myself until she was sixteen years old. And now with you, it's the other way around. You're the baby I got to hold and love and nourish and teach. And now you're leaving me. But then I guess that's the way it's supposed to be, isn't it, especially with a son."

His own eyes filled with tears. "You've been a good mother," he assured her, leaning forward and kissing her cheek. "I love you, and I'm sorry for some of the trouble

I've caused—hurting your feelings and all. I've always thought you should have things better, but it's never seemed to matter to you, as long as you were with Pa."

She nodded, a tear slipping down her cheek. "Don't hold him to blame, James. It's all the prejudice that's to blame. He's worked hard, and he's loved me more than any woman could hope to be loved. There are few men as good and strong and brave as Caleb Sax. You remember that, and remember that all those qualities are in your own blood. Please, don't leave without telling him you love him."

He sighed and nodded. "I have to go, Mother. Everybody is waiting outside. Pa will want to get going so he can get back here before dark. You know how he worries about you."

She forced a smile for him, patting his arm and handing him a leather bag packed with dried meat and a variety of vegetables, homemade jam, and other items of sustenance. "I love you, James."

He took the bag and she followed him out, walking straight and sure, ignoring the pain in her joints this day. She did not want her son going away with the sight of his mother in pain as his last memory. She met Caleb's eyes when she got outside. He sat astride a big Appaloosa mare, ready to ride with his son to Bent's Fort. He rode up closer to her.

"Are you all right?"

She nodded, but he frowned with concern. He knew the torture this was for her. He looked over at Lynda, who was hugging James. She let go of him, and James turned to the rest of the family. "You stay near your mother today," Caleb told Lynda.

Lynda walked over to the woman, putting an arm around her. "You don't have to tell me that."

Caleb smiled, then waited for James to load his last bag of supplies and mount up. The boy looked at his father, taking a deep breath. "I'm ready."

Caleb nodded. "Let's go then."

James took a last look at his mother, wondering if he would ever see her again, and realizing with some guilt that his own hatred of his Indian blood was the reason for all of this. "I'll write, Mother. I love you."

He struggled not to break down and cry like a child. He was not a child. He was a man. For a brief moment painful childhood memories swept through him, all the struggles in Texas, the few good times he had had as a much younger boy, when he was still friends with Cale.

But then there had been the war and the Indian haters. He tore his eyes from his mother and urged his own horse into a moderate run, realizing the horse represented one of the few good memories he had. His father had brought it to him as just a colt, after they had had to leave Texas.

He did not look back. He couldn't. Soon Caleb was riding beside him. James stared straight ahead. He was riding beside a man who belonged in this land. But James was sure he belonged someplace else, someplace where he could be white, no questions asked. He became more and more sure of it as he studied the vast emptiness of the rolling plains, then watched his father whenever the man moved ahead of him, long hair blowing in the wind, the fringes of his buckskins dancing with the gentle lope of his horse. In the distance a heard of buffalo grazed, looking like a huge, black spot on the wide plains.

Caleb saw them and pointed. "I'm afraid that's a sight that's getting more and more rare. There ought to be some Cheyenne around the fort. I'll let them know about the sighting. Maybe Cale will be there and you can see him again before you leave."

James said nothing, and Caleb turned to look at him. "Maybe," James finally replied.

Caleb turned away. "You're itching to see the cities of the East, James." He kept his horse close beside James. "I've seen all that—St. Louis and New Orleans, at least. Of course, it's all probably grown a lot since I was there. It's been thirty years or more. From the stories we get at the fort, those places are sure a lot bigger than when I knew them. But that's not for me." He made a sweeping motion with his arm. "This is life, James. Out here a man can be a man, find his peace with the spirits, be on his own. Back there—" He shook his head. "Be very careful,

James. There are dangers there, too. Just a different kind. Men fight with papers and laws rather than brawn and weapons; and they'll smile at you and stab you in the back at the same time."

"It won't be as hard for me, Pa."

Caleb didn't look at him as he pondered the meaning of the words. "No, I don't suppose it will."

The man said nothing more, and James felt the old ache of having botched the moment again. Caleb wanted to talk. These were their last moments together. James was at a loss for words. What could he say? His father knew perfectly well why he was leaving.

It was nearly a half-day's ride to the fort, and they barely spoke the whole way. James was surprised that he was almost disappointed that Cale wasn't there. There were times when he missed his nephew more than he ever thought he would. And in spite of his sureness and determination to leave this land, he felt a last-minute panic as he watched his father talking to Willie Taylor.

Everything seemed to happen too quickly then. They ate together. Caleb bought some supplies and packed them into his gear, then turned to James.

"I have to get back before dark. Willie's leaving in the morning." Their eyes held. "Good luck, James. I'll pray for you."

The boy's eyes teared. "Will you, Pa?"

"Of course I will. I'm just sorry—" The man's voice suddenly choked. "I'm sorry to be the cause of your unhappiness."

James hung his head. "Pa, it's not you—not directly. You're my father. I love you."

Caleb swallowed. "And I love you. Much as you don't believe it, I love you just as much as Tom or Lynda or Cale or any of them. Someday you'll understand that, James. But you've got some growing up to do, some learning, some decisions to make. You're probably right to get away from here for a while. I'll miss you, Son."

James met his eyes, then spontaneously hugged his father around the middle. Caleb hugged him back.

"Good-bye, James," he said, his voice husky with emotion. "Write us as soon as possible."

"I will, Pa."

They embraced for several long seconds before James finally pulled away. "You better go," he told Caleb, keeping his eyes to the ground.

Caleb stood there awkwardly for a moment, breathing deeply to stay in control. There was no sense in making it harder on the boy. "When I see you again, I expect you'll be a grown man, James. You do what you want in life. Just be the kind of man your mother and I would be proud of. Work hard, and don't let anyone cheat you or use you."

"I won't, Pa." The boy sniffed and wiped the back of his hand across his nose, finally looking up at Caleb. Caleb was struck by how little he had realized how much the boy had grown. James was approaching six feet in height, and with his blue eyes and sandy hair and broad shoulders, he was very handsome. This child was the result of the reawakening of the passionate love Caleb Sax had had for his Sarah. And somehow he had let this son slip through his fingers. "By, Pa."

Caleb touched the young man's face for a moment, wondering if he would ever see James again. He could not speak. He squeezed James's shoulder reassuringly, then turned and mounted his horse.

"Nemehotatse."

James's chest tightened. The word meant "I love you" in Cheyenne. He opened his mouth to answer in Cheyenne, but the words "I love you, too" came out instead, as though to accent his denial of his Indian blood.

Caleb stared at him sadly a moment longer, then turned his horse.

James felt a strong urge to run after the man, but his feet would not budge and a voice told him to let it be. He must leave. He must forget. He watched Caleb ride into the open plains. At a considerable distance the man turned once and waved, and James felt an odd chill move down his spine at Caleb's almost ghostly appearance. He waved back. "By, Pa," he whispered.

* * *

Juanita stood beside the man who in moments would be her husband. Father Juarez moved through the long ritual of a proper Catholic marriage, while Luisa watched, crying through the entire ceremony. Tom held Juanita's hand tightly, feeling her trembling, keeping hold of her even in the moments when they were supposed to be apart for the ceremony. He refused to let go for fear she would change her mind and run away. He could never catch her. There would be no more running for Tom Sax. A slow, limping walk was all he would accomplish the rest of his life, most of the time with the support of a cane. He decided to be grateful that he could at least still ride a horse and that he could use his firearms as good as ever.

For today he had left the cane aside. He would stand as Juanita's husband without any support. Today she was the one who needed the support. He ached with the thought of consummating this marriage, yet knew he might have to wait for weeks, maybe months. He had given her his solemn vow that they would be no more than companions until she was ready to be a wife. At least she would finally belong to him and his loneliness would be erased.

He heard himself repeating vows, heard her voice saying the same, and finally it was over. They were pronounced man and wife, and even Father Juarez had tears in his eyes. Tom turned to his new wife, carefully lifting the lace and veil from around her face, meeting her trusting eyes. "I love you," he said quietly before bending close to meet her lips. He kissed her lightly, then straightened, smiling down at her. He could take her now if he wanted. She belonged to him. But she was actually more delicate now than she was when still a virgin and had not known the worst side of man.

"I love you, too." A tear slipped down her cheek.

In the next moment Luisa was hugging the girl, then Tom; followed by a host of nuns and a few church members who liked to attend any wedding just for the beauty of it. Most of them didn't even know the couple involved, but they supported the love such marriages represented. Tom and Juanita were led to the open court of the mission where roses bloomed profusely, filling the air with their perfumed scent. A cake and gifts awaited them. Tom found himself wishing his father could be with him now, and he decided he was finally ready to write to his family. He would send something off right away and hope he could find someone willing to travel over the Sierras with the letter. But it was unlikely the note would ever reach Caleb before the next spring.

Juanita nervously opened gifts, and they ate cake and drank wine. She cried at the thought of what her wedding should have been—a grand celebration at her father's estate, with a *fiesta* that would last for days afterward. But that life was gone now.

Father Juarez took them aside, giving both of them an embrace. "Have you thought about where you will live, Tom, what you will do?"

Tom sighed, shaking his head. "I only know I want to work with horses. With the money Juanita has left and some I had, and my ability to round up wild mustangs on my own, I think I can get a herd started. But I don't know what to do about a place to live." His eyes showed a little of the old hatred. "It might not be easy trying to buy land with so many Americans here now. They will make it difficult for people like Juanita and me."

The priest smiled, taking a piece of rolled and tied paper from a large pocket in his robe. He grasped Tom's hand, turning it up and placing the rolled paper into it. "Not to worry. You now own some land, and no one can take it away from you."

Tom frowned, looking down at the paper, then back at Father Juarez. "What do you mean?"

"I have put some land into your name. It is land that was willed to the mission by one of our own—a man who lost his entire family in a terrible fire many years ago. He was broken and no longer cared about his farm. He willed his land to the mission, and although I talked to him and tried to comfort him, he took his own life. Now there is this land—about a thousand acres, I believe—for which the church really has no use. I am giving it to you. These papers are legal. No one can take this land away from you, Tom. It belongs to you and Juanita now."

Tom looked down at the rolled papers in astonishment, temporarily at a loss for words.

"There is a map rolled up in there, explaining where the land is. It is somewhere in a nice valley—east of Sonoma, I believe. Is a thousand acres enough for raising horses?"

Tom looked at Juanita, whose eyes were wet with tears. He looked back at Father Juarez. "Father, I can't take it. It isn't right—"

"Why not? It is just sitting there, and it is land the Americans cannot touch. It belongs to the church, and the Americans have been careful not to offend the church. God wants the two of you to have a new start, to be together. It would not be easy for you to get land on your own. And it cost me nothing, or the church, so where is the loss to us? There is none, nor is there going to be any argument about it. Just promise me you will always be happy together, and that you will have many children and you will let me know when you do—and bring them here for their christening."

Tom looked down at the paper again. "A thousand acres," he murmured. He looked at Father Juarez, smiling through tears. "Yes. It is enough."

"It will be up to you to get the horses. The land is all I can give."

Tom put an arm around Juanita. "Thank you, Father. Land is the best gift of all! My father would understand that. I think I will write him and tell him. Maybe he will even come here and help me. He would like that. And the climate would be good for my stepmother."

The priest touched his arm. "You miss your father very much, don't you?"

"Very much. We were very close."

The priest nodded. "You are free now, Tom. Go and settle this land and raise your horses. And may God grant you many children."

Juanita reddened as Tom hugged her tighter. "Thank you, Father. I don't know what else to say."

"You do not need to say anything. I can see it in your eyes." He touched Juanita's arm then also. "Just take good care of my Juanita. Be good to her. She will make a fine wife and mother. I know this in my heart."

"So do I, Father." Tom's voice was a near whisper from emotion. He turned to Juanita, fully embracing her. "Land, Juanita! We already have some land. Everything will be good now. You will see."

"There are many *californios* looking for work now, Tom," Father Juarez said. "Hire some, and they will help you protect your land from the miners."

Tom frowned, releasing his hold on Juanita. "Miners?"

"Yes, Tom. Gold has been discovered at the mill near Sutter's Fort. Already San Francisco is growing from new people coming in—suppliers and the like. You have been quietly healing here at the mission and do not know what has been happening. But they are saying that next spring thousands will come from the East seeking the gold. But that land belongs to you. No one can touch it, and you have the right to defend it. Just be careful, my son, and get some men to help you with your new *ranchero*. Legal title has been registered in your name. Perhaps you can even supply the miners with horses, and food, if you farm some of the land. You could become a rich man from this."

Tom looked down at Juanita, already feeling protective of his woman and his land. "Gold," he said aloud to her. He looked back at the priest. "Do you really think many will come?"

The priest smiled sadly. "I am afraid California will never be the same, Tom. Think about the things your father has told you about the white men and their love of wealth. They will come. Believe me, they will come."

Tom sat down on the edge of the bed and pulled off the boot from his good leg, then held out his left leg to Juanita, who sat stiffly in a chair nearby.

"I'm afraid you'll be helping me boot and unboot this foot for a long time, Mrs. Sax. I'm sorry."

She looked at him warily, feeling a damp perspiration rise on her skin as she reached over and helped pull off the boot. Tom winced with pain, holding his leg until the boot was off.

"Are you all right?" Juanita asked softly.

Tom slowly lowered his leg. "I will be in a minute." He sat there breathing deeply, and the little room where Tom Sax had slept for months was suddenly too quiet for Juanita. There was only the bed, and a washstand and basin in one corner, as well as a dresser. Juanita's own things were still in her own room, and she sat staring at her hands now, wondering if it might not be better to go there. She realized with sudden clarity that she was alone in a room with a man who was now her husband.

"That land already feels like home, Juanita." Tom stood up and gingerly walked on the game leg to a wall with pegs on it for clothes. He began unbuttoning his shirt. "I haven't even seen it yet, but I know it is beautiful, just because it is ours." He turned, smiling happily. "I thought a couple of times about going back to my father in Colorado, but I want to stay in California. It is so beautiful here. There are two things the Americans cannot spoil—the land and the climate. I will write my father, and he will come here. You'll see. And you will like Caleb and Sarah very much."

She nodded, glancing at the door as though ready to dart through it. He pulled his shirt from his pants, then noticed her eyes widen as he bared his chest. She had seen him naked while he was sick, even helped wash him. But this was different. He was well now, and he was her husband. Tom frowned, keeping his shirt on.

"What do I see in those eyes, Juanita? Fear?" He walked closer. "What happened to your promise to trust me?"

She looked at her lap again. "I am sorry."

He knelt in front of her, wincing from the pain in his leg. "I will tell you something. My first wife and I were married under conditions much like this—spent our first couple of nights at a mission. She was afraid, too, and I did not touch her the first night; nor would I have touched her the second night if she had not been willing."

She studied the dark hands that he wrapped around her own small hands. "But she was afraid . . . for a different reason. You were . . ." Her voice choked. "You were her first."

His grip tightened almost painfully. "And I will be *your* first," he said almost angrily. "*Look* at me, Juanita!"

She met his eyes, surprised at their commanding fire.

"Unless you have given yourself to a man willingly, you have not given yourself to him at all! Do you understand?"

She swallowed, tears slipping down her cheeks. "Do you really believe that?" she whimpered.

"You damned well *know* I do! I will be your first man, Juanita, because I will be the first one you desire—the first one you want to share your body with. When the time comes that I take you, you will know. You will know to whom you belong—one man. Tom Sax. And I will, by God, make it so you never again give a thought to those others. I am your husband now. You will listen to me and trust me. And I am telling you now to never again say that I was not your first man—the only man who has truly touched you." He put a hand against his chest. "In here— in your heart. They touched only your body. I will go much deeper than that."

She stared at the fiery eyes and knew he meant every word. "Please, do not be angry with me on our wedding night," she said quietly.

Tom closed his eyes and sighed, bending down and kissing her hands. "Go to sleep, Juanita. Get into your gown and get some sleep." He rose then. "I will go out while you change if you want me to. But I will sleep beside you tonight, and you will not be afraid of me." He leaned down and kissed her hair.

"When will we leave for our new home?" she asked as he headed for the door.

He hesitated at the door. "I think we can be ready by the day after tomorrow." He opened the door. "Tell Luisa to be ready. She will go with us. You need her."

"No."

He turned, surprised at the remark.

"Luisa is like a mother to me, and I will regret saying good-bye to her. But it is best we are alone at first, don't you think? All I really need is you, Tom. I must learn this."

The anger left his eyes and a smile passed across his lips. "Yes."

"And I think . . ." She swallowed, rising from the chair.
"I think the trail there might be hard for us—and once we
get there we will be living in a wagon until we build a
house."

He frowned, confused by what she was trying to tell
him. "Yes. That's true."

"So . . . so if we are to be husband and wife—" She
looked at the floor. "It would be easier to do that soon . . .
before we leave . . . while we are here where it is peaceful
and comfortable."

He walked closer. "Juanita, you're confusing me."

"I know. I'm sorry." She looked up at him. "If . . . if you
keep your promise about tonight, then perhaps tomorrow
night—"

He put his fingers to her lips. "No, Juanita. It will not be
planned. And you will not lie down for me out of some
kind of duty. It will be because it is right for you. And I
will know if you truly want me. I refuse to have you just
lie there and bear it as though some kind of wifely submission. That would be little different from what you have
already known. It will be as I said before—you will want
me as you have never wanted a man, and you will know
who is the only man in your life. It will be right, whether
it's before we leave or after we get settled. Now you get
into bed. I will be back soon."

She raised her eyes to meet his. "Thank you," she whispered.

He leaned down and kissed her cheek, then left, feeling
the near pain of being unable to touch his beautiful young
wife on their wedding night. His patience and willpower
were going to be sorely tested for a while. He decided he
would have to draw on that certain strength his father had
always told him only those with Indian blood had. The
thought made him grin.

"I bet you never had to be this strong, Father," he muttered. "I think I will outdo you on this one."

Chapter Twenty-one

Tom studied the white stallion quietly from his hiding place, a huge rock upon which he had climbed and on which he now lay flat, watching his prey. The animal was a prize catch indeed. He had been watching it for days, gauging the best time and place to try to rope it. The proud steed grazed now with its brood of mares in the lush, green valley below.

The stallion reminded Tom very much of Valiente, and he often wondered what had ever happened to that grand animal that he had so faithfully trained just to make an impression on Juanita. Those days of the gentle life and the rich Spanish heritage that was California seemed to be fading. Not only had Americans filtered in steadily since the Mexican war, but the steady stream of newcomers had increased to amazing numbers. It seemed incomprehensible that thousands more might come the next spring, once the Sierras were again open to those who were hungry for gold.

Father Juarez had been right. Finding help in protecting his land had been easy for Tom. He hired several men before he even left San Francisco, for many of those who once helped run the vast *rancheros* now divided up by the Americans were now jobless. Some had taken to the hills to look for gold themselves, but most preferred the kind of work they had always known, and the chance to help run a horse ranch was enticing, even though Tom could offer little in the way of wages for the time being.

Tom had hired four men in San Francisco, men who had their own horses and guns but nothing to do but work sweeping floors in the stores of American merchants, or walk the dusty streets cleaning up horse dung. They jumped at the chance to head for the country and do the work they knew best; as well as being proud to protect the lovely Señora Juanita, the beautiful wife of the man called Tom Sax.

As Tom moved toward his new home he picked up three more men, using his keen insight and knowledge of people as his only guide as to whether they could be trusted. There were no "Emanuel Hidalgos" in these men, no traitors.

Tom had never quite gotten over his uneasiness about being back outside, away from the shelter of the mission. Would anyone recognize Juanita, perhaps add things up, and determine that Tom Sax was the mysteriously vanished Indian leader of Los Malos? The notorious painted Indian seemed all but forgotten now. The raids had stopped and the rest of The Bad Ones were dead. Most people seemed ready to look ahead and not behind. He had even heard a few people talk about the raids and the Indian leader right under his nose.

But rather than find the man, people seemed happier that he had not been found. It was food for talks around potbellied stoves and card tables, and the vanished Indian leader had seemed to take on a bigger-than-life reputation. Tom was amazed at the stories people had concocted about him, all the way from being a ghostly spirit that still rode the hills of California, to an inhuman being that lived with the animals somewhere in the Sierras.

Tom sat up quietly. The stallion did not notice him. He lit a small cigar, grinning to himself at the reputation he had built as the leader of The Bad Ones. It was not unlike the reputation his father had among the Crow, who still feared him. And it seemed ironic that both reputations had been built over the love of a woman.

That love had become an aching need that was at times unbearable for Tom. He had been married three months, and still his marriage had not been consummated. They had come close once or twice, but always Juanita stiffened and began to panic, and he knew she had again tried to please him out of a sense of duty. He wondered how much longer he could go on this way before resigning himself to simply taking her out of his own husbandly rights. But he knew he could never really bring himself to do that.

He had done all that he could. He had built a small cabin for themselves, what he called their temporary house until he was rich enough to build her a better one. And just yesterday he had made a long trip into Sonoma just to buy her some special material to make curtains. She seemed content with her new little house, and she was a good housekeeper and cook—a perfect wife in every way but the one way he needed most.

In order to stay away from her he had poured his energies into building his ranch, spending long hours building fences and outbuildings, riding the borders to check for squatting miners, riding down mustangs to begin to build a herd. He was usually so tired at night that he could fall asleep quickly, so that he did not have to lie beside his beautiful wife and go mad from the temptation to force himself upon her.

He scraped the end of his cigar on a rock to put it out, then put it back in his pocket, slithering down the rock to his horse.

"Come on, boy," he said quietly to the animal. "Time to rope down that white stud below. I think he's in just the right place this time." He quietly worked his mount toward the valley below, keeping to rocks and rises and brush so that the wild-eyed stallion would not spook and run.

Juanita watched, and the hired help who were nearby cheered as Tom came thundering home with the white stallion roped and tied to the pommel of his saddle. Juanita moved down the steps of the little porch of the cabin, her heart swelling with pride. It reminded her of the day Tom had come riding back with the black stallion her father had challenged him to tame, and suddenly the pride and the warm passion she felt for him then moved through her now.

It was the first time she could clearly remember how she felt that day, the odd sensation deep inside, a desire unmarred by the ugliness of rape. Her eyes teared at the realization that she had been nothing short of cruel to Tom, denying him what he most longed for. She did not doubt that if he could claim her, it might even help heal the last remnants of hatred that still boiled deep inside; for if he could have her completely, he would have won the final battle.

He rode up close to her, grinning. "Is he not beautiful?"

The husky white steed reared and pulled on the rope, and Juanita laughed. *"Sí,* he is wonderful!"

"I will get him in the corral. Then I will be in for supper." He turned and rode off with the animal, and she studied his broad shoulders, the way he sat a horse. She knew capturing the stallion was not just a victory over the wild horse, but also over his physical handicap.

"No more," she muttered softly. "I will deny you no more, my love." Her heart pounded with the realization that this time she truly wanted him. This time was different, and she felt like laughing out loud with the joy of it. All day she had been thinking of Tom differently, ever since he had awakened with the recurring nightmare of seeing all his friends shot down. She had been reminded of what he had gone through in avenging her wrong and saving her from the horrors in which he had found her.

Juanita turned and went inside, her breath actually coming hard because of her excitement. She would surprise him. She hurried into the bedroom and began undressing.

It was almost a half hour after that when she finally heard him. He stopped on the porch to wash in a basin she kept there for him, and she snuggled deeper into the quilts when she heard him come inside.

"Juanita?"

"I am in here." She felt scared and silly and excited and terribly in love all at the same time. His footsteps came closer and he drew back the curtain.

Tom frowned. "What are you doing in bed? We haven't even had supper. Are you sick?"

She closed her eyes and drew a deep breath. "No, my husband, I am not sick." She held his eyes. "I am just . . . in love." She pulled one arm out from under the covers, and he could see one shoulder was bare. "Bolt the door and come to bed, Tom, before I lose all my courage."

His heart quickened, and he just stared at her at first, trying to determine if it was different this time. He felt his blood rushing hot and his skin felt prickly. "Juanita, I can't . . . I don't think I could stop this time."

She smiled, and there was something different about her, something alive and beautiful. Desire! He finally saw desire in her eyes. "You won't have to stop this time."

He watched her a moment longer, then turned and walked across the outer room of the little two-room structure to bolt the door. He actually felt light-headed as he moved back into the bedroom, watching her eyes every moment as he began removing his clothes. She had seen him undress before, but she had never watched him as she was watching him now. He stripped down and moved to sit on the edge of the bed, leaning close to her, reaching out and hesitantly touching the long, dark hair that tumbled over her creamy shoulders. "What happened?"

Her eyes began to tear. "I . . . I do not even know. All day I have thought about you. Perhaps God planted you there, in my mind. And then I saw you coming back with the stallion—so proud and sure and handsome—and I thought about how quickly you have made a home for us here, how hard you have worked."

"Juanita, it can't be a payment—"

"No. I do not think of it that way. It is . . . it is different this time. I . . . I felt like that day . . . that day you came riding in with Valiente. I wanted you so that day, even though I was so young. Now I am eighteen, Tom. I am a woman, and I want to be a complete woman. And most of all I want a baby to hold and love. You should have a son, Tom Sax."

He swallowed, instantly on fire, gently taking his hand from her face and grasping the quilts, carefully pulling them down to her waist and exposing her full, firm breasts. His only glimpse of them had been when he had first brought her to the mission. Now their dark nipples peaked with the stimulation of his gaze, and he touched them ever so lightly with the back of his hand.

"Yo te amo, querida," he whispered.

She reached out and touched his thick, dark hair, pulling

his head down to the fullness of her breasts. *"Mi esposo,"* she whispered in reply.

He shuddered with the beauty and wonder of it, the glory of tenderly kissing the smooth skin of her breasts, of hearing a light whimper from her lips, a whimper that bespoke desire, not dread. He could not keep his lips from moving to the nipples, and he groaned as he lightly sucked them, finding a force akin to power move through him at the act, as though doing this gave him some kind of new strength and nourishment.

Her breathing quickened into enticing little gasps as he lingered at her breasts, laying her back and moving under the covers, running his hands over her tiny, soft body. He sucked and kissed her breasts while his fingers found what they were hoping to find, a silken moistness deep in the soft folds between her legs that said this time she desired what was to come.

Juanita knew now that she did not want him to stop. The past was something to put behind them, and these wonderful things they could share were all that lay ahead. Once she let go of her fear and put all trust into this man who loved her, it all seemed so simple and easy and wonderful.

She was quickly lost in him, the room swirling with lovely, romantic Spanish words of love; muscular, dark shoulders hovering over her; moist, gentle kisses pouring over every part of her body; expert fingers bringing out desires she didn't even know existed deep in her womanly being. His own groans and whispers told her this moment was just as exciting and important for him, and suddenly he was moving between her legs.

She felt a hint of the old panic, but he kept whispering her name so lovingly, drowning her in kisses that left her breathless. His big hands moved under her small hips, and suddenly it was done. Her man was inside her. It was nothing like the ugly horror of her rapists. It was like rising up to the clouds of ecstasy, floating in the beauty and splendor of love that was greater than all fear—love that conquered memories and pain. He moved with a beautiful rhythm that she found herself responding to, arching up to him in return.

Never had Tom Sax felt this way with a woman. Taking his first wife had been a beautiful experience. But Bess had never suffered what this beautiful child had suffered, and it was his duty now to erase all of it for her, to make it as beautiful as he possibly could. His joy at feeling her respond as she should, realizing her genuine desire, was overwhelming. It took tremendous willpower for Tom not to release himself too quickly, for never had he known such exquisite pleasure as he felt being inside his new wife.

Tom felt her throbbing climax as she whispered his name with each breath, her eyes closed, her body shuddering. She took him almost wildly, so relieved and overjoyed that it could be as wonderful as he had promised. She cried out almost as though in pain, but he knew that instead it was ecstasy.

"My God, Juanita, it's so beautiful," he groaned, surging inside of her in hard thrusts, changing at times to teasing circular movements that made her grasp his arms tighter and whimper his name. He held back for as long as possible, not wanting the glorious moment to end, but the thrill of it finally brought forth an almost agonizing climax, as he fought it all the way, spilling his life into her unwillingly.

He breathed deeply a moment longer, as she lay there with here eyes closed. He looked down at her tiny body and flat stomach, wondering how he had even fit inside her.

It was done. She belonged to Tom Sax, finally, completely. No other man would ever touch this one again. Those who had already done so had lived to regret it.

He met her eyes as she opened them. *"Gracias, querida,"* he whispered.

She smiled, tears in her eyes. "You liked it?"

He laughed lightly, embracing her tightly and staying on top of her. "I've never felt like that in my whole life. I love you, Juanita. I love you so much." He kissed her hair. "Things are going to be good now. So good. This has been the best day of my life."

He raised up and looked down into her eyes again. "Are you all right? Did you enjoy it?"

She reached up and traced slender fingers over his lips. "You could not tell?"

He grinned. "I could tell. I just wanted to be sure."

Her eyes teared more. "It was beautiful. I wish I would not have waited so long." She swallowed. "Perhaps we should make up for all the lost time."

She felt her cheeks growing hot under the bold remark, and his dark eyes glittered with heated desire.

"Perhaps we should." He met her lips again.

"Dear Folks," Sarah read. *"I reached St. Louis and decided to stay right here."* She glanced at Caleb, pain moving through her. She and Caleb had both found love in St. Louis and had also found tremendous suffering and the agony of separation. How ironic that their son was now there, living in that very city. That had all been so many years ago, another time, another Caleb and Sarah.

"Well? Keep going, Grandma," John spoke up anxiously. "Is Uncle James all right?"

Sarah blinked back tears and returned to the letter. She had asked Jess and Lynda to join them for supper so they could read the letter together. It had come that same day. It was mid-February, 1849, and for once Sarah had had a winter free of major illness. Everyone was healthy, and they prepared to leave for California. Caleb could not bear another year of wondering about Tom, nor could he put off taking his Sarah to a place where the climate meant it would be possible to add years to her life. It was now or never. One never knew what another winter would bring.

"I looked right away for a job and found one within two days with a big supply merchant here. While I work, I am using some of my money for special tutoring so that I will get the equivalent of a college degree when I am through. My boss's name is Gilbert Hayden, and he said he might even send me to even bigger cities farther east someday to hunt for good buys and find out the latest fashions—things like that. The way you used to describe St. Louis to me, you would be surprised if you saw how big it is now. There will even be a railroad built into the city soon, connecting us with all the major cities in the East, and with Chicago."

Memories. They came flooding in. Sarah and Caleb had grown up like brother and sister at Fort Dearborn when that was all it was, just a wooden fort. Now it was a city called Chicago. Her eyes met Caleb's again, and he realized he had better keep some humor in the situation or his wife would break down.

"Too bad they didn't have a locomotive between Chicago and St. Louis when I had to get down there to find you all those years back. Sure would have saved me a lot of time, wouldn't it?" He puffed on a pipe, his eyes twinkling.

She smiled sadly. "We've never even seen one of these locomotives they talk about at the fort. I wonder how big they are."

Caleb shrugged. "Pretty damned big, so I'm told. Big and noisy and dirty. But fast. And contrary to what a horse can do, they can go on forever, as long as you keep feeding wood into their bellies."

"They sound like monsters," John spoke up. "I bet they scare away animals."

Caleb nodded, wondering what the effects of the railroads would be on the peaceful plains and the Indians and buffalo that lived there. Maybe they would never get this far west. Still, he no longer underestimated the power and will of the progressive white man. More would come, and they would bring their railroads with them.

"You going to finish that letter, woman, or do I have to take it from you and read it myself?" Caleb asked.

She smiled, taking a deep breath and continuing. *"I am just fine. We had no problems on the way here. Right now I mostly just stock shelves and take inventory, and Mr. Hayden is teaching me how to keep books. I stay in a room right over the store, so if you want to write me, you can send your letter to Hayden's Mercantile, River Street, St. Louis. I expect to be here a long time, so I will get the letter.*

"I suppose you have heard by now about gold in California. Because of the gold rush, Mr. Hayden is doing a booming business and has already opened a second store. St. Louis is filling up with thousands of people getting

ready to head west. There are so many that there is a tent city growing outside of town. This will be a benefit to all of you, as there will be a lot of people going to California and it will be easy for you to find a wagon train to travel with. With so many wagons the trip should be safe, and there should be lots of help if anything goes wrong.

"It is exciting to be around so many people. I never knew there could be so many in one place. There are schools here, theaters, opera houses, saloons, barbers, doctors, and even places called factories where they make machinery and things. I can't believe the difference between the East and the wide open plains.

"It's hard to believe the West could ever be like this, but some people here say that someday it will be. Most people think the West is wild and dangerous, and a lot of people going there for the first time ask me about it. It makes me feel kind of important to be able to tell them I grew up there.

"I do wish you could see St. Louis again, Mother. I know you often wondered what the latest fashions are like now, so I enclosed some sketches for you that can be bought here at the store and used for patterns."

Sarah stopped, looking into the envelope and taking out more folded paper. She opened it, smiling and holding up the sketches for Lynda. "Lynda, look! We *are* out of style. We had better get the needles going and bring ourselves up to date."

They both laughed lightly, realizing how silly it was to worry about style in the middle of Indian country.

Sarah returned to the letter. *"You and Lynda will have fun with these patterns, Mother. I would send material, too, but I'm not very good at that. You had better buy your own.*

"It's late and I have to get some sleep and get this to a messenger in the morning, so I'll close now. Send me a letter and let me know if you're going to California. I'm tempted to go myself, but this is a good job, and just working at a supply store in St. Louis means getting in on some of the excitement. This job is a sure thing, but running off

*to find gold doesn't sound to me like anything very depend-
able. Besides, I just got to the city. I don't relish the
thought of turning right around and going back out to the
'wild West' as they call it here.*

"My love to all.

"Sincerely, James."

Sarah put down the letter. "Well, he sounds as if he's
doing fine." She tried to sound cheerful. But somehow she
could not shake the feeling that she would never see her
son again.

Caleb nodded, rising from his chair. "Sounds like. I've
got a pregnant mare to check on. You and Lynda can ponder those patterns." He looked at Jess. "You want to come
see how Paint is doing?"

"Sure." The man rose, excusing himself from the table.
Caleb looked at Sarah again before he went out. She knew
what he was thinking. It was unlikely that James Sax was
telling any of his new friends that his father was part Indian. And he had made no mention of how people in St.
Louis felt about the Indians.

Juanita put the finishing touches on the cake. Tonight
she would tell Tom what she was sure of now—that she
was pregnant. Glorious spring had brought green to the
foothills and melted snows in the high Sierras—and it had
brought life to the womb of Juanita Sax. She guessed she
was perhaps four months along. That would mean the baby
would come around October. She wondered if the letter
they had sent to Tom's parents would reach them soon.
They would have to send another, telling them the latest
good news. Tom had urged them to come to California,
and they anxiously awaited the reply. It was already May,
but with the winter snows it was possible the letter would
not reach them before July.

She went into the bedroom to take another look at herself in the mirror. She smoothed her dress, wondering if
Tom had noticed her waist was getting thicker. How many
times had she thanked God that none of her rapists had

gotten her pregnant? God had saved that sacred event for cfthe man she truly loved, and this baby would be perfect.

She heard someone riding hard then and dashed out into the main room and to the door to see Tom coming, riding as though something was wrong. But then he let out a yelping cheer and laughed. She waited with a pounding heart, wondering what on earth he was so happy about. There was no chance to tell him about the baby as he thundered up and dismounted before the horse even came to a halt.

"Juanita! Wait until you see," he shouted, grabbing a leather pouch from his gear. He limped up the steps and grabbed her hand, dragging her into the house. "Look at this!" He opened the pouch and dumped out several nuggets that sparkled gold.

Juanita stared at them, picking one up and studying it. "It . . . it looks like gold."

"It *is* gold! Gold from our own stream that runs through the north quarter and comes from Mission Mountain—*our* mountain! It's lying all over in the bed of the stream, Juanita, which means there is lots more up higher in the mountain!"

She looked at him, blinking in near shock. "Gold?"

His eyes teared and he grasped her hands. "Gold! And it's ours! Juanita, we are rich—richer than this ranch could ever make us!"

Her eyes teared with joy. "Oh, Tom, are you sure?"

"As sure as I am that I love you."

She smiled, hugging him. "Oh, Tom! If it is true—"

"If it is true, I can build you a grand home. You will live the way you once lived, only even better. You will have servants and—"

"All I need is you. You and our baby."

He grinned. "I know, but life will be so much better for us, Juanita. We deserve this after—" He stopped, watching her eyes. "You say 'baby' as though, as though you mean . . ."

She smiled and nodded. "Around October, I think."

He put a hand to the side of her face. "That is even

better news than the gold," he said softly. He enveloped her in his arms. "I never thought I could be this happy, Juanita. We will be rich, and you are with child. How I wish my father could be here, but he probably will not be able to come. He is probably well settled now, or perhaps Sarah is not well." He drew back. "Do you think he will understand in my letter how much I want him here?"

She laughed lightly. "Tom, I don't even know him. How would I know what he will think?"

He hugged her again. "I miss him so much. I want to share all this with him. Here he could give Sarah the life he always wanted to give her."

She leaned back and looked up at him. "We have much to celebrate. I baked a cake for the baby. I was going to make this a special night, tell you the news."

He sighed, kissing her forehead. "And I spoiled it with news about the gold. The baby is so much more important." His eyes teared. "It makes me very happy, Juanita." He sucked in his breath, hugging her close and swinging her around. "What a day! Gold in my land and a baby in my woman. No man could be happier than I am this day."

He set her on her feet, and she looked up into his dark eyes, eyes once full of vengeance and hatred, but now glittering with love and joy. "We must give part of everything we make from the gold to Father Juarez and the mission," she told him. "It is the right thing to do."

He nodded, still finding it hard to believe that so much hell was behind him. "Yes." He kissed her cheek. "I must go to Sonoma tomorrow and have these nuggets checked out, file a legal claim, and make sure this land is properly registered."

"Father Juarez said it is."

"Just to be sure."

She grasped his wrists. "Be careful, Tom. I hate it when you go there. I cannot quite get over the fear of someone knowing—"

"No one knows and they never will. It is all behind us now." He knelt down and hugged her around the hips, kissing her abdomen. "All we need now is for you to have a healthy baby and that you have no problems with the birth."

She ran her fingers through his hair. "I know in my heart all will go well. God has blessed us richly, Tom. He has answered all of our prayers. And He will bring your father. You will see."

• Chapter Twenty-two •

Sarah watched the approaching Indians. They appeared to be all men and gave every appearance of being a war party. She moved closer to Jess, who waited with his repeating rifle ready.

"What do you think, Jess?"

"They're riding in easy. It must be Caleb. They'd be riding hard and yipping it up if they were on the attack."

She shaded her eyes, straining to see if it was Caleb. She was not really afraid. After all, she was the wife of Blue Hawk, and Caleb had left instructions on how to explain that very fact in sign language—giving them his name in Cheyenne. The Cheyenne were not really in the habit of attacking lone travelers, although they had been wrongly blamed for several attacks on supply trains. As a result they were constantly chased by soldiers.

The Sax family was camped along the South Platte, on their way to Fort Laramie, where they would join a wagon train and head west. It seemed the right time to go. Trade with Santa Fe had dwindled to unprofitable proportions, and a cholera epidemic had swept through southern Colorado, chasing off most of the terrified Indians, who suffered the greatest losses from the "white man's" disease. Loss of trade, both with Santa Fe and with the vanished

Indians, had caused a disappointed and despondent William Bent to burn Bent's Fort to the ground. The man had already sent his Cheyenne wife and their children north with other Cheyenne, away from the cholera scourge in the Santa Fe Trail vicinity.

There was nothing left now but to leave the small Sax ranch and again find a new place to settle. Survival in southeast Colorado was next to impossible. But Lynda refused to go any farther without finding Cale and making sure he was all right. She had to see her son once more, and Caleb had gone to find the boy. Sarah trusted that if anyone could locate a Cheyenne camp, Caleb could. Now as the warriors came closer she saw her husband, who was taller and broader than the rest of them. He raised his rifle and called out. "It's all right, Jess."

Jess lowered his rifle as Caleb and another rider rode harder, the others halting and staying several yards behind them.

"Jess, it's Cale," Lynda said excitedly, starting to run out to him.

Jess grabbed her arm. "Wait. You know what Caleb told us. Cheyenne men don't show their affection in public. Don't embarrass him, Lynda."

"But it's Cale."

Jess felt her agony, but as he watched the boy come closer he realized this was not the Cale who had left them almost two years ago. He was all Indian. He wore buckskin leggings and moccasins and a buffalo-hide vest, his horse and uncovered parts of his body painted. The blue quill necklace hung around his neck, and he sported a feather tied into his long black hair, which was braided to one side. The feather was clipped off at the top in a diagonal line. Jess had talked with Caleb about the Cheyenne enough to know what that indicated—killing an enemy by cutting his throat.

"This isn't the Cale you're remembering, Lynda," he said gently as grandfather and grandson rode up close.

Caleb quickly dismounted, looking lovingly at Sarah. She knew he wanted to embrace her but would not do so in front of the others. "I had a harder time finding them than I thought I would."

Sixteen-year-old Cale watched his mother, smiling as he swung his foot around and slid off his mount with agility. "Mother! It is good to see you."

She reached out for him, but he stepped back a little, turning to Jess and putting out his hand. Jess put out his own and Cale grasped the man's wrist firmly. "Hello, Jess."

Jess grinned, returning the grip. "I can't believe it's you, Cale. You've grown so much."

Cale smiled proudly. "I have even ridden against the Pawnee." He pointed to his feather. "Do you know what this means?"

"I do, Son." Jess looked him over. "You all right?"

The boy tossed his head proudly. "No Pawnee can get the best of Heammanahku."

Jess nodded. "That's right. We're to call you Bear Above. It's hard for us to think of you with any name but Cale."

Sarah watched Caleb, whose eyes brightened when Cale just spoke. For a few days her husband had been one of them again, riding wild and free.

"Bear Above brought some of his friends along," Caleb explained. "It's getting too dangerous for an Indian to ride this country alone now. There are so many Easterners moving through on their way to California, and they all think nothing of taking potshots at Indians." His eyes had lost their joy and had turned to anger at the remark.

Cale nodded, his own anger showing. "Many things are changing."

"Yes," Lynda said sadly, realizing Jess was right. This was not the Cale of her memories. He was nearly seventeen now, so tall and strong. The little boy she had once known was gone, and in his place stood a Cheyenne warrior.

Cale glanced at his grandmother, seeing her need as well as his mother's to embrace him. "Come," he told them. He moved past them and around to the other side of one of the covered wagons, then turned to Lynda, reaching out to her. She quickly embraced him, breaking into tears.

"Oh, Cale, I was so worried—the soldiers, the cholera. I couldn't go any farther without seeing you once more."

"I am glad you sent Grandfather to find me. I wanted to come and see you, but we were all afraid to come around the fort and the Santa Fe Trail. When we come there soldiers chase us, and there is all the disease."

He pulled away gently, turning to his grandmother and embracing her. "How have you been, Grandmother?"

Sarah struggled against her own tears. "I had a good winter, Cale. I'm fine."

He glanced at his grandfather, who had already told him about Sarah's frail health. He saw the fear and sadness in Caleb's eyes and the boy understood just how devastated his grandfather would be if anything happened to this woman. He prayed that it would be many years before poor health took its toll on his grandmother.

It was good that Caleb was taking her to the place called California. There it was always warm; perhaps she would get stronger there. And this was a good time to go.

Cale let go of his grandmother, turning to nine-year-old John and grinning. "This cannot be my little half brother. He has grown so much!"

John grinned, excited at seeing his wild brother. "It's me, Bear Above," he said proudly.

Cale laughed and hugged the boy, then turned to his mother. "And where is my new baby sister, whom I have not even seen yet?"

Lynda smiled through tears. "Jessica is in the wagon sleeping. Come and see her, Cale."

The boy ignored her insistence on using his given name. He followed her to the back of one of the wagons and helped her climb in. There was barely room inside for the mattress on whose end little Jessica lay sleeping. Lynda scooted over to the girl.

"It's a little crowded in here," Lynda explained. "Usually Jess and John just sleep outside under the wagon so Jessica and I can have more room."

Cale crawled across the mattress to the baby, and Lynda

pulled away the blanket. "She's nineteen months old already, Cale," she said softly.

Cale stared at a chubby girl with dark, curly hair and fair skin. Her lips were pursed, a finger stuck between them, and she was curled into a little ball. He reached out and touched her hair. "I know she is beautiful without her even being awake," he said softly. "Does she have your blue eyes, Mother?"

Lynda smiled. "How did you know?"

Cale looked at her lovingly. "I was only hoping. You have beautiful eyes. I would want my sister to have your eyes."

Their eyes held for a moment, and Lynda could no longer control her emotions. She covered her face with her hands. "Oh, Cale, I might never see you again." She wept.

Cale grasped her wrists, pulling her hands away. "Mother, do not cry. I am so happy—truly. And you do not have to see me to be with me. I have learned so much living with the Cheyenne, and from Grandfather. Life is just a great circle, like this stone he gave me." He put one hand against the blue quill necklace and the round, painted stone attached to it. "I have learned that the only real thing is spirit. We are spirits first, then are given life. Then we return to the spirit. And the spirit is very strong. My father's spirit is strong. He is with me and with you— always. You and I will not be separated by death like my father, only by miles. But even so, we will always be together; for you will always think of me, and I will think of my mother and pray for her. I miss all of you, yet I am always with you, and you with me."

She sniffed, wiping at her eyes. "But what if I . . . don't see you again?"

His own eyes filled with tears and he leaned forward, kissing her forehead. "I will always know that you love me. And someday we will all be together again anyway. It is only a matter of time before we all walk *Ekutsihimmiyo* to the heavens where we will ride free and have full bellies and be happy and strong. Until that time *Maheo* has given you Jess and John and a new baby daughter. And all sons leave their mothers. The only difference is I have chosen to be with the Cheyenne."

She touched his face. "I was so worried about you during the cholera and all."

"Again I was spared, just as I was when cholera killed John and Bess in Texas. It did not touch me. And I thank the spirits that it did not touch Séhe."

"Séhe?"

The boy suddenly looked embarrassed, and he grinned bashfully. "It means Snowbird. She is Buffalo Boy's young sister."

She thought a moment, then grinned. "Cale! Are you interested in a girl?"

He sat back against a crate. "She is still too young. But when she is a woman—" He shrugged. "We will see. She is very beautiful, and we are good friends, except that now I cannot talk to her anymore. She has had her first flowing, and she cannot be around the young men. When her father allows her to marry, I intend to be ready. Already I have proven my skill and strength through the Sun Dance and in raids against the Pawnee. I have killed buffalo and captured wild horses, as well as stealing horses from the Pawnee. And Buffalo Boy's father is fond of me." He put on the proud air that was so common to Indian men. "When the time is right, Snowbird will be mine."

She smiled lovingly. "You do seem very happy then."

He nodded. "I am. It is a hard life. It is getting harder and harder to move from hunting ground to hunting ground. So many white men come now because of the gold, and sometimes soldiers attack our camps for no reason, blaming us for things we have not done. And still I love the life, Mother. I would have it no other way." He glanced at Jessica again. "Most of the white men not only go through our land, but they cut down all the trees and leave their dead animals in our streams. That is why so many get sick. It is the white man's filth that does it."

He sighed deeply and looked back at her. "We are told by Broken Hand Fitzpatrick that the white man's leader in Washington wants to make some kind of treaty with us. Fitzpatrick is a white scout who is a good friend to the

Indian and often speaks for us to the soldiers and the men in government. He tells us that soon important men from Washington will come here and show us what land is ours, where we can live safely, hunt all we want, be free of white settlement. Grandfather is afraid it will never work, but we have little choice. We must trust these men and know where we can live freely without worrying about our women and children being slaughtered by white settlers. I just hope the whites will stop killing and scaring off the buffalo. Without the buffalo we cannot survive."

She watched him sadly, wiping at her eyes. "Oh, Cale, I hate to leave you to all of that."

"It would not matter, Mother, if you are here or far away. I will still be with the Cheyenne. This is what you must remember. You must go on with your own life—with Jess and John and Jessica. Remember what I told you, Mother. Life is one great circle. And the spirit has much power. We are never really apart from our loved ones."

She reached out and grasped his hands. "You have learned how to be so strong, Cale. I will remember your words." Her eyes teared again. This was her son, the baby she had nurtured at her breast, the seed of Lee Whitestone, her strong, loving Cherokee husband. She leaned forward and embraced him. "God be with you, Cale."

It seemed so strange that he could be so wild and yet such a loving son. "Thank you for coming, Cale. I was so afraid we'd reach Fort Laramie before finding you, and then it would be too late. Please stay the night. Your friends can camp nearby. We have plenty of coffee and tobacco. Is there anything you need?"

He grinned at her motherly concern. "No. The spring hunt was good, and we traded robes at Fort Laramie for other things we need. But I will stay if you wish. Then I can see my sister when she is awake."

Lynda turned to the baby, patting her bottom. "She'll never know you, Cale."

He touched the thick curls of his sister's hair again. "She will know me. You will tell her. You will not let her forget

that I exist. She will know me as well as if we were together, because you will make me live for her, just as you
always made my father live for me by telling me so many
things about him. I feel I knew him well, even though I
never got to see him." He smiled, meeting her eyes.

"Yes, she will know you, both as Cale and as Bear
Above."

Jessica started to stir and Cale moved to the back of the
wagon. "I will go and tell my friends that we are staying
until sunrise."

He climbed out, talking more with the others outside the
wagon before mounting up and riding back to his friends.

Lynda heard him call out something to them in the
Cheyenne tongue. She leaned down and drew Jessica into
her arms, tears coming again. It would not be easy leaving
her firstborn for a second time, perhaps forever.

The night was still, except for the constant singing of
crickets and the occasional sound of voices somewhere in
the distance—men gambling around a campfire, the occasional cry of a baby, a dog barking, a couple arguing over
something in the confines of their wagon, trying to keep
their voices down.

The Saxes were a part of a huge wagon train that was
camped now not far from Fort Hall in Unorganized Territory. They were deep in the Rockies, not far from the western slopes that would lead them to the Humboldt River and
through the broad desert of northern Nevada and on to the
Sierras.

At Fort Laramie, Caleb had sold the small herd he had
brought along. It was an easy sale and a profitable one, as
the United States army had just that year purchased the fort
from the American Fur Company. Fur trade had all but
vanished, and with so many thousands of people migrating
westward, problems with Indians had increased, and citizens shouted for more protection. Now more and more of
the old fur trading posts were being converted to army
forts.

The flow of people headed for California was overwhelming to the Saxes. Some of the people who were a part of their wagon train were simple farmers, people fleeing worn-out land and higher taxes in the East, searching for something better. But in this year of 1849, most were going to California to prospect for gold.

There were hordes of people along—merchants, blacksmiths, prostitutes, and some Caleb was convinced were criminals fleeing the law back East. Most of them weren't even using a wagon, but traveling only with pack mules. Many of the men were single, but there were plenty of married ones along who had left whole families behind. It amazed Caleb that a man would leave his family for gold. It was as though they had been drugged with some strange, powerful craving. "Gold fever" was what some called it, and it seemed to make a man sick in the mind instead of in body.

Men traveling alone often passed whole wagon trains, determined to be among the first to arrive in California, the first to get at the gold that some seemed to think spilled out of the mountains in virtual rivers. The migration of some of the more degenerate looking was good cause to keep a close eye on Lynda and Sarah. But most took one look at Caleb Sax and thought twice about bothering his women.

Caleb did not doubt that many of those who hit California would get rich not from the gold, but from feeding the needs of the prospectors. Some of the wealthiest would no doubt be the prostitutes, and he grinned at the way one had been flagrantly batting her eyes at him on the whole trip, making Sarah a bit cranky.

The trip had not been without its hardships. Two people had accidentally shot themselves, greenhorn farmers who simply did not know how to handle pistols. Wagon axles sometimes snapped; mules and oxen often ran off in the night; wagon wheels sometimes shrank away from their iron braces. People got sick; and some couples got into all-out shouting matches, arguing over why they had come at all. Many had sold whole farms or businesses, sacrificing everything to search for something better, or to find the gold Caleb was sure would be elusive to most.

It had not taken long for Caleb to overcome the initial shunning they suffered because he was Indian. His skill and knowledge of the land soon made him popular, a man to whom they often turned for advice; and a man they were glad to have along the day a huge party of Crow warriors confronted their train, blocking its movement and demanding a great quantity of food items valuable to the travelers, as well as blankets and tobacco. Their demands might have been met, if not for the fact that they also demanded two young white women, grinning as they gripped tomahawks and rifles they had stolen from other travelers, threatening to burn every wagon.

To Sarah's quickening heart it was Caleb who met them head-on, speaking to them in their own tongue mixed with sign language and telling the wagon master their demands. When it came to demanding the white women, there was a flat no from Caleb, who proceeded to tell them they couldn't have any of the other things either. The words became more heated as Sarah and Lynda and Jess watched with dread, Jess gripping his rifle. Suddenly the two Crow with whom Caleb spoke looked wide-eyed with surprise at Caleb. They turned to the others and shouted something, and the rest of them looked at Caleb as though he were some kind of spirit.

One of those close to Caleb raised a tomahawk, and Caleb pulled his huge hunting knife while women gasped, some covering their children's eyes. Caleb shouted something threatening to the man, as though goading him into using the tomahawk. He circled his horse, which sensed the excitement, and Caleb shouted at all of them. He let out a series of war whoops while every Crow man there just stared.

Suddenly their apparent leader reached out to his friend and ordered him to put away the tomahawk. Caleb slowly lowered his knife, and there was more conversation between them before Caleb rode back, telling the wagon master they would settle for some tobacco and sugar and a couple of blankets. Travelers quickly donated the necessary items and Caleb took them to the Crow, who turned and left, some casting lingering stares at Caleb.

Caleb rode back to his own wagon, and Sarah saw the fire and pride in his eyes. For a moment he had been Cheyenne again, and his old hatred of the Crow had been rekindled.

"What on earth happened, Caleb?" Sarah asked as he dismounted.

"Those warriors looked at you as if you were a ghost," Jess put in.

Caleb could not help a proud grin. "I was, in a way. It was simple. I just told them who I was." He looked at Jess. "Blue Hawk. When they doubted it I told them things only Blue Hawk would know. One of them thought for a moment about being the one to finally kill the old legend. But he seems to have changed his mind." He winked at Jess. "I guess this old warrior still has what it takes."

Jess broke into a light laugh, and now Sarah could still hear it, still envision the episode. She sighed deeply and she felt Caleb stir now, moving a leg over hers and rubbing his hand over her stomach.

"You all right, Sarah?"

"Yes," she answered quietly. "I'm just thinking about our run-in with the Crow. All these years away from that life, and you handled it as though you were one of them, as though you never left at all."

He moved closer and kissed her cheek. "Actually I was hoping the one would use that tomahawk. I was itching for a good fight."

"Oh, Caleb!" She pushed at him and laughed, then settled back against the pillow. "Do you realize all we've been through, all the places we've lived? Now here we are in the middle of the Rockies, on our way to yet another new land. We should be a hundred years old, Caleb."

He rested his hand on the curve of her hip. "I agree with you there."

Sarah sobered, reflecting. "What's happening? Sometimes that's how old I feel. All these people. It makes a person wonder if there is anyone left back East."

"Oh, there are plenty left all right. I don't have to go back there to know."

"I remember what Washington was like—alive with people and progress—and that was such a long time ago. And I remember how those people would joke about the land west of the Mississippi, calling it the Great American Desert. They thought it was all so worthless. Now look at them—climbing all over each other to get out here. They've taken Texas and made it a state, and now they have New Mexico and Arizona and most of Colorado, California, and a bunch of territory they just call 'unorganized.' Everything is so different from when we were children at Fort Dearborn. It's so hard to imagine there is a city there now." She turned to face him. "All those years ago, and I can still picture you then. The day I had to leave and go to my father in St. Louis..." She shivered. "I'll always remember watching you standing there on the banks, so handsome. I was only thirteen, but I knew I loved you. God, I loved you, even then."

He met her lips, kissing her tenderly. "I'm just glad your health is holding up on this trip. I'm sorry, Sarah, for having to live this way. It will be different when we get to California. I've put you through so much."

She touched his face. "You know I don't mind, as long as we're together. It's the right thing this time, Caleb, I'm sure. And we're going to find Tom, I just know it."

"I hope so," he whispered. He pulled her closer. He had begun sleeping in the cramped wagon with her just for warmth. Nights in the Rockies were very cold, even in July, and his worst fear was that she would again contract pneumonia.

He nibbled at her lips. The hard trail life had meant virtually no sex since they had left Fort Laramie, and suddenly Caleb's needs became painfully clear.

"It's been so long," he whispered. "Do you feel rested enough? We might not get another chance before reaching California. I hear the trip through the desert is pretty miserable."

"I've been wanting the same thing," she whispered.

He moved his tongue between her lips, pushing up her gown and deftly removing his long underwear. He moved on top of her and ever so gently entered her, moving softly so as not to draw attention from outside.

She breathed deeply, trying not to make any sound. But she could not keep from moaning softly as she hungrily returned his kisses. Her desire for him seemed more intense this night, passion heating her blood. His big hands moved under her hips, and he filled her completely.

She thought about the first time Caleb had done this to her, in a cave somewhere in the wilds of Missouri after they had fled St. Louis. She was so young, so innocent, and so much in love. He had been gentle and careful, so sweet and understanding. She wondered how different everything might have been if she had not gotten sick and they could have kept going and settled together.

They had shared so much. Suffered so much. Now they were seeing the changes, feeling the years slipping away. Every day was precious now. More hardships lay ahead for them on the grueling trail to California, but Sarah was not afraid. No man could take better care of her on such a journey than Caleb Sax. Ahead of them lay California— and a new life. Perhaps in these mellowing years they could at last find that special peace and beauty they so deserved.

They had left their mark in so many places, and now their descendents were becoming scattered across the land —James in St. Louis, Cale riding the wide plains with the Cheyenne. If both of them married and had children, who could tell how much more scattered the Sax blood would become?

Sarah moaned as her husband's life spilled into her. Yes, the blood of Caleb Sax would certainly continue—through Lynda and James and their children and grandchildren. And it had all started so long ago, in the wilds of what was now called Illinois, at a little place called Fort Dearborn, where a small white girl was introduced to a lost and orphaned Indian boy called Blue Hawk.

• Chapter Twenty-three •

"Well? What do you think?" Caleb turned to Sarah, halting the lumbering wagon atop a rolling foothill that looked out over the Sacramento Valley. They had just split off from the rest of the wagons and were now traveling only with Jess and Lynda. To Caleb it felt good to be away from so many others. And he was sick of walking along beside oxen.

No team of horses could handle the arduous trip over both the Rockies and the Sierras, let alone the deserts, at least not while pulling a wagon behind them. So Jess and Caleb had purchased oxen at Fort Laramie, trading more of the horses they had brought to the fort to sell and taking on oxen instead for pulling their wagons. But oxen had to be led with whips and curses, and both Jess and Caleb had literally walked nearly the entire journey. They had kept four saddle horses, which they had tied to the backs of their wagons, and both men couldn't wait to get camped somewhere safe and get back on a horse.

As soon as everyone was settled temporarily, Caleb intended to promptly look for Tom before going any farther. He had deliberately steered clear of the main road the prospectors took to get to this valley, wanting to keep the women away from the streams of strange men, many of whom had not been near a woman for a long time.

Sarah sucked in her breath at the scene below, momentarily speechless. The journey through the Nevada deserts and over the Sierras had been rigorous and dangerous; many lives had been lost. An early snowstorm had set in while they were in the mountains, halting the wagon train and making everyone wonder if they were doomed to spend the winter buried. And Sarah had been sick through much of the bitter cold.

Finally the storm had abated, and they struggled over the crest of the mountains to lower elevations where there was less snow. They finally made it to the foothills, where there was no snow at all and the warm sun began to burn out the bitter cold everyone still felt in his bones. Caleb knew now he was here to stay. He would never again subject his Sarah to a trip over those mountains.

"Oh, Father, it's beautiful," Lynda called out from her own wagon.

"Caleb!" Sarah said softly, tears in her eyes. "It's like . . . like heaven." She stared out over hundreds of miles of open land, dotted here and there with vineyards, orchards, and pecan trees. Cabins could be seen scattered miles apart, as well as larger ranch houses and outbuildings. In the distance some horses ran free, and Sarah spotted a string of mules far to the left, loaded down with supplies, a few men walking with them. Prospectors. She thought how sad it was that so many were coming here hungry for gold, paying no heed to the beauty and peace of the land into which they had come. "So much green," she said softly.

The sun was setting far into the horizon, over an ocean that could not be seen from this far away. Dusk brought a hazy look to everything, the greens turning to violet, the sky red in the distance.

"Everything looks like velvet," Sarah said. "There's a certain peace here, Caleb. Do you feel it?"

He nodded, turning to watch her and putting an arm around her shoulders. "How do you feel?"

She took a deep breath, putting a hand to her chest. "Better. Much better. The pain in my chest is nearly gone."

Caleb rubbed a hand over her back. "This place is going to be good for you, Sarah. You'll see. No more long, cold winters and bitter winds and deep snows. In Texas it was just the opposite—too hot and dry and brown. Here it's just right. You can grow flowers and have a garden, you can sit in the sun without sweltering, and you can enjoy that sun all year round."

She held his eyes. "Wouldn't it have been nice if we could have come here when we were young?"

He felt the old pain move through his chest, and he didn't answer. He stood up and called out to Jess. "We'll head down a little farther and make camp. Tomorrow morning I'll saddle up and see if I can find out something about Tom."

Jess nodded and Caleb sat down, heading the wagon farther down, hoping they could continue to avoid prospectors. But that would not be easy. They had passed through several camps already, but at least most of them were higher up in the Sierras.

He had deliberately avoided the several mining towns that had already sprung up, realizing they must be wild, lawless places unfit for women—especially when one of those women looked Indian and the other was married to one. Sometimes at night when they made camp they could hear piano music and laughter, carried on the mountain winds, a sign that much of the peace that the hills of California once enjoyed had been rudely interrupted by gold-hungry newcomers. But that wouldn't last forever, and it would take more than a few thousand prospectors to truly destroy the devastating beauty of the land into which they had come.

They made camp, enjoying the fact that even though the sun was down it was still warm, and no insects bothered them. Far up in the higher foothills and mountains camp-fires peppered the black night—the campsites of prospectors.

Caleb sipped coffee, watching Sarah stir some stew. Yes, this land would be good for her. He was sure of it. He could stand to live far from the Cheyenne and the other world he had known, if it would help his Sarah live longer. Now all he had to do was find Tom.

Caleb stared at the double oak doors to the sprawling and still-unfinished home perched on a hillside overlooking the vast hacienda that supposedly belonged to his son. His heart pounded with a mixture of joy and apprehension. He had searched every mission in San Francisco until he had found a priest who admitted to knowing Tom, then had gladly spilled out the whole story and Tom's whereabouts when he realized Caleb was the boy's father.

The story Father Juarez told tore at Caleb's heart. He ached with the sorrow of not having been with his son through the horror of what had happened to Juanita, not having been there to stop him from waging his war of revenge and risking his life, not having been there through his terrible suffering after being wounded.

Thank God there had been the kind priest to help them. Juanita was healed and they were married, and no one better deserved the good fortune they were experiencing now. Juanita was pregnant and they had found gold on their land, enough to make Tom Sax a very rich man. The news when he went back to get Sarah and the others would bring great rejoicing, but he was too anxious to see his son to take the time to go and get them first. They were not so far away. He would get the rest of the family as soon as he saw for himself that this was his Tom. It was almost too good to be true, and he waited hesitantly while one of Tom's hired hands went inside first.

A continued distrust of Americans or any stranger had left Tom Sax cautious. Caleb had been met at the outskirts of the sprawling ranch by several Mexicans who took his weapons and demanded to know who he was. One of them had brought Caleb this far and now went inside to tell Tom, with orders that Caleb should wait outside—unarmed. The man returned momentarily. "Come in," he told Caleb.

Caleb went inside. The doors opened into a cool hallway that led in two directions, left and right, while ahead of him was an open door that led into an open court, where Caleb could see roses blooming. A young man walked toward him from the court, using a cane. Caleb felt a piercing pain at the man's limp. His hair was cut short, but there was no mistaking who it was.

"*Nehoe!*" Tom walked faster, his eyes already tearing.

Caleb grinned, walking toward him in long strides. "*Nahahan,*" he said lovingly, hurrying to Tom and embracing him tightly. Tom dropped his cane, unable to control his tears with any more discipline than his father, who also wept. What had this precious son been through? How hard it must have been for him to suffer it alone. How much he must love the rest of his family not to burden them with it.

They exchanged loving words in the Cheyenne tongue, laughing and crying at the same time, neither of them wanting to let go of the other.

"I cannot believe you are really here," Tom said, finally pulling away slightly. "You must have got my letter."

Caleb shook his head. "I got no letter. It must have come after we left. I just came to find my son. I was going crazy with worry, Tom."

The boy grinned, wiping at tears and standing back a little, looking the man over. "Do you never change, Father? Look at you, still so tall and strong. You never age. You still look like a man I would think twice about crossing." He sniffed and grasped the back of a wrought-iron garden chair while Caleb took his own inventory.

"Well what about you? You're thinner, Tom. And that leg—I've seen Father Juarez. I know all about the wound. You should have told me sooner."

Their eyes held, then Tom looked away. "I couldn't. You had your own problems. I brought it on myself."

Caleb walked closer, putting his hand on the young man's shoulder. Tom was as tall as his father, and normally as strong and broad. But his healing was still not done. "Tom, those raids—"

"I had to do it. I made a vow that until Juanita was well again, I would kill every American I could find and destroy their farms." He sniffed and swallowed. "I knew what might happen, but it didn't matter." He turned and faced the man. "It was as when you went after the Crow when my mother was killed. Surely you understand that feeling. What they did to Juanita—" He looked down and sighed. "It was worse than death, for both of us. For a long time she was like a crazy woman."

"I know. Father Juarez told me. You don't have to go over all of it now."

Tom shook his head. "Even after she got better and agreed to marry me—she was so afraid." He picked at a rose that bloomed near him. "I did not touch her for nearly three months after we were married. I could not do it until she was herself ready for such a thing. Even though she loved and trusted me, that part of it terrified her. But finally—" He smiled sadly, shrugging. "Finally my love and patience won her over." He met his father's eyes again. "But I would have waited forever if I had to. We are such good friends. You will understand when you meet her. I just wanted to be near her. She is my strength, Father. It is as with you and Sarah."

Caleb nodded. "I understand." He put an arm around the young man, leading him to a garden bench where they both sat down. "What about the leg? Does it still give you pain?"

Tom rubbed at it. "Sometimes. Not all the time. Today it is bothering me a little. I don't always use the cane as I have been today. I can ride and do ranch work." He smiled, forcing himself to ignore the ugly memories. "How do you like my ranch! Is it not beautiful?"

Caleb grinned at the heavy Spanish accent Tom used now. "It's very beautiful. And what is this about gold?"

Tom laughed, grabbing the man's hands. "I am a rich man, Father. The land is mine—legally—through Father Juarez. I have hired a mining company to mine the gold for me. I want to spend my time with Juanita and with the ranching. That is what I really love. And now I have the money to build it up all I want. Life is good now, Father. God has blessed us greatly. Juanita is even going to have a baby."

Caleb grinned as Tom looked around. "Where is Sarah? The rest of the family?"

"They're camped a few miles from here. I'll go and get them soon. I just couldn't wait to see you first, to know for sure it was my Tom Sax who lived here." Their eyes held, and they embraced again. "This reminds me of the day you came riding to me across Blue Valley," Caleb said, his words broken. "Everyone was so sure you'd been killed at the Alamo, but I refused to believe it. And then there you were, coming back to me from the dead." He squeezed the boy tighter. "My son. You're my only son now."

Tom frowned, drawing back. "What do you mean, Father? What has happened to James?"

Caleb reluctantly let go of Tom. He wiped his eyes and rose, taking a thin cigar from his pocket. "James left us to see the big cities of the East. He's working for some big merchant in St. Louis now. I doubt I'll ever see him again." He met Tom's eyes. "James hates his Indian blood. You know that. And he didn't look Indian. None of us doubts he's living there in St. Louis pretending to be all white. I've lost him, Tom, just as sure as if he were dead. And I can't help but wonder if it's because of all the things that happened in Texas. Right after the war, when things were so bad, I wasn't a very good father to him. And he saw the ugly side of being Indian. I could never quite get through to him after that, and never could share the closeness with him I've shared with you."

Tom watched him lovingly. "We grew up in a different time, Father, different circumstances. For many years I was all you had, and you were all that I had. Even when you married Marie, that didn't really change. It has never really changed. And don't you worry about James. For all you know there is nothing you could have done about it. Each man chooses his own way, Father. You know that."

Caleb lit the cigar and took a puff. "That's true. Cale isn't with us either. He's with the Cheyenne—living with them. He even participated in the Sun Dance ritual last summer."

Tom stared at him for several long, quiet seconds. "And you would like to be with him."

Caleb grinned a little. "Sometimes. But there is something more important to me and that's Sarah. I've brought her here hoping the climate will be good for her." He sobered—sitting back down. "She hasn't been well, and the trip here was pretty rough on her. Her lungs get congested so easily, and she has bad pains in her joints a lot of the time. I thought maybe a place where it's not as hot as Texas and not as cold as Colorado would be good for her."

Tom put a hand on his arm. "Then you have brought her to the right place. It is beautiful here, Father. I don't think I could ever leave California now, in spite of some of the bad memories. But that is over. God has given us a good life, and it will be good for you, too. Is Lynda with you?"

Caleb nodded. "Lynda and Jess and John—and they have a baby daughter now, Jessica."

Tom grinned. "This is truly a happy day. We can all live right here and be together again."

Caleb took another puff on the cigar. "Well, now, Jess is itching to have a place of his own. He never has, you know. For one reason and another he's never been able to strike out on his own, and of course he's stayed with us partly because of Lynda. But he's an independent man and I don't blame him for wanting to try something new now that we're in California. He and Lynda will go on a ways."

Tom nodded. "I can understand that. But you and Sarah. You will live with us. Surely you will."

Caleb frowned, meeting his son's eyes. "Tom, I didn't come out here to live off my son. I'll get settled somewhere and—"

"Father, you would not be living off me." Tom's eyes teared again as he slowly shook his head. "My God, Father, look at all the years I lived with you. You have done more for me than I could ever repay. I need you, Father. There are days when I can't get on a horse and do the things a man who runs a ranch needs to do. You could do that for me. There is nothing you know better in the world than raising horses and running a ranch. Here you can realize the dream that was stolen from you in Texas. I have got it back for you, something I always hoped to do. Here at last you and Sarah can find the peace you deserve, and Sarah can live in total comfort. We even have servants. It is the kind of life you always wanted for her, and if you think you need to do something in return, you will be earning it right out there with those horses—and by staying with me when I need you most."

Caleb saw the pleading in his son's eyes. Tom grasped the man's forearm firmly. "Please say you will stay, Father, right here. We have many rooms. And it would be good for my Juanita. It has been many years since she had a mother, and I can think of no woman who would be better for her or love her more than Sarah. And if Lynda is moving on, then Juanita could be a companion and friend to Sarah. Besides, Juanita will deliver soon. I would like nothing better than for Sarah to be here for her. And after that she can help take care of the baby, and she would have another grandchild to hold."

Caleb smiled sadly. "You make it all very tempting."

A tear slipped down Tom's cheek. "The last couple of years have been hell," he said, his voice gruff with emotion. "Seeing you is better than finding the gold. The important thing is that my Juanita is well, and now my father is here. Don't leave, Father."

Caleb put a hand over Tom's. "All right. We'll try it for a while, at least; but I'll by God do my share."

"I have no doubts about that." Tom smiled through his tears. He looked past his father. "Juanita! I told them not to disturb you from your nap."

He rose, and Caleb turned to see a young woman with a swollen belly entering the garden. He was struck by her provocative beauty, seeing immediately why Tom Sax had fallen so madly in love in spite of the gap in their ages. Tom limped to Juanita's side, putting an arm around her and leading her toward his father.

"I woke up," she was telling Tom. "They said your father is here."

Caleb rose, meeting the girl's eyes as they came closer. She seemed to be reddening under his gaze, but she smiled.

"Juanita, this is my father, Caleb." Tom smiled proudly. "Father, this is Juanita. See for yourself how beautiful my wife is."

Juanita looked down bashfully. "Tom, you make me embarrassed."

Tom just laughed, and Caleb reached out and took her hand. "You are indeed beautiful—not just in looks, Juanita. You are beautiful because you love my son."

She raised her eyes at the remark, already loving this new father-in-law. "I know you are a good man. Tom thinks so much of you, talks about you all the time. I feel I already know you. And now that I see you, I know why my Tom is such a strong, good man. I am grateful that you raised such a fine son, and that he is my husband."

She suddenly hugged him, and Caleb patted her shoulder, feeling the softness of her dark, long hair against his hand. Already he could feel some of the rage Tom must have felt at what happened to this treasure. She was so young and sweet, and it was easy to see what an innocent she must have been. She pulled away, sniffing and wiping at her eyes.

"You are here to stay? You will live with us, won't you?"

Tom put an arm around her. "I have already talked him into it. My stepmother and my sister and her family are camped not far from here. I will ride with Father to go and get them. I am anxious to see my family. Do you mind, Juanita?"

"Of course not. I have plenty of protection here. I will have the servants get rooms ready for them." She looked up at Caleb. "Those that are finished anyway. The house is still not completed. But enough is done to accommodate my husband's family."

Caleb was struck by her gracious manners. This girl was well-bred. "We don't need anything fancy. Lord knows we haven't lived fancy in a long time."

"Oh, but Tom has told me much about his stepmother. She is a fine lady who deserves all the comforts. I will see that she gets them." She looked back at Tom. "I will have plenty to do to get ready. You go with your father. When will you leave?"

Tom looked at Caleb. "It's up to you." He threw up his hands. "I haven't even asked you if you are tired. Would you like something to drink, or are you hungry?"

Caleb grinned. "A little. Why don't we have some lunch and then leave. We can make the camp by nightfall." He looked Tom over. "Are you sure you feel up to it? You seem to be in pain today."

Tom shrugged. "I am used to it."

Caleb noticed the pain and sorrow in Juanita's eyes. All of Tom's suffering had been for her. Surely every time she watched him limp she remembered those awful days.

"I can ride." Tom turned to Juanita. "Honey, why don't you go tell Luisa to get some lunch ready?" He kissed her cheek and she blushed.

"Yes, I will do that." She looked up at Caleb again. "I am so happy you are here. It is another prayer that has been answered. So many have been answered for us lately."

She turned and left, and Tom watched her lovingly, then turned back to his father. "Luisa used to be a nursemaid to Juanita when she lived with her father—before all the bad things happened. We sent for Luisa after we got settled and built this bigger house. I knew Juanita could not take care of it all by herself, and I don't want anything to go wrong with the pregnancy. Now that Sarah will be here, I feel extra good about it. It is very important that Juanita have a nice healthy baby to love. I am not sure she could handle it emotionally if anything went wrong. She has had enough loss and pain."

Caleb sighed deeply, meeting his son's eyes. "She's beautiful, Tom—more beautiful than I anticipated."

Tom smiled proudly. "I wanted her the first day I saw her, in spite of her youth." He turned. "Come. I will show you around, and then we will eat."

"Tom."

The young man turned, waiting.

"What about Los Malos?"

"What about it? That is over now."

"Father Juarez said all of them were killed the day you were wounded—but that later you discovered one had lived and was hung. What is the possibility that someone knows who led The Bad Ones? Maybe the one who lived told someone."

Tom shrugged. "If he did, someone would have come for me by now. I am known in Sonoma. The leader of Los Malos is a legend. If anyone knew who it was, they would jump at the chance to expose him and be the one to capture me."

Caleb studied him thoughtfully. "I suppose you're right. It just gives me an uneasy feeling."

Tom put on a grin, hiding his own similar concern. "Well, now my father is here, so it does not matter. If something goes wrong, between the two of us we can fight it and win, right?"

Caleb smiled himself, deciding not to go into it any further and spoil this happy moment. "Right."

The two of them embraced once more. Caleb had not felt this happy in several years. Being with Tom even helped ease the pain of saying good-bye to James. This would be a good life for Sarah. At least she would live the way she deserved to live. This place called California was going to be a happy chapter in their lives.

•   **Chapter Twenty-four**   •

Caleb stretched out in the huge, comfortable bed. The room Tom had given Caleb and Sarah was quite large, decorated with richly polished mahogany furnishings handmade by a Spanish carpenter Tom had hired. Paintings of matadors and mountains hung on the walls, as well as a picture of a Mexican man with his head bowed, covering himself nearly completely with his large sombrero as he took his afternoon siesta. The stucco walls of the rambling Sax home kept the rooms cool, and there were so few insects in the air that most of the time Caleb and Sarah slept with their windows open, breathing the fresh night air.

"I never dreamed it would be this beautiful, Sarah," Caleb told her. She lay curled up beside him, reaching her arm over his bare chest when he spoke.

"And it's so good for you. You actually seem younger and stronger, Caleb."

He laughed lightly. "I never thought working so hard would actually give me more energy. Tom's got me riding down wild mustangs, training horses, teaching the other men the best breeding practices, building fences, herding horses and cattle; we've even been going out to the mine and doing some work there."

"You do seem to put in a full day," she said jokingly.

He grinned, moving an arm under her and pulling her closer. "I love it. But mostly I'm just so damned happy to see Tom doing so well. He's smart not to be counting on that mine. He takes all that money and turns right around and invests it in this place. He knows someday that mine will probably play out and when it does he'll have plenty of other resources. I can't believe how wealthy my own son is."

She smiled, kissing his shoulder. "But still the same good man. He is so unaffected by it. And he's so much in love with Juanita. She's so beautiful, Caleb, so sweet. With Lynda moving on, it helps having Juanita. I already look at her like a daughter. I just pray she'll never suffer again—that life will always be good to her now. I hope she has a nice healthy baby."

Caleb rubbed a hand over her back and hips. "I think Jess will be happier, too, having a place of his own. According to that letter, he's got a nice little spread started already. I promise to take you there as soon as I get a free day."

"They'll do fine. Jess is such a capable man. But I do miss Lynda so."

He lightly kissed her hair. "I know. But Tom says the town they live near is only a two-day ride from here."

Sarah sighed, snuggling closer. "I'm so glad we came, Caleb. That awful trip was worth it. I just pray God will be with Cale . . . and James. It's so strange to think of them being so far away."

"It wouldn't have been any different if we had stayed, Sarah. Always remember that. They made their own choices." He turned to face her, studying her lovely face in the moonlight, somehow always failing to see the age lines about her eyes and the gray that was overcoming the red-gold splendor of her hair. "This is the best place on God's earth for you. We've only been here a month, and you already look so much healthier. There is more color in your cheeks, a brighter light in your eyes, and you've even put on a couple of pounds."

She laughed lightly. "That's because you're all babying me and waiting on me hand and foot. Caleb, it's absolutely pitiful! I am not an invalid, you know."

He kissed her lightly. "I know. But you deserve to have servants doing things for you, so you can have time to just sit in the sun and read and sew and do all the things you haven't had time for in years." He put a big hand to the side of her face, gently caressing her hair. "This is the life I always wanted to give you. I'm just sorry I've had to do it through Tom."

She grasped his wrist. "Caleb, you tried so hard. Don't ever forget how well you did in Texas. None of the things that happened there were your fault. And you know as well as I that Tom absolutely loves being able to do this for us. He's never been happier. He wants to give something back to you, and he needs your help. He's in pain so much of the time. I'm glad we're here for him, and for Juanita. I just want to forget all the ugly things from the past and enjoy this wonderful place and Tom's good fortune."

He gently stroked her hair, leaning closer and kissing her again. Neither of them needed to say it. It was said in the touching, the kissing. In these moments they were young lovers again. The magic had never left them, for their love went far beyond physical attraction. It ran deep, strengthened by years of hardships, by the memory of how it felt when each thought the other was dead. But some of the memories were beautiful, to be forever treasured and bringing a glorious excitement to their lovemaking in their later years—memories that could not be stolen from them no matter what the outside world did to them.

He searched her mouth, exploring with his tongue in the titillating way he always used to bring her desires to the surface, always a master at bringing out all that was woman about her.

She soon forgot the pain in her joints that had plagued her all day, thanking God for this beautiful man. Caleb's big hands moved over her, touching places so familiar to him now, yet always touching her as though it was the first time with her, near worship in his gentle caresses.

He didn't have to ask. Years together told him when she was ready for this and when she wasn't. He said nothing. He only moved his lips down her neck, unbuttoning her gown and pushing one side off her shoulder, seeking out the pink fruit of her breast and cupping it higher with his hands to gently taste it, his lips and tongue so soft that increasing desire moved through Sarah in a rush that made her dizzy.

She grasped his hair, her breathing deepening, her eyes closed as he pushed up her gown. His lips lingered at her breast. His fingers explored, experienced in just the right ways to bring out the sweet nectar that would make inter-course soft and satisfying. She gasped when his fingers entered her in an intimacy she had allowed only this man to know. He moved them rhythmically, drawing out the mois-ture needed to enter her, and in moments he was on top of her.

She grasped his powerful arms as he pushed into her. She arched up to meet his thrusts. Caleb held out for a very long time, grasping her hips and moving in hard rhythm, letting her enjoy the sweet ecstasy of the moment before finally giving in to his own pleasure and releasing his life.

Sarah wondered for a moment how many children they might have had if they could have been together all those lost years they were separated. But she quickly swept away the thought, one that always saddened her. She could only thank God she had found Caleb again.

He stayed inside her a moment, raising up on his knees and moving his hands over her breasts and belly, then along her hips and thighs. "I was going to go right to sleep," he told her.

Sarah grinned, moving her own hands over his hard thighs and up over his forearms. "I'm sorry I kept you awake."

He came down on her, kissing her lightly. "I guess it's all right." He kissed her again, several times over, until suddenly someone tapped on their bedroom door.

Caleb moved off her, pulling up the covers. "Who is it?"

"Father, it's me," came Tom's voice through the door. "I'm sorry to bother you, but Juanita has gone into labor. Can Sarah come?"

"Yes! Yes, I'll be right there." Sarah sat up. "Give me a few minutes to get dressed."

"Thank you, Sarah. I'll be in our room. Luisa is with her now."

Caleb and Sarah both detected the near panic in his voice.

"Oh, dear, I hope this all turns out all right," Sarah fretted, hurrying over to the washstand.

Caleb got up and began dressing. "I think I'll have a harder time with Tom than you will with Juanita. Sometimes this is worse for the men than the women, you know."

She laughed. "You've never had a baby, Caleb Sax. I'd be willing to bet the Sun Dance ritual isn't much worse."

Caleb walked over to where she stood, moving his arms around her from behind. "So much for our good night's sleep." She turned, looking up at him, and he embraced her. "I'll be close by if you need me, Sarah." He gave her a squeeze. "She'll have a fine, healthy baby, and we'll have another grandchild."

"I hope so. It's so important to both of them, Caleb."

Antonio Galvez Sax was born in October, 1849, a strapping, healthy son for Tom and Juanita. Little "Tony" was a matter of great pride to the entire family, as well as another step toward a total healing for Juanita, who knew the moment she held her son to her breast that she had every reason now to live, and that she had done the right thing by marrying Tom Sax. There would be many more children for her husband. She vowed it would be so.

The entire family traveled to San Francisco, where Tony was christened by Father Juarez, whose own pride and joy were so evident the man looked as though he might burst with happiness. On the way home they all visited Jess and Lynda to see the small ranch near a town called Henderson where the two had settled.

Seeing how happy Jess was with his own place warmed

Sarah's heart, for having Jess happy made Lynda happy. It was good that they were living separate lives, good for Lynda to begin breaking the powerful need she had always felt to be close to her parents.

In all their years together she was sure that coming to California was the wisest thing they had ever done. She only wished Cale and James could be with them, too. So far away . . . over two mountain ranges and beyond. She fought to keep from allowing the nagging question to burden her heart, but still, it was always there, just beneath the happiness she now knew, the only thing that spoiled her present joy. Would she ever see her son James again?

Tom looked up from his desk as one of his men came inside with a Mexican who looked familiar to Tom.

"What is it, Daniel?" Tom asked his hired hand.

"This man wishes to speak to you alone, he says," Daniel answered in Spanish. "I took his gun."

The man scowled at the one called Daniel. "You got no right to take my gun."

"When you come onto Sax land, you go by Sax rules," Daniel answered. "You will get your gun back when you leave."

The man sniffed. "You take orders from an Indian?"

Daniel's eyes flashed with anger. "El señor Sax is a good *patrón*. He pays us well, and his heart is Spanish."

The man nodded, a strange, knowing look in his eyes as he turned them to Tom. "*Sí.* So I am told."

"By whom?" Tom asked. "What do you want here? And what is your name?"

The man looked at Daniel, then back to Tom. "Make him leave first."

"Go ahead, Daniel."

Daniel cast the stranger a warning look, then left, closing the door behind him.

"Come and sit down. Who are you?"

"My name is Francesco Fajardo." He moved closer but did not sit down, looking ready to run at any moment.

Tom eyed him challengingly, a warning, distrusting look in his eyes. "You look familiar. Do I know you?"

Fajardo fingered the hat he held in his hand. "*Sí*. I used to work for el señor Galvez. I remember you. You are the one who trained the black stallion for him . . . the one who was sweet on his pretty little daughter."

Tom frowned, all senses alerted. "So?"

"So, they say in Sonoma the daughter of Antonio Galvez, who disappeared after her father's ranch was attacked by Americans, and after those Americans were all murdered . . . is now your wife."

Tom told himself to stay calm. He must not give anything away. "Why don't you get to the point, Señor Fajardo?"

Fajardo shrugged, glancing at the corners of the room as though there might be men there watching. "My point is, señor, that two or three years ago, after Juanita Galvez disappeared, there were many attacks on Americans by a gang of guerrillas called Los Malos. You have heard of them?"

Their eyes held challengingly. "I have heard of them. They were all killed."

"All but their leader—who was, by a strange coincidence, an Indian. At least he painted himself as one." The man's eyes moved over Tom. "And they were not all killed. One called Rico lived to hang. I was the cleaning man at the doctor's office where they kept him. I talked to him often when he was in great pain and needed a friend."

Tom struggled to show unconcern and irritation, rummaging through some papers. "You are wasting my time, Señor Fajardo. I could not care less about Los Malos. It is all a legend now, from what I hear in town."

"*Sí*. The people like to talk about it—like to wonder whatever happened to the leader, who has never been found. He was"—the man glanced at Tom's game leg—"wounded, so they say, the day the rest of them were killed. And this Rico, he said once in great pain, he said, 'Tom. Tom.'"

Tom glanced at him and Fajardo smiled. "Now perhaps you see what I am driving at, Señor Sax."

Tom's face darkened with rage. "How dare you insinuate I would be that man!"

"I do not insinuate," the man growled. "I accuse!"

A fearful look of bitter hatred came into Tom's eyes. "I might remind you that you are alone here, Señor Fajardo, and I have many men. If I were this man, don't you think you are taking a great risk by coming here to accuse me?"

Fajardo fingered his hat more vigorously, swallowing before speaking. "I thought of that. So I told many of my friends where I was going. I told them that I was coming here to look for work. If something happens to me, they will wonder and come looking for me. This would draw much attention to you, señor, if something happened to me. There would be many questions asked. Perhaps it would upset your poor wife."

In an instant Tom was storming around the desk toward him, towering over the shaking Fajardo as Fajardo inched back toward the door. "You make trouble for my Juanita, and I don't care what happens to me—you're a dead man, Fajardo," he sneered at the man, his dark eyes showing then all the fiery revenge they once showed as the leader of Los Malos. "You are insinuating I could be this Indian leader of The Bad Ones. But you have no proof, and if you pursue this, I will crush you!" He raised his fist close to the man's face, and Fajardo backed up more.

"I need no proof. You are surrounded by American settlers, Señor Sax, many of whom still hold much hatred for The Bad Ones and want very much to catch their leader for once and for all. I have never told anyone what the man Rico said in his pain. I was saving it, so that I could be the one to find out who this leader was. When I heard Tom Sax was back and had his own ranch and was married to Juanita Galvez, I thought and thought, until it all made sense." The man took a deep breath for courage. "It would not take much to set them all to thinking the same thing I am thinking. That could lead to a hanging for you, Señor Sax, if the people were angry enough. I could make them that way, and you would be hung, probably without even a trial. Your poor wife would be left all alone."

Tom stepped closer again.

"Or I could say nothing!" Fajardo quickly finished.

Tom scowled, then broke into a grin that showed only hatred. "It's money, isn't it? You want money, you son of a bitch!"

Fajardo cleared his throat and swallowed, wondering if he had done the right thing by facing this man. If he truly was the leader of The Bad Ones, the man was capable of savage murder. "You are a rich man now. They say in Sonoma how Tom Sax has much money—what a big ranch he has, with a gold mine right on his own land. What would it hurt you to give a little of that gold to Francesco Fajardo, if it would save you from disgrace and hanging, save your wife from being left all alone."

Tom's jaw flexed in rage. He couldn't kill this man, and yet he despised the idea of paying him. That was no more than an admission of guilt, which Fajardo might still turn around and use against him to get him hung anyway.

"You see the situation, señor? Even if I am wrong"—a slow smile moved across Fajardo's mouth—"it does not matter. With so much hatred left for The Bad Ones, it would be easy to turn the Americans against you and make them think you are the one. But for"—he shrugged—"maybe fifty thousand dollars, all the trouble can be avoided."

"Fifty thousand!"

"I have checked around. Bank tellers sometimes talk when they are drunk. I know you have much more than that. Surely you can spare fifty thousand—and perhaps another fifty thousand next year."

"And the year after that?"

Fajardo only grinned more. "You should be grateful, señor, that I have never said anything about this to anyone else."

"Oh, I'm very grateful," Tom sneered. "Perhaps some day I can show you just *how* grateful."

Fajardo swallowed. "Think of your family, señor—all that you have here."

Tom held himself in check, scrambling to think straight. He eyed the man squarely. "You have had a lot of time to think this over and decide what you will do. Give me the same privilege—a day or two at least."

Fajardo looked around the room again. "All right. But remember you would have some explaining to do if any of your men should harm me when I leave here. All of my friends know I am a peaceful, hardworking man. They would not believe it if you said I came here and made trouble."

"Don't worry, Fajardo," Tom sneered. "You're safe—for now. But I would advise you that if I pay you any money, you had better go someplace very far away from here— very very far. And if you should still make trouble for me even if I pay you, I or my men will make sure you die!"

Fajardo took a deep breath, straightening his shoulders. "For my own safety, señor, I think you should come to Sonoma to pay me—in two days. I do not want to come back to this place. I live in a room at the Gold Coast Hotel. Do you know it?"

"I know it. It's a dump, where only trash stay," Tom sneered.

Fajardo reddened. "I live there with friends. I told them I came here to look for ranch work. That is what I do best. I do not like working in the town. They will suspect nothing."

"I can't meet you there. They'll wonder why someone with my money is meeting a worthless *gusano* there!"

Fajardo clenched his fists at being called a worm. "Two o'clock, the day after tomorrow. Behind Stuart's Livery then. Bring the money, Señor Sax, or hang." He moved quickly to the door.

"Fajardo."

The man hesitated, wanting nothing more now than to get out fast, wondering if he was too much a fool challenging this man who could very well be the real leader of Los Malos.

"I find it amazing the dangerous and stupid things a man will do for gold," Tom sneered. "You had better ask yourself if this is worth it, Fajardo. It is possible I will pay you, but you will spend the rest of your days looking over your shoulder. I don't care to have a man walking around who is capable of destroying me with his lies."

Fajardo quickly left, and Tom stared at the door, shaking now with the realization of what one man with a big mouth could do to him. He waited a few minutes, watching Fajardo ride off with Daniel, then went outside to speak to another man.

"Miguel!"

"Sí, Señor Sax?" The man hurried over from where he was trimming roses.

"My father is out helping build more fence. Have someone ride out and tell him I must see him right away."

"Sí." Miguel put down his trimmers and hurried away to get a horse, and Tom went back inside to wait, glad Juanita and Sarah were both napping. Neither of them knew of Fajardo's visit. He didn't want Juanita to see the distress that at the moment he could not hide. Somehow he had to think what to do, to keep this from Juanita. Nothing must happen to bring back all the ugliness for her.

He went back to his study and poured himself some brandy, nervously pacing in spite of the pain he suffered today that had kept him out of the fields. Caleb was over two miles from the main house, and it took nearly a half hour for him to arrive. He came through the door of the study without knocking, sweat on his forehead. He wore buckskin pants and vest, and the dark skin of his arms was growing even darker from working out in the sun. He stopped short at the sight of his son drinking in the middle of the day and pacing on his painful leg. More than that, it was the look in Tom's eyes that alarmed him.

"What the hell is going on, Tom? I just got back to work from lunch. Is something wrong with Sarah?"

Tom sighed, setting his empty glass on his desk and

stepping closer to Caleb. "Father, a man was here. He calls himself Francesco Fajardo. He used to work for Juanita's father, the same time I did. I never really noticed him, but that's beside the point." He turned, running a hand through his dark hair. "He knows, Father. He figured it out—who I am. He wants money or he says he'll turn the people in Sonoma against me and get me hung." He began pacing again.

Caleb felt his heart tighten. "Does he have some kind of proof?"

"No, not really, just that he talked to my friend Rico— the one who lived and was hung. He says Rico said the name Tom—and he knows I was once sweet on Juanita. Now I am married to her. He just . . . he put it all together. He—"

"Tom, calm down."

"What am I to do? I have to think of Juanita. If he starts something, they could drag Juanita in on it, question her, bring it all back for her. She couldn't take it! She couldn't take it! But I couldn't kill him, either. People would ask questions. He told his friends he was coming here just to look for work." He stopped pacing, facing his father and looking helpless. His eyes shone with a mixture of desperation and bitter hatred. "That bastard!" he hissed. "It is not me that I am worried about. It's Juanita! It took so long to get her back to normal. Everything is so good now."

Caleb walked closer and grasped Tom's shoulders. "And it's going to stay that way. Stay calm and tell me everything he said."

Tom closed his eyes and sighed, turning and sitting down wearily in a stuffed leather chair. He rubbed his eyes as he began the story, while Caleb listened closely. Afterward, Caleb walked to the window, gazing out over the beautiful ranch that belonged to his son. He said nothing for several long minutes. A mantel clock ticked quietly.

"There is a way we can beat this thing completely, Tom —without your having to pay that man a cent or even worry about his telling others," Caleb finally spoke up, turning to face his son.

Tom frowned. "How? I can see no way, Father, short of killing him."

"You won't have to kill him." Caleb came closer. "Tom, he never saw me. He probably doesn't even know I exist. We have never even been to Sonoma yet since we've been here. I came straight from San Francisco here, and Sarah and I have yet to go into town. No one who knows you in town has met me."

"So what?"

"I can clear you, Tom," Caleb said, his voice cool and sure. "You go to Sonoma—challenge this man to go ahead and talk. Go straight to the law there and tell them what has happened—tell them you wish to have this thing cleared up right away. Let them accuse you all they want. Don't worry that some of them think you might be guilty."

Tom shook his head. "Father, I don't understand—"

"While you're in Sonoma and everyone is arguing over your possibly being the leader of Los Malos, the *real* leader will strike again!"

Tom stared at him for several long seconds; again the only sound was the ticking clock. Then Tom's eyes widened and he felt a chill. "You?"

Caleb's eyes glittered with sure victory for his son. "Why not? All you have to do is tell me how you dressed —how you painted yourself. I'll attack one or two American settlements. I'll try not to kill anyone—just do some damage and put a good scare in them—enough that they will come running into town to tell everyone the phantom Indian man has struck again. You will have the best alibi of all. You will be right there among them."

Tom held his eyes, his love for his father never more intense. "It would be dangerous, Father. They would shoot at you. You could be hurt—or killed. It's too risky."

Caleb grinned almost wickedly. "I can do it, Tom, and no one will know the difference. All I do is lie low afterward for a long time. I will strike at night, while the men all think I'm in the house sleeping with my wife. During the day I'll be at my chores as always. I'll strike the night before you leave and again the night you are there so that the news comes quickly."

"What about Sarah? What about the men wondering why you didn't go into town with me?"

"If they find out what is happening in town and wonder why I am not at your side, I'll tell them Sarah isn't well, and that Juanita is very upset over the reason you went into Sonoma. You will give the same story. We'll tell Sarah but not Juanita. We'll try to keep it from her, at least until it's over. It will take a few days for the news even to get back to your men."

Tom sighed, standing up. "Sarah will be so worried. And so will I. I don't like it, Father."

"It's the only way, and you know it. You'll be taking a risk yourself, you know. An angry crowd could gather. That's why I have to attack settlements closest to town so that the news gets there quickly. If it works, you're a free man. No one will doubt you again. And the phantom Indian will simply disappear again."

Their eyes held. "If you got hurt or killed, I would never forgive myself, Father. I have suffered enough guilt over feeling responsible for what happened to Juanita in the first place."

"If something happened to me, you would never have to feel guilty. It's what I *want* to do. It's my idea, not yours. And I would die helping my son. I can think of no better way to die. You would do the same for Tony, whether he was a baby or forty years old. I want to do it, Tom."

Tom turned away, swallowing back tears. "Apparently there was a reason God sent you when He did." He breathed deeply. "You would have to be very careful. There are many who would like to say they are the one who captured or killed the legendary leader of Los Malos."

Caleb walked up and grasped his son's arm. "I am Blue Hawk, Tom. I might be getting older, but I'm still capable and strong. The only way out of this is to clear you completely so you never have to live with that cloud hanging over your head."

Tom met the man's eyes. "I am afraid it makes sense." His eyes were watery. "I will explain to you how you must dress and paint yourself." He suddenly embraced the man. "God be with you, Father."

· Chapter Twenty-five ·

Sarah waited impatiently, pacing in the dark room while the rest of the household slept, including Juanita, who thought Tom had only gone to town on business. She would probably find out he was in trouble soon enough, but so far not even the men at the ranch knew why he had gone.

This was Sarah's second night without sleep—and Caleb's. The first night he had ridden out after the men were bedded down for the night. Caleb knew where guards were kept and how to get around them so that none of them knew he had gone. He was back at dawn, having already washed off his war paint. He rode into the fields and corrals as though he had been up early and was already out getting some work done.

In order to keep things looking normal, Caleb was forced to put in a regular day's work so that no one would suspect he had not slept at all the night before. That made this second night even more dangerous. He was tired and would be forced to put in yet another day's work when he returned, taking only a short nap when he came in at dawn and perhaps catching some sleep at lunchtime.

This second night he had ridden out before sundown, telling the hired hands he was going to the mine. They wouldn't really notice that he did not return that night. They had their own lives and chores. None would be aware that after leaving the mine Caleb would again go on into the hills, where he would paint his face and don his Indian dress and weapons and hit a settlement before full dark, so that the settlers would get a good look at him.

Again, that second night, a wild-eyed, painted Indian

rode screaming through farms, yelping war whoops and spooking cattle. Caleb continued his rampage well after dark to ensure there would be plenty of alarmed settlers who would go running into Sonoma. At two o'clock in the morning he attacked his fifth settlement: trampling crops, running off horses and cattle, knocking down fences, smashing windows. He had to smile to himself at how easy it would be to truly destroy these settlers single-handedly if he was serious. He had shot at several of them, deliberately missing. But it would have been easy to shoot them down, most of them were so frightened and inept.

The raids brought Caleb's Indian blood to the surface, and he could sometimes feel the true anger of his relatives who were themselves becoming more and more belligerent against the whites who continued to infiltrate their land. He trampled through a cornfield, wielding his war club and riding right next to the settlers' cabin, smashing the club through a window. The part of him that understood the hard life these people led made him feel remorseful, but he reminded himself that he was doing this for his son.

Someone inside the cabin screamed, and moments later a man came out carrying a rifle, watching a dark figure on a horse that circled behind the cabin and then came toward him. Man and horse cleared a fence and headed right for the front porch. Orange fire spit from the end of a pistol the "wild Indian" fired, and a bullet bit the doorway no more than an inch past the settler's head, startling the man so that he ducked and fumbled with his rifle. The Indian rode right up onto the porch, pinning the settler against the wall while the man's wife screamed his name from inside the house.

"American trash," the Indian hissed. "Go back to where you came from!"

He rode off the porch and disappeared into the night.

"Alfred! Alfred, what is it!" the woman inside screamed.

The man slowly rose, hurrying to aim his rifle. He got off a shot but was sure he had hit nothing. The ghostly figure was gone. The settler's wife opened the door and yelled for him.

"I'm right here, Jane."

"What happened!"

"I don't know. I . . . I think it was him."

"Who?"

"That Indian. That one they talk about that used to lead The Bad Ones. In the moonlight . . ." He swallowed back his fright. "I could see his face—painted. It must have been black and white like they say—one side was real bright in the moonlight. The other side I couldn't even see."

"Oh, Alfred, what's happening?"

"I don't know. But come morning I'm going into Sonoma to tell the authorities that bastard is back. They'll find him this time!"

Neither of them knew that in Sonoma the town was already buzzing with gossip. "The Indian" had already hit three settlements the night before, casting doubt on the story of one Francesco Fajardo, who claimed he knew who the Indian leader of Los Malos was, angrily accusing a man who had won the respect of many of the townspeople, Tom Sax.

Fajardo was furious that Tom had refused to pay him any money and had himself gone directly to the sheriff. Fajardo was sure it would have been easy to gain glory by revealing the identity of the infamous phantom Indian. But to his surprise the people of Sonoma supported Tom. After all, Sax had a lot of money in their bank. His huge ranch and gold mine meant a good deal of business for several Sonoma citizens. And the man had a beautiful young wife and a new baby boy. How could he possibly be the phantom Indian? Why would he strike the night before and turn himself in the next day? And those who had recently suffered the Indian's newest attacks claimed he had long hair, just as he did in the earlier days. Tom Sax had short hair, and it had been short since they had known him. Tom Sax was soft-spoken, a true gentleman and a man of wealth. Why would he return to raiding, even if he was the infamous Indian leader? And Tom Sax had a bad leg, injured by a wild mustang. All the new friends Tom had made around Sonoma believed that. After all, Sax worked with horses all the time.

Tom sat in a jail cell that very night while citizens debated the ridiculous charges of Francesco Fajardo. Francesco himself was in near shock. And while he angrily drank away his problems in a saloon, Tom sat praying for freedom to go back to Juanita before she discovered what was happening, and Caleb Sax headed back home, hoping he had done enough damage to save his son from hanging.

In the morning Caleb showed up, riding in from the north range as though he had been out early again. There was no sign of paint on his face, no trace of the wild and infamous phantom Indian. He told one of Tom's men that his shoulder was bothering him and that he was going to the house for a while. The man smiled and nodded and went about his business.

Caleb rode up to the house, and a very tired-looking Sarah greeted him at the door. "Come to the bedroom," Caleb told her. "I don't want Juanita to see me yet. Where is she?"

"She's in the kitchen feeding Tony."

Her heart tightened at the odd pale look of her dark-skinned husband. It was more than just being tired. He walked to their room and closed the door, then hurried to the bed, sitting down on it. "I've been shot, Sarah," he groaned.

"Oh, my God," she whimpered, hurrying over to him.

"Stay calm." He kept his own voice steady and reassuring. "Help me get this shirt off. The bullet ripped right through, under my right arm. It bled a lot—but I don't think it hurt anything vital." He grimaced as she pulled off the cotton shirt he wore to see bandages wrapped clumsily around the wound.

"Oh, Caleb, you could have been killed!" she fussed, unwrapping the bloody bandages.

He reached up and squeezed her arm. "You've got to try to hide this, Sarah, even from Tom."

"Caleb, he should know—"

"No! I don't want him carrying that burden. I can hide it."

"Caleb, I can tell already that you can hardly move your arm." Her eyes were tearing as she threw aside the bandages and hurried to bring over a pan of water and a clean rag. "Are you sure the bullet went through?"

"I'm sure. I don't dare go to a doctor, for obvious reasons. You've got to clean it out and rewrap it, and I've got to go put in a day's work as if nothing is wrong."

"Caleb, you can't!"

"Yes, I can. You've got to help me do this, Sarah." Their eyes held and he squeezed her hand. "Be strong for me."

She stiffened and nodded as he lay down on his left side. With much effort he moved his arm straight out so that Sarah could wash the hole just under his right shoulder blade and the one just beneath his right breast where the bullet had exited. How he loved her for the strength and calm she could summon when necessary. That strength had seen her through a lifetime of hardships.

"Pour some whiskey in it. The last thing I need is infection. If I can keep from getting an infection, I can hide it."

She worked over the wound, struggling not to break down and cry. "What about Tom?" she asked.

"If he's in a lot of trouble, someone will come and get us. Otherwise, I expect he'll be riding home himself soon. A couple of the men have to go to Sonoma today, so we'll know soon enough. I'll get him out of town myself, if things go wrong. But after last night I don't think anyone will question whether or not Tom is the culprit."

She cleaned and wrapped the wound as best she could. She set the pan aside as Caleb rolled onto his back, grimacing and breathing deeply. Sarah knelt down beside the bed, putting her head down on the edge.

Caleb touched her hair, the one small movement taking great effort. "Come up here beside me, woman."

She moved onto the bed, lying down on his left side. He put his arm out and held her close, kissing her hair.

"It's done, Sarah. I'll be all right. You just get a little rest and try not to let Juanita see you looking all upset."

"I'm so tired." She broke into quiet tears. "I could have lost you!" she whispered, clinging to his arm.

He sighed deeply. "I'm sorry, Sarah, to put you through this. It was all I could think of to help Tom."

"I know," she whispered. How she loved him for the sacrifices he was always willing to make for his children. If only James had recognized that side of his father. "I hope Tom is all right."

"We'll know soon enough."

"Caleb, if they ever figure out it was you . . ."

He gave her a squeeze but with little strength. He felt suddenly very weak. "They won't find out. If they do, I'll just go down in history as the infamous phantom Indian. That's not such a bad way for somebody like me to go, is it?"

The sheriff of Sonoma and the bank president, Miles Sherman, both came to Tom's cell only hours after Caleb had returned to the ranch after his second night of raiding. "You're free to go, Tom," Sherman told him.

Tom looked up at them, rising from his cot.

"The Indian hit again last night," the sheriff said. "It's pretty obvious where you were. There's nothing left to discuss and no reason to hold you." He opened the cell door. "I'm sorry I had to put you in here at all, but we had to check it out. In fact, you have every right to have this Francesco Fajardo arrested for trying to blackmail you, if you want."

Tom followed the man out into the main office, where he picked up his pistol and rifle. "The hell with Fajardo. I just wanted to get it all straight. Now I want to go home." He put on his hat. "Thank God this phantom Indian, or whatever people call him, decided to strike again." He kept his eyes cool, forcing himself to show no emotion. "Anybody catch him or wound him?" he asked casually.

Sherman shook his head. "No. He got away again. I don't know how he manages to disappear like he does. By the way, a couple of your men are outside. Came into town this afternoon and heard you were in jail. The whole town has been talking about the Indian. They couldn't help but hear what was happening."

Tom strapped on his gun. "It's too bad he can't be caught. A lot of people would sleep better."

"Well, we'll search the hills again," the sheriff spoke up. "But I don't expect to find much of anything. At least no one was killed this time. But just as before a lot of property was damaged." He handed Tom his wallet and money. "You had better get going. Your wife must be worried sick. You should have let us send a man out to tell her what's been going on."

"No. She gets upset very easily. I told her I came to town on business. I was hoping things would work out and I could leave her completely out of it." He shoved his money into his pants pocket, looking at Miles Sherman. "Thank you, sir, for supporting me and keeping a mob off my back."

"No problem, Tom. I know a good man when I see one."

Tom met his eyes with mixed emotions. Sherman was the very kind of man he had hated with a passion for many years—a wealthy white man who put money above all things. He knew good and well that was the only reason the man had supported Tom. Tom Sax had a lot of money in Miles Sherman's bank.

In general, the Americans in Sonoma had supported him. It was almost laughable if not for all the past tears. But it was time to put it all behind him now, and he had to learn to get along with these people for the sake of peace, and to recognize there were many good people among them. He shook hands with Sherman, wondering how he would be treated if he lost all his money. He felt like a little boy who had just gotten away with eating stolen candy, and he broke into a handsome grin.

"I have to get going. I will come back another time to talk about those palominos I want to buy."

"Anytime, Tom."

Tom nodded, walking outside and greeting his men.

"*Patrón*, what is this about your being the phantom Indian?" one called Daniel asked.

Tom just shook his head. "It was all a big misunderstanding because I am Indian. But I hear the Indian himself struck again two nights in a row. I guess if I am sitting in jail, I cannot also be out there attacking the American farmers now, can I?"

They all laughed, heading for the livery to get Tom's horse. Tom sensed someone approaching him from across the street and glanced sideways to see Francesco Fajardo coming toward him. He stopped and waited, grinning.

"How did you do it?" Fajardo growled.

"I didn't do anything. Your timing was just bad, Fajardo."

"This is the man I brought in to see you a few days ago," Daniel spoke up.

"*Sí.* He tried to accuse me of being the Indian who led Los Malos and wanted me to pay him money." His eyes drilled into Fajardo. "Two weeks ago, my friend, you might have convinced the people I was that man. But then think how you would have felt when the *real* phantom Indian struck again!" His eyes turned to an angry dark brown, his smile vanishing. "Get out of my sight, Fajardo! And don't ever let me catch you on my land or I'll have you shot. I could get away with it now. People would understand."

Fajardo blinked, visibly trembling. His entire plan had failed. And the look in Tom Sax's eyes meant business. "You lucky bastard," he sneered. "You are the phantom Indian. I know it!"

Tom suddenly backhanded the man with a jolting blow that sent Fajardo reeling sideways. He landed on the ground, tasting dirt, and Tom planted a boot on the man's back while his men and others watched, none of them blaming Tom for his anger. "You remember what I told you, Fajardo," he growled. "Don't ever come onto my property. You are a liar and a troublemaker. Go find someone else to blackmail. It will *not* be *me*!" He pushed hard with his foot, then left the man and headed for the livery. By the time he rode out, his men and the others who had watched Tom hit Fajardo were shoving Fajardo back across the street, ordering him out of town.

Tom grinned, feeling more victorious than ever. He had

no doubt that he would not see Francesco Fajardo again. His worries were truly over now.

"I am heading home," he told his men as they walked back to him. "You men can stay here and finish whatever you came here for."

"*Sí, patrón,*" Daniel answered. "I hope your father is better."

Tom's smile faded, and his eyes took on a look of grave concern. "What do you mean? What has happened to my father?"

"Oh, it is nothing serious, Señor Sax. He has been getting up too early, I think. He was out riding the fences before the sun was up. This morning he went to the house early because he had a sore shoulder. But he is a big, strong man. I am sure whatever it is, it will go away soon. He has been working too hard. You make him slow down, Señor Sax. Your father, he is a good man, but he is no longer so young, you know."

Tom's heart tightened. A sore shoulder? Caleb Sax never complained of such things. He was as healthy as a man thirty years younger. Surely he had been injured after all! Tom nodded good-bye to his men, trying to hide his grave concern. He turned his horse and rode toward home, keeping to a light gait until he was out of sight, then breaking into a gallop.

Four hours later Tom entered his own land. This should have been a moment of sweet victory and celebration, but there would be no celebrating if something bad had happened to Caleb. He rode straight to the house, and before he could dismount Sarah was at the door. He greeted her on the porch.

"Tom! You're all right. Is it all straightened out?"

He touched her arm. "Yes, but I saw two of my men in town. They said Father was down with a sore shoulder. He was hurt, wasn't he?"

Sarah closed her eyes and nodded her head. "He didn't want you to know. But there's no way he can hide it, Tom. He can't move his right arm at all. I'm sure it will get better in time. The men think he did it working too hard."

"Damn!" Tom turned away. "Did you send for a doctor?"

"Tom, we can't. He won't hear of it. Right now he can't be seen with a bullet wound. No one must know. The bullet went clear through, under his shoulder blade. I cleaned it the best I could."

He sensed the stress in her voice and turned, touching her shoulder. "You tell Juanita you are not feeling well yourself and get some rest. What about Juanita? Does she know?"

"No more than the others."

"My men will be back tonight, and they all will know what happened in town. I will tell her myself later, before they get here. Now that it is over I can tell her without alarming her. Right now I will go and see Father."

She met his dark eyes, seeing the tears in them. "He wanted to do this for you, Tom. You shouldn't blame yourself. And I'm sure he'll be all right in a few days."

"And in the meantime he suffers because of me." Sarah saw the pain in his eyes before he turned away. "I must go and see him."

He left her, going to Caleb and Sarah's room and slowly opening the door. Caleb looked up from where he sat in a chair rubbing his arm. "Tom!" His face lit up and he rose from the chair. "It worked. It must have worked!" He stopped short of embracing the young man when he saw the sorrow in his eyes.

"You were shot." Tom almost groaned the words.

Caleb frowned. "Who told on me?"

"I knew it the minute my men in town said you went in early with a sore shoulder."

Caleb sighed deeply. "I didn't want you to know, but I guess I couldn't have done a very good job of hiding it. I'll be all right, Tom."

Tom pressed his lips tightly together, his jaw flexing in an effort to stay in control. He swallowed before speaking. "If you had been hurt bad, or killed—"

"But I wasn't. And now it's over, Tom. The one cloud that hung over your head has been cleared away, and there can be nothing but happiness ahead now for you and Juanita. Believe me, a stiff arm is a small price to pay for that!"

The sudden and unwanted tears came then, as all the agony of the past mixed with the sudden relief of feeling truly free swept over Tom. He reached out and embraced his father, trembling with a wild mixture of emotions.

"It's over now, Tom." Caleb gave him a firm embrace with his good arm. "It's time to let out all the rest of the hatred and be rid of it. You've been full of hatred ever since Texas. It's done now."

Jess got out his list of needed supplies as he plopped a sack of flour on the counter in front of the supply store owner.

"Morning, Mr. Purnell." The man smiled.

"Morning. I need quite a few things, Handy."

"Well, just name them."

Jess went down the list. He liked the people here in Henderson. They were some of the better Americans, not like the first ones who had come here, robbing and killing and destroying the old established haciendas. These Americans seemed to be trying to get along with the *californios*. It was obvious they had to make the mixture work. The real troublemakers were the prospectors who came here and never found their dream—drifters, some of them outlaws who had fled the East, who for lack of money were now turning to their old occupations to get it. Most of them didn't dare try to jump a man's claim. Claim jumpers got hung real fast. So they turned to preying on the settlers instead. But here in Henderson things were peaceful enough, and they were only a two-day ride from Caleb and Sarah to the southeast, and one day from Sonoma to the southwest.

"Do you think they'll ever catch that there phantom Indian?" Handy was asking him. "He's raided around here before, too, you know. You'd best keep a good eye out for your woman and kids."

"Oh, I will." Jess smiled to himself. They had just returned from visiting Caleb and Sarah, and he knew the whole story. Caleb Sax never ceased to amaze him in the distance he would go to help his family. And Tom, in his joy at truly being free now, had held a huge *fiesta* in honor of his sister's visit, inviting every hired hand and their wives and girlfriends, and hiring an *orquesta* that played gay Spanish music for a party that lasted three days. The best part of the visit, especially for Lynda, was to see her mother looking so well. Thank God Caleb was recovering from his wound. Tom Sax would have been a very broken man if his father had been killed or maimed in the incident.

Jess was setting a sack of potatoes on the counter when he heard a scream from outside. Lynda! He threw down his list and ran to the door, followed by Handy, who came around from behind the counter to see what the commotion was.

"You leave my ma alone!" Ten-year-old John was standing near their wagon, fists clenched, looking ready to dive into five men who were armed and one of whom had hold of Lynda, locking her arms behind her. Three-year-old Jessica stood in the back of the wagon crying.

"Well now, boy, she's just a squaw," one of the men jeered at John. "Don't you know squaws is for the takin'? We been up in the mountains, boy, pannin' for gold. Ain't seen anything this pretty that was free for the takin' in a long time."

"Let her go!" Jess demanded, moving up beside his son. He stood unwavering in front of the men, while people stared from windows and from behind shelter.

One of the men just laughed. "Says who?"

"Says her husband."

"Whoooo-weeee," another jeered. "The man has got himself a pretty little squaw! He done found out squaws is a lot more fun in bed than white women."

"Let her go!" John hissed, tears in his eyes. He made a move and Jess reached out and grabbed his arm.

"Get your sister and go inside the store."

"But, Pa—"

"Do it! Now!"

John knew when his father meant business. He ran to the wagon, grabbing Jessica and carrying the kicking and crying girl inside the store. Handy hurriedly let him in and closed the door again, watching from a window. It had only been lately that some of the scum in the mountains had trickled down into town, causing trouble. There was no law in Henderson, and these men knew it.

One of the five men outside stepped away from the others, leering at Jess. "Well, now, we got us a real brave man here." His eyes looked Jess up and down, sizing him up. He took inventory of Jess's powerful build, but he figured that was from pushing a plow. "Trouble is, you farmers don't know how to use a gun, and we do," he goaded. "So we're gonna take the pretty squaw with us for a while, farmer. When we're done with her, you can have her back, I promise."

They all laughed, but Jess stood unflinching. Lynda quit her initial struggling, realizing that if Jess was going to do anything at all, the less movement, the better. She watched her husband with complete faith and trust in his skills. His sure, strong ways were much of what she loved about him, and since being more on his own, those qualities had shone through even more, making her realize he was more man than she had even realized.

The men holding her sobered when Jess stood his ground and showed no sign of fear. He kept his eyes on the one who had just spoken to him. "A long time ago, mister, back in Texas, my wife suffered at the hands of trash like you. I promised her that it would never happen again, and I aim to keep that promise. Touch her, and you're a dead man, even if she goes down *with* you."

Their apparent leader smiled nervously. "Well, now, that's a pretty brave statement, comin' from a farmer who probably don't know better than to shoot his own foot off with his pistol." The man's eyes fell to the repeating pistol at Jess's side. "Does it make you feel good, wearin' a gun, farmer? You know how to shoot more than the side of a barn?"

Jess just grinned. "Try me."

There was a tense moment of silence and hesitancy while Jess's keen eye watched every man facing him.

"I don't like the look in his eyes, Bates," the one holding Lynda grumped. "Ain't no Indian woman worth gettin' killed over."

"I ain't backin' down from no farmer," Bates answered.

He moved toward Lynda, grinning again. "Go ahead, Davis," he told the man holding her. "Grab yourself a handful. I'll take care of the farmer."

The one called Davis locked Lynda's arms behind her with just one of his own, moving the other arm around her waist and up toward her breasts. But before he could touch them Jess's pistol was out and fired with amazing accuracy, opening a hole in the man's head. Lynda actually felt the bullet whiz past her face.

After that all was a blur of action to Lynda, guns firing all around as she dropped to the ground. She covered her head, terrified for Jess, who had already put a bullet in the one called Bates when the man pulled a gun on Jess the split second after Jess fired the first shot that killed Davis. Jess rolled on the ground to avoid getting hit, coming up and shooting a third man who was firing at him. The other two were scrambling for cover.

"Lynda, roll under the wagon!" Jess shouted, saying a quick prayer she had not been hurt.

She quickly obeyed as more shots were fired. Jess made a dash for a water barrel, ducking behind it and taking careful aim at the fourth man, who darted out from behind a watering trough. Jess fired, and the man cried out and landed in the trough.

Jess searched desperately for the fifth man, but moments later a horse galloped off in the distance.

All was quiet. Jess waited a moment, then came out from behind the barrel. He holstered his gun and hurried over to the wagon, helping a shaking Lynda from under it while townspeople began filtering out of doorways and alleys. Jess grasped Lynda close, and her fingers dug into his arms.

"Jess, they could have killed you!"

"I'm all right. What about you?"

"I'm not hurt." She looked into his eyes then, her own eyes widening with sudden realization. "I felt your bullet go right past my face."

He kissed her cheek, tears in his eyes. "I know. I'm sorry. I went crazy watching him." He held her close again. "My God, if my aim had been off—"

"I wasn't afraid. I knew if I just held still you could do it."

John ran out beside them, hugging his mother from behind, while little Jessica clung to her skirts, crying. John moved beside his father.

"You all right, Pa?"

Jess reluctantly released his hold on Lynda. "As far as I know."

"Wow, Pa, I never knew you were *that* good! I never saw anything like it!"

"Mr. Purnell!" Handy hurried up to Jess. "What shooting! You are something with that pistol."

Others gathered around him, praising his courage and skill. The general commotion turned to talk of needing protection against men such as those Jess had just faced down, and before the excitement was over, the people were urging Jess to consider being their sheriff.

"That's an excellent idea," one of them shouted.

"We could pay you well, Mr. Purnell," Handy told him. "We would gladly pool our money and give you a good wage and build you a nice house right here in town to live in for nothing. You might make better money than you do ranching."

Jess frowned, confused himself at the moment. "I don't know . . . you don't even have a jail here."

"We could build one easy enough," another spoke up. "Our blacksmith could make an iron cell."

"Oh, Mr. Purnell, we need a lawman here so badly," a woman put in. "Men like those you just faced have been coming here more frequently lately. If we don't put a stop to it, they'll take over the town eventually, and it won't be a fit place to live. Please, think about it, Mr. Purnell, for the sake of the women and children, if nothing else."

Jess looked at Lynda, seeing the worry in her eyes at the thought of her husband's taking what could be such a dangerous job. Lynda in return saw a hint of eagerness in Jess's eyes. He wasn't really happy just ranching. He had been doing it nearly all his life, and he was tired. Somehow being a sheriff seemed to fit a man like Jess. But the thought of it terrified her.

"It's something my wife and I would have to discuss alone."

Lynda knew what that meant. Jess Purnell was already considering becoming the first sheriff of Henderson.

• Chapter Twenty-six •

It was destined to become one of history's most memorable Indian treaty gatherings. The summer of 1851 found Cale headed for Fort Laramie with every Cheyenne man, woman, and child along. There they would join several other tribes, even enemy Crow, to discuss a treaty with men representing the white man's government and to finally learn just what lands they could call their own.

Over the next several days a total of over ten thousand Indians gathered. Generations later they would find themselves still wondering why they didn't stick together right then and there and wipe out all whites from Canada to Mexico. But at that time the Indians were still trusting, still ready to discuss what land would be theirs, still hoping for a peaceful solution to white filtration into their lands. The various tribes still had their own quarrels: whether or not to sign a treaty within each tribe; and quarrels with other tribes that stemmed from ancient grievances never resolved; quarrels that prohibited them from holding together against their common enemy—the white man.

Cale had more than the treaty on his mind. This would be a good year for him. They would hold their treaty council and finally have peace; and soon after the council, he would marry Snowbird. He was seventeen, but soon to be

eighteen and he had more than proven his manhood.
Snowbird was fifteen—a woman in his eyes and in the
eyes of the Cheyenne. And to Cale she was the most beautiful woman among his tribe. His only regret was that his
mother and grandparents could not be present for the celebration of his wedding and would probably never know
Snowbird. She was so grown up from when Caleb had met
her when he attended the Sun Dance ritual with Cale.
Some might think him too young to be a husband, but
death seemed always so near now, as more and more
whites were coming, bringing disease; bringing more conflict. He felt like a man, and Snowbird's father approved.
He did not want to waste any precious years with Snowbird, and he wanted to be one with her.

If only Blue Hawk could be here. But he was so far
away now, living in the white man's world, because of his
love for Sarah Sax. Cale wondered how many years it
would be yet before his grandfather came home to the
Cheyenne. He prayed the man would not die before he
could see him again.

All those years he had lived with his grandparents and
his mother and Jess seemed like another time, another
Cale. How could it all seem so long ago, when he was now
only seventeen? Texas. It nudged at his memory often,
especially deep in the night—mostly in the form of remembering James and how close they once were. He could
not help wondering how James was doing now, where he
was and if he was happy.

All thoughts of the past vanished during the next few
days. The number of Indians around Fort Laramie swelled
until the treaty council had to be moved to Horse Creek, an
area thirty-five miles south of Fort Laramie, where there
was fresh grass for the thousands of horses that had already
overgrazed the area around the fort.

This was an important moment for the Indian. There
were a few skirmishes between members of enemy tribes,
but most of them seemed to recognize that it was important
to show their own skills and power to the important white
men present.

How Cale wished his grandfather could see the grand

spectacle the Sioux and Cheyenne presented! On one occasion nearly a thousand Sioux warriors rode in a column four abreast to the commissioners' tents, bringing gifts. The white men gave gifts of tobacco and vermilion in return. There were demonstrations of the Indians' riding skills, a display of the various positions from which a good warrior could shoot an arrow with remarkable accuracy, daring trick riding that made the white men gasp.

Cale had no doubt that these days of treaty-making were going to be days he would long remember—days of feasting with other tribes and celebrating in a hundred ways. And, of course, the marriage. His blood burned hot with the thought of it. He had only to wait for Snowbird to finish their wedding tipi. "One more day," her mother had told him. He had hardly caught a glimpse of Snowbird. She was teasing him, staying out of sight, deliberately not allowing him to see or talk to her before their wedding day.

After what Cale considered eloquent speeches by Cheyenne leaders, words that sometimes left the schooled white men surprised and speechless at the wisdom of the Indian, a treaty was finally drawn to mark the boundaries within which the Cheyenne could supposedly ride freely. It included the southeast corner of what the white man called Wyoming, and most of the northeastern quarter of Colorado, all the way down to the Arkansas River near the site of old Bent's Fort, the western border being the foothills of the Rockies and the eastern border along the territories the white man called Kansas and Nebraska.

The thought of how the Indians' territory had been narrowed saddened Cale. The white man considered the area they had "allowed" the Indians quite large. But once the Cheyenne roamed all the way from Canada to Mexico, west beyond the mountains, and much farther east. It was necessary to move with the seasons and the buffalo. He could not help wondering just how they would continue to survive and grow when confined to such a small amount of land. The white men said they would be "subsidized" with "government annuities," which supposedly meant that the white man's government would provide them with food, tobacco, clothing, utensils, whatever the Indian needed that he could no longer get from the land.

That disturbed Cale. Didn't it mean a loss of pride? Were they to begin taking handouts, like beggars? The white men talked of helping the Indians learn to farm. Farm! What Indian wanted to farm? It all left a heavy feeling in his heart, for he knew from living in Texas and from long talks with his grandfather that the white man often spoke out of both sides of his mouth. Would they really come through with the "annuities"? He wished his grandfather were present to discuss these things, to help him decide if this new Laramie Treaty was a good thing. Everyone seemed satisfied, but Cale was not.

The treaty was signed. And as they all waited for the first wagons full of "annuities" that the white men promised were coming right away and that they would hand out before the Indians left, Snowbird finished her wedding tipi. It was time to forget about his worries over the white man's promises. Snowbird would be his wife. If only Blue Hawk could be here to see her now!

Sarah laughed as Caleb began sticking wildflowers into her hair. He had pulled the pins from it, letting the slightly graying but still beautiful tresses fall to her waist. He grasped her across the bosom and laid her back on the blanket they had brought along, then moved on top of her and kissed her, raising up on his elbows to study the velvety skin of her face.

"You look like a young girl like that."

She smiled and pulled a daisy from behind her ear. "Then I'd better do this more often. It isn't easy for someone my age to look young."

He leaned down and kissed her eyes. "In my eyes that's how you always look."

They lay on a grassy hill under a huge ponderosa pine that Caleb guessed had to be over a hundred years old. This had become their favorite spot to come to when they wanted to be alone. It was on a hill far above Tom's house, and there was enough growth of smaller trees and bushes bordering the spot that when they lay down, no one below could see them. They had made love here several times. Here it was just Caleb and Sarah and no one else.

Sometimes Sarah felt self-conscious when she lay naked under the sun. Surely she no longer had the body she had when this man fell in love with her, yet his own dark, magnificent build never seemed to change. But Caleb never touched her any way but with utter gentleness and near worship.

His lips moved to her throat, and he moved a big hand over one breast and to the buttons of her dress. She breathed deeply, looking up at the aging, sprawling branches of the old pine tree. "Oh, I love it here, Caleb. It's like this is our special place. When we come here, it's like leaving the rest of the world behind."

He sat her up and pulled her dress to her waist, then began unlacing her undergarment. "I knew you'd like it the first time I saw it. We'll come here often, Sarah, as often as you want. I know what you mean. Here, alone with you, I feel as if we've never had a problem in our lives— almost as if we're starting all over."

"In so many ways we are. Coming here has been like being given a second life. I just hope God allows me enough years—"

He put his fingers to her lips. "When we come here we don't talk about anything but good things, remember? And today you feel good and look beautiful." He pulled open her undergarment, reaching inside with big, calloused hands and running them over her breasts. She felt her cheeks going crimson. He pulled off the undergarment, and she was naked to the waist. He pulled her onto his lap and kissed her, the kiss lingering.

Nothing more was said. He nibbled and teased with his lips, and soon she found herself lying back on the blanket again, her clothes coming off. In the next moment he stood next to her in raw, naked splendor, his body hard and magnificent as he came down to her.

A sweet breeze caressed Caleb's skin as he moved between her legs. He stayed on his knees and lifted her hips, guiding himself into her and enjoying the little gasp that came from her lips. He liked looking at her this way. It seemed so much more natural to do this in the open air under the big ponderosa. Perhaps it was the Indian in him that made it seem as though nature and making love with his woman should just go together. He had never liked beds all that much, but again, that had just been a part of the white life he had long ago accepted in order to be with her.

At least Sarah willingly agreed to some of the little things he sometimes wanted to do that went against her upbringing as a white woman—like this moment, lying naked in the open air with the grass beneath her, letting her man take her in a perfectly natural need. He moved one hand under her hips and pressed his other hand against her belly, supporting her as he rhythmically urged forth her gentle climax. Her natural muscle reactions drew him even deeper, telling him all he needed to know.

He came down close to her, whispering sweet Indian words into her ear as he thrust himself deep, holding out as long as possible until his own life pulsed into her.

For several minutes neither of them spoke. He pulled away from her, picking up a second blanket and covering her with it, then lying down beside her. He stared up into the branches of the pine, watching them sway gently with the wind. He wondered about Cale and the Sioux and Cheyenne. He had not told Sarah yet about the major treaty-signing he had heard about from men who had been to Sonoma. Would it really mean peace? He doubted it. The government and white settlers had yet to keep to any treaty agreement. Why should this one be any different?

A bird cried out somewhere, and again he felt the distant calling, the restless spirit in his soul craving to be released. The wind made a soft moaning sound through the pine needles overhead, and all the years and their hardships seemed to be represented in that big, old tree. It had been standing there tall and strong since many years before he was even born, and he did not doubt it would be there for many years after his death. It made life seem so frail and short. He pulled Sarah closer.

* * *

James entered Gilbert Hayden's office, greeting the man warmly. Hayden had become like a father to James, a guiding hand that had taught him everything a young man needed to know to be successful in the world of the merchant. And James had become a valuable asset to Hayden; so competent and so excited about the added responsibilities Hayden gave him that he had never stayed in any of the Eastern cities to which he had traveled as a buyer for Hayden. He had always returned to St. Louis and the man who had sent him off, coming back with new items that helped Gilbert Hayden expand his business.

James wore a suit of the latest fashion. It was 1857, which meant a man wore peg-top trousers by day and tighter-fitting trousers in the evening, both with a side band of a different color striping the outer seam of the pants. Waistcoats were a must, with lapels that buttoned back, and a knee-length outer jacket was always worn. His ties were either tied into large bows at the neck, or he wore a large scarf tied neatly at the neck and fluffed out down the front of his shirt and tucked into his waistcoat.

James liked to look good. It helped win customers and helped in dealing in buying and selling. He was proud of the gold watch Hayden had given him the year before for James's excellent job of supervising the bookkeeping and inventory, the job he held when he wasn't off on another buying venture.

James stood as tall as his father, the father Gilbert Hayden knew nothing about. He was twenty-four now, a handsome young man with thick, sandy hair that had a hint of red to it in the sun; bright, blue eyes; and an even, sincere smile. His high cheekbones and straight, proud nose only enhanced his good looks, and his big hands always gave a firm, friendly handshake.

James Sax was a man destined to be wealthy and successful. That was what Hayden was always telling him. The man had seen that James got some special tutoring, for he had been denied higher learning in Texas, or so that was what Hayden understood. According to the story James had given Hayden, James had grown up in Texas and had worked hard helping his parents run a farm there. His parents had been killed by Comanche, and after a long struggle to keep the farm going, James had given up and had come to St. Louis, to a place more civilized, where he hoped to find work and be able to make something of himself.

James had received a few letters from someone named Sax in Colorado, but he had told Hayden the letters were from an uncle who had been too destitute himself to help James after his parents had been killed. The letter had gone unanswered. Hayden felt sorry for the boy with "bad memories" of Texas who wanted to better himself. He had taken the young man under his wing.

"Have a seat, Jim," the man told him with a warm smile. Hayden sat behind a huge walnut desk. He was sixty, balding and gray. He was a slender man, a man who had worked hard all his life, building a mercantile empire and putting so much of his energy into that enterprise that he had never remarried after losing his wife in death over thirty years ago. He realized now that all the hard work had just been his way of getting over the terrible grief. He had loved her dearly. There had never been another.

"What do you need, Mr. Hayden?"

Hayden laughed lightly. "Jim, I wish you'd call me Gil. You know you're free to do so."

James smiled and shrugged. "It's kind of hard to do. After all, you are my boss."

"And you're a young man who respects that. I understand. But, please, do call me Gil. You have come much too far, and I have known you too long now, for you to be calling me mister."

James nodded. "If you say so."

Hayden laughed lightly and nodded. "I say so." He looked James over quietly for a moment. "How old are you now, Jim?"

"Twenty-four, sir."

Hayden nodded. "You were no more than a boy when you came here looking for work. I still remember the day."

James thought of the day he had left Colorado, the way

his father had turned and waved, silhouetted against the horizon. A brief stabbing pain moved through his chest. Why had he stopped writing them? "Yes, sir, I was pretty young."

"Well, now you're a man, and nothing short of a partner in this business of mine." The man leaned forward, resting his elbows on his desk. "How would you like to be just that—legally? A partner?"

James stared at Hayden in surprise. "Partner? You mean . . . own half of your mercantile business?"

Hayden nodded again, smiling warmly.

James struggled for a moment with the shock of the offer. Hayden was a rich man. To be his partner . . . "Sir, I wouldn't feel right about it. I've only been here nine years."

"Long enough for me to know the right man when I see him." The man leaned back in his chair. "Jim, I'm getting old. I have no family, no one to whom I can leave all of this, at least not anyone I could really trust. You've proven your intelligence and ability many times over. You're young and personable, a hard worker. I can't think of a better person to inherit all of this someday. I don't want my business to fall into the hands of courts and the state of Missouri. I want someone to take it over who will care about it and keep it going. I've worked too hard at this to let it all just crumble when I leave this world. Would you be willing to take this over when I'm gone?"

James swallowed, looking away, overwhelmed by the man's kindness and suffering a sudden guilt. What would Hayden think of him for lying about where he had come from? What would he think if he knew James Sax had Indian blood? Would it matter? He should tell the man. He had always meant to, but there never seemed to be a right time. Indian! Why did he have to be part Indian?

He faced Hayden again. Damned if he was going to let his Indian blood destroy the best chance for success and wealth a man could ever stumble upon. This was the ultimate opportunity to live the life he had always dreamed of living. Maybe someday he could even use it to help his poor mother, to give her the kind of life his father had never given her. But then how would his mother feel about the lies he had told to get this far?

"I . . . I don't know what to say, Mr. Hay—I mean, Gil. You know that I would very gladly carry on your business. I just feel as if I don't deserve it."

"Of course you deserve it. For years I've been looking for just the right man to take all this over. But for one reason or another, none of those who have worked for me in the past had all the right qualities. You have everything, Jim: guts, determination, intelligence—and you're handsome and presentable, a man who can make deals and win customers over with a smile and a handshake. Your parents must have been very fine people to raise a man of such fine qualities."

James struggled to keep a smile on his face, but again the awful pain stabbed at him. "Yes, sir," he managed to answer, this time sincerely. "They were good people." Why did he feel this strange lump in his throat? "They taught me a lot about hard work and . . . honesty."

Hayden opened a drawer and took out a cigar for himself, offering one to James. After James refused, Hayden lit his own. "Jim, I'm making out a will tomorrow. It will name you as my partner and will give you full rights to everything I own when I'm gone."

James shook his head, his eyes actually tearing. "I don't know what to say, sir."

"Don't say anything. I know gratefulness when I see it." The man moved around to sit on the edge of his desk. "There is only one thing I ask of you. It will give you the best experience you've had so far—sort of a chance to know what it's like to start from the ground up."

James ran a hand through his hair. "Anything you say, sir."

Hayden puffed the cigar a moment, then stood up and walked to a big map on his wall, pointing to Colorado Territory. "The West, son. This is where our future lies."

James felt an odd chill, apprehension. Colorado!

"A territory growing very fast, Jim. And it's centered in the heart of the central route between here and California, a route that will be taken by thousands over the next several years, mark my words. The base of the Rocky Mountains —that's the most logical place to stop and stock up on supplies before going on over the Divide and through the deserts and the Sierras to California and other points west."

Hayden left the map and came closer. "And I'm laying odds that there will be a railroad out of St. Louis straight into that territory someday, Jim." He set the cigar aside in an ashtray. "I want to open a store in there, and I want you to do it for me—run it for me—do everything that needs to be done to build a business. We'll take some time to consider the best spot, but I'd be willing to bet that before you're through I'll have more than one store there—maybe even keep going and have a Hayden's Mercantile opening somewhere in California. What do you say, Jim? It would be a great experience for you."

Never had James struggled more to keep his composure. Colorado! It was the *last* place he wanted to go—back to uncivilized country, Indian country. From what he read, the Cheyenne were still riding wild in Colorado, disobeying the treaty agreement, sometimes attacking settlers. He didn't want to go back to that country—back to all the things he had deliberately left so long ago.

He rose from his chair, walking to a window, trying to think straight. He didn't want to disappoint Gilbert Hayden. The man treated him like a son and was now offering him a virtual merchandising empire. It was impossible to tell him so. He loved Gilbert Hayden almost as he would love a father.

Father. He had a father, one he also loved but had deserted a long time ago. He had to think of Mr. Hayden now, and all the man had done for him. He couldn't let his own selfish desires get in the way. Besides, it couldn't be all that bad. Surely the place was becoming more civilized now. And a young man in his position could become very important in a new and growing territory. If that was all it took to seal this wonderful offer, why shouldn't he go? After all, his family was all gone from Colorado now—all but Cale. But then how much chance was there that their paths would ever cross again?

He turned, facing Hayden. "I'll miss you, Gil. But I'll go. It sounds exciting." He struggled to show some enthusiasm.

Hayden smiled almost sadly. "I'll miss you, too. But if you're going to be my partner, it's going to be a real good experience for you, Jim. You can keep in touch by telegraph"—he rolled his eyes—"unless the damned Indians cut the wires. I hear they do that a lot."

James felt the old shame—the fear of being found out mixed with the guilt of pretending he was something he was not.

"But don't you worry about the Indians. I hear Colorado citizens are working very hard on ways to rid the whole territory of them." Hayden stepped closer to James and put out his hand. "Well? Are we agreed, partner?"

James breathed deeply to get rid of the hurt in his chest. He took the man's hand firmly. "Agreed. I'll never forget this, Gil. I'll always feel indebted to you, and I promise to do everything in my power to help Hayden's Mercantile expand even more."

Hayden squeezed his hand. "'Hayden & Sax' you mean. I'm officially changing the name on the front of all my stores, Jim. When you open a new store out west, you call it 'Hayden & Sax Mercantile.'"

James could not get over the irony of it. He had left Colorado in near poverty, the very place where his parents had struggled desperately just to survive. Now their son would be going there a rich man. He wished he could share this moment with his parents, but he dared not even tell them. They might come and see him.

He buried the old longing to see them again, as well as the terrible burden of guilt that seemed to be getting heavier. He had set his course in life and he would not go back, nor would he let his Indian blood destroy all that he had worked so hard to achieve.

• Chapter Twenty-seven •

Late 1857 found the Saxes in Henderson, attending a dance for that town's new mayor, Jess Purnell. A huge barn had been cleared and decorated, a side of beef roasted, and wine was passed around freely. Seventeen-year-old John was proud of his father and had dreams of his own now of one day being the sheriff of Henderson. He was good with a gun, and he had watched his father handle men. John was taller than Jess but carried the same powerful build as his father. He was a most handsome young man, with his mother's dark skin and hair and his mother's and grandfather's striking blue eyes.

Jessica, almost ten now, still had very curly hair. It was a shining black color, and her eyes were also blue, but her skin was fair and creamy, seeming even whiter against her dark hair and lashes. She danced now with her grandfather, giggling at how Caleb had to bend over to keep a hand at her waist. Fiddles played, and Caleb and Jessica moved in circles to the music while others watched. A few women gossiped about the new mayor's "Indian" wife and father-in-law; about the gracious and lovely white woman who was his mother-in-law. None suspected that the new mayor's wealthy but also "Indian" brother-in-law, Tom Sax, was none other than the infamous phantom Indian who had led Los Malos and brought terror to many of the very people who watched him now. Nor did they know that yet another tragic story had birthed the love Tom Sax shared for his Mexican wife.

That love could not be more obvious as Jess attempted to introduce Tom and Juanita and their now five children to one of the town's more prominent businessmen. Jess and

Tom had both been drinking, and introductions became a comedy as Jess held up his hand and insisted on taking care of the matter himself, challenging Tom that he could name each child and his or her age.

Tom bowed and Juanita laughed. "Be my guest, brother-in-law," Tom told him, his dark eyes dancing teasingly as he lined up his children. One little girl who could barely walk stood beside Juanita, clinging to her mother's skirts, and Juanita held a very new baby in her arms.

Jess stood back, studying each one. "Now give me a minute," he told them, followed by helpless laughter.

Caleb walked Jessica over to the gathering, moving to stand beside Sarah. "What's going on?" he asked her.

"Jess insists on naming all of Tom's children for that man—a Mr. Mathewson, a friend of Jess's."

Caleb grinned as Jess stood back, eyeing the row of Sax descendants. "Okay, okay, here goes."

His friend folded his arms, grinning. "I am waiting, Purnell."

Sarah watched Jess. He was happy. Age seemed to be good to him. He was still hard and handsome. And he had been a good husband to her Lynda. It was good to see that at least Tom and Lynda were happy and settled now. If only James and Cale could be with them. James . . . why had he never answered their letters?

"This is Antonio Galvez," Jess told his friend, pointing to the oldest boy. "And he is . . . uh . . . nine. Nine?" He looked at Tony, who grinned and shook his head. "I will be eight soon," he giggled. The others laughed as Jess made a face at being wrong.

Every one of Tom's children was dark, a grand mixture of Mexican and Indian and that hint of white that made them all handsome boys and beautiful girls. Tom Sax had a family some men envied, but Caleb knew he deserved it. Yes, he by God deserved it.

Tom moved behind the second child, who stood just a little shorter than his older brother. He put his hands on the boy's shoulders from behind. "And who is this?" he asked Jess.

"This is number two son, Ricardo Jesus. And he is three years younger than Tony, so he is five."

"Very good, señor," Tom teased. He moved to the third child.

"Andres . . . Andres . . ." Jess frowned. "I don't remember his middle name. Hell, I'm doing good to remember their first names." He laughed.

The others laughed with him.

"I am thwee yews old," Andres spoke up, still unable to say his "r's". He held up his chin as though he knew everything and no one else knew anything.

They all laughed again, and Tom moved to child number four, waiting for Jess. Jess grinned.

"Ah, this is the first daughter. How can I forget her? This is Rosanna Marie." Jess bent close to the chubby-cheeked and exquisitely beautiful child who clung to her mother's skirts. "And Rosanna Marie is about two years old."

Tom shook his head. "You are doing better than I thought you would."

Jess folded his arms, nodding proudly. "And the one in Juanita's arms is a new arrival—another daughter—Louise Juanita." He turned to Tom. "There, you see?"

Tom grinned, picking up Rosanna, who started to cry. "Jess, you amaze me."

"Well, actually, I told Lynda to help me remember all this before you came," Jess admitted. It brought another round of laughter and another round of drinks, before they all moved to the picnic tables spread with every conceivable kind of homemade dish.

Sarah held back, and Caleb turned to see her watching the children and grandchildren with tears in her eyes. He walked back to her, taking her arm. "What's wrong, Sarah?"

She looked up at him, smiling through tears. "Look at them, Caleb. I guess we did a few things right after all, didn't we?" She swallowed and wiped her eyes. "They're so happy. I just wish James and Cale could be here with us." She met his eyes, her own tearing more. "I'm not going to ever see my James again, am I?"

He grasped her shoulders. "Don't do this, Sarah. There are some things in life we can do nothing about, or at least you reach a point where you've done all you can."

"But why doesn't he answer our letters?" She sniffed, grasping the front of his shirt. "Oh, God, I know why. And it makes me sick, Caleb. I'm so sorry for what he's doing."

"*You're* sorry?" He walked her around behind a shed and pulled her close. "Don't you ever, ever be sorry about anything. Whatever has happened to any of the children, or to us, it was not your fault, or even mine. You said that yourself, remember? It has taken me years to stop blaming myself. Don't go turning it on yourself now."

She cried for several quiet minutes, while Caleb checked his anger at James Sax. He patted her shoulder, thinking how frail she felt in his arms.

"I just get these fits of depression, and I can't seem to control them, Caleb." She pulled away and took a handkerchief from the pocket of her dress, dabbing at her eyes. "And more and more I'm forgetting the most common, everyday things, yet I can remember so vividly things that happened thirty or forty years ago. It scares me." She looked up at him, so tall and strong. "Isn't that a sign of old age?"

He laughed and hugged her, trying to keep the moment light. "Sarah, take a look at other women your age and then look in the mirror. You're the prettiest woman here. Now the whole family is waiting for us."

Lynda came around the building looking for them, stopping short when she saw her mother crying in her father's arms. "Mother! What's wrong?"

"Just having a little sentimental cry," Caleb told their daughter. "You know how women are—they cry when they're sad, and they cry when they're happy. And us men have to try to figure out the difference. It's a damned hard situation you females put us in sometimes."

Their eyes held. Her father's smile did not fool Lynda. She saw the pain behind the smile, the worry, the terror. She took a deep breath and put on a smile of her own. "Oh, Mother, don't you dare spoil this day for yourself and the rest of us. Now do come and eat. You're much too thin anyway. Come and let all those fat old women around the picnic table envy the way you can stuff yourself and still be prettier and more slender than they could ever hope to be. Besides, a lady friend of mine wants to meet you. She knows all about you and Father, and she thinks you're quite remarkable."

Sarah laughed lightly, blowing her nose and wiping her eyes. "Remarkable? That's one I've never heard before." She looked up at Caleb. "How about that, Caleb Sax?" She blew her nose again. "You have a remarkable wife."

He nodded, smiling sadly. "Well, it really isn't a bad description. You *are* a remarkable woman." He leaned down and kissed her cheek. "Especially in bed," he whispered in her ear.

"Caleb Sax!" She pushed him and walked off with Lynda, clasping her hands in joy when Lynda told her she was going to come and visit for two weeks.

Caleb watched them walk away, his heart hurting so bad that he put a hand to his chest. *Yes, quite a remarkable woman,* he thought. He walked toward the picnic table, where thirteen of the people there were Saxes or married to Saxes. Sarah was right. They had done something right. Here was the proof, the seeds of their love. But some of those seeds still remained scattered. And some had been snuffed out completely and lay buried—in Texas. Their lives had moved in a wide circle, covering half this country called America. He looked up at the sun and thought of Cale and the sun stone. His own circle was not yet complete.

James watched out the window of the stagecoach as the land became painfully familiar. Broad, empty plains moved into a sea of rolling hills that led toward the base of the snowcapped Rockies.

This was the land he had fled and hoped never to see again. Now here he was, as though fate had dragged him back to laugh at him and torture him with memories. It was 1858. Ten years had gone by since he left. And yet it seemed on every ridge he could see his father, sitting proudly on a big horse—his long, black hair flying in the wind, his face painted, the man dressed in buckskins and adorned with weapons. He could see the thin, faint scar on Caleb's left cheek, put there by a white man when his father was just a boy.

Why did James always feel his father watching him? Was this what a man's conscience did to him? Thank God his parents were at least in California. He would not have to face them.

He sighed deeply, reminding himself what was at stake. He had to like this place, had to make it all work. He was going to a new town called Denver. The stage driver had told him Denver was just a one-street town with log buildings, but there had recently been a gold strike there, but no one was sure how profitable it would prove to be. Easterners were headed for the area, the call of gold again beckoning those who dreamed of riches. James guessed that most would find nothing but hard work and despair. But a gold rush meant growth, and James would take advantage of that growth and establish one of the first mercantiles in the area.

He moved his handsome blue eyes again to the young woman who sat across from him. She was traveling with her mother to Colorado, where her father had already gone to establish a small bank to grubstake prospectors, an easy means of getting rich without doing the back-breaking work of actually panning and picking for gold. The young woman's name was Willena Treat, and James thought her the prettiest young lady he had ever set eyes on. Her golden hair fell in a cascade of waves down her back, the sides of it drawn up into pretty curls on top of her head. Her big, inquisitive eyes were green, and when she smiled her lips exposed white, even teeth and provocative little dimples appeared in her cheeks.

He already knew that Willena Treat was nineteen and well schooled. Her family had money, and she dressed beautifully. He couldn't help but wonder how she stayed so fresh-looking on this hot, dusty trip, and he admired her courage in coming to a land still uncivilized, where she planned to start a school in Denver for the children of prospectors who had families with them. Willena had enough schooling herself to teach, and although her mother had wanted her to stay in Philadelphia where they had lived before, Willena would not hear of it. Her father loved the Rocky Mountain area and wanted to stay. He had come home and sold everything except the bank he owned, then moved his wife and daughter temporarily into a relative's home in Philadelphia until he was more settled in Colorado. Their home would be a log house for now, but Willena's father already had plans made and material ordered to build his family a fine brick home, or so Willena and her mother had told him.

He liked Willena. She was not only pretty, she was smart, and very sweet. He continued his own lie about his past, but could at least tell her he was familiar with the wild West as she called it, which made for good conversation. Willena wanted to know all about it, and he could tell she looked to him with great admiration and curiosity—and there was no mistaking the physical attraction each had for the other.

Her mother was kind and attentive and didn't seem to mind her daughter's talking for hours on end with James Sax. After all, James Sax was co-owner of one of the most successful mercantile chains in the Midwest. Making his acquaintance could only be beneficial for her daughter.

But James knew Willena didn't look at it that way. She was a genuinely sweet girl. Like his father, James Sax was a good judge of people. He had learned first from Caleb Sax, then sharpened his eye through his work with customers for Hayden & Sax Mercantile. He had been too busy building his career in the last several years to think much about any woman in a permanent way. There had been a few in St. Louis, as well as enough willing ones for James to know all he needed to know about sex. Wealth and good looks certainly helped attract any woman he wanted. But he was not one to use women that way, and the young lady he spoke with now was not the kind a man toyed with. She was too sweet, too honorable. And in many ways her personality reminded him of his mother.

. "James, look!" Willena blinked at dust as she stared out the side window where she had rolled up the dust flap for fresh air. They had traveled in the same coach together all the way from Independence and by now were on a first-name basis. James turned to look, seeing a party of Indians lined along the top of a distant ridge, sitting on their horses and quietly watching the coach. "They aren't going to attack us, are they?" Willena asked in alarm.

James studied them with mixed emotions. There had been more Indian trouble lately as the latest gold discovery brought thousands of settlers into what was supposed to be Indian country, according to the Laramie Treaty. Already that treaty was being abused, and the Indians, especially the Cheyenne and Sioux, had retaliated. He studied the Indians in the distance, seeing a few women move down the ridge, walking beside their warrior husbands, some leading horses that dragged travois loaded down with personal belongings.

"I don't think so," he answered, watching carefully. "It isn't a war party. There are women and children along. They're probably moving camp to a site where they know they can find game."

She turned and watched him, fascinated by his knowledge of this land. "Do you know any Indians, James? Have you ever fought any or befriended any?"

He kept staring at the Indians in the distance, unable to look at her yet. He had to keep his composure. *My own father is an Indian*, he was tempted to say. *My own nephew lives among the Cheyenne*. Finally he turned and met her soft green eyes, struck by the feelings she gave him. He wanted her. Never had he had such intense feelings for a woman in such a short span of time.

"I knew some Cherokee down in Texas," he told her, thinking that at least that was the truth. "That was before they were all sent to Indian Territory. And as I told you, my parents were killed by Comanche," he lied. "The Comanche are a pretty vicious tribe, but most of them have been routed out of Texas now, too, I hear."

Yes, he thought, *all Indians were kicked out of Texas,*

including my own father. We lost so much just because we had Indian blood.

Willena's mother sat with her head back on a pillow, having fallen into an exhausted sleep. The coach ride was taxing, a matter of hanging on over bumps and coping with the constant swaying motion, the noise, the heat, the dust. The woman slept so hard now that those things didn't even bother her. Willena and James spoke softly so as not to wake her.

"Father says it won't be long before Colorado gets rid of its own troublesome Indians," Willena said. "They're talking about forming their own militia. Father says he thinks the states will be at war in another two or three years—all this awful bickering over slavery and all. He says if that happens, the few soldiers we have in Colorado will be called back East, and then we'll be left with no protection against the Indians. He thinks they will commit full-scale raids. He and others are working very hard to form a volunteer army out of Colorado citizens. But he says they might be hard to control because they wouldn't be regular soldiers, and a lot of men in Colorado are not of the finest quality—prospectors, men who have fled the law back East and such."

James nodded. "You're probably right there. Your father sounds as if he's had military experience."

"Oh, he has! He fought in the Mexican war. He was a lieutenant."

James studied her perfect complexion, the lovely way her lips moved. *My father fought in the war for Texas independence,* he wanted to tell her. *My half brother, Tom, was at the Alamo but by the hand of God was sent out with a message and escaped the massacre. My father and my sister's husband fought at San Jacinto under Houston, where Santa Anna was defeated.*

"I was still living in Texas during the Mexican war," he told her. "But I was too young to fight in it. When my parents were killed, I came to St. Louis, hoping to be successful in more civilized places." He grinned, throwing up his hands. "Now look at me! Right back in the wild West, as you call it."

She laughed lightly, and it was like music to his ears. "I think it's beautiful country. I'm very excited about going to Denver. And I'm so happy you're going there, too."

Their eyes held. "You are?"

She reddened slightly. "Yes. How wonderful for you that the kind Mr. Hayden you told us about made you a partner. You must be very intelligent, James, and a very hard worker. I like that in a person. My father does, too."

He smiled softly. "And you are very brave and strong to come out here. I like that in a woman. You're very dedicated to teaching to be willing to come to a place such as this just so the children out here can learn."

She blushed more and looked at her lap. Just then her mother's handbag slipped to the floor, and both of them leaned over to pick it up at the same time, their faces close. They both grasped the purse, looking at each other and laughing lightly, neither of them eager to sit back again. How tempted he was to cover her mouth with his own! But he checked himself. Her mother could wake up at any moment, and perhaps Willena herself would be offended. He felt drowned in the wide, green eyes, so close to his own.

"Willena, I . . . I would like to call on you once I get settled in Denver. May I?"

To his surprise, it was she who moved first, leaning closer and kissing his cheek. "Yes," she whispered. "I would like that very much."

They sat up, watching each other, neither of them aware that Willena's mother had seen everything through narrow slits of eyes pretended to be closed. She had deliberately feigned sleep to allow them time to feel more alone, and she was very pleased with what she had just seen. This James Sax was no doubt a prize catch for her lovely daughter.

The woman stretched then, mumbling about what a good sleep she had had, and Willena handed her mother the handbag. James looked back out the window. The Indians were gone.

• Chapter Twenty-eight •

Caleb carried Sarah to the courtyard, which was alive with green plants and hundreds of rose bushes. Sarah's health had grown worse during the past three years. Now the pain was so bad that there were more days like today than good days—days when Caleb had to bathe and dress her, carry her to the table to help her eat, and then to the courtyard, where she could sit and enjoy the sunshine.

Sarah rested her head on his shoulder. She often wondered if Caleb got tired of doing this, wished for someone young and healthy at his side. He never complained or gave one hint that he minded any of it. Her Caleb was as rock hard as always. She knew he was capable of making love with as much virility as a younger man, yet in her heart she also knew she needn't worry that he might go find someone else to fulfill those needs.

On her better days they could still share that part of their love, but not nearly as often now as they once did. Yet it didn't seem to matter. What they had ran so much deeper. Just being together, touching, talking, was often all they needed, and Caleb made a point of taking her at least once a week to the grassy hill where they sat under the huge ponderosa Sarah had grown to love, calling it "our tree."

He set her in a cushioned lounge chair with a canopy overhead so that she didn't get too much sun. Other than the spot under the big pine, this was Sarah's favorite place, surrounded by roses of every breed and color. The air was full of their fragrance.

Tom's fortune had grown, right along with his brood of children, which with the birth of Rodriguez Miguel in

1858, and of Edwina Marie just this spring of 1860, brought the number of Tom and Juanita's children to seven —four boys and three girls. Juanita was plump and healthy and a very happy woman. But it brought pain to Sarah's heart that she had never been able to give Caleb more sons and daughters. There were only Lynda and James. And James was lost to them. It was as though they had never had him.

"Comfortable?" Caleb asked, tucking a light blanket around her legs.

She sighed deeply, looking up into the brilliant blue eyes. "I'm such a burden, Caleb."

"Like hell. God knows you deserve to be waited on hand and foot, and I don't mind doing it. You know that."

"And you'd rather be outside more, or maybe back on the Colorado plains riding with Cale."

He grinned and shook his head, leaning forward and kissing her cheek. "You've been my best friend since you were six years old, Sarah Sax. My greatest enjoyment is being right here with you." He straightened. "Can I get you anything?"

She put her head back. "No. It's nice just sitting here, listening to the birds, smelling the roses."

He smiled. "You rest awhile. I'm going into Sonoma today to see if there is any news about the problems back east."

"Oh, Caleb, I can't imagine that this country could actually get involved in a civil war. Do you think James will get mixed up in it? I'm so worried about him."

Caleb quelled his anger with James for never having answered any of their letters and putting his ailing mother through so much torment. He had considered going east to find James, but he could not bring himself to leave Sarah for such a long period of time, her health was so precarious. But he had sent a letter off with a man headed for St. Louis, telling the man to try to find James personally and advising him to try a place called Hayden's Mercantile first. If the man found James, he was to give the young man the letter, which all but begged James to come to California as soon as possible and see his mother. Caleb had not told Sarah about sending the letter, for fear of her being too disappointed if the messenger could not find James.

"I'm sure he'll be all right," he reassured her aloud.

She grasped his hand. "You won't go getting involved, will you, Caleb? I don't want any more wars in our life."

He squeezed her hand gently. "Tom and Jess and I have all had our fill of war, Sarah. Besides, you know I would never leave you like that now."

Their eyes held, and he suddenly remembered the visit from White Horse all those years ago, back in Colorado. Sarah! He felt like a lost little boy. "I'll be back tonight." He put on a smile for her in spite of the wretched pain in his heart.

"Caleb," she spoke up as he turned to leave.

He looked back at her.

"You'll check again? For a letter?"

He masked his anger at James. She refused to think or say anything against her son. "You know I will."

James headed for the little schoolhouse, reading the news article as he walked. The Cheyenne were causing many problems for the newcomers to Colorado, who were settling on land the Indians had been granted by the Laramie Treaty. But now that gold had been discovered around Pike's Peak, towns were springing up everywhere, and the settlers and prospectors had decided a new treaty must be struck. It was everyone's decided opinion that the Indians were simply in the way and must get out. They must be made to understand that the land was going to fill with even more settlers; that changes were coming and the Indians must change along with everything else, or die.

As a merchant whose supplies were often destroyed or stolen by raiding warriors, James had to agree with the rest of the settlers. His new store had already suffered losses in goods already paid for that never reached him. Settlers in outlying areas were in constant danger. Relations with the Cheyenne were going from bad to worse, and citizens were scrambling to form a militia. Because of mounting tensions back east and rumors of possible war, soldiers were being called there from duty in the West, leaving few men to protect the vast, open lands of Colorado.

But James read more into what he heard and saw. He knew firsthand how good the whites were at exaggerating some events, at doing their best to make the Indians look as bad as possible. The same thing had happened in Texas. A chosen few knew just the right things to say to stir up the rest, cleverly downplaying the Indian point of view and ignoring the fact that there was a legal treaty that was being ignored. Just the year before James came to Denver, soldiers had raided a peaceful Indian camp, using superior weapons against the Indians in a surprise attack. Once the Indians were chased off, a huge supply of food stored for the winter was deliberately burned by the soldiers, along with every tipi and any other goods left behind. The attack and destruction had nearly crippled the Cheyenne, sending them running in two different directions. Some went north to join the Sioux. Others headed south, to places they considered safe. But there was no safe place for them, and they continued to be hounded and attacked, returning their harassment with more attacks on whites, so that it all seemed to be tumbling out of control.

James wondered where it would end. He well knew how easy it was for such things to get out of hand, and that surely innocent Indians would suffer. How the Cheyenne were being treated right now was the very reason he had decided long ago to be the white man he looked as if he were. He wanted no more of those black days, the harassment and degradation that came with being an Indian. And now he lived among settlers who for the most part hated the red man with a passion.

It had all been easy in St. Louis, a place already long settled and free of its Indians. People in the East didn't worry about Indians anymore. Now he had been thrown right back into the bitter controversy, but for James the battle was even harder, for he struggled with his own guilt over hiding his Indian blood. His concern over Indian troubles was the same as that of his business neighbors, but he also understood all too well the Indian side of the story; and living in both worlds was even harder for him than it had been for his father. James had a greater understanding of the white point of view and a deeper commitment to that world; and he lived in constant terror of his Indian blood being discovered.

He often wondered where Cale might be. Perhaps he was no longer even alive. Between disease and soldier attacks, the Cheyenne numbers had dwindled. They had split up for the most part now, to the extent that they were now called Northern and Southern Cheyenne. To make matters worse in regard to James's own inner struggle, Willena's father was one of the founders of the Volunteers, which was being formed to protect Colorado citizens against the raiding Indians, but the group was not yet solid. James loved Willena. Of that he was certain now. What would it do to their relationship if she and her family learned he had Indian blood? It had become more important than ever to hide that fact.

In spite of the Indian problems and lost supplies, the new Hayden & Sax Mercantile was doing well, as was James's relationship with Willena. He reached in his pocket and fingered the ring that had finally arrived from St. Louis. He had ordered it special for her, writing Gilbert Hayden and requesting the man special-order a specific diamond of the finest quality cut. He already knew her ring size, having gotten it from Willena's mother after requesting Mr. Treat's permission to marry his daughter. The man had readily agreed, finding James Sax a handsome, likable, successful young man. Two years had passed. James had established himself and at twenty-seven he had proven his worth to Willena's father. Willena was twenty-one. It was time to settle. James wanted her for his wife—wanted a family.

Again James shook off the fear of what Mr. Treat would say if he knew the truth. He couldn't risk it. He could not tell them, and especially not Willena. He loved her too much. And he would have her for his wife, if she would agree. He could not imagine that she would say no, but he supposed all young men worried about being turned down by the women they loved.

He reached the schoolhouse steps. Nearly every day

James came to walk her home. There were too many disreputable men in this town now to allow Willena to walk alone, and on lovely days like this one, she always insisted on walking rather than taking a buggy to the fine two-story brick structure on a foothill overlooking Denver that the Treats called home. James was already planning to build her just as fine a home of their own, and the thought of living with her, sleeping in the same bed with her and invading her body whenever he wanted, brought a wonderful warmth to his blood.

He leaped up the steps two at a time, his legs long like his father's. He had taken special care with his hair today, and wore an expensive suit. He walked through the door, his eyes resting on Willena as she sat at her desk at the other end of the room. But his bright smile faded when he saw the young boy standing beside her.

All the other children were gone but this one, a child of perhaps eight, who stood next to Willena, reading to her. James felt a chill. The boy looked like a full-blooded Indian, something rarely seen in the civilized parts of Denver! Willena looked up, her green eyes glowing.

"I'll be right there, James. Daniel needs a little extra coaching."

James stared as the boy finished reading a page from a little reading book, stumbling over some of the words, which Willena helped him pronounce. She praised him, then hugged him, sending him on his way. James watched the boy run out, then looked back at Willena, who was clearing her desk.

"Who the hell was that?"

Willena looked at him in surprise. He had never before used profanity in front of her. "He's a new student."

"I can see that. He's *Indian*! What's an Indian boy doing going to school here in Denver?"

She felt a touch of anger at the prejudiced remark. "He has to go to school somewhere, doesn't he?"

"There are schools on the reservations, which is where he is supposed to be."

She frowned, taking her shawl from the back of a chair. "James, why does one little Indian boy upset you so?"

He felt his cheeks redden slightly, realizing he had over-reacted. "I don't know. I mean, with all this trouble we've had . . . I'm just surprised to see him here."

She threw her shawl around her shoulders. "Well, I feel a little sorry for him. The children aren't very nice to him. His mother is white, and she couldn't stay on the reservation." She saw the bewilderment in his eyes. "His mother was captured by the Sioux a few years ago. And contrary to what I can see you're thinking, her son is not the result of some forced relationship." She was too refined and embarrassed to use the word *rape*. "She ended up caring very much for one of the young men. She was only ten when they took her, so she learned their ways. It's really quite an interesting story, James. When she was older she married one of them. Then he was killed by soldiers, and she considers reservation life unbearable. I don't blame her, from the way she described it to me. It's disgraceful how those poor Indians are treated."

"Poor Indians! They're out there killing white people!"

"Of course they are, and one can hardly blame them. After talking to the boy's mother, I've learned a great deal about what's going on on the other side." She closed and locked her desk. "At any rate, since she is white, she was allowed to leave. The poor woman is struggling to make a good life for her son, but she is certainly not being treated very nice around here. I gave her a job cleaning the schoolhouse." She folded her arms. "James, I know it sounds unbelievable, but the woman truly loved her husband. To her he was just a man, not an Indian. Can you imagine that—a white woman loving an Indian the way any woman loves a husband? It really opened my eyes."

He had to turn away. All he could think of was his own mother. But her love for an Indian had nearly ruined his life and was still interfering with his happiness. It would be the same for the little boy who had just left. He would be torn and battered his whole life.

"James, what's wrong?" Willena came around from behind her desk.

He just shook his head. "Nothing," he said quietly. He

forced a casual attitude. "I suppose you're saying *you* could marry an Indian?"

She faced his almost accusing eyes, but she sensed more, that the question was more probing than it sounded. "Well, I . . . I hardly think so."

"There!" He sounded almost victorious. "You can understand it, but you could never do what that woman did. And you know why? Because you're intelligent enough to see the fruitlessness of such a marriage. The two cultures are too different. Even that woman, who grew up with them, can't live on the reservation. I can't imagine living on a reservation."

There was a hint of something close to fear in his eyes, as though he thought it could happen to him.

"Then you understand how bad things are for them."

James frowned. "What is this sudden sympathy for the Indians? I thought you hated them."

She stepped closer, totally confused by his almost nervous demeanor. "James, I never once said I hated them. Yes, I fear them somewhat. And I agree something must be done. The raiding, the loss of lives on both sides has to stop. But they do have a point. And I can't bring myself to hate them individually."

He forced a sarcastic smile. "Face it, Willena, when it comes down to basics, you feel superior to them as all of us do. Don't let your sympathy for one little boy turn your head to the truth."

"The truth? And what is the truth, James?" She stiffened at his attitude.

"The truth is that no matter how hard we try, the true Indian spirit cannot be changed, Willena. To get too involved will only hurt you in the end and bring you ridicule and hatred from your friends. The white man will never make the Indian like himself. They have a certain . . . a certain spirit that no white man can touch, and deep inside they have a wild streak, a need to be free. They aren't going to be changed overnight, or even in our lifetime. There's a certain something that calls them away from anything you might teach them, calls them to a spirit world you could never understand, makes them need the land, the animals, the freedom—"

He stopped short, a pain piercing his chest, realizing that for the first time in his life he was talking about himself. It actually surprised him, but it also angered him, for he had allowed that tiny part of himself to surface, and he hated himself for it. In that one moment he vowed to fight harder than ever to deny that part.

"James!" She spoke the name softly but almost in shock. "You talk as though you truly understand them." She blinked, studying the handsome blue eyes that she loved. "How do you know that much about them?"

He stiffened, his jaw flexing against his own emotions. At the moment he could see his father so vividly, watching him, inwardly weeping over the lie his son was living. Why was he so cursed?

"I just...when my parents were killed by the Comanche...some people tried to comfort me by trying to explain the Indians' point of view—that we were intruding on their lands. I don't know. I...I just made it a point to understand them as much as I could so that maybe some of the bitterness over my parents' death would leave me."

Her green eyes turned to total sympathy. "Of course." She stepped close and touched his shirtfront. "Your parents. I'm so sorry, James. I shouldn't be standing here defending Indians. It must be hard for you to do that."

He sighed, grasping her arms. "Just don't get too involved, Willena. It will tear you apart, believe me. Things are going to get worse, and I've lived in places where anyone who sympathizes with Indians gets treated pretty bad. There's a lot of hatred going on around here. So don't go getting involved in Indian problems."

She rested her head against his chest. "I won't. But not because of that." She looked up at him. "I simply can't, because of what happened to you. It wouldn't be fair to the man I love."

He felt almost sick with guilt, but here stood the woman he loved and desired beyond all reason. That was all that mattered. To tell her the truth would be to lose her forever, especially in times like these. Her own father was forming a militia to fight Indians.

"I love you, too, Willena." His eyes actually teared. "More than you could ever imagine."

She saw a sudden vulnerability, a momentary loss of the strength he usually exhibited, as though he were suddenly a lost little boy about to cry. She was sure it was because she had brought up the bad memories of his parents' deaths. She patted his chest. "No more talk of Indians, I promise."

He forced a smile, nodding. He kissed her forehead, moving his lips to her eyes, her mouth. He suddenly wanted her more than ever. It all seemed so urgent now—make her his wife before she found out about him by some horrible twist of fate. He kissed her almost savagely, pressing her close, moving one hand to her hips and pushing her against his hardness as his lips left her mouth and traveled down her neck.

"James," she gasped.

"I love you, Willena," he repeated, almost weeping the words. "I love you and I want you. Marry me, Willena. I've already asked your father."

She smiled, relishing the feel of his lips at her throat as she threw back her head. "You know I'll marry you."

He lifted her slightly, and she felt weak and on fire as he kissed her breasts through her dress, repeating over and over that he loved her. She knew she should protest. He had never taken such liberties with her, yet both of them had dreamed of these things in the night.

"Sunday. Marry me Sunday," he told her. "I don't want to wait any longer than that."

He lowered her slightly so that her face was close to his. Her green eyes were glassy with awakened desires. How she loved this man!

"All right. If it's all right with my parents, I'll marry you Sunday."

He kissed her again, exploring her mouth with his tongue. The hardness she felt against her belly made her both frightened and terribly curious. He was so much man, so strong and handsome and successful. She had no doubt he would be as good at making her a woman as he was at everything else.

He reluctantly released her, taking the little box from his pocket and handing it to her. "Here. I meant to give this to you before asking you."

She smiled with delight, opening the box and gasping at the size and beauty of the ring inside. "James! I've never seen anything more beautiful!"

"Put it on."

She removed the ring and slipped it on her finger, holding out her hand for both of them to see. "Oh, James, it's magnificent."

He took her hand, pulling it to his lips and kissing the ring. "Sunday you will be Mrs. James Sax." He touched her face gently. "I'll be a good husband, Willena." He studied her lovingly. "I'll never give you reason to be ashamed of me."

She frowned at the curious remark. "Ashamed? James, what could ever make me ashamed of you?"

His face reddened slightly. "I don't know, I . . ." Again he was tempted to tell her. But to risk losing her now was more than he could bear. How he wanted her! There was no reason for her to know. "I just want you to be proud of me. I mean, I'm so proud of you and all. I'll have the most beautiful, wonderful wife in Colorado."

She laughed lightly and hugged him. "And I will have the most wonderful husband."

He hugged her tightly, almost desperately.

· Chapter Twenty-nine ·

The messenger Caleb had secretly sent to St. Louis returned a year later. He had not delivered the letter. "There's no James Sax at Hayden's in St. Louis," he told Caleb. "Just old man Hayden himself. He said he's full partner with a young man named James Sax, but that the man isn't in St. Louis anymore. He was sent to Denver, Colorado, to open a new Hayden Mercantile there—only it's called Hayden & Sax Mercantile now. Sax and Hayden are full partners—rich men, I might add. At any rate, old man Hayden said this Sax couldn't be the one I was looking for because the Sax he knew didn't have any parents. They was killed by Comanche down in Texas. I done told him his pa was mostly Indian, and Hayden said then he was *sure* it couldn't be the James Sax he knew. Said he didn't look a bit Indian and he didn't care much for them, seein' as how they killed his folks. I expect he's right figurin' it couldn't be the same man. I'm sorry I didn't find him, Mr. Sax. By the way, I come back right quick. There's all out war back east, Mr. Sax. I didn't much want to get mixed up in it."

The man handed back Caleb's letter, while Caleb thanked him and struggled to keep his composure. He stood alone in Tom's office, where he had met with the man, and a mixture of intense anger and terrible sorrow swept through him. James had apparently totally disowned his parents, did not even acknowledge they were alive. What kind of lies was he living? Was he enjoying his riches, knowing he had betrayed his own blood to get them?

How could he tell such shattering news to Sarah? Let her

believe the best that she wanted to believe. Deep inside she surely knew the truth, but she didn't know the whole truth, and Caleb was not about to tell her.

Denver! How ironic. His son had been sent back to the very country he had run from years before. A partnership with Hayden must be extremely lucrative to make James Sax go back to Colorado. Yet he felt relieved that James was at least in an area unlikely to become involved in the war.

The whole matter became just an extra burden on Caleb's heart as he watched the woman he loved beyond his own life struggle daily with a failing body. He vowed he would tell no one what he had learned, not even Tom or Lynda. He had sent the letter on his own, unsure what the outcome would be. He hadn't wanted to get Sarah's hopes up. Now he knew it was a good thing he had kept it to himself. The pain of it was often close to unbearable. He threw the letter into the fireplace and watched it burn.

Hayden & Sax Mercantile stores in the East flourished during the war, mostly through furnishing the Union army with supplies. James felt lucky to be away from the bitter arguing Hayden wrote him was taking place in Missouri.

In Denver things were also going well. James Sax knew his business, and with a wife and two children by 1864, he worked even harder, determined they would live a grand life forever. His Willena would not suffer just because he had Indian blood, the way his own mother had been forced to live a life less than her worth, a life of struggling and hardship. He would continue to hide his heritage, and he would work as hard as he could to keep building his merchant business.

He built Willena a two-story brick home that overlooked Denver, a fast-growing city that was becoming a trade center, just as Gilbert Hayden had predicted. In his sanctuary in the foothills James could get away from the very busy life he now led in Denver and enjoy his beautiful Willena and their children, Elizabeth Ellen, born in 1861, and James David Jr., born in 1863.

To their father's great relief, neither child showed any

Indian blood. Elizabeth was blond like her mother, and even had Willena's green eyes. "Jimmie" had his father's sandy hair and blue eyes and was even more fair than James. Success and the passing of time buffered James's long-buried guilt at keeping his secret. It seemed there would never be a reason now to reveal the truth.

He was happy. Willena was a wonderful wife, and she loved him dearly. He could never take the risk of losing that love by revealing to her that she was sleeping with a man who had Indian blood. Hatred for the red men of the Plains was running high in the Denver area, which often suffered from supply shortages, because of Indian attacks on supply trains, and the cutting of telegraph wires. Settlers in outlying areas were less safe than ever, for the rapid growth of white settlement in the area had brought bitter reprisals by the Cheyenne. And with war still raging in the East there was little soldier protection.

Exaggerated stories of Indian atrocities ran rampant in the newspapers, stories most citizens believed. Few realized that some acts of theft and murder were even committed by white men disguised as Indians—white men who hated the Indians and would do anything to keep the hatred against them alive; white men eager to get their hands on more Indian land rich for farming, or land that might contain more gold. The ultimate goal was to rid Colorado of all its Indians, and scare tactics seemed the best method to bring cries of outrage from Colorado citizens. A Colorado militia made up of citizen volunteers was becoming a solid reality.

Increased tensions began to reawaken old guilts in James's soul. He was good friends with those who ran the newspapers, and he turned his head when they discussed the best ways to dress up stories of Indian attacks to keep the people angry. He smiled with the rest of the important people of Denver when they made jokes about the Indians —the white man's view of their sex life, their "uncivilized" mannerisms, their ignorance.

"Take away the buffalo, that's what I say," some said. "The dumb bastards would die within a week."

"We're already working on it," another would reply.

"There's a growing demand back east now for the hides. I'll tell you one thing—you want to see a pissed-off Indian, let him find a dead buffalo with its hide stripped and the rest of it left to rot."

More laughter. James would join in, an odd heaviness in his chest. Sometimes he felt like an actor, deciding he must be a very good one. No one seemed to notice anything different about him when the conversation turned to Indians.

"I say they should declare open season on them," another would say. "We've got the superior weapons. Just take cover and pick them off wherever we find them."

"The damned government says we nice boys shouldn't do those things. It will just make them madder. They remind us we aren't even supposed to be here."

"Like hell. It's those mother-loving redskins who don't belong here. All the wealth this land represents—and they don't take advantage of any of it. They don't have the tiniest idea of how to be successful. They just go on living as they did thousands of years ago. If they're that stupid, they deserve to die."

"Well, they do seem to understand the balance of nature," James put in once. "They don't pollute the rivers and creeks, and they don't dig up the mountains. I mean, there must be something we can learn from them. Maybe if we tried to—"

"You defending them, Sax?" The question came from a prominent banker.

"Well, no. I just . . . well, we can't fight forever. We've got to find a way to make peace."

"There's a way, all right. Kill them all off," the banker answered.

There was a round of laughter. It was the last time James Sax spoke up in their defense.

Outrageous behavior by citizens continued. Whiskey was deliberately and illegally pushed on the reservations. A drunk Indian soon turned into a useless Indian, and a drunk Indian was easy to cheat. Some citizens even paid whiskey to Indians to steal other settlers' horses for them, keeping the horses while the theft was conveniently blamed on the Indians. Some white men and even soldiers helped steer Indian women into prostitution, convincing them that was the only way they could "earn" their badly needed food and supplies.

There were, of course, no news stories of abuse of Indians by white men. No one was told of unwarranted attacks on innocent Indians, murders and rapes, or of blatant cheating of Indians by reservation agents and suppliers, some of whom made fortunes on government issue while the Indians starved.

The governor of Colorado Territory, anxious to please his wealthy friends who were eager for more Indian land, took up the "cause," declaring he would do everything in his power to stop the "Indian problems." He fully recognized and legalized the Colorado Volunteers, who were put under the leadership of "Colonel" John Chivington, a former preacher of questionable authority and experience. But he was the perfect man for Governor Evans and his cohorts. Chivington was an avid Indian hater, his own wife having been killed by Indians. He hated them beyond all Christian reasoning, in spite of calling himself a man of that faith; and soon the Cheyenne called him *Zetapetazhetan*, meaning "Big Man" or "Squaw Killer." The title was very fitting.

James suspected matters were worse than he cared to face. He quietly sat back while his friends and the Volunteers began a campaign of harassment that would, they hoped, force the Indians to leave on their own, or at least force them into all-out war, which would give the Volunteers the right to ride down hard on them and attack the starving, poorly armed tribes without mercy.

James understood the tactics all too well. It had happened to the Creek, Cherokee, and other southern tribes, now crowded into Indian Territory—and to all the Indians in Texas. It was happening to the Apache, many of whom were already on reservations much smaller than the lands afforded the Cheyenne under the Laramie Treaty. As long as those Cheyenne and Sioux and other Indians involved continued to insist that treaty promises be kept, which was their right, there would be trouble for them, big trouble.

James had listened to a speech by Chivington in Denver, and he had no doubt the kind of man he was.

Now James sat in his study, taking a drink of whiskey. It seemed he was drinking more and more lately, and he cursed his damned conscience. "I suppose I inherited that from you, too, dear Father," he muttered, drinking down another slug.

He twirled the glass in his hand, thinking about Chivington's roared words against Indians. It gave him the shivers. It brought back all the memories of Texas, and the Indian haters there who would have killed his whole family if they had not got out in time. He thought about his pet dog that Indian haters had killed and tears came to his eyes. Sometimes he still felt like that little boy, especially around men like Chivington, who threatened his very existence. Little did the man know that one of the men in the crowd was part Cheyenne himself.

Just as he poured himself another drink, Willena came inside the room looking for him. She stopped short at the sight of the glass in his hand and was startled by his watery eyes. She closed her eyes and sighed.

"James, what's wrong with you lately?" she asked with sincere concern. "You never used to drink so much."

He shrugged. "I have a right to drink if I want, love. Don't start nagging me about it." He swallowed the shot and she folded her arms, a discerning look in her eyes.

"I suppose you do. But it isn't like you, and I think I have a right to know what's bothering you."

"Nothing!" He slammed down the glass and she jumped slightly, but she stood her ground, facing him with chin held high.

"Is it me?"

He met her eyes, then let out an almost disgusted sigh, smiling sadly. "Don't be ridiculous. You're the best thing that's ever happened to me."

She moved closer, dropping her arms and leaning over his desk. "What then, James? You know how much I love you. I would understand anything you tell me."

He stared at her for a long time, then began laughing lightly. "You have no idea what you're saying." He shook his head. "No, my beautiful Willena, you would not understand. But it will pass. It's just..." He had to think. "It's just that sometimes I get to thinking about my parents, how I felt when I was left alone. I just get spells where I wish I could have helped them somehow—makes me feel a little guilty."

"Oh, James," she said softly, coming around the desk.

It had worked again. He had used the story about his dead parents to soothe her anger and make her quit asking questions about what was bothering him. It was his parents, all right, only they weren't dead at all. He actually found himself wishing they were. It would all be so much easier then, and he wouldn't have to worry about Caleb Sax's showing up at his door someday.

Willena cradled his head against her stomach, stroking his hair. "Please stop the drinking, James. You can bear it without this crutch. It frightens me to see you drinking so much."

He wanted to laugh and shout it. *Your husband's a drunken Indian! He can't handle the whiskey because he's part Indian!* It was all a sudden and ludicrous vision. How little she knew!

"You do still love me, don't you, James?"

He grinned, kissing her stomach. "You know I do." He pulled her onto his lap, hugging her and nuzzling her breasts. "You're the most wonderful thing in my life."

"Excuse me, Mr. Sax." A maid walked in, suddenly flustered when she found Willena sitting on her husband's lap. "Oh!" She backed away. "I'm sorry, sir, but there is someone here to see you."

James scowled at the timing, wishing the woman hadn't come in. He would like nothing better right now than to take Willena upstairs and have a good round with his wife. The whiskey was enhancing his manly needs. "Who is it?"

"Your father-in-law, sir, and a Colonel Chivington."

James paled visibly. Two of the most active men in the Volunteers. What on earth did they want? Willena quickly rose, and James got up on shaky legs. "Send them in, Lucille."

"Yes, sir."

The woman left, and James took a deep breath for self-control. "Wonder what they want," he said, looking at Willena.

"It must have something to do with the Volunteers."

"Yes," James answered, feeling light-headed and apprehensive. They both heard footsteps, and a moment later Willena's father came inside, accompanied by the tall, stern-looking, bearded Colonel Chivington. James saw something in the man's dark eyes that bordered on insanity.

"James," Willena's father said, coming closer with a grin on his face. "It's our turn, son."

James blinked in bewilderment. "Our turn?"

"To do our part to support the Volunteers. We businessmen can't just throw money at them. We have to show Denver citizens that we mean what we say, and that we're willing to go out there and fight to protect property and lives. It's good business, James."

James ran a hand through his hair, wishing he hadn't drunk so much whiskey. "What are you talking about?"

Treat took a deep breath, looking strong and firm in spite of his age and his gray hair. Willena's father had a powerful influence on a lot of people, and James had gone his father-in-law's way on most things, more out of his deep fear of somehow betraying his Indian blood than anything else. He felt an obligation to constantly please the man, and he hated his inability to stand up to him. He was not a man to be bullied about, but that one dark secret seemed to interfere with his very manliness.

"We're going to ride out on a campaign with Colonel Chivington, James," Treat said excitedly.

James paled visibly, and Treat frowned.

"Good God, man, it's just one campaign. We're all taking one turn, just to show our support. Surely my big, strapping son-in-law isn't afraid to ride with the Volunteers."

James cleared his throat, forcing his voice to come. "Of course not. I'm just . . . surprised. I mean, I have my store to look after, and Willena and the children—"

"We're all in this together, James. Those who stay behind help run the businesses and watch over the loved ones of the rest. There's no problem. You needn't worry about the family."

"We need you, Mr. Sax," Chivington spoke up in a deep voice.

Willena moved closer to James. She didn't like Chivington, and she was not certain everything the Volunteers did was completely proper. She had argued with her own father over the Indian issue and had been given orders to never voice their defense in public.

James's mind raced wildly. A campaign! Against the Cheyenne? Against his own father's people? Perhaps against Cale himself? But surely Cale was not even in this area. He could be anywhere, most likely in the north where most Cheyenne had fled. Maybe he was even dead. He struggled to keep his composure. "Where to? Do you have a specific mission?"

He watched Chivington's dark eyes glitter. "We always have a mission, Mr. Sax, and it is always the same. To kill Indians and rid Colorado of the scum that keeps us from progress. The men are useless and ignorant, the women nothing but breeders of more lice-infested children who grow up to be just as useless as their parents. We will ride through the southeast and be gone only a few weeks. We will make sure there are no Indians in places they should not be. They insist on calling the Laramie Treaty lands their own. But they have been told that can no longer be, and they must understand we mean what we say."

"Your opinion of the Indians is much too biased and unreasonable, Colonel Chivington," Willena spoke up. "It is one thing to—"

"Willena!" Her father interrupted her angrily. "You're speaking out of place. Colonel Chivington is a guest in this house, and he has done much for Colorado! If not for him, perhaps you and the children would be in danger this very moment."

She glared at Chivington, who met her gaze sternly. She turned and looked at James. "Are you going?"

He met her eyes, his emotions torn. So much was at stake. His standing in the community, his father-in-law's opinion of him, his need to make very certain his Indian blood would never be known. What better way than by riding on a campaign with Chivington? It couldn't be all that bad. He didn't have to kill anyone himself if he didn't want to. And who from his own family would ever know? "I have to, Willena. It won't be for long. I can't shun my duty if everyone else is taking a turn."

She blinked back tears and left the room, and James turned to Chivington. "The only Indians I know of in the southeast are peaceful ones—Black Kettle and his band. I thought they were camped at Sand Creek, waiting for some word from the government on annuities and where they're expected to go next. Black Kettle is known for his desire to remain at peace."

A wicked smile came over Chivington's face. "There is no such thing as a peaceful Indian, Mr. Sax. If they pretend to be, it is only to buy time, until they are strong enough to attack again. You apparently don't know much about Indians, Mr. Sax, but you will learn after riding with me."

James's eyes hardened. He could tell this man plenty about Indians. A tiny flicker of Indian pride moved through his blood, the kind of anger his father would have felt at this moment. But he ignored it, forced it back. "I'm sure I will. When do we leave?"

• Chapter Thirty •

Jess removed his string tie and his suit coat, then his shirt, as Lynda lay in bed, watching from under the covers. She was proud of her husband's still-broad shoulders and firm physique; his handsome face was tanned from the California sun, the age lines only making him look more appealing, a man experienced in the hard knocks of life. Jess had just returned from a town meeting. He was one of the most respected men in Henderson, still the mayor, but also the owner of a food store for which most of the produce, including meat, fruits, nuts, and wine, was supplied from Tom's ranch.

Tom had long ago expanded from just raising horses to raising cattle and produce, as well as developing a winery that was doing more business every year.

Jess's store was doing so well that he was thinking of opening a second one in Sonoma. Henderson itself had grown to many times its size since when they had first settled there, and now the current sheriff had several deputies; there was a town council, and law and order now prevailed in Henderson, something for which Jess Purnell was more than a little responsible.

Lynda was proud of her husband, glad she had agreed to let him come here and lead his own life. The years while he was sheriff had not been easy for her. She had lived with a constant fear that some unsavory character would come along some night and think nothing of shooting her husband in the back. She could not imagine a life without him now, and she smiled as he came to the bed, wearing only his underwear.

"John get back yet?" he asked her as he moved under the covers and turned down the oil lamp next to the bed.

"No. I hope he's all right."

"He's almost twenty-four years old, Lynda, and he's made that supply run between here and Tom's many times."

"Well, I hope you can keep him interested in helping you with the store. I don't want him doing that, Jess."

"Well, he's damned good with a gun. And a man has to do what he wants to do, Lynda. We've been over that before. But I agree. I hate to see it, too. I'll do my best to keep him in the produce business. At least with his skills he can take care of himself if he gets bushwhacked on the trail."

"Oh, Jess, don't say that."

He grinned and turned to her, pulling her close. "Quit worrying. Jessica sleeping by now?"

"Yes."

Their eyes held, and he traced a big, rough finger around her full lips. "You know, the nice thing about marrying a woman with Indian blood is she doesn't seem to age as quickly. Something about that pretty, dark skin. I wanted you twenty-seven years ago, and those feelings haven't changed a bit." He kissed her lightly. "Have I told you lately that I love you?"

She pursed her lips. "Mmmm, I think so—a few days ago."

He laughed lightly, pulling her closer and nuzzling her neck. "Life's been good to us since we came out here, Lynda, hasn't it? We've been pretty damned lucky."

She sighed deeply. "Mother and Father are so happy about it all. Ten grandchildren." She lay there quietly as he kissed her neck more as he began unlacing the front of her gown. "Except that one of those grandchildren we don't know anything about anymore. Maybe even *I* have grandchildren, Jess."

He raised up and met her eyes. "Caleb won't go to his grave without finding out about Cale, Lynda. You know that. And Cale is a thirty-two-year-old man now."

She met his eyes. "If he's alive."

He kissed her eyes. "What did he tell you about the spirit and the great circle of life? He's alive. You know it—" He put a hand against her chest. "In here. Your son is all right, Lynda."

She smiled sadly. "I love you, Jess." She reached up and touched his thick, sandy hair. "It's hard for Mother, too— not knowing about James. How sad that he never kept in touch. Sad and cruel. Cale has a reason—the way he lives. But James has no reason, living back East somewhere, knowing how to send a letter."

"Hey—you're spoiling my plans with all this sad talk."

Her eyebrows arched. "What plans?"

He pulled the gown down over her shoulder. "I want my woman. That's what plans," he answered, his voice suddenly gruff with desire.

She ran her fingers down the thick hairs of his powerful chest. "I'm sorry. I'll stop talking."

She met his eyes, and in the next moment his mouth was caressing hers while his fingers lightly teased a nipple. He pushed her gown down farther and she helped wiggle out of it while they remained kissing. She curled up against him, reaching down to unbutton his underwear. She reached inside to feel his soft swelling need of her, and he moved out of his underwear. He tossed them to the floor and moved between her still-slender legs, remembering the first night he had taken this woman—that wonderful, passionate, desperate night before he had left to go fight for Texas independence, that night of ecstasy when he had discovered the steamy desires and passion that lay beneath the cool exterior of Lynda Sax.

That first time they were so eager they didn't even undress all the way. It just seemed important to be inside of her, without all the foreplay that usually goes with making love. But afterward the clothes had come off, and they had made love again—and again.

He had never lost his desire for her. Moving inside Lynda Sax Purnell carried the same thrill as it had then. She had a way of pulling him inside herself that drove a man crazy with ecstasy, and she did it to him again now.

Lynda sucked in her breath with Jess's first thrust. How she loved her sweet Jess, the homeless drifter she had taken in to keep forever. They moved in a steady rhythm, finely tuned to each other's needs, until he felt the pulsations of her climax. He met her mouth, thrusting his tongue deep as he thrust himself into her, making her groan with the ecstasy.

They hung in that magic moment where a man and woman are oblivious to anything around them, glorying in the excitement of the moment, until finally his life spilled into her in several explosive throbs. He let out a long, satisfied sigh, going limp beside her and kissing her damp hair.

"I hope I can always keep up with you, woman," he told her teasingly.

She laughed lightly, but quickly sobered when they

heard a horse ride up close to the house at a hard gallop. Jess was quickly out of bed and pulling on his underwear as they heard someone come pounding up onto the porch and begin unlocking the door. It could only be John, but why would he come in such a hurry and this late at night? And why on horseback? He was supposed to come back with a wagonful of supplies.

Before Jess could get to the bedroom door John was tapping on it. "Pa?"

"Just a minute."

Lynda pulled the covers up close to her neck, and Jess opened the door. John had been with women enough to know when someone was fresh from lovemaking, and his cheeks reddened slightly when he looked at his father's disheveled hair and perspiring face.

"I'm sorry, Pa. It's Grandma. She's worse. Grandpa said Mother should come. The quicker she goes back, the better."

Lynda felt her heart beat harder. Sarah! She had been expecting this, and yet now it hit her like a terrible weight. It had been many years since Lynda had lost someone close to her, but she had never quite gotten over the sting of it, the hatred of the inevitable.

"We'll head out at the crack of dawn," Jess said. "Thanks for riding back yet tonight to tell us, Son."

"I would have gone ahead with the supplies, but it would have slowed me down."

"It's all right. All that's important is to get Lynda to her mother as soon as possible."

"I'll go up to my room and try to sleep a little. I've got to go cool down the horse first. It's one of Grandpa's best."

Jess closed the door and turned to Lynda, who suddenly looked like a lost little girl. She and her mother were as close as any two people could be. "I'm sorry, honey," Jess told her, feeling helpless.

Her eyes brimmed with tears. "Come and hold me, Jess."

He came to the bed, taking her into his arms, and she wept bitterly.

"Get it all out now, Lynda." He petted her hair. "Don't cry in front of her."

He did not look forward to the next few days, or hours —however long Sarah Sax had left to live.

Cale turned to Snowbird, who to him was more beautiful at twenty-eight summers than she was when they were wed. Knowing their tribe would go with Black Kettle's people to the hated new reservation farther south made Cale so full of sorrow that it tired him. He had seen once-proud Cheyenne warriors turn into women from the hated whiskey, and he remembered how his grandfather used to preach against it. His good friend Ten Stars had accidentally shot and killed himself one night after drinking too much, something he and other young warriors had come to do all too often. Cale often wondered if the shooting had really been an accident; there was so much despair among the young men. Buffalo Boy, Snowbird's brother, and another of Cale's good friends also drank heavily now. They had ridden north to be among the Northern Cheyenne and the Sioux, who were responsible for many of the raids for which the Southern Cheyenne were being blamed. It was safer here in the South, or so Cale thought, and so he had kept his family here.

So much had been lost. They were surrounded now by the enemy—white settlers who wanted their land. Where was their hope? It was true the Sioux were waging a good battle in the North, but Cale had knowledge of the white world, and that knowledge told him now in his older years of wisdom that no matter how many battles the Indians might win presently, in the end it would all be the same.

It saddened him, mostly because of his children. He had a boy eleven summers, a daughter eight summers, and another son only four summers. Cale wanted very much to go north and continue the fight, for he was a warrior at heart and buried deep inside was the old spirit and pride that had never really left him. But he had to think of his family. Soldier attacks were vicious now, especially toward the more warlike Indians. They used the big cannon from the hills, showering Indian villages with shrapnel that killed from far off, setting tipis on fire. Women and babies were murdered with no more feeling than a white man felt killing a rabbit. There seemed to be no honor in the way they fought, and even when mostly women and children were killed in an attack, it was called a "victory" for the brave bluecoats.

He wanted peace, and life, for his wife and children. If that meant staying with Black Kettle and leaving for a new reservation, then he would do it. He only wished his grandfather could be here now. It would be easier to make these decisions. And how he missed the man! How he missed his whole family. But he kept in mind his own words to his mother all those years ago—how long had it been? At least fifteen years. They would always be together in spirit. He wondered what his sister looked like. Surely very beautiful now. And he had no doubt his mother was still beautiful. How old would she be now? Close to fifty? Surely that was impossible! He wondered if they had found Tom, or if his grandfather was even still alive.

He would not give up his hope that Blue Hawk would one day return to the Cheyenne. He could not imagine his grandfather dying out there in the place called California. He would come back to his people, and Bear Above would see his grandfather again. Blue Hawk would die fighting like a true warrior, and Bear Above would take him to the mountains and give him the proper Cheyenne burial.

He sighed, dismissing the longing thoughts that brought an ache to his heart. He moved an arm around Snowbird and kissed her neck. They both lay naked under a robe, while the children slept nearby. It was not yet light, but Cale could not sleep. Snowbird turned to him, smiling.

"This is not the time, my husband."

Cale nibbled at her lips. "Anytime will do. Who says a man can take his woman only certain times?"

"I am not sure. But it was probably a woman."

They both laughed lightly and Cale moved on top of her. "I have a need. I feel . . ." His smile faded. "I feel I must hurry and make love to my woman, before someone takes her away."

She opened her legs readily. Never once had she turned

him away. Why should she, when she took as much pleasure in him as he took in her? "And who is going to take me away? We are a few Indians alone here, waiting only for word from the white man's government when our supplies will come and where we must go to be safe."

He studied her lovingly, coming down to meet her mouth. They soon moved together, while outside an American flag flew from the tent of Black Kettle, symbolizing the Indian leader's desire to cooperate with the white man.

Dawn began to break just slightly as Cale and Snowbird shared bodies in joyous pleasure. Soon his life spilled into her womb, and Snowbird hoped that this time the seed would take hold and she would give her husband another son, even though another mouth to feed would be difficult. She would do anything to keep Bear Above from falling into the terrible depression some of his friends had felt, some of them even committing suicide. Bear Above loved his children. He felt a great responsibility toward them. Many children would keep him a happy man, even if they had to live on a reservation. And he knew a little bit about the white man's ways of ranching and farming. Perhaps they could be happy on a reservation, at least a little happier than most.

Cale moved off her, stretching out on his back, then sighing deeply. "Something is wrong, Snowbird."

"I feel it too."

His eyes suddenly teared. "I have this . . . terrible feeling. I don't feel safe here. I don't feel safe at all. We should have gone north."

"But we are protected here. The white men, Agent Wynkoop and Major Anthony, both told us to wait here until they get word at Fort Lyon what we should do. I trust them."

"I also trust them. It is others I do not trust. There is much hatred in this land, Snowbird. And I feel the eyes of the Squaw Killer."

She shivered and moved closer, moving her arms around him. "Perhaps you are right. But we have done nothing wrong. They cannot harm us as long as we stay here as we are told."

He sighed deeply, pulling her into his arms, his heart strangely heavy.

James could hardly believe what had taken place—panicked settlers everywhere they went. None cared if it was Sioux or Northern Cheyenne or Southern Cheyenne who had attacked them. Some horses had been stolen, some homes burned, some people killed. Yet dispatches to Fort Lyon verified that Black Kettle's band remained camped peacefully at Sand Creek. They could not possibly be the culprits.

Yet now here they were, camped above Black Kettle's quiet, lazy village below, just barely able to make out the smoke curling from the tipi holes from fires that warmed their occupants against the November air. Quietly, very quietly, men positioned the twelve-pounder mountain howitzers. When they had reached Fort Lyon, Chivington had actually talked of collecting scalps, and Major Anthony had told the man he had been waiting for some extra manpower to help him attack the "warring Cheyenne" who he knew were camped along Sand Creek.

Warring Cheyenne? James studied the village below. It could hardly be considered as belonging to a war party. Many tipis, campfires, and meat and hides hanging to dry all pointed to the fact there were women along. Back at Fort Lyon one man had dared to tell Chivington that to attack these particular Indians would be nothing short of murder. Chivington had gone into a tirade, damning the man for defending the Indians, claiming he had come to kill Indians and that it was right and honorable to do so.

James realized he was riding with a crazy man. He couldn't leave and disgrace himself in front of Willena's father. He had agreed to come along and to leave would be desertion. He had to stick this out. Surely it wouldn't be all that bad. A couple of shots from the howitzers and those below would surrender soon enough and that would be that. Not too many lives would be lost. And Chivington and the others could claim another "victory."

He felt suddenly sick to his stomach. For years he had buried so many of his feelings that now he really didn't know who he was anymore. He wondered how much longer he could continue this pretense. Drinking had seemed his only comfort lately. If he didn't stop, he would lose Willena. But if he told her the truth, he would still lose her.

"Get ready," someone close to him said, shaking him from deep thought. "We're going to get rid of the lice."

James rose from where he sat leaning against a rock. He adjusted his saber and climbed onto his horse, putting on his hat and resting a hand on his pistol. His heart pounded painfully, and he felt a lump in his throat so big that he wondered how he was breathing. He could almost see his own father below, almost hear the man talking to him, warning him that he could not forever deny his Indian blood. Here was the moment of truth—here he could finally cut any remaining emotional ties and prove his Indian blood meant nothing.

A howitzer exploded, and seconds later a tipi was ripped apart. There were screams below. The "battle" had begun, a surprise attack at dawn on a peaceful village of perhaps six hundred Cheyenne, mostly women and children—Cheyenne who thought they were safe.

Volunteers around James let out war whoops as more howitzers were fired and Indians began pouring out of their tipis. Men pulled sabers and descended upon the village.

"Grab the children and run!" Cale shouted to Snowbird as she hurriedly pulled on her tunic. *"Hopo! Hopo!"*

Snowbird's eyes were wide with panic. Their strange uneasiness now had an explanation. The big guns! Why! Why were they being attacked?

Another explosion ripped the tipi near their own, and Snowbird screamed while Cale, tying on only his loincloth, grabbed a tomahawk and an outdated rifle. He shoved his wife and children outside to see bluecoats descending fast. Snowbird picked up the youngest son. She knew what to do. The old ones would help women and children scramble for safety, while all men able to fight would stay behind and fight the enemy, buying time for their loved ones. Women and children must be protected. They were the seed and hope for the future.

But the soldiers were everywhere. Several rode close to Cale, amid thundering hooves, whinnying horses, and screaming women. Dust rolled, and Cale quickly lost sight of Snowbird and his children as he turned to swing his tomahawk at the approaching horse, landing it hard into the animal's chest. He had wanted to bury it in the rider, but all was confusion. The animal screamed and reared, and the soldier on the animal fired a pistol at Cale, stinging Cale's shoulder with a glancing blow that sent him reeling backward. The soldier disappeared and Cale quickly got to his feet again and stumbled blindly in a circle for a moment, stunned and dizzy.

Everything from then on seemed to move slowly for him, as though some horrible nightmare. He realized some of these soldiers were not even in uniform. He saw one strike down a woman with his sword, then dismount and cut off her arms while she screamed and pleaded for her life. Then the man split open her dress, ripping open her belly and cutting through her private parts.

Cale was numb with the havoc going on around him. This was not fighting. This was slaughter, wicked, maniacal slaughter. Guns fired all around. The soldiers had come in so fast and with such surprise there was no hope of fighting them. Thinking themselves safe, the Indians had failed to post any scouts. In the distance he could see soldiers riding toward the fleeing women. Snowbird!

Cale ran toward the women, still gripping his tomahawk. He felt a soldier riding down hard, and he turned and fired, grazing the man's leg. He cried out and turned in another direction, while more men rode toward the women. Cale could see Black Kettle in the distance waving a white cloth as he stood in front of his tipi, the American flag still flying from it. Some of the Cheyenne men were waving their arms and shouting that they were at peace, that they did not want to fight. They were shot down. A few women and warriors gathered around Black Kettle, but more soldiers opened fire on them. Horses and sabers were everywhere, drawing innocent blood, while white men let out war whoops as wild as those of the very Indians they were murdering.

Cale again headed in the direction in which he had seen Snowbird flee with the children, then stopped short at the sight of a warrior covered with stab wounds, stripped, his privates cut off. Nearby a woman lay with her breasts cut off. She was still alive, both her arms broken and bleeding from a saber. Cale shuddered with the horror of it, walking up to her and meeting her wild, pleading eyes. He shot her himself with his pistol.

Cale ran toward a low bank where he knew several of the women and children would be. He was oblivious to his bleeding shoulder. Somehow he had to save Snowbird and his children. But soldiers thundered past him toward where many women were crouched over their children to protect them. Something hit Cale hard from behind and he stumbled forward. Moments later he heard the awful screams as the women and children in hiding were rousted out and indiscriminately murdered and maimed. Many were stripped, their privates cut out, skulls smashed. Cale lay still a moment, hearing more shots, laughter.

"Look what I got," one man shouted. "I got me a trophy!"

Cale moved his eyes in the direction of the voice to see a man holding up what looked like the reproductive ovaries of an animal. He realized with a lurching stomach they must have come from a woman. The man rode past and Cale struggled to get to his feet.

Snowbird! He stumbled toward the ravine, then fell to his knees, a blow from a gun butt stunning his spine so that he could not quite stay on his legs. A soldier came walking up from the ravine, leading his horse by the reins. Cale noticed him stop and vomit. Cale did not move for a moment, feeling a creeping chill move through his blood at the realization there was something familiar about this man.

After several seconds of vomiting the soldier began walking again, sniffing and wiping at his eyes. The man stopped short when he realized a warrior was watching him. He gripped his saber defensively, yet could not seem to bring himself to use it. He walked slowly closer, while in the distance indiscriminate killing and celebrating continued.

Cale did not know that Black Kettle had finally managed to escape, along with a very few others. Undisciplined Volunteers, still full of whiskey they had drunk during the night before the raid, had killed hundreds of Indians, mostly women and children, in one of the most shameful massacres in the history of the Indian wars. But the two men who faced each other now knew nothing about the historical importance of what had happened this day. The soldier's eyes widened as he came even closer, standing in front of the Indian.

"Cale!" he groaned, his eyes wild and red.

"You!" Cale growled through gritted teeth. "My... Uncle!" He spit the word bitterly at James Sax.

"You don't... understand..."

"I understand," Cale hissed, struggling to his feet. "I understand what you have become! Grandfather's eyes are on you, James Sax! You will burn in hell and never sleep again for what you have done this day!"

"Sax!" someone shouted. Another man came riding up. "What the hell you doin', Sax? Carryin' on a conversation with this degenerate?"

James whirled, pointing his rifle at the man. "Touch him and you're a dead man!"

The man backed off, his eyes glaring. "You've not got much stomach, do you, Sax? I reckon' somethin' like this separates the men from the boys. You got some growin' to do, boy. Chivington won't like to know that." The man turned away and trotted his horse past them.

James turned wild eyes to Cale. "Lie down as though you're dead."

"I will not!"

"Do it, damn it! They'll cut you down!"

Cale grudgingly lay down. James took out his pistol and fired, hitting the dirt past Cale's head. Men turned to look, and the one who had just left them laughed and put up his fist. "I knew you could do it, Sax!"

James shoved his pistol into its holster and looked down at Cale. "I wish . . . we could talk . . ."

"About what, squaw killer?" Cale growled. "I do not know you."

"I didn't kill any women or kids. I swear."

"You were with them. It is the *same*! And if I did not want to live to find my woman and children, I would kill you now with my bare hands and let them shoot me down. It would be *worth* it!"

James swallowed, struggling not to break down. "How many . . . children, Cale?"

"My name is Bear Above! And unlike you I am proud of it! My woman and my two sons and little daughter headed for that ravine. If they are dead, you, my loving uncle, will find it hard to have pleasant dreams. Whatever is over there, your nephew's woman and children are probably among them!"

James made a choking sound. "Cale . . . Bear Above . . . you don't understand . . . truly. I didn't kill any women—"

"Do not make excuses, James Sax. James Sax," he said louder, "son of Caleb Sax! Son of Blue Hawk! How long has it been since you have seen your father? Do you pretend to those scum you call friends that you are lily-white?" He spit into the dirt. "Go! I do not know you! Go back to wherever you came from, to the pretty white woman you probably married, and to your children who do not know they have *Indian* blood. Go back to your friends and laugh and celebrate the great victory you have had this day!"

"Cale—"

"Leave me before I change my mind and *kill* you!" Cale interrupted, his voice gruff with emotion. He could hear heavy breathing and again a choking sound.

"Cale, I . . . I didn't know . . . it would be like this. I didn't even want to come. And I never thought . . . you would be with them."

"Does that make it any more right?" Cale turned his face away. "There is someone else here today. Only in spirit. But he is here. And he weeps."

James felt revulsion and guilt ripple through him in

lurching jolts. He turned away and vomited again. He knew very well of whom Cale was speaking. James stumbled toward the others, struggling to keep his composure, his mind reeling with horror so forcefully that his head ached fiercely.

"James!" His father-in-law rode up to him. "We're leaving now. These Cheyenne won't be giving us any more trouble." He waited while James stood hunched over. "James, what the hell is wrong with you?"

James straightened, turning and mounting his horse with great effort, then turning tear-filled eyes to his father-in-law, his face crimson with agony. "No, sir, they won't give you any more trouble," he said brokenly. "Not even my nephew."

Treat frowned, looking his son-in-law over and wondering if he had lost his mind. "What on earth are you talking about?"

James rode closer, gritting his teeth. "This was a camp of women and children, peacefully waiting for orders from our government. You can be proud of what happened here today, dear Father-in-law, but I'm not. And the worst part is that even though I didn't take part in this slaughter the way you and the others did, I'm more guilty than *any* of you. You keep going with Chivington. I'm through!"

"James! Where are you going?" Treat demanded.

"I'm going home. You can stay and ride with the Squaw Killer if you want. I'm going home to Willena"—he whirled his horse—"to tell her her children have *Indian* blood!" He grinned almost like a madman.

Others turned to stare at him in shock, most thinking the attack had somehow affected his mind. Perhaps he had taken a blow to the head. He would get over it in time.

Treat watched James disappear, then turned his eyes to a rise where John Chivington sat tall and stern in his saddle, the proud "victor." Treat did not share the feeling of victory the others did, nor had he taken part in the maiming and degrading of the women. He agreed something had to be done about the Indians, but this was not what he had in mind. He was accustomed to fighting with honor. There was no honor here today.

He rode after James, concerned for his daughter's husband. He hoped the man would regain his senses before reaching Denver.

Cale lay still until the last soldier was gone. He managed to get to his knees, crawling toward the ravine, shuddering and weeping at the gruesome sight all around him. His heart lay heavy with grief and his mind reeled with terror at what he would find. He got to his feet, stumbling toward the ravine and down into it, groaning as his eyes scanned the bodies of women and children.

"Snowbird," he wept. "Where are you?"

He searched in agony, then heard the voice of his youngest son, four-year-old Little Eagle. Cale turned, catching his breath. "Little Eagle!"

The little boy ran to him and Cale swept him up in his arms. "My son! My son!"

"They killed Mother," the boy wept, clinging to Cale. "The men with the blue coats stuck her with the big knife —and they stuck Yellow Wolf and Blue Flower."

Cale put the boy down. "Show me," he choked out.

Little Eagle led his father to the spot where Snowbird lay sprawled, stabbed and stripped, their oldest son and their daughter lying dead nearby.

Cale threw back his head and let out a great, long cry, a cry more piercing than that of any wild animal which roamed the plains.

• Chapter Thirty-one •

Light from a rising sun shafted through the bedroom window on Tom and Juanita, moving together in the sweet rhythm so familiar to them. They had been together fifteen years now. Juanita was thirty-three, and to Tom she only grew more beautiful with the years, filling out in a womanly way that only made him love and want her more. She had given him seven children, and no woman could be a better mother and wife than his Juanita.

This morning they had made love out of a need to remind themselves that life went on, for a great sadness hung throughout the household. The Purnells had been there for three days already, waiting along with Caleb, Tom, and Juanita as Sarah's health dropped substantially. Father Juarez, who had been asked to come, was with her now.

Tom stretched and lay thinking. Sometimes he felt the aches of his own vanishing youth, and he still walked with a limp. But he was still strong and virile and eager to keep his ranch a success and leave his children a vast fortune. The mine had finally played out, but it had not ruined its owner. Tom had saved and invested wisely. His hold on his land was solid, and so was the love he shared with Juanita.

"Yo te amo, querida," he told her, pulling her close and kissing her cheek.

She smiled, patting his arm. *"Yo te amo, mi esposo."*

He raised up on one elbow, leaning down and kissing her bare breasts, which had grown huge from nursing many children. "I have stayed in bed much too late this morning. We both have. We are usually up at sunrise."

She breathed deeply. "It is best you stay close to the house today anyway, I think," she said, a sadness coming into her voice. She met his eyes, and he knew what she meant. Sarah Sax could not possibly live through the day.

He sighed and lay back, staring up at the ceiling. "I don't know what to do for my father, Juanita. All my life he has helped me, guided me, been there through times of terrible grief. Always he was so strong for me. But I am not so sure he is strong enough for this. Now it is my turn to be strong for him. But I fear if he loses her, there may be nothing any of us can do to help him with his grief."

Juanita's eyes teared. "I love her like a mother, Tom."

He patted her arm. "I know."

Someone tapped at the door. "Who is it?" Tom called out.

"It's me—Lynda."

"Just a minute." He got up, and Juanita pulled the covers close around her neck. Tom pulled on some underwear and a pair of pants, buttoning them and running a hand through his hair as he went to the door and opened it. Lynda stood there fully dressed, tears in her eyes.

"She is worse?"

Lynda nodded. She could see past him to Juanita. "Father says she wants to see everyone—all the grandchildren. I'll go start helping the little ones dress."

Lynda turned to leave, but Tom grabbed her arm, his eyes tearing now. "What can we do for him, Lynda? I feel so helpless."

She looked down, putting a hand over his. "I don't know. He just . . . walks around like a lost soul. He talks to the children as though nothing is wrong, trying so hard to be strong around the little ones. And he talks about mother as though . . . as though she'll be here weeks from now. He keeps saying he should build them their own little house so Mother will have her own place for the next few years." She shook her head and broke into tears, and Tom pulled her into his arms. She rested her head on his bare shoulder.

"I know how hard this is on you, Lynda—what she means to you. You've always got Jess, you know, and Juanita and me. I hope you realize Father just might leave after she's gone. I know he means the world to you, but there is something he will have to do once he's lost Sarah. He'll go back, Lynda—back to the Cheyenne. Don't make it harder for him than it will already be. We are his descendants. We will go on and bring pride and honor to the Sax name."

She pulled away, nodding. "Yes," she whispered. She left him, and Tom turned to Juanita, closing the door. "We had better hurry."

Juanita wiped her own tears, then raised her eyes to the high window through which the sun shed its light. "At least the sun is shining," she said almost absently. "She loves the sun."

* * *

Caleb stood near a window, looking out at men herding some horses into a corral. Life went on. It was all around him in the form of his grandchildren, who all stood around Sarah's bed dressed in their best suits and dresses, a few of them sniffling.

Caleb felt numb. He would not let the reality of this sink in yet. He could not. He kept looking out at the horses as Sarah, propped up against a mass of pillows, hugged and spoke to each grandchild one by one.

"Don't go the way of the gun, Johnny," he heard her say in a weakening voice. "Don't worry your mother that way."

"Stay close to your mother, Jessica. A mother and daughter should always be friends," she told her oldest granddaughter.

Then came the sons and daughters of Tom Sax, and Sarah's words of how proud she was of each beautiful child: Tony, fifteen; Ricky, twelve; Andres, ten; Rosanna, nine; Louise, seven; Rodriguez, six; and little Edwina, four. She had something to say to each one.

"Come here, Tom," Caleb heard her say. "You have been a better son to me than the son of my blood."

Again Caleb felt a bitter anger toward James. He didn't want to feel it. James was his son, too. But he should be here with his dying mother.

"Life will always be good for you now, Tom," Sarah was saying. "You have put down the sword that was in your hand and shed the hatred in your heart."

Tom said something in return. Caleb could not hear him. He didn't want to hear. He didn't want to feel.

Sarah then spoke to Juanita. "Such a good wife you have been to Tom. And how lucky you have been to know so much joy of motherhood . . . to have so many beautiful babies. I wanted so much to have . . . many children."

Caleb felt as though he were struggling just to breathe. So much had been denied Sarah Sax. Such a beautiful person she was, inside and out. What a wonderful mother she could have been if she had been allowed to lead a normal life. The sweet, caring, happy little girl he had known at Fort Dearborn had never been given the chance to truly fulfill all that was inside her. She had been denied the joy of watching her daughter grow up, and the one baby she had been able to keep from birth had deserted her. The abuse she had suffered at the hands of Byron Clawson had cost her so much—more babies, her health, lost years. And all because she had dared to love Caleb Sax.

"She wouldn't have had it any other way and you know it, Father," he heard Tom say behind him. They both stood in the hallway outside Caleb and Sarah's bedroom. "It's just as Sarah always said. It was others who did those things to both of you. No man could have loved her more than you do, and everybody damned well knows it."

Caleb remained turned away. "Get me . . . a shot of whiskey," he managed to choke out.

Tom sighed deeply. "Yeah. I'll be right back." He left for a moment, and Caleb stared at a huge painting of a rearing black stallion. In the bedroom it was Lynda who now hugged her mother.

"My precious daughter," Sarah said softly. "How wonderful that God brought us together . . . and helped us find your father. We cannot mourn the lost years, Lynda."

"I need you, Mother," Lynda whispered. "I love you so."

"Of course you love me. But you don't need me the way you think. You have your Jess and Johnny and Jessica. And you have Tom and his family."

"Thank you, Jess, for being so good to my Lynda," Sarah said. "You're a good, good man. Thank God . . . you came along."

There was a moment of silence. Caleb heard footsteps behind him and recognized Jess's walk. The man said nothing, unable to find the right words. He walked farther down the hall.

"Mother," Lynda groaned from the bedroom.

"My beautiful . . . precious daughter, my . . . Lynda." Sarah struggled to hang on, feeling the hands of death grabbing her. Not yet! Not yet! There was one more thing she had to do. "Get Caleb."

Lynda leaned down and kissed her cheek, then rose. She

struggled not to break down and weep in front of Sarah. She took a deep breath and walked out into the hallway, while all the grandchildren and Juanita remained standing around the bed.

Out in the hall Caleb was downing a shot of whiskey. "She wants to see you, Father," Lynda told him.

Caleb turned, and Lynda almost gasped at the look on his face. He had aged overnight. For the first time he was beginning to show his sixty-nine years, at least in his face. He was still so tall and strong looking. The thin white scar on his cheek seemed to stand out even whiter against skin that had grown darker over the years, and against age lines that were becoming more predominant.

He said nothing as he handed Lynda the small glass and went back into the bedroom. As he leaned close to Sarah, her eyes brightened. "My Caleb." She smiled, a sudden beauty to her face that made her look younger. "Take me . . . to the tree . . . our tree."

Caleb frowned. "Sarah, you can't even get out of this bed."

"You can carry me." Her eyes suddenly teared and filled with near panic. "Please, Caleb," she begged. "Please . . . take me there! Don't let it happen . . . here. I want to be . . . with just you . . . under our tree."

A tear slipped down the side of her face into her ear. He wondered how much longer he could stay this strong for her. "All right," he told her softly. He straightened, wiping at his eyes and going out into the hallway. "Get a buggy ready. I'm taking Sarah to the big ponderosa where we used to go to be alone."

"What! Father, you cannot move her," Tom protested.

"I can do anything I damned well please," Caleb barked. "Sarah wants to go there and I'm taking her!"

Lynda turned away, grasping her chest. Tom held his father's eyes a moment longer, then nodded. "I will get a buggy ready." He turned away.

"Tom," Caleb called out.

Tom turned to face him.

"I didn't mean to snap at you."

Tom smiled sadly and shook his head. "You didn't really

think you had to explain, did you?" He blinked back tears. "I will get the buggy. You go back inside with Sarah."

He walked off and Caleb turned to Lynda, going up to her and putting a hand on her shoulder, squeezing it as he bent down and kissed the top of her head. "You understand, don't you? She wants to go there, Lynda. She's dying anyway. She doesn't want to die in that bed."

Lynda nodded. She couldn't turn around or she would break down. She couldn't break down yet. He needed her to stay strong, just a little longer. Jess rose and came back down the hall, taking her in his strong arms. Caleb left them and went back into the bedroom, telling Juanita to take the children to the kitchen and have the cook give all of them something to eat. She met her father-in-law's eyes and knew there was nothing more to say or do. The time that was left was for Caleb and Sarah.

Caleb took Sarah from where she lay bundled in the back of the buggy. He picked her up and carried her up the hill, his arms still so strong, her body thin and emaciated. She rested her face against his shoulder, breathing deeply of his familiar scent of buckskins and the out-of-doors. She thought of the utterly handsome Indian man who had appeared at her doorway back in St. Louis all those years ago—the boy Caleb grown into a man, an Indian man called Blue Hawk. Oh, how she had instantly loved him!

He carried her to the tree, and she looked up at massive, outstretched branches as he sat down with her in his lap. She wondered how old that tree was. Surely much older than they. Nature had a way of making a person feel so small, of making a human lifetime seem like hours instead of years. The tree reminded her of Caleb, old but still tall and straight and strong.

P"Are you warm enough?" Caleb asked her. It was December, 1864. One could hardly tell winter from summer here in the Sacramento Valley. But the last few days had been cooler than normal.

"I'm always warm in your arms." She looked up into his face, alarmed at how he had aged. "Caleb, don't look that way. We knew . . . years ago, didn't we? This time we've had here in California has been so beautiful and peaceful. I've had everything I needed...even servants!" She smiled. "I always felt funny...having servants. You thought I should have...those things. But I didn't care. I would have lived in a tipi with you if necessary."

He struggled to keep his composure. "I know, Sarah." She seemed so happy, so peaceful. Her eyes were full of love and joy, and she seemed to have a sudden surge of unusual energy. The past few months she usually couldn't have kept up a conversation for long without tiring and falling asleep.

For weeks he had watched her slip away at a rapid pace. She had lost all control of her bodily functions, and he had cared for all her needs almost completely on his own. Her appetite had dwindled to the point where over the last few days she had not eaten at all. It was useless, for nothing would stay in her stomach. There had been moments when Sarah didn't even know where she was or know Caleb or her grandchildren. But today she had awakened with an odd spark of life to her, completely lucid, wanting to talk and talk. But Caleb knew what it all meant. He took no hope in this sudden improvement. God was giving them this last moment.

"Caleb, I want you to make me a promise...two promises."

He gently smoothed back her hair, which was now nearly all gray. The shining, cascading red-gold, waves were gone.

"I know you never break promises. And I want to go in peace, Caleb." She watched the compelling blue eyes that at one time had all but hypnotized her, eyes that had beheld her body in her youth, eyes that told her so much without his saying a word.

"James." Yes. The eyes hardened slightly. "You must find him...and forgive him. Tell him I love him, and have always loved him. I hold...nothing against him, except that he didn't...love his father enough. But now if you would just see him, I know he would realize how much he loves you."

"Sarah, I don't know if I can forgive him for what he's done to you."

"You must," she said, some strength in her voice. "Please! You must promise me, Caleb. He's our son. He deserves to be loved just as much as the others. At least tell him he was always loved to the end. Promise me you will find him and forgive him and make everything right."

Caleb studied her pleading green eyes. He had never been able to deny her anything. He certainly was not going to start now as she lay near death.

"I promise," he said quietly.

She took a deep breath. "The other promise . . . is one you made to me a long time ago. Tell me again, Caleb, that you will go back to the Cheyenne. Go and find Cale, and get word to Lynda if he is all right. Then stay with your people, where you have always belonged. I want you to do it, not just for you, but for us." A sudden bitterness came into her eyes. "I want you to ride with them against the soldiers—the whites who caused you and me so much grief; the very kind of people who tore us apart and made us lose all those years we could have had together."

The words surprised him. Her jaw was set tightly, and there was fire in those green eyes.

"Do it for us," she almost hissed. "And when you die, you will die the only way . . . a man like my Caleb can die! You will be Blue Hawk, fighting for what is right—fighting for the rights of your people. And one day soon you will join me, and we will be together forever and ever. And there will be nothing that can ever again come between us."

A faint smile of utter victory moved across her mouth, and he felt as though someone were lifting a very heavy weight off his chest. She was happy, and she knew that it would not be that long before they were together again in a world where there would be no tears, no death, no pain.

"I'll go back," he said gently. "I will find James and find a way in my heart to forgive him. And I'll find our grandson. Cale and I will ride together. I've had my time with our other children and grandchildren. Now it will be James's and Cale's time."

"Yes," she whispered. "The family. With you as the link they will truly... all be together. And it all started in that cave when you made love to me for the first time and planted the seed that grew into our Lynda. I can remember that cave so vividly, Caleb."

"So can I." A lump in his throat made it ache almost unbearably.

"Kiss me, Caleb. Kiss me as you kissed me then."

He smiled softly, pulling her close and meeting her lips, kissing her gently, feeling the breath coming out of her as he did so, drawing that last breath into his own lungs as though by doing so he could keep a bit of her life in his body forever.

He knew. He knew it happened at that moment. He moved his lips to her cheek. "I love you, Sarah Sax," he whispered, holding her close. He could not let go. Not yet. To let go meant realizing she was dead.

Below, Tom, Lynda and Jess sat in the courtyard amid the hundreds of roses Sarah had loved. They said nothing. They only sat waiting, listening to the birds singing. And suddenly a cry interrupted the normal sounds of nature. It was a long, eerie, mournful wail that resembled a wounded animal. The birds stopped singing and the soft breeze died down. There was a sudden total silence in the air.

Tom and Jess watched Lynda, who rose and stared out at the hills that rose in the distance. She looked in the direction of the big ponderosa.

"She's dead," Lynda said quietly.

Tom knew it, too, and where the cry had come from. It was no animal. It was Caleb Sax.

· Chapter Thirty-two ·

The slaughter at Sand Creek was followed by some of the fiercest Indian retaliation the settlers had yet known. Black Kettle moved south of the Arkansas River to join the Kiowa and Comanche, still determined to remain peaceful. But most of the Southern Cheyenne went on a rampage of murder and theft. In February, 1865, they burned the town of Julesburg in Colorado Territory, stealing valuable food and provisions. They also seized and chopped up an army payroll, and the Indians whooped and hollered as they threw pieces of the white man's paper money into the wind.

The revitalized spirit of the Cheyenne warriors gave them strength and determination. Their hearts were "bad," full of bitter grief and revenge. Victorious Cheyenne held a dance right in front of Fort Rankin after killing all but eighteen of the sixty men holding the fort, then isolating those left by cutting down all the telegraph poles and using them for bonfires. By the time the Indians left the fort, many of the men remaining were nearly dead from starvation.

Then they headed north, some led by the one called Bear Above, who had lost his woman and two children at Sand Creek. The warriors looked highly on Bear Above, for he was the grandson of Blue Hawk. The warring Cheyenne left a trail of slaughtered cattle and scattered items once belonging to peaceful settlers. They also left a trail of dead bodies.

With every victory the Cheyenne regained more spirit and willingness to fight for what was rightfully theirs under the Laramie Treaty. Joining with the Sioux and Northern

Cheyenne, their numbers were so vast that troops at Fort Laramie were ordered to vacate the fort.

This was the spirit that reigned the summer of 1865 as the Civil War came to a close. It was a good time for the Cheyenne, for the war in the East had left the plains virtually without protection. The Indians enjoyed their remaining days of glory, giving no thought to the fact that the moment the white man's war ended in the East, soldiers would be sent back west . . . in much larger numbers.

He sat high on a ridge overlooking the sprawling Cheyenne village below. The wind whistled and moaned around him, thick stands of trees hiding him from sight. He breathed deeply of the sweet air of the sacred Black Hills. The wind blew his long, black hair away from his ageing face, revealing a lingering handsomeness, but also the hardness of a man who had known far too much suffering. A thin white scar moved down his left cheek, meeting the tassle of a beaded hair ornament.

He was as Indian as any of those in the village below, from the war paint on his face and on his Appaloosa to his beaded moccasins. He carried a tomahawk, one he had stolen himself from enemy Chippewa when he was only nine years old. That had been a proud day for him, but was it possible it had all taken place sixty years ago? How could it be? How could time move so swiftly; and why was he the one who remained . . . ?

The wind whipped up dust that stung his eyes, but he hardly flinched. He sat straight and strong, a repeating pistol strapped to his waist and a rifle resting in its boot on his gear. Animals peeked at him from behind rocks and brush and from the branches above him.

He took another deep breath, hoping to draw strength from this land he loved most of all. Perhaps here he could manage to find a way to want to live, but it seemed as if Sarah Sax was everywhere, sleeping beside him, riding in front of him on his horse, talking to him around his night campfires.

Sarah! How was a man to bear this loneliness? He caught a whiff of smoke from fires below. He was home.

This was the only way to bear the pain. He had to live a life far removed from the one he had led with his Sarah. That meant he must be Indian again. He would never again be Caleb Sax. He was Blue Hawk. And he had come to fight the enemy—the very kind of men who had nearly destroyed his greatest love.

Sarah had asked him to do this, and he knew she was watching, riding beside him. Her spirit was as powerful as the wind that caressed his face, and there were times when he was sure he heard her voice whispering his name. *Caleb. My Caleb.* He looked down at the aging skin of his hands, and he knew it would not be long before he was with her forever.

He headed his horse down toward the village below, praying he would find out that his grandson was still alive. Two scouts quickly rode up to meet him, demanding to know who he was. He looked at them sadly—such young men. Of course they did not know him. He had been away many years from this life. He quickly identified himself in the Cheyenne tongue: Blue Hawk, grandfather of Bear Above.

"I have come looking for my grandson."

They both sat straighter at the mention of his name. "You are the Blue Hawk of whom stories are told around winter campfires?" one asked.

Caleb smiled sadly. "I am."

They looked him over, taking inventory. Yes, he was an old man. But they were not fooled by the gray at his temples and the lines in his face. This man was still strong and vital, and they sensed that he would be a dangerous foe in battle.

"Bear Above is with us," one of them answered.

Caleb felt joy and relief move through his soul. "Take me to him," he said quickly, his eyes lighting up with the first joy he had felt since losing Sarah.

"Come." The warriors turned their horses and led him into the village, shouting in the Cheyenne tongue that Blue Hawk had come. "We have good luck! Now we will truly be strong," one of them shouted.

The name Blue Hawk was muttered as they rode through

the village, and women stared at the noted warrior. Dogs barked and jumped around the horses. Caleb scanned those who gathered around, some coming out of tipis. There was a sense of victory in the air. He smelled it. But he also sensed the distant fear and hopelessness. He spotted a few men tipping whiskey bottles, and he didn't like the faces of the women, long and forlorn.

As they neared a tipi where one of his guides had already ridden, a young man ducked out of it, looking up wide-eyed at the visitor. Caleb halted his horse and stared, his heart leaping with joy. Cale!

"Grandfather!" Cale whispered. His eyes teared and he quickly ducked back inside. Caleb knew why. He must not show his emotions. As Caleb dismounted a man and a woman and several children came scurrying out of the tipi, staring curiously at Caleb. Caleb held back the entrance blanket and went inside, leaving the entrance open for light. It was a warm day, and part of the tipi skins were turned back to let in more light, and skins were pushed up from the bottom stakes for ventilation.

Caleb stood straight in the roomy structure, feeling as though he had finally come home.

"Bear Above," he said gruffly, his eyes tearing as he faced the handsome man who stood staring back at him. He saw grief in his grandson's eyes, but also great joy in the moment.

"Grandfather," Cale groaned, coming closer and embracing Caleb.

For several long seconds there were no words, only the embrace. Then Caleb noticed a little boy of perhaps five watching them in wide-eyed wonder. The child was a replica of Cale. He finally managed to pull away from Cale. "Is this your son?"

Cale turned. *"Ai.* He is all that is left of my family. My Snowbird, and another son and daughter, were killed at Sand Creek."

Caleb looked at Cale in alarm, realizing what a great loss his grandson had suffered. He had heard about Sand Creek when he stopped at Fort Hall after crossing the Sierras. The Sierras—California—his beautiful family. He would not see them again. But that was as it should be. He had promises to fulfill, and he still had family right here. He walked closer to the little boy, reaching out and touching his hair, trembling with the awesome realization that he had a great grandson. "What is his name?"

"He is called Little Eagle."

Caleb could not control his tears. If only Sarah could see this child! He drew the boy close and the child did not resist. "Little Eagle," Caleb said softly.

Cale swallowed back an urge to break down completely. "Grandmother? She is . . . dead?"

"Yes," Caleb answered softly. "I promised her I would come and find you . . . and that I would live out my years with the Cheyenne."

Cale's heart swelled with pride. "You will bring us good luck, Grandfather. Many bad things have happened. But we are stronger now. We are proud and we are angry. We are tired of broken treaties."

Caleb gently let go of the little boy, petting his hair a moment before rising and facing Cale. He looked him over. "You look well, but I see the sorrow in your eyes."

"You are a man who understands sorrow." He motioned for Caleb to sit on a blanket nearby. "Sit and rest. Are you hungry? Thirsty?"

"No. Since your grandmother died, it seems I have no feelings of any kind. I am just numb, except for this moment." He sat down wearily, and Cale sat down across from him.

"Words cannot express how I feel at this moment, Grandfather. This is the most happiness I have known since marrying Snowbird. It was right after the great gathering at Fort Laramie in 'fifty-one." He closed his eyes against the pain. "Tell me everything, Grandfather, about my mother, and Tom. How were things in that place called California?"

Caleb told him of Tom's good fortune, and also of the Bad Ones and the Mexican War. Cale sat listening to all of it, happy to learn he had so many new cousins through Tom and Juanita.

"I made your grandmother a promise. I will have to leave you again for a while. I am going to find James."

Cale stiffened, and bitter hatred filled his eyes. "James!" He spit. "You do not know?"

Caleb frowned. "Know what?"

Cale's jaw flexed in anger. "James was among the Colorado Volunteers . . . at Sand Creek."

The pain of the news cut through Caleb like a knife, and he sucked in his breath and bent his head as though in pain.

"Grandfather! I am sorry. I told you too quickly."

Caleb shook his head. "It's all right," he groaned. "I don't know why, but somehow I knew." He raised tired eyes to meet Cale's. "I made your grandmother a promise —that I would find him and forgive him for never seeing or contacting us again. Sarah never got to see her son. It will be hard for me to forgive him, Bear Above, but I gave my word. For the sake of Sarah's memory, you must try to find it in your own heart to do the same." His eyes teared. "I don't know what led him to go so far against his blood, but surely James suffers a sorrow far greater than our own, the sorrow of betrayal."

Cale closed his eyes and sighed deeply. "I am not sure I can ever forgive him, except that he spared my life." He opened his eyes and met his grandfather's eyes, surprised at how bright they still were, and still such a beautiful blue. "A soldier told him to shoot me, but he only pretended to shoot me. And I saw a look on his face I will never forget. I think you are right. I think he is living in hell, walking in it every day. He swore to me he took no part in the killings, but . . . he was there." The man's voice choked. "I only thank God that you did not have to see what I saw that day, Grandfather—women and children with their heads smashed, breasts and arms cut off, bellies cut open, and warriors' manparts severed. Many of us still have nightmares and our hearts are bad, Grandfather, and so full of vengeance. We have made much war, and we will keep on making war to the last man."

"I know the feeling, Bear Above. And I will be fighting at your side."

Cale looked surprised. His grandfather had to be at least seventy years old. Caleb smiled softly. "I know what you are thinking, but I am still strong and still a good shot. And the only honorable way for me to die is among my people. Sarah always knew that. She made me promise to come here. And as long as I'm here, I want to do what I can, Cale. Don't worry about the danger. I will die a happy man if I can die fighting with the Cheyenne. And then I can be with my Sarah."

Cale reached out and touched his arm. "Grandfather, I know how you loved her. I know how you must suffer."

"Grief is no stranger to me, nor to you now. But we go on." He grasped Cale's hands, squeezing them firmly, screaming with grief on the inside—not just for Sarah, but for the fact that his own son had been a part of the massacre at Sand Creek. Sarah had no idea the burden she had put upon him by telling him to find the man and forgive him. Little did she know how much had to be forgiven.

"You will stay a few days before you leave again?" Cale was asking. "This dwelling belongs to Basket Woman, an aunt to my Snowbird, who has given Little Eagle and me shelter now that I have no woman of my own. Basket Woman and her husband would be honored to have Blue Hawk stay with them. There will be much celebrating tonight, Grandfather. You are a sign of good luck." He kept a tight grip on his grandfather's hands. "I need the strength and power you bring, Grandfather, for I have lost the blue quill necklace."

Caleb frowned, feeling a painful loss, remembering how much the necklace meant to him. It was a part of Caleb's own mother, the Cheyenne mother he had never known. "How?" he groaned.

"At Sand Creek. I searched and searched, but then we had to get out of there, for the soldiers were returning to find anyone left alive. It has left a bitter emptiness in my heart, Grandfather. I would rather cut off my arm than lose that necklace. It was my power, my precious gift from Blue Hawk. You gave it to me when I was a newborn baby, all those years ago in Texas. I grew up being taught its meaning, and then you gave me the sun stone to tie on to it when I suffered the Sun Dance."

"It's all right, Bear Above. You have not lost that power. The spirits simply have some kind of new purpose for that necklace, one we might never know in our own lifetime. But the power comes from the blood, Bear Above, from the love that flows from me to you. You don't need the necklace for that."

Cale's eyes teared. "I wanted to give it to Little Eagle. What do I have to give him now, Grandfather? What will his future be? We will fight, and probably die. But the children, they must go on. And one day the soldiers will win. I am not fool enough to think otherwise. He will grow up on that stinking reservation. I do not want that for him. It is no life, Grandfather. There is no pride, no hope. On the reservation many of the young men take their lives, and those left live on the firewater. There is disease, and reservation agents cheat us. What am I to do about Little Eagle?"

Caleb sighed deeply. "I don't know. I have many things to think about, Bear Above. Before I can consider them all, I must find James. I am glad I came here first. When I get to Denver, I will send a messenger to tell your mother that you are well, and that she has a grandson. It will gladden her heart. She needs such good news after losing her mother."

Cale nodded, still holding Caleb's hands. He leaned forward and kissed the man's cheek. "Be careful in Denver, Grandfather. It is a very dangerous place for a man like you. Very dangerous."

Caleb smiled bitterly, thinking of James. "But not for Indians who look like white men."

Willena slowly rose as the rider approached. The sun was behind him, making it difficult at first to determine who it was. But she could see the dancing fringes of buckskins. As she walked to the steps of the veranda, which ran the full length of the front of the Sax mansion, she saw that he was an Indian. He stopped short of the steps, looking over the house with strangely sad eyes, then moved those intense blue eyes to meet her green ones.

She wondered why she was not afraid, why she didn't call for one of the male servants to get a gun. This man was old but certainly not feeble, and he looked as wild as she would picture the Cheyenne warriors who had been leaving bloodstains on settlers' lands all over the plains. He nodded, watching her almost knowingly.

"You are James's wife." He made it a statement rather than a question.

She nodded, feeling frozen in place.

"I can see why," the man said in perfectly clear English that surprised her. "You are very beautiful, and you look very much like his mother. Perhaps that is what drew him to you."

A prickling realization moved through her blood then. "You're his father!"

Caleb rode closer and dismounted, then walked up the steps, holding her eyes. "I asked at a neighbor's house where James Sax lived. I knew it would be in this area, where it is obvious the wealthier citizens of Denver live. I had no doubt my son was wealthy and successful. After all, he paid quite a price for all of it, including abandoning his mother and denying his own blood."

She caught the bitterness in the words and her eyes teared. She held his eyes boldly. James needed help, and this man was the only one who could help him. She must not let this moment be wasted. "It isn't like that, Mr. Sax. James is a fine man, and I love him very much. He was just... afraid of losing all he had worked so hard for... and of losing me. He should have trusted in my love enough to know he could have told me and it wouldn't have mattered."

Caleb frowned. Apparently his son had finally spilled the truth, and there was something about this young woman he liked. She was strong and beautiful and not afraid to say what she was thinking. Yes, she was very much like a young Sarah—the Sarah who had stood against her father in defense of her love for Caleb Sax.

She stepped closer. "Thank God you've come! You have no idea how happy I am to meet you. My prayers have been answered." She grasped one of his hands. "Come inside and we'll talk, Mr. Sax. Don't judge your son just yet. The way you treat him could be a matter of life and death."

Caleb was struck by how she grasped his hand—so

much like Sarah, so welcoming and spontaneous. A light breeze ruffled his long, loose hair, and little bells that were tied into a hair ornament tinkled with the wind.

Willena found it incredible that this man was so Indian. He was much more Indian than James had even described, except for the amazing blue eyes; and she sensed a man of compassion behind them.

"What do you mean—life and death?"

She blinked back tears. "Do you know he was at Sand Creek?"

"I do. I have already found my grandson Cale, among the Northern Cheyenne in the Black Hills. He told me."

Her eyes widened. "You . . . rode right into their camp?" She let go of his hand, as though realizing just how Indian he really was.

He grinned a little. "I am Blue Hawk. I am one of them, in case you didn't notice."

Her cheeks flushed a little and she smiled through tears. "Of course." She sighed deeply. "What I meant was that James—" She folded her arms, trembling obviously. "He's suicidal, Mr. Sax. He's despondent, drinks too much, and a few weeks ago I walked into his study to see him standing there with the barrel of a pistol in his mouth." She looked down. "If I hadn't come in when I did, I have no doubt he would have . . . pulled the trigger."

Her tears started to flow. Caleb closed his eyes against the pain. *Forgive him,* Sarah had told him. *Find James and forgive him.*

He saw several riders coming then and moved back, sensing danger.

"Your neighbor lady was scared to death of me. I think she decided maybe you would need some help. There are riders coming."

Willena quickly wiped her eyes and walked down the steps, taking the reins of Caleb's horse and tying them to a hitching post as several of her neighbor's hired help rode around the neatly trimmed shrubs of the well-manicured lawn, keeping to the stone riding path that was laid out in a grand circle in front of the house. Every man carried a rifle, and Willena stepped out to greet them.

"You got trouble here, Mrs. Sax?" one of them spoke up. "Mrs. Hornby said this big Indian was headed for your place."

"It's all right. He's my father-in-law."

Caleb smiled a little at the bold and quick answer. There was no hesitation, no attempt to hide his identity.

"Father-in-law!"

"My God, the rumor is true," another spoke up.

"No wonder Sax lost his beans after Sand Creek," another spoke up jokingly.

"I'll be damned."

"And I would appreciate it if you all left." Willena curbed her anger. They had, after all, come to see if she needed help. "I appreciate your concern."

They all gawked at Caleb, some fingering their rifles eagerly. Then they began moving out. One lingered behind to look insultingly at Willena. "Seein' as how you're married to one of them, don't expect us to come ridin' to your aid again, ma'am," he sneered.

Willena stiffened. "I think I can get by without your help, Sam. When I need help, I'll call on a *real* man to help me."

Caleb grinned and Sam scowled at Willena, then rode off. Willena turned and came up the steps, meeting Caleb's approving eyes.

"You've got courage."

"It isn't courage. It's plain old anger," she answered, fire in her green eyes.

Caleb looked her over. She had a shape that would entice any man. His son may have done a lot of wrong things in his life, but marrying this woman was one of the smartest things he ever did. "I don't even know your name."

She smiled a little, the anger leaving her eyes. "It's Willena. Come inside and we'll talk. James is in town. I don't doubt he'll find out very quickly that his Indian father is here. Someone will ride in and tell him. I'm not sure what that will do to him, but I expect he'll come home. At any rate, there are a few things you need to know before he gets here."

She led him through double doors into a cool hallway. A

huge chandelier hung overhead, and a spiral staircase led to upper rooms. Its rail was polished mahogany, but the bars and steps were painted white. Huge plants were scattered about, and expensive-looking paintings hung on the walls. She noticed Caleb taking inventory of his son's mansion.

"These things don't mean anything to me, Mr. Sax. I would gladly give it all up to have James healthy and happy again." She led him to the left, into a grand parlor decorated in a soft green. "Sit down, Mr. Sax. I'll get the children. You can meet them before we talk."

He sat in a love seat covered with green satin brocade, feeling awkward and out of place. Children? Did he have more grandchildren? If only Sarah could see all of this. If only she could have seen Little Eagle—and now to see James's children! Moments later Willena returned, leading a little girl and boy along, the little girl wearing a ruffled dress, the little boy dressed neatly in a shirt and cutoff pants, his hair slicked back as though freshly combed.

"Children, this is your grandfather. You don't have to be afraid of him. He is Indian, and he is a fine man. Your father has told you all about him, remember?" She brought them closer. "Mr. Sax, this is your granddaughter, Elizabeth Ellen. She's four years old. And your grandson James Jr., who is two."

Caleb stared at two beautiful children, the girl looking so much like Sarah that renewed grief swept through him with painful force. His eyes teared, and he reached out to lightly touch her chubby cheek. "The first time I met Sarah, I was nine years old—a wild, orphaned Indian boy that her uncle brought home with him," he told her softly. "Sarah was only six, not much older than you. And you look just like her—just like your grandmother."

"My grandma's name is Sarah?"

He breathed deeply to stay in control. "It was. Your grandmother is dead now, Elizabeth. But she would be so proud to see you. She was a very beautiful woman, so I'm sure you will be, too."

Looking at her brought back so many memories—little Sarah, his sweet little friend! Where in God's name had the years gone?

Willena swallowed back a lump in her throat. So, Sarah Sax was dead. She felt an odd sorrow that she would never get to meet the woman. She had suspected she must be dead, suspected that was the only reason Caleb Sax had come back from California. She watched him turn to little James, quickly winning the boy over with a genuine love and warmth that any child could sense. In spite of his size and appearance, neither child seemed to be afraid.

"Both of you run back upstairs and play now. Your grandfather and I have many things to talk about."

"Can he stay and eat supper with us?" Elizabeth asked.

"Of course he can. He can stay as long as he likes."

A maid walked into the room and gasped when she saw Caleb sitting there, then looked wide-eyed at Willena.

"It's all right, Joanne. This is my father-in-law. Please bring us—" She looked at Caleb. "What would you like, Mr. Sax? Coffee? Tea? Some brandy, perhaps?"

"Maybe just some water for now." He smiled and watched his grandchildren run out of the room. He was glad he had come. Two more grandchildren and a great-grandson! He had always wanted family and identity, though all his life he had struggled between two worlds. Now it was obvious his family would help blend both of those worlds. Surely Sarah was up there watching. Surely she knew about Little Eagle, Elizabeth, and James Jr.

He leaned forward, resting his elbows on his knees. "Tell me about James, Willena. I didn't come here to condemn him. I admit there is a lot of bitterness in my heart. I don't mind what he did to me. I have broad shoulders. But it's hard for me to accept what he did to his mother. I'm here at her dying request, Willena. She made me promise to find James and to forgive him, and that's what I'm going to try to do. Maybe it would help if I knew what's going on around here. If you caught James threatening to shoot himself, then my son needs help badly."

"Oh, yes, he does!" Willena moved to sit down beside him. "Sand Creek nearly destroyed him, Mr. Sax."

He sighed deeply. "Call me Caleb. Or Father. Anyone who marries my son becomes my daughter."

Her eyes teared and she looked at her lap. "I can't imagine James would overlook the love you obviously carry for your family, or turn away from it the way he did. I don't know if you realize how much he was affected by the things that happened to him in Texas, how afraid he was that those he loved would suffer because of his Indian blood. We're all different, Mr.—I mean, Caleb. Who can explain why certain things affect us the way they do?"

Willena rose as the maid brought in a tray with ice water on it. She set it down and quickly left, as though she feared losing her scalp. Caleb poured himself a glass of water and let Willena talk.

"At any rate"—she moved to stand beside a grand piano, her back to him—"it's true James lived a lie most of his life. But deep inside, he loved you very much. We've talked a lot since Sand Creek. He told me everything— from his boyhood in Texas to the day I caught him with that pistol in his mouth."

She turned to face him. "I think you understand, Caleb. Suffice it to say, Sand Creek brought it all to a head. He had what amounts to a nervous breakdown after that. He deserted the others and came straight home and just—" She sighed and shook her head. "He fell to pieces. For several days he just stayed in bed and cried. I couldn't get him to tell me what was wrong. Luckily he had reliable men helping to run the mercantile. I told outsiders he was sick and couldn't come to work."

She walked to a window and looked out at the lush, green lawn. "Then he started drinking, getting abusive. One night he—" She folded her arms and remained turned away. "He wanted to make love to me, only he was mean and forceful. When I protested he said, 'What's wrong? Don't you like making love with an Indian?'"

She turned to face him, her cheeks crimson. "That's the first time I realized what was bothering him. I asked him what he was talking about, and he spilled it all out then. 'I'm Indian! I'm Indian!' he shouted at me. 'Your husband is part Indian, and so are your children! What do you think of that, Mrs. James Sax!'"

She rubbed her arms. "I was so shocked I'm afraid I ran out of the room. I spent the rest of the night locked behind the door in the children's room, waiting for him to sleep it off, thinking about what he had said. So many things made sense, things he had said or done before that I couldn't understand. As God is my witness, Caleb, it wasn't what he told me that upset me. It was the fact that he didn't trust in my love enough to tell me in the first place. It wasn't fair of him, and it wouldn't have mattered. For years I have disagreed with my own father on the treatment of Indians. And I might add that since this all came out my father has disowned me." Her eyes teared. "But that is something I guess I will just have to live with."

He studied her lovingly. "You're so much like Sarah I can hardly believe it."

She smiled through her tears and turned away again. "At any rate, the next day James told me everything. We had a long, long talk. I think he understands that it doesn't matter to me and that he's not going to lose me. And I think he can even stand up against the friends and the father-in-law he has lost because of it all. It even hurt business a little, but we'll survive. The man James was partners with died about three months ago, so James is sole owner now of Hayden & Sax Mercantile, which includes a lot more stores than just here in Denver."

She sighed deeply. "Your son is a very rich man, Caleb. But he is a very unhappy man. Even though he has owned up to his Indian blood, he can't live with the guilt of denying that blood for so long. He can't live with the knowledge that he never contacted or saw his mother and father again. And he can't live with the memory of Sand Creek and seeing his own nephew there. He wakes up with terrible nightmares, then he cries like a baby, and too often he turns to whiskey to soothe the hurt. I've done all I can do to help him. I've loved him the best I can. But I'm not the one who can really help him fully heal, Caleb. It has to come from you—from someone in the family he deserted. If he can't get things right in his heart and learn to forgive himself, I'm afraid he's going to get out that gun again—" Her voice choked. "And the next time I might not walk in in time."

She leaned on the piano and broke into tears. Caleb walked over to her, putting a hand on her shoulder. "He's my son, Willena. A man can get angry with his son, but he never stops loving him. I'll go into town right now and talk to him."

"No! No, you mustn't go into Denver." She turned and faced him. "It would be much too dangerous. For James's sake, don't go into town and get yourself shot. That would destroy him completely. Let him come home."

He nodded. "All right, if you think that's best."

She grasped his arms. "At least he has faced up to his heritage, Caleb. He has told all his friends, and he has lost some of them because of it. But none of that really bothers him now. He's a strong, wonderful man. It's the inner guilt that is destroying him. If he could get rid of that, he would be stronger than ever before, and he would find the happiness he has never really known in his whole life. He's a good husband and father, and he's very intelligent and hardworking. There are too many wonderful things about that man to let him slowly destroy himself on the inside. You can stop it. I know you'll have that power."

She wiped her eyes and Caleb grasped her arms. "I'll do what I can to help, Willena. He just needs to heal. Maybe I can help close the wound."

She looked up at him, then suddenly hugged him. "You can, I know you can. Thank God you came! I've been going crazy trying to think what else to do. I've been so lonely. It's like God sent you here for us."

He moved his arms around her, thinking how much Sarah would love this young woman James had married. What wonderful instincts his Sarah had had. Somehow she knew their son needed him desperately. He felt the anger leaving him. He had come here to fulfill a promise. He would do it, but not just for Sarah. He would do it because it was in his own heart to forgive his son.

"No, Willena, it wasn't God who sent me. But it was a spirit, a gentle spirit named Sarah."

It had taken years of separation, and the horror of Sand Creek, to bring the closeness he had always wanted with James, if, in fact, he could find it now. How sad so many years had been lost, and that he had only a few days to make up for all of them. He closed his eyes. *Help me, Maheo,* he prayed.

• Chapter Thirty-three •

All the way home James felt uneasy, the kind of feeling a man got when he sensed something was wrong. Perhaps it was something he had inherited from his father. Caleb Sax always seemed to know when someone he loved was in trouble. Someone he loved. Was that it? Was something wrong at home? He rode a little faster, leaving a growing Denver behind him and heading into the foothills toward the only tiny piece of happiness he had left—Willena.

Poor Willena. She was being so patient and understanding. Never in his wildest dreams did he think she would still love him if she knew. It felt good to have it out in the open, but there still remained the fact that by riding with the Volunteers he had chosen the ultimate betrayal.

He headed up the road to his house, slowing his horse as he ascended the circular driveway. A horse was tied at the front of the house— a big Appaloosa. It was the kind of horse he would expect his father to ride, and as he slowly drew closer he realized the horse only carried a small Indian saddle and an Indian blanket. A rifle boot on the gear sported a fancy repeating rifle, and a sun was painted on the horse's rump.

His blood tingled and his hands suddenly felt sweaty. Utter dizziness came over him when he rode around the other side of the horse to see a blue hawk painted on the other side of its rump. He looked quickly at the front doors to see Willena coming outside. For a moment they just stared at each other. She came down the steps.

"Your father is here. He's up in the big pines behind the house. He said it would be better to talk alone with you there."

James sat frozen in place. Willena came closer and touched his leg. "He knows everything, James. It's all right. Go and see him."

He began shaking, his hands gripping the reins tightly. "I knew he'd come . . . one day . . . and yet it always seemed as if it would never really happen."

"I like him, James. I like him very much, and so do the children. You really should go and see him. You don't have to be afraid. Get it over with, James."

He swallowed, glancing up at the hills beyond the house. He was up there, the man he loved but in his own mind could never please. And now he knew all of it, all the shame, the ugly truth! His eyes teared at the sudden realization of why the man had come. "My mother is dead, isn't she?" he choked out.

"Yes. She died last autumn, and she had nothing but loving thoughts for you."

He closed his eyes, a little gasp of grief making his chest jerk. "My God," he groaned.

"James, she was surrounded by children and grandchildren. They lived with Tom, and he has seven children. And Lynda lived nearby with John and a daughter, Jessica. Tom is very wealthy, James. They discovered gold on his land. Your mother lived a very good, comfortable life, just the kind of life you always thought she deserved. Your father says their years in California were wonderful, peaceful years. Your mother wanted for nothing. And she never once held anything against you."

He drew in his breath, tears moving down his face. He kept taking deep breaths, wiping his eyes. "I can't face him crying like a little boy, can I?" He forced an embarrassed smile.

"James, it wouldn't matter. You know yourself that your father has shed his own share of tears. There's nothing wrong with a man mourning the death of his mother."

He looked down at her. "It must have been quite a shock for you to see him. There's no mistaking he's Indian, is there? Can you believe he's my father? I mean, look at us. Two men couldn't be more different."

She smiled softly. "In looks, yes. But in talking to him, I know where you got your strength and your size, and on the inside I don't think you're as different as you think you are. Go and see him, James."

He breathed deeply again, sitting a little straighter in the saddle. "I had a strange feeling all day that something was amiss. I felt him, Willena. That's the way it is with my father. He gives off a kind of power. I guess that always intimidated me a little. He probably never meant it to. That's just the way it was."

"He would never want it that way. If he intimidates you, it's all in your mind. Open your mind, James, and your heart. Let go of the past."

He sniffed and wiped his eyes again, nodding and turning his horse. He headed around the side of the house and up a pathway that led into thick pines in the hills above. Every nerve end felt alive and on fire. He actually wondered if he would get so light-headed that he would fall off his horse. It occurred to him that the contrast between father and son would be made even greater by the expensive suit of clothes he was wearing. But there was no time to change into anything else. He dreaded this moment, yet wanted nothing more than to have it over with.

He moved several hundred yards uphill until he reached a clearing in the trees that was hidden from the house. Then he saw him, sitting on a large rock watching.

Caleb's own heart quickened. James! He was a grown man. Until this moment he had been unable to picture him as anything but the teenager who had left them in Colorado. James halted his horse and slowly dismounted, standing at a distance. Caleb could see the young man was practically frozen where he stood. Caleb had to make the first move. He walked in long strides toward his son.

James stared at an ageing, graying man, realizing for the first time his father had grown old. Just as Caleb had pictured James not even grown, James had always pictured his father the way he looked when he left. But he was not surprised that Caleb Sax still stood tall and looking rock hard.

All the lies and guilt swept through James as he hung his head and broke into unwanted tears. In a moment the man who should hate him more than anyone was embracing him firmly. Much as he fought it, James could not control his weeping. He flung his arms around his father, feeling like a child, begging his forgiveness.

"I forgive you, Son, if you'll forgive me for anything I did that kept us from being close."

James felt the odd heaviness he always felt in his chest begin to lighten, and he couldn't bring himself to let go of Caleb. Caleb's heart went out to him, and his own tears came. He thanked *Maheo* that this young man had not taken his life before Caleb could get to him.

How long they stood there holding each other neither was sure. Finally Caleb kept an arm around James's waist, leading him to the rock. "Come and sit down, James. Everything is going to be all right."

"But . . . Mother . . . Mother . . ." He couldn't get all the words out, and he pulled a handkerchief from his pants pocket and blew his nose and wiped his eyes.

"Your mother always thought the best of you, James, and her years in California were good ones. She died happy, and her last words were of you and Cale. I promised I'd come back and find both of you before I'm gone, too."

They sat down on the rock and James hung his head. "Cale. When you see him—"

"I've already seen him."

James turned red, swollen eyes to meet his father's, realizing then that Caleb Sax's eyes were the same as always, a deep, discerning blue. It was his eyes that made him seem younger than he really was. They were still handsome and compelling. "You've seen Cale? And you can still come here and act as if everything is all right?" He looked away. "My God, Father, don't you realize what I did?"

Caleb sighed deeply. "James, a man can't live his whole life worrying about the mistakes he's made. He can only learn from them and go on from there, especially when he has a wife and family who love him and depend on him. I'm here to make things right, not just for Sarah, but for myself, and for you. When I met your wife and saw those children, I knew that in spite of his mistakes, my son also did a lot of things right. And because he has his mother's blood in him, he also has a hell of a lot of good in him. When Willena told me what happened after Sand Creek, I knew you had suffered enough. Why should I add to it by coming here and condemning you? You're my son. No matter what kind of mistakes he made, you would never stop loving little James Jr., would you?"

James wiped his eyes again. "Of course not."

"And I've never stopped loving you. It's out in the open now. You've told people you're part Indian. You understand now that a man can't deny his own being. And Willena still loves you."

James swallowed, breathing deeply to stay in control. "Willena. She's so good to me, Father. She's a good wife. She reminds me so much . . . of Mother."

Caleb put a hand on his arm. "Yes, that was my first thought when I met her."

James met his eyes again. "You saw it, too?"

He realized then what great sorrow his father must be suffering. Losing Sarah had to be the worst loss of the man's life. "Of course I saw it. But then sometimes I see Sarah in everything, James—in the sun, the flowers, in every grandchild. I even see her in Tom's children, even though her blood doesn't flow in their veins. But she was so good to them, and they loved her so much. Her influence somehow radiates in them."

James stood up, walking a few feet away. "How can I make amends, Father? There must be something—"

"There is something you can do. It would really be more for Sarah, and for your sister Lynda."

James faced him. "What, Father? I'll do anything."

Caleb saw sincerity and love in the young man's eyes. "Cale lost his wife and two of his children at Sand Creek."

James closed his eyes and sucked in his breath. "Sweet Jesus," he groaned. He clenched his fists and gritted his teeth. "I should have ... pulled the goddamned trigger ... before Willena got to me."

In the next second his father was grasping his arms and shaking him. "I didn't tell you that to make you feel worse again, James. I love you. We all love you. Look at me, James."

James met the man's eyes, trembling with agony over Cale's loss. "You can help Cale, James."

More tears ran down James's face. "How in God's name can I do that now?"

"He has one son left. He's only five years old, a beautiful child called Little Eagle. He's my great-grandson, James, mine and Sarah's. Cale knows that in the end the Indians will lose. He doesn't want Little Eagle to grow up on a reservation. I want you to take him to California for me—to Lynda. Lynda never got to see Cale again and probably never will now. Nothing would lift her heart more than to see her grandson, to keep him and raise him."

James nodded. "Yes. That would surely be best for the boy ... and for Lynda."

"Bringing Little Eagle to Lynda to raise would be wonderful for her. Cale loves his last remaining son, but he intends to fight to his death for what he knows is right. He is afraid Little Eagle will get killed or end up living out his life on a reservation. I told him I'd find a way to get the boy out to Lynda."

James looked at his father in astonishment. "And you really want *me* to do it?"

"Why not? I can think of no better person to be in charge of Little Eagle. While you're in California, you could visit your mother's grave and could see the rest of the family— see Tom and Lynda and all your nieces and nephews. If you want, you could leave all the unhappiness you've known here in Colorado and start a whole new life in California, open another store there, maybe in San Francisco.

The way I hear it, you're always looking to expand Hayden & Sax, right?"

James studied his eyes. "But what about you? You aren't going back?"

Caleb let go of him. "No. I'm never going back. I've left that life behind me. The only way I can bear going on without Sarah is to leave that life all together—to leave Caleb Sax back in California."

James frowned, then his eyes teared anew. "You're going to Cale, aren't you. You're going to live out your life with the Cheyenne."

"It's the only way for me now, James. Sarah even made me promise that's what I would do."

"But . . . they're making war everywhere! They're hunted like wolves! The worst is yet to come, Father. You'll be killed."

Caleb smiled sadly, shaking his head. "I thought after all that's happened you would understand that side of me, James."

James breathed deeply, nodding slowly. He smiled a little himself then. "You *want* to go down fighting with the Cheyenne."

"Is there any other way for me to die? Would you have me die a crippled old man, shriveled under the blankets of my deathbed?"

James stood a little straighter. "No. My father would never die that way."

Caleb nodded. "Now you understand. In a way even I denied my blood for a lot of years, James, because I knew your mother couldn't live the life I would have lived if I hadn't got mixed up in her world. Now I am going back to the life I was meant to live, for what little time I have left. And my presence will help comfort Cale. I was born Blue Hawk, James. And I will die Blue Hawk. And I will die knowing that my sons and daughters and grandchildren are all well and happy and together. That is what Sarah would have wanted. Will you take Little Eagle to California?"

James held the man's eyes boldly. "Yes. You go and get him, and I'll see that he gets out to Lynda. But there is something else I wish you would do first." He swallowed, his emotions rising again. "For me."

"Whatever you need, James."

"I want . . ." He breathed deeply again to keep his composure. "I want to go up in the mountains with you . . . just you and me. I want you to teach me about the Cheyenne—their beliefs, enough that I'll have a little something to teach my own children. Help me understand. I want to understand why Cale chose to go with them and why you are going with them now. I want to feel that . . . that spiritual power that you have. Somehow I never felt it inside myself, not like Tom and Cale. Even Lynda had some of it. I don't care if I have to suffer some kind of physical pain to find it." His eyes were pleading. "I want to know, Father. I want to smoke a peace pipe with you. And I don't just want to know about the Cheyenne. I want to know *you*."

Caleb felt the wall tumble for the first time. He nodded, breaking into a warm smile. "All right. We'll leave in the morning. Will Willena understand?"

James smiled lovingly. "Willena understands everything. She's the only right choice I ever made in my life."

"Until now."

James nodded. "Until now." He took a deep breath. "I love you, Father. I always loved you."

"I know, James. And I've always loved you." Caleb stepped closer, grasping his shoulders. "You're going to be all right, and when you come down from the mountains with me, you will have an Indian name. I'll pick one for you."

James swallowed, his jaws flexing as he struggled with his emotions. "I would like that, very much."

Caleb smiled warmly, turning James and leading him toward his horse. "Let's go below and have some supper. I want to see my grandchildren again."

James picked up the reins of his horse, and father and son walked down the slope together. A hawk circled overhead, coming down to light upon the rock where James and Caleb Sax had found each other again.

* * *

Caleb Sax's journey in life had taken him from the deep woods of an uncivilized Minnesota to Fort Dearborn, which one day became Chicago, Illinois. It led him to New Orleans, and the famous battle there against the British; to St. Louis, where he found and claimed the love of his life; to Texas and its war for independence; to California in the years of the gold rush; and finally back to his roots—to the Cheyenne. Blue Hawk again rode with his people and made war.

Along his trail in life the graves of loved ones were left behind. But also left behind were the sons and daughters and the descendents of Caleb Sax, who would proudly carry on the name of the little adopted half-breed boy who once reached out and took the hand of Sarah Sax, to be led into a world foreign to him, but one he had lived in—for her.

Sarah Sax would never have had it any other way. Her life had also been a long journey, closely following the pathway of the man she loved beyond her own life. The marker at her grave in California was fitting:

HERE LIES SARAH SAX, A REMARKABLE WOMAN.

One other remnant of the man called Blue Hawk was also left behind—a blue quill necklace, lost at Sand Creek.

But that is another story.

I hope you have enjoyed the "Blue Hawk" series. If this is the first book in the series you have read, you will want to look for SAVAGE HORIZONS and FRONTIER FIRES, both from Popular Library. Through those books you can go back and read about the beginnings of the Sax family. I am sure you will enjoy those stories also.

—*F. Rosanne Bittner*

The Best Of
Warner Romances